THE COMPLETE STORIES
OF
MORLEY CALLAGHAN

THE COMPLETE STORIES

OF
MORLEY CALLAGHAN

Volume Four

Introduction by
Margaret Atwood

EXILE
editions

Library and Archives Canada Cataloguing in Publication

Callaghan, Morley, 1903-1990
    The complete stories of Morley Callaghan.

(Exile classics series ; no. 22-25)
Introductions by Alistair MacLeod (v. 1), André Alexis (v. 2), Anne
    Michaels (v. 3), and Margaret Atwood (v. 4).
Includes bibliographical references.
ISBN 978-1-55096-305-2 (v. 2).--ISBN 978-1-55096-304-5 (v. 1).--
ISBN 978-1-55096-306-9 (v. 3).--ISBN 978-1-55096-307-6 (v. 4)

    I. Title. II. Series: Exile classics ; no. 22-25

PS8505.A43A15 2012   C813'.54   C2012-906213-8

Design and Composition by Digital ReproSet~mc
Cover Photograph by Brian Summers
Printed by Imprimerie Gauvin

Published by Exile Editions Ltd ~ www.ExileEditions.com
144483 Southgate Road 14 – GD, Holstein ON, N0G 2A0
Printed and Bound in Canada; Publication Copyright © Exile Editions, 2012

The publisher would like to acknowledge the financial support of the Canada
Council for the Arts, the Government of Canada through the Canada Book Fund
(CBF), the Ontario Arts Council, and the Ontario Media Development Corpora-
tion, for our publishing activities.

Conseil des Arts   Canada Council
du Canada   for the Arts

Canadä

ONTARIO ARTS COUNCIL
CONSEIL DES ARTS DE L'ONTARIO

Ontario
Ontario Media Development
Corporation

North American and International Distribution:
Independent Publishers Group, 814 North Franklin Street,
Chicago IL 60610   www.ipgbook.com   toll free: 1 800 888 4741

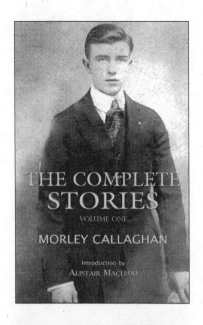

THE COMPLETE
STORIES

VOLUME ONE

MORLEY CALLAGHAN

Introduction by
ALISTAIR MACLEOD

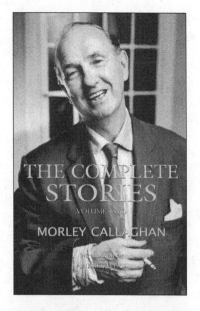

THE COMPLETE
STORIES

VOLUME TWO

MORLEY CALLAGHAN

Introduction by
ANDRÉ ALEXIS

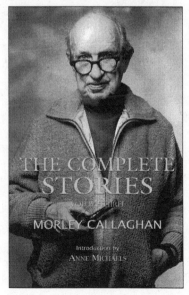

THE COMPLETE
STORIES

VOLUME THREE

MORLEY CALLAGHAN

Introduction by
ANNE MICHAELS

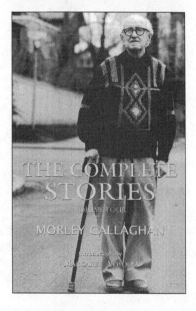

THE COMPLETE
STORIES

VOLUME FOUR

MORLEY CALLAGHAN

Introduction by
MARGARET ATWOOD

INTRODUCTION

by *Margaret Atwood*

Morley Callaghan, long considered the most important Canadian story writer of his generation — which he was — has also long been a literary misfit; people never knew quite what to make of him. Doubtless this was how he liked it: he took pleasure in baffling expectation. He's important, he's very important, they say; but why? Even the American critic Edmund Wilson, lavish in his praise of Callaghan in his 1964 book *O Canada*, spends a lot of time scratching his head. Callaghan's effects, he says, are so subtle, so modulated, yet so simple, that it's hard to describe them. And so it has often gone.

For those Canadian writers who began in the early 60s, cutting their teeth on beatniks and post-war French existentialists and the Theatre of the Absurd, Callaghan was neither fish nor fowl. He wrote of a time before our time, but not so long before that we had no memories of it. In some ways the world he depicted overlapped with our own age — we knew about the squalor of rooming houses, and grubby Depression-scarred lives lived on the financial margins, and the fear of unwanted pregnancy — but in those instances it represented parts of our lives we wanted to change, or hoped we had escaped. Such things held no glamour for us.

The esthetics of Callaghan's minimalist style, devoid of fancy words and metaphors — a style he hoped to render "transparent as glass" [1] — had excellent antecedents in the English tradition, from Addison's efforts to divest the

---

[1] *That Summer in Paris*, as reprinted in *Canadian Novelists and the Novel*, ed. Douglas Dayman and Leslie Monkman, Borealis Press, Ottawa, 1981. pp. 143-146.

eighteenth-century English stage of bombast and superfluous rhetoric, to Wordsworth's attempt, in *Lyrical Ballads*, to get back to the poetic basics, to Orwell's prose like a window-pane, intended to give us an unimpeded view of real life, like so many raw steaks in a butcher's display case. All such purifiers see their efforts as a sort of excavation: a fraudulent accumulation of grotty old barnacles called "the literary" or "the academic" must be scraped away in order to get to the deep-down freshness and newness of the actual — to truth, to honesty, or, in Callaghan's words, to "the object as it really was." [2]

However, if you're a writer, all this must be done through language, which is — how can the purifier get around it? — man-made, and therefore artificial. But if you must have speech, then make it plain speech; if words, then short words. Awkwardness is to be preferred to an overly carved and varnished elegance; and if elegance, then the elegance of a Shaker chair. These tendencies too can turn mannerist. Taken too far, you'd end up with a literature of monosyllables that would read like a *Dick and Jane* primer, but Callaghan avoided this trap.

Style in every art swings like a pendulum from the plain to the ornamented and back again, with "nature" and "artifice" being the polarizing catch-phrases; but we whippersnappers in the early 60s hadn't thought much about that. To us, the hard-boiled school — decades old by the time we came across it — seemed an almost comic affectation, like talking out of the side of the mouth in gangster films. The young are cruel, and they are most cruel to the quasi-

---

[2] *That Summer in Paris*, as reprinted in *Canadian Novelists and the Novel*, ed. Douglas Dayman and Leslie Monkman, Borealis Press, Ottawa, 1981. pp. 143-146.

parental generation preceding them, as Callaghan himself was cruel to the aesthetes of the turn of the century — "show-off writers,"[3] he termed them, fixated on demonstrating their own cleverness. It's a necessary cruelty, I suppose, or we would all be replicants.

Callaghan's legend — as opposed to the milieu depicted in his work — did have glamour for us, however. He'd been our age in the 1920s, and had written through the Great Depression and the War — eras that were now so far away that they were already furnishing the costumes for fancy-dress parties. In Paris, still thought of as the proper destination for an artist of any kind, he'd consorted with Hemingway and Fitzgerald — writers we'd studied in school, and who for that reason alone had an aura of semi-divinity, while at the same time being ridiculously hoary. Unlike those two, however, he'd become neither a drunk nor a suicide, and was said to be living in Toronto — Toronto! — an unromantic, second-rate city in which no real writer — surely — would live by choice. Why wasn't he stowed away in Paris or New York, where we wouldn't have to bother about him? Why did he stick around, like a burr?

What was it about Callaghan that made us uncomfortable? For one thing, he was doing something thought to be impossible: he was making a living in Canada, as a writer, albeit through sales in the United States and in England. That was a challenge, since it was a truism among us that you'd have to leave the country to get anywhere. We were — of course — provincials, who believed that the Great Good Place was somewhere else; and he was a non-provincial who

---

[3] *That Summer in Paris*, as reprinted in *Canadian Novelists and the Novel*, ed. Douglas Dayman and Leslie Monkman, Borealis Press, Ottawa, 1981. pp. 143-146.

understood the provincial — having once partaken of it —
and who had chosen this very provinciality as his material.
(He was a student of — among others — Flaubert and de
Maupassant, who had done the same.) We youngsters
weren't the only folk made nervous by this. As Edmund
Wilson said in 1960,

> The reviewer ... is now wondering whether the primary
> reason for the current underestimation of Morley
> Callaghan may not be a general incapacity — apparently
> shared by his compatriots — for believing that a writer
> whose work may be mentioned without absurdity in
> association with Chekhov's and Turgenev's can possibly
> be functioning in Toronto.[4]

Northrop Frye was another to put his finger on the
Canadian uneasiness with Callaghan. After having stated
that by 1929 Callaghan had established himself as perhaps
the best short-story writer in Canada, he later said,

> Morley Callaghan's books, I think I am right in saying,
> were sometimes banned by the public library in
> Toronto — I forget what the rationalization was, but
> the real reason could only have been that if a Canadian
> were to do anything so ethically dubious as write, he
> should at least write like a proper colonial and not like
> someone who had lived in the Paris of Joyce and
> Gertrude Stein. [5]

---

[4] Edmund Wilson, *O Canada: An American's Notes on Canadian Culture*.
Farrar, Strauss and Giroux, New York, 1964. Some essays 1960. page 21.

[5] *Northrop Frye on Canada*. Ed. by Jean O'Grady and David Staines.
University of Toronto Press, 2003. page 549.

Not surprisingly, Callaghan — who was nothing if not a scrapper — kicked against the pricks. He took the piss out of what he saw as the back-scratching mediocre sham literati in Canada, calling them — among other things — "local medicine men feasting and having a big cultural pow-wow," [6] and homegrown critics took the piss out of him for it, and he took the piss out of them back. One of these fracases took place live on television, after Callaghan had been praised by Edmund Wilson, and then predictably denounced for it by a two-bit academic, live on a talk show. Callaghan, no stranger to rancorous debate, did not take this sitting down. It was an object lesson in self-respect to the young, and one we needed; for at that time, in Canada, to be a writer was to be thought next door to a junk-bond salesman: shifty, not above pinching the silver, to be sneered at and viewed with suspicion.

Self-respect. Respect. Respectability. These are key concepts in Callaghan's work: in fact, "respect" is the last word in the last story in this collection. Almost every Callaghan character desires to have and to earn "respect," the admiration of others. "Self-respect" — that quality of inner integrity, the ability to hold up your head when you look in the mirror — is also highly valued. "Respectability" is ambiguous. You need it to get and hold a job, which connects you with money — the ability to earn a living, to show a girl a good time, and to buy coveted objects — often articles of clothing, for people were judged very much by their wardrobes in those days. Money is never out of the picture, because, for Callaghan's characters, it doesn't grow on trees. But "respectability" is also a negative. It's the lack of *joie de vivre*, the

6. From "The Plight of Canadian Fiction," (1938), reprinted in Dayman and Monkman, page 150.

absence of passion and energy; it's conformity; it's hypocrisy; it's mediocrity; it's a dingy grey stifling fog. It's also next door to self-righteousness, and self-righteousness was not a quality Callaghan admired, although it occupied him greatly as a subject.

Callaghan has frequently been compared with Fitzgerald and Hemingway, yet the concerns of the three are very different. In a Western shootout saga, Fitzgerald would have been interested in the cattle barons hiring the gunmen, Hemingway in the gunmen themselves; but Callaghan, though he might have paid some attention to both of the other groups, would have focused on the jittery townsfolk who were crouching behind the dry-goods counter. Fitzgerald was drawn to rich people, Hemingway to adventurous people, but Callaghan to people — men, usually — who might long to be rich and adventurous but who cannot actualize their longings, either because life has not provided them with the scope or because their own makeup defeats them. Their sense of their own worth is tenuous, as is their sense of their own bravery: both can stand or fall on an accident, an incident, a misunderstanding, an added pressure brought to bear. We identify with such characters because we've known people like them, but also because, given a change in circumstances, we could so easily find ourselves in their shoes.

As a story writer, Callaghan has been likened with many: Chekhov and Turgenev, Sherwood Anderson, Katherine Mansfield, de Maupassant, the Joyce of *Dubliners*, even O. Henry. His specialties were the small and thwarted life and the brief but exactly sketched state of emotion. Typically, his characters live in rooming houses or cramped apartments; they're unemployed, or in danger of losing their jobs or modest businesses. They borrow money they can't repay, or they get drunk and blow it, or they skirt the edge of minor criminality. If they are women, their husbands may have run off, or — and Callaghan's sense of gender interaction is exact for his times — they may be resented and even physically abused for having jobs when their men do not. If they are children or young people, adults let them down. If they are dogs, they are unfortunate.

Most of them indulge in irrational hopes and yearn for better things, but it's not likely they'll get them. They see themselves reflected in the eyes of others and the reflection does not please them, unless they are puffed up by a soon-to-be-deflated vainglory. Desiring to be looked up to, they more often feel belittled or small: size does matter. Occasionally someone will score points — the boy in "The New Kid" gains status through combat, the umpire in "Mother's Day at the Ballpark" is cheered by the crowd — confusingly for him — because he's punched a mother-insulting heckler. Amid the malice and the disappointment and the rage and the bitterness in these lives there are moments of generosity and joy, however unfounded; but such states of grace, we know, are temporary.

In literature, irony is a mode in which the reader guesses more accurately about the character's fate than he does himself, and in this sense Callaghan is a profoundly ironic writer. Life is not only a struggle, it's a puzzle. Another puzzle is why Callaghan, in *That Summer in Paris*, would claim to applaud the art he admires— his example is Matisse — as "a gay celebration of things as they were." [7] "Why couldn't all people have the eyes and heart that would give them this happy acceptance of reality?" he con-

---

[7] Dayman and Monkman, page 146.

tinues. Happiness and gaiety and acceptance of things as they are may have belonged to the author of Callaghan's stories, but they are not frequently found among his characters. Perhaps the stories are, in part, an attempt by Callaghan to answer his own question — to provide a "because" to go with the "why " — with the lamentable scarcity of the right kinds of hearts and eyes.

The next four words in the curious passage quoted above are "The word made flesh." The context might lead us to believe that this is an endorsement of a philosophy of immanence, of the divine *isness* of things — "The appleness of apples. Yet just apples," as Callaghan had just said of Cézanne. Yet they are also a signpost pointing towards Callaghan the Christian writer.[8]

This side of Callaghan is not obtrusive or doctrinaire, and yet it's there — the ground beneath the house, not always seen, but necessary. It's more obvious in the novels, and avoidable in "The Man with the Coat," the last short fiction Callaghan ever wrote — a transitional form, termed a novel in the 1955 issue of *Maclean's* magazine in which it appeared, but really a novella. Callaghan expanded it and changed the plot, and this version later appeared as *The Many Coloured Coat*.

"The Man with the Coat" is an adroitly constructed piece in which several characters take turns sneering at and belittling one another. Scorn is handed from character to character, like the hot object in a game of Pass the Package, until the sequence of blame leads to a tragic consequence.

---

[8] Right after this, Callaghan makes a dismissive remark about St. Paul. Christians often see themselves as having to choose between the road of St. Paul, which leads to Rome, and that of Christ, which leads to Cavalry. Not much doubt about which Callaghan preferred.

The motion is not circular, but spiral: its end is not its beginning. It's possible that this story was written as an attempt to work out a problem: how to write a tragedy in the age of the common man. Arthur Miller's *Death of a Salesman,* for instance, is pathetic rather than tragic in its effect, because the salesman can't fall from a high place, having never achieved one. The true tragic hero must plummet like a falling star, and his descent must be due in part to a weakness or flaw in his own character. Or so went the theory. Callaghan was widely read, and perfectly aware of the requirements. As he was a Christian writer, the flaw needed to be a flaw in Christian terms: more a sin than a flaw.

The story begins with a trial, and ends with one. The description of the physical ambiance — the smell of wet wool, the annoying *whoosh* of galoshes, every little thing — is spot-on, as is usual in Callaghan. Harry Lane, the hero, starts out as a sort of Timon of Athens before his reversal of fortune, or a Hamlet before the black-suit phase: he's the observed of all observers. He's a celebrated war hero, handsome, well-off, easy-going, generous, careless in a lily-of-the-field way, admired by all, and with a top-of-the-line girlfriend. The initial event in the plot is driven, like the acts of Cassius in *Julius Caesar,* by envy: a bank manager named Scotty uses Harry as the cat's paw in a fraudulent transaction, hoping to profit by it himself. But he gets caught, and is put on trial, and then kills himself, and Harry — undeservedly — has the moral guilt pinned on him. People look down on him. They expect him to feel small. They no longer respect him. For a Callaghan protagonist, this is awful.

Struggling to regain the esteem of his society, Harry passes the parcel of scorn to Scotty's friend, a tailor and ex-pugilist named Mike Kon. The vehicle is a coat with a faulty lining, made by Kon, interpreted by Harry as a gesture of disrespect towards himself. By spreading its story and wearing it everywhere, Harry makes Kon appear dishonest and a fool. (Kon passes on the scorn in his turn, and so does Molly, the upper-class girl with the cold heart who has thrown Harry over due to his disgrace.) But neither Harry nor Kon can resolve the conflict between them, because both suffer from the sin of pride. Both demand "justice."

The plot develops in rounds, like the boxing match that signals the climax of the action. In the course of vindicating themselves, defending their self-respect, and standing up for their honour, the characters wallop one another both verbally and physically, and are walloped in turn. There are three arbiters, or umpires, who stand outside the ring. One is the owner of the prestigious bar where all gather, or want to. He's the social arbiter: he decides, literally, who's in and who's out. The second is Mike Kon's father, an old man who's suffered a stroke. He's the spiritual arbiter. He can't talk, but he can write, and he delivers himself of a shakily-printed oracle that probably says *Judge not*. (The rest of the phrase, not supplied by the old man, is, . . . *lest ye be judged*. And so it is: all who judge are indeed judged in their turn.)

The third arbiter is Annie Laurie, a woman of large heart and easy morals, who unfortunately — like mermaids — has a jinx on her. The Annie Laurie in the song of that name gives promises true, and Callaghan's Annie also tells the truth, because — having no respectability — she has nothing to lose. She's got those coveted Callaghan qualities, honesty and the ability to show the object as it really is, and the reader trusts her. But the Annie Laurie in the song is a creature for whom men would lie down and die, and Callaghan's Annie

Laurie also has this effect on men who stay too long with her: they end up prone and breathless.

Are we intended to see her as a sort of *femme fatale*? I think not: she's connected with truth, not with poisonous wiles. Possibly one way of understanding her place in this story is to refer back to *Everyman*, that other simply written and episodic Christian tale of a man's progress towards the grave. Most of Everyman's companions — Kin, Good Fellowship, and the like — desert him when times get tough, as Harry's pals do. The one left at the end is female, and her name is Knowledge. It could be that Annie Laurie is no fatal woman, but instead a kindly psychopomp, a tender conductress of the soul, a helpful companion on Harry's fated journey. She does try to warn him away from the paths of pride: she's got the kind of knowledge he needs. But he won't listen.

It is Annie who is present when Harry is killed, and Annie who testifies at the trial. Like many a prophetess, she isn't much believed; in her case, because of her dubious sexual reputation. It's Mike Kon, Harry's erstwhile enemy and slayer, who — exonerated by the same legal system that earlier caused Harry so much grief — ends up as the shield-bearer, the Horatio figure, the teller of dead Harry's story. He has learned what it is to judge and to be judged, and has opted for the hidden alternative to justice, which is mercy. It's a conclusion both deeply ironic and oddly compassionate.

Which, underneath everything else, would seem to be the appleness of apples at the very bottom of the Callaghan barrel. Irony and compassion. The Callaghanness of Callaghan. Yet just Callaghan. The object as it really is.

THE
RED HAT

———◆◇◆———

*I*t was the kind of hat Frances had wanted for months, plain
and little and red with the narrow brim tacked back, which
would look so smart and simple and expensive. There was
really very little to it, it was so plain, but it was the kind of felt
hat that would have made her feel confident of a sleek appearance. She stood on the pavement, her face pressed up close
against the shop window, a slender, tall, and good-looking girl
wearing a reddish woolen dress clinging tightly to her body.
On the way home from work, the last three evenings, she
had stopped to look at the hat. And when she had got home
she had told Mrs. Foley, who lived in the next apartment, how
much the little hat appealed to her. In the window were many
smart hats, all very expensive. There was only one red felt
hat, on a mannequin head with a silver face and very red lips.

Though Frances stood by the window a long time she
had no intention of buying the hat, because her husband
was out of work and they couldn't afford it; she was waiting for him to get a decent job so that she could buy clothes
for herself. Not that she looked shabby, but the fall weather
was a little cold, a sharp wind sometimes blowing gustily up
the avenue, and in the twilight, on the way home from work

with the wind blowing, she knew she ought to be wearing a light coat. In the early afternoon when the sun was shining brightly she looked neat and warm in her woolen dress.

Though she ought to have been on her way home Frances couldn't help standing there, thinking she might look beautiful in this hat if she went out with Eric for the evening. Since he had been so moody and discontented recently she now thought of pleasing him by wearing something that would give her a new kind of elegance, of making him feel cheerful and proud of her and glad, after all, that they were married.

But the hat cost fifteen dollars. She had eighteen dollars in her purse, all that was left of her salary after shopping for groceries for the week. It was ridiculous for her to be there looking at the hat, which was obviously too expensive for her, so she smiled and walked away, putting both hands in the small pockets of her dress. She walked slowly, glancing at two women who were standing at the other end of the big window. The younger one, wearing a velvet coat trimmed with squirrel, said to the other: "Let's go in and try some of them on."

Hesitating and half turning, Frances thought it would be quite harmless and amusing if she went into the shop and tried on the red hat, just to see if it looked as good on her as it did on the mannequin head. It never occurred to her to buy the hat.

In the shop, she walked on soft, thick, gray carpet to the chair by the window, where she sat alone for a few minutes, waiting for one of the saleswomen to come to her. At one of the mirrors an elderly lady with bleached hair was fussing with many hats and talking to a deferential and patient saleswoman. Frances, looking at the big dominant woman with the bleached hair and the expensive clothes, felt embarrassed, because she thought it ought to be apparent to everyone in the shop, by the expression on her face, that she had no intention of taking a hat.

A deep-bosomed saleswoman, wearing black silk, smiled at Frances, appraising her carefully. Frances was the kind of customer who might look good in any one of the hats. At the same time, while looking at her, the saleswoman wondered why she wasn't wearing a coat, or at least carrying one, for the evenings were often chilly.

"I wanted to try on the little hat, the red one in the window," Frances said.

The saleswoman had decided by this time that Frances intended only to amuse herself by trying on hats, so when she took the hat from the window and handed it to Frances she smiled politely and watched her adjusting it on her head. Frances tried the hat and patted a strand of fair hair till it curled by the side of the brim. And then, because she was delighted to see that it was as attractive on her as it had been on the mannequin head with the silver face, she smiled happily, noticing in the mirror that her face was the shape of the mannequin face, a little long and narrow, the nose fine and firm, and she took out her lipstick and marked her lips. Looking in the mirror again she felt elated and seemed to enjoy a kind of freedom. She felt elegant and a little haughty. Then she saw the image of the deep-bosomed and polite saleslady.

"It is nice, isn't it?" Frances said, wishing suddenly that she hadn't come into the store.

"It is wonderfully becoming to you, especially to you."

And Frances said suddenly: "I suppose I could change it, if my husband didn't like it."

"Of course."

"Then I'll take it."

Even while paying for the hat and assuring herself that it would be amusing to take it home for the evening, she had a feeling that she ought to have known when she first came into the store that she intended to take the hat home. The saleswoman was smiling. Frances, no longer embarrassed, thought with pleasure of going out with Eric and wearing the hat, tucking the price tag up into her hair. In the morning she could return it.

But as she walked out of the store there was a hope way down within her that Eric would find her so charming in the red hat he would insist she keep it. She wanted him to be freshly aware of her, to like the hat, to discover its restrained elegance. And when they went out together for the evening they would both share the feeling she had had when first she had looked in the shop window. Frances, carrying the box, hurried, eager to get home. The sharp wind had gone down. When there was no wind on these fall evenings it was not cold, and she would not have to wear a coat with her woolen dress. It was just about dark now and all the lights were lit in the streets.

The stairs in the apartment house were long, and on other evenings very tiring, but tonight she seemed to be breathing lightly as she opened the door. Her husband was sitting by the table lamp, reading the paper. A black-haired man with a well-shaped nose, he seemed utterly without energy, slumped down in the chair. A slight odor of whiskey came from him. For four months he had been out of work and some of the spirit had gone out of him, as if he felt that he could never again have independence, and most of the afternoon he had been standing in the streets by the theaters, talking with actors who were out of work.

"Hello, Eric boy," she said, kissing him on the head.

"'Lo, France."

"Let's go out and eat tonight," she said.

"What with?"

"Bucks, big boy, a couple of dollar dinners."

He had hardly looked at her. She went into the bedroom and took the hat out of the box, adjusting it on her head at the right angle, powdering her nose and smiling cheerfully. Jauntily she walked into the living room, swinging her hips a little and trying not to smile too openly.

"Take a look at the hat, Eric. How would you like to step out with me?"

Smiling faintly, he said: "You look snappy, but you can't afford a hat."

"Never mind that. How do you like it?"

"What's the use if you can't keep it."

"Did you ever see anything look so good on me?"

"Was it bargain day somewhere?"

"Bargain day! Fifteen bucks at one of the best shops!"

"You'd bother looking at fifteen-dollar hats with me out of work?" he said angrily, getting up and glaring at her.

"I would."

"It's your money. You do what you want."

Frances felt hurt, as if for months there had been a steady pressure on her, and she said stubbornly: "I paid for it. Of course, I can take it back if you insist."

"If I insist," he said, getting up slowly and sneering at her as though he had been hating her for months. "*If I insist.* And you know how I feel about the whole business."

Frances felt hurt and yet strong from indignation, so she shrugged her shoulders, saying. "I wanted to wear it tonight."

His face was white, his eyes almost closed. Suddenly he grabbed hold of her by the wrist, twisting it till she sank down on one knee.

"You'll get rid of that hat or I'll break every bone in your body. I'll clear out of here for good."

"Eric, please."

"You've been keeping me, haven't you?"

"Don't, Eric."

"Get your fifteen-buck hat out of my sight. Get rid of it, or I'll get out of here for good."

He snatched the hat from her head, pulling it, twisting it in his hands, then throwing it on the floor. He kicked it across the room. "Get it out of here or we're through."

The indignation had gone out of Frances. She was afraid of him; afraid, too, that he would suddenly rush out of the room and never come back, for she knew he had thought of doing it before. Picking up the hat she caressed the soft felt with her fingers, though she could hardly see it with her eyes filled with tears. The felt was creased, the price tag had been torn off, leaving a tiny tear at the back.

Eric was sitting there, watching her.

The hat was torn and she could not take it back. She put it in the box, wrapping the tissue paper around it, and then she went along the hall to Mrs. Foley's apartment.

Mrs. Foley, a smiling, fat woman with a round, cheerful face, opened the door. She saw Frances was agitated and felt sorry for her. "Frances, dear, what's the matter with you?"

"You remember the hat I was telling you about? Here it is. It doesn't look good on me. I was disappointed and pulled it off my head and there's a tiny tear in it. Maybe you'd want it."

Mrs. Foley thought at once that Frances had been quarreling with her husband. Mrs. Foley held up the hat and looked at it shrewdly. Then she went back into her bedroom and tried it on. The felt was good, and though it had been creased, it was quite smooth now. "Of course, I never pay more than five dollars for a hat," she said. The little felt hat did not look good on her round head and face.

"I hate to offer you five dollars for it, Frances, but . . ."

"All right. Give me five dollars."

As Mrs. Foley took the five dollars from her purse, Frances said suddenly: "Listen, dear, if I want it back next week you'll sell it back to me for five?"

"Sure I will, kid."

Frances hurried to her own apartment. Though she knew Eric could not have gone out while she was standing in the hall, she kept on saying to herself: "Please, Heaven, please don't let me do anything to make him leave me while he's feeling this way."

Eric, with his arms folded across his chest, was looking out of the window. Frances put the five dollars Mrs. Foley had given her, and the three dollars left over from her salary, on the small table by Eric's chair. "I sold it to Mrs. Foley," she said.

"Thanks," he said, without looking at her.

"I'm absolutely satisfied," she said, softly and sincerely.

"All right, I'm sorry," he said briefly.

"I mean I don't know what makes you think I'm not satisfied — that's all," she said.

Sitting beside him she put her elbow on her knee and thought of the felt hat on Mrs. Foley's head: it did not look good on her; her face was not the shape of the long silver face of the mannequin head. As Frances thought of the way the hat had looked on the head in the window she hoped vaguely that something would turn up so that she could get it back from Mrs. Foley by the end of the week. And just thinking of it, she felt that faint haughty elation; it was a plain little red hat, the kind of hat she had wanted for months, elegant and expensive, a plain felt hat, so very distinctive.

TIMOTHY HARSHAW'S FLUTE

*A*lthough both were out of work, Timothy Harshaw and his wife were the happiest people in the Barrow Street house. Timothy was a very fair young man who never thought of wearing a suit coat with trousers to match, and yet somehow he looked carefully groomed and even distinguished.

In the evenings, Mr. Weeks, a bank teller who lived in the one-room apartment behind the Harshaws', heard Timothy playing his silver flute. When Mr. Weeks could stand the flute-playing no longer, he rapped on the Harshaws' door and pretended he was making a social call. Mrs. Harshaw opened the door. A plain gray sweater made her look slim and attractive. She was at least thirty-two, but she was so effusive, with her short, straight black hair, her high-bridged nose and her sparkling eyes that she seemed like a young girl. Mr. Weeks was welcomed so enthusiastically by the Harshaws that he began to feel ashamed of his surliness; both bowed politely and hurried to get him something to drink. They explained that Timothy had learned to play the silver flute at the Sorbonne in Paris, where he had had a scholarship.

Louise Harshaw had never been to France but she talked about Paris as if she knew every boulevard, bistro, *bal musette*, and café, until she was ready to laugh at her own eagerness. On this night both the Harshaws seemed jubilant, as if they had suddenly settled all their important problems. Mr. Weeks couldn't help asking, "What's making you so happy tonight, Mrs. Harshaw?" and she burst out at once, "We've just decided we'll never get anywhere in this country. We're going to go away for good and live in Paris, aren't we, Timothy?"

Mr. Weeks looked at Timothy, who was sitting cross-legged on the bed, holding his silver flute loosely in his hand. The Harshaws had cut the posts off their bed so it would look more like a couch. "That's right, Louise," Timothy said, his face brightening. "There's nothing here for us, Weeks. I ought to have seen that long ago. I'll live as a translator in Paris. The main thing, though, is to get there."

"Are you going right away?"

"Oh, no," they both said together, "we're awfully poor now."

"How are you going to do it, then?"

"We'll both get a job and work," they said. "Then we'll save."

The Harshaws went out every morning looking for work. At noontime they met in Childs' restaurant and amused each other, mimicking the peculiar mannerisms of everyone they had encountered. They seemed to have all of the shining enthusiasm that makes every obstacle a stimulation. Timothy was the first to get a job, in the advertising and publicity department of a publishing house. The more he talked about it to Louise, the more he felt like celebrating, so he borrowed five dollars from the bank teller, who loaned it with reluctance, though he became more cheerful when Timothy, slapping him on the back, invited him to help spend the money. They went to a delicatessen store to buy some cheese.

"People don't seem to understand that a gentleman ought to know his cheeses every bit as well as his wines," Timothy explained, and he bought brie, camembert, gorgonzola, munster, and gruyère. He also bought a bottle of red Italian wine. When they got home, Mr. Weeks thought Mrs. Harshaw might resent Timothy's initial extravagance, but instead she moved around getting plates and glasses as though they were about to start playing a new, delightful game. It occurred to her, too, to phone her friend, Selma Simpson, who did publicity for a small theatrical producer, so they would have more of a party.

That night the Harshaws talked a good deal about France. Timothy had been so happy at the Sorbonne. And, there were the trips you could take to places like Chartres: Louise was dying to see the cathedral.

"We'd like to take over the whole darn tradition, if you see what we mean," Timothy said, leaning forward.

"It sounds swell. Maybe I'll take a trip like that some day," Mr. Weeks said. "When are you going?"

"In the spring. Everybody goes to Paris in the spring — it's the season. Why don't you come with us?"

"I may at that," Mr. Weeks said, ashamed of himself for lying. Timothy was making forty dollars a week and they put ten in a bank that gave them a red bank book. In order that they would not sacrifice money on foolish pleasures, they decided to stay home at night and Timothy would teach Louise French. When they began the lessons, Louise learned rapidly. Timothy was full of joy, and they were both so pleased with themselves they thought their friend, Mr. Weeks, might like to take lessons, too. At first, Mr. Weeks tried seriously to speak French, but they were both so eager to help him he became self-conscious and made a joke of the whole business.

In the second week of November Timothy lost his job at the publishing house, for a reason that perplexed and angered him. As he told it to Louise, walking up and down rubbing his hand through his hair, it seemed ridiculous. He had got into an argument with his boss about theosophy and had suggested that modern Americans might be the ancient Egyptians reincarnated. The boss, slamming his fists on the desk, had begun to tell Timothy everything that was wrong with him — when he wrote advertising, he couldn't understand he was appealing to the masses; he was always making sly jokes for his own amusement; and anyway, it was obvious he couldn't adapt himself to the routine of the office. Timothy was fired. "There was something underhanded about it, Louise. We didn't seem to face each other like gentlemen at all." He kept looking anxiously at his wife.

Louise wanted to cry. Her face was white and pinched, as if once again in her life she had reached out and tried to touch something that had always eluded her. But she said earnestly, "It's all right, Timothy. You can't destroy your character for such people. I'll get a job and we'll go right on saving."

There were two difficult weeks when they hardly spent a cent for food, because Louise wouldn't draw money out of the bank. They ate canned soups and cereals, and were most hungry when they talked about the good times they would have in Europe in the spring.

Then they had an unbelievable piece of good fortune. They could hardly believe such luck: Louise's friend, Selma, quit her job to get married, and she asked Louise if she would like to take it. Louise wouldn't say anything; she kept swallowing hard till she went around to see the producer with Selma. He listened while Selma swore there wasn't a girl like Louise in the whole country; then he smiled benevolently. Louise got the job.

For a while the Harshaws were happier than they had been at any time since they were married; they had a splendid goal ahead of them — Europe, with a tradition and environment that would appeal to Timothy — and they had some money in the bank. Louise worked hard, rebuffed her sly, sentimental employer sweetly, and hurried home every night to Timothy, who cooked the dinner for her. He stood at the window waiting for her, with one of her aprons around his waist. He had taken a fancy to cooking.

Toward the end of December, the Harshaws had the calmness and deep inner contentment of people who can see ahead clearly. They had one hundred and twenty dollars in the bank. They talked of going third-class on the boat. Whenever they talked for very long about it in the room, they became silent, almost hushed with expectancy, and then one night they put on their coats and hats and went out together to walk through the rain without talking at all. They went into a church and knelt with their heads down and prayed, and when they had finished praying, they sat there in the pew instead of going home. They sat there, close together.

Then, Louise began to get very tired and nervous. Timothy noticed that she was sometimes short-tempered. When Selma, who often dropped in on them, came around intending to speak to him about Louise, he was so happy and confident he made Selma feel like an old chaperon who was not wanted, so she said: "Keep your eye on Louise, Timothy," and looked at him searchingly. Timothy smiled, thanked her for her solicitude, and became silent and very worried.

One night when Louise came home from work, she was so tired she couldn't eat. She sat looking at Timothy with a kind of helpless earnestness, and then she almost fainted. When he was rubbing her forehead and her wrists, she told him she was going to have a baby, and she watched him with a dogged eagerness, her whole manner full of apology. At last he took a deep breath, and said, "Good, good. That gives a man a sense of completion. Let's hope it's a boy, Louise." He became very gay. He played his flute for her. He explained he had bought a neat little machine for rolling his own cigarettes, and his good humor so pleased her she let herself whisper, "Wouldn't it be wonderful if we could have the baby born in France?"

She worked the rest of the winter, but in March she had to stop. The baby was born early one gray morning in May. Timothy had got a young obstetrical specialist who was willing to take the case without having Louise go to a hospital. It never occurred to Timothy that he would have to pay him. All that damp spring night the doctor and Timothy sat in the kitchen waiting. Timothy was polite, but he looked sick. With a mild graciousness, while the light overhead shone on his fair bright head, he talked about the Sorbonne, though sometimes he halted and listened for sounds from the other room. The doctor liked him and nodded his head patiently.

At five o'clock in the morning, the doctor called Timothy into the other room, and he went in and kissed his wife. For a moment he was so relieved he could only grin without even thinking of the baby. Louise, looking waxen-faced and fragile, smiled at Timothy and said, "We've got a boy, even if we're not in Paris, Timothy."

"It's splendid," he said, beaming with pride and relief and making her love him. He bent down and whispered, "Last time I was in Paris in the spring, it was cold and damp. The fall is a far better time, dear. Paris'll wait. It'll always be there for us."

Then the doctor beckoned to Timothy and they went back to the kitchen. The doctor said, "I might as well tell you, Mr. Harshaw, you'll have to give your wife your undivided attention for a while. However, I congratulate you." They shook hands very solemnly. "Remember, be cheerful. Don't let this interfere with your wife's plans. Do what you want to do."

"We were going to go to Europe. We won't be able to do that for a while."

"No. Not for a while, of course."

"Of course not. Not for months, anyway," Timothy said. Then they were both silent.

"If I can be of any assistance at all," the doctor said diffidently. Timothy, reflecting a moment, said eagerly, "By the way, tell me, do you know a good indoor tennis court? When Mrs. Harshaw gets up, I'd like her to take exercise. We don't want her to lose her shape, you know. She wouldn't want this to make any difference."

"I'll let you know if I hear of one," the doctor said, as he picked up his bag to leave.

Outside, the gray, misty morning had become a morning of fine, thin rain. On the street the doctor stopped suddenly, listening. He stood looking back at Timothy's place, hearing faint flute music.

A REGRET
FOR YOUTH

*T*he first time Mrs. Jerry Austin's husband went away, she cried and wrote a long letter home, but in two months' time he came back. They had dinner and agreed never to quarrel again and he promised not to feel restless any more. The second time he left her, she didn't bother looking for a job. She told the landlady, Mrs. Oddy, that Mr. Austin had gone traveling and was doing well. Mrs. Oddy, who had red hair, a toothy accent and a loud voice, said that whenever Mr. Oddy did any traveling she liked to keep him company, but after all, it was none of her business.

Mrs. Austin had paid a month's rent in advance. She was friendly with Mrs. Oddy, who occasionally invited her to go motoring. Mr. and Mrs. Oddy sat in the front seat and Mrs. Austin sat in the back seat. Mr. Oddy was in the civil service, a good job, but his wife got twice as much money from her three rooming houses. Mr. Oddy always drove the car as fast as possible along Lakeshore Drive and Mrs. Oddy made a long conversation over her shoulder about a trip she had planned for Europe next year.

In the long summer evenings Mrs. Austin was sometimes lonesome. She sat on the front step till dusk talking to Mrs. Oddy, then she went upstairs to her kitchen to sit down at the window and look out through the leaves on the tree across the street to the well-kept school ground, the shadowed building and the few stars coming out over the roof of the school. Four men standing underneath a lamppost at the corner were trying to make harmony with their voices, but only one fellow had a good voice, the others were timid. She listened, leaning out of the window, hoping they would follow through with the next piece instead of laughing in the middle of it. She heard a loud laugh and the men moved farther down the street, singing softly, lazily. Disappointed, she pulled down the blind and turned on the light.

She heard the Oddys talking downstairs, Mrs. Oddy's voice loud and sharp because her husband was a little deaf. She talked to everybody as though they were a little deaf. That was mainly the trouble with Mrs. Oddy. Mrs. Austin got out her ironing board, adjusting the electric plug in the wall. She patted the board two or three times, hesitating till she decided she didn't feel like ironing at the moment, so she went to her bedroom and looked at herself in the large expensive mirror her mother had given her. Mrs. Austin patted her hair, the knot at the back of the neck, and the wave at the side. She had fine, fair hair. Her nose wasn't a good nose and she was too plump for her height. She was only thirty but looked at least five years older. Her legs were short and plump but shaped nicely at the ankles. She wanted to get thin but couldn't diet for more than five days at a time.

She combed her hair carelessly, staring in the mirror, not concentrating but simply passing time, pleasant thoughts in her head. In the next room she heard a noise and knew the young man, Mr. Jarvis, would be going out soon. She hoped he would speak to her as he passed the open door and maybe ask her to go for a walk. Before Jerry went away she had thought of Mr. Jarvis only occasionally, after a quarrel usually, and had been unhappy when she found herself thinking too often of him. Now that Jerry had left her she enjoyed having long imaginary conversations with the young man and was glad her ankles were slender. She was at least eight years older than he, and really didn't know him very well but liked his small hands, and his slim body, and was sure he had a good education, and would probably wear spats in the winter. Once she had given him a cup of tea and another time had made his bed. She liked making his bed. Vaguely she thought of Jerry, missing him merely because she was used to him. The idea of his walking in the door didn't excite her at all.

She knotted her hair again and returned to the ironing board. Mr. Jarvis, going along the hall, passed the open door and called, "How's the little lady tonight?"

"Fine and dandy," she said.

He passed quickly and she caught only a glimpse of him, but his shoes were shiny and his suit well pressed. She thought of going downstairs and suggesting to Mrs. Oddy that they ask the young man to go motoring with them some night, but realized that Mr. Oddy, who didn't like Jarvis, would say something unpleasant. Oddy had often said the young fellow was too deep for him.

At the end of the month Mrs. Austin had a hard time paying the rent. The landlady suggested Jerry was indeed a peculiar traveling man, and the suggestion irritated Mrs. Austin, so she took twenty-one dollars out of the bank and for three dollars sold a small bookcase to a second-hand dealer who called at the house once a week for rags, bones, and bottles. At four o'clock in the afternoon, Mrs. Oddy, not quite so friendly now, came upstairs to examine critically Mrs. Austin's furniture. She offered to buy the mirror because it was an awkward size and not much use to anybody. Mrs. Austin said her husband might object. Mrs. Oddy eagerly disagreed for she had been waiting a long time to talk plainly about Mr. Austin. She talked rapidly, waving her arms till Mrs. Austin said, "For heaven's sake, Mrs. Oddy, you'll have a hemorrhage if you don't watch out."

But afterward she cried, eager to leave the city and go home, but was ashamed to tell the folks Jerry had left her again. Besides, Jerry would be back soon. Stretched out on the bed, she dabbed her nose with a handkerchief and was glad she had at least been dignified with Mrs. Oddy, practically insisting the woman mind her own business. She got up and looked out of the window at the clean streets in the sunlight. She decided to go out for a walk; many people passing on the street would be company for her.

She took off her housedress and before putting on her blue serge suit with the coat that was a little tight, she stood in front of the mirror, patting her sides and hips critically, dissatisfied. She needed another corset, she thought. She had only a few dollars in the bank, and a little food in the house, but was worried mainly about having a good strong corset. She nodded vigorously at her image in the mirror, many angry words that she might have used to Mrs. Oddy coming into her head.

It was a hot day, there was bright sunlight and men were carrying their coats. She walked all the way downtown. In one of the department stores she bought a corset and arranged to have it sent C.O.D. It was five o'clock before she started to walk home. At her corner she saw Mr. Jarvis getting off the streetcar. He raised his hat, slowing down so that they could walk home together. She talked eagerly about Mrs. Oddy and about being a little lonesome. He had many splendid words he could use carelessly. Nearly all the words pleased her and made her feel happy. He was carrying a yellow slicker though it didn't look like rain, carrying it neatly hooked under his arm close to his hip. She liked his clean fedora at a jaunty angle on his head and was sorry his mouth turned down a little at the corners.

Opposite the Women's Christian Temperance Union they turned the corner. Some boys were playing catch on the road and over in the schoolyard girls were playing baseball.

"I don't think I'll go right up," she said. "I think I'll sit on the steps a while and watch the kids play."

"Want some company?" He grinned at her.

"Oh, I nearly always like company."

They sat on the stone alongside the steps. Mr. Jarvis went on talking, enjoying his own jokes and Mrs. Austin's laughter. For a while she tried watching the girls playing, her eyes following white and red blouses and light and dark skirts on the green grass across the road, and she listened to high-pitched shouting, but losing interest in the game, she wondered how she could keep him talking.

She saw Mr. Oddy turn the corner, a paper under his arm. He came along the street, a big man. He turned up the walk. He nodded curtly and went in the house.

"That guy's an egg," Mr. Jarvis said.

"A what?"

"Boiled a little too long."

"I don't like him much myself."

Mr. Jarvis, getting up, held open the door, and followed her upstairs where he smiled good-naturedly and said good evening. She heard him going downstairs.

She took off her hat and coat and smiled at herself in the mirror. She fingered her hair. For the first time in months she looked closely at her hair and was glad it was so nice. She smiled and knew she wouldn't feel lonesome for some time. She moved around the room glancing in the mirror to catch glimpses of herself, pretending she was not alone. She ate some supper and found herself comparing Mr. Jarvis with Jerry. She didn't think of Jerry as her husband, simply as a man she had known a long time before he had gone away.

Three days after the walk along the street with Mr. Jarvis she wrote home to tell her mother Jerry had gone away again. Her mother said in a long letter that Jerry was a good-for-nothing who would never amount to a hill of beans in this world, and enclosed was the railroad fare home, if she wanted to come. There was some gossip in the letter about people she had known, two or three girls she had known at school were married and had babies. Thinking of these girls with their babies made her feel bad. Rather than go home and meet these people she would try and get a job in one of the department stores. She put the money for the railroad fare in the bank.

She went downtown but it was hard to get a job because of summer holidays and the slack time in all the big stores. In the evening, wondering what she could sell to the second-hand dealer, she selected two chairs. She put the chairs in a corner, and standing a few feet away, her hands on her hips, made up her mind to pay rent by the week from now on.

Mrs. Oddy rapped on the door and wanted to know how Mrs. Austin was getting on with the rent money.

"At the end of the month I'll start paying by the week," Mrs. Austin said.

"Oh, that's up to you, of course."

"Yes, it's up to me."

"Are you sure you can get it? Of course it's none of my business."

"I'll get it all right."

Mrs. Oddy looked around the room and saw the chairs in the corner. Not sure of herself, she said, "Maybe you'll need to be selling something soon."

"Just a thing or two. I don't know what's the matter with Jerry, he should be back any day now." She knew she didn't want Jerry to come back.

"Well, if you're selling stuff, I'll always take that mirror for a fair price."

"Oh, no thanks."

"How much do you want for it?"

"I really wouldn't sell it."

"No?"

"Really no."

Mrs. Oddy, sucking her lips, said mildly, "The girls across the hall say you're a bit cuckoo, you and the mirror, I mean."

"Well, I certainly like the nerve of those hussies."

"Oh, I don't know, they say you're looking for a husband in the mirror."

"Very clever."

"I thought so myself."

The girls across the hall had seen her combing her hair a few times, Mrs. Oddy explained. Mrs. Austin, listening politely, became indignant. Mrs. Austin had intended to speak fiercely but said, "The mirror is company for me in a way."

Mrs. Oddy laughed good-humoredly. "We do have some queer people around here, quaint, I mean. You and the uppish Mr. Jarvis. We'll find out a thing or two about him yet and out he'll go."

Mr. Jarvis had been two days late paying his room rent, she explained.

"What's the matter with him?" she asked.

"There's something fishy."

"How do you mean, Mrs. Oddy?"

"For one thing, where does he work?"

"I don't know. Do you?"

"He doesn't work, that's the point, and he's so superior."

"I don't think so."

"And much above everyone else around here, a mighty suspicious character, I tell you."

Mrs. Oddy went out. When the door was closed Mrs. Austin started to laugh at her, a suspicious woman, a ridiculous woman with a long tongue and a loud voice, but suddenly remembering the girls across the hall she felt unhappy. Two waitresses found her amusing; commonplace girls with huge hands who took off their coats as soon as they got into the house and sat around in their vests. She had never seen Mr. Jarvis without his jacket on. Then she worried Mr. Jarvis would go away and there were things she wanted to say to him. Before going to bed that evening she combed her hair, smiling at herself in the mirror, wondering if she would be able to find the right words so she could tell him how much she liked him and would be happy if she could please him.

For the first time she looked carefully at the mirror, the handsome oak frame, the wide bevel. She laughed out loud, thinking of Mrs. Oddy and the girls across the hall.

A week later Mrs. Oddy told her that Mr. Jarvis was again late with his rent and that they had come to a definite conclusion about him, and Mr. Oddy was going to give him so many hours to get out. Mr. Oddy had two minds to go over to a police station and see if the young man had a record.

Mrs. Austin waited for Mr. Jarvis to come home at five-thirty that evening. She imagined herself talking to him till she had convinced him she really loved him and they would be happy together in another city after she divorced Jerry. She was excited, feeling timidly that there was an understanding between them so she could talk freely.

He came up the stairs about half past five. Mrs. Austin heard Mrs. Oddy follow him upstairs. Then Mr. Oddy came up slowly. Mrs. Austin opened her door. Mrs. Oddy was saying, "My husband has something to say to you, young man."

"That's unusual," Mr. Jarvis said.

"I've got nothing much to say," Mr. Oddy said. "You'd better clear out, that's all. This ain't a charity circus."

"No."

"You heard me."

"All right. You mind telling me what's eating you?"

"You got two hours to get out," Oddy said. "I know all about you, I had you looked up."

"You're a stupid man, Mr. Oddy."

"Don't worry about that," Oddy said.

"You're a great ox, Mr. Oddy."

Mrs. Austin, stepping out in the hall, looked coldly at Mrs. Oddy and put her hands on her hips.

"You just can't help being ridiculous, Mrs. Oddy," she said.

"Well, I like your nerve, Mrs. Austin," the landlady said. "An abandoned woman like you," she said. "We've too many people like you. The house'll get a bad name." Mrs. Austin said she would certainly leave the house the next day.

Alone in her room, Mrs. Austin sat down to write home. She was excited and felt she wouldn't really go home at all. She lay awake in bed wondering if she would be able to talk to Mr. Jarvis before he went away.

At noontime the next day he rapped at her door. He smiled and said he heard her say she was going home and he would like to escort her to the train station. He was polite and good-humored. The train didn't go till four, she said. He offered to come at three. When he had gone she phoned an express company and arranged to have her furniture shipped home. She worked hard for an hour packing and cleaning. She dressed slowly and carefully. She took many deep breaths. She put on the blue serge suit and wore a small green felt hat fitting her head snugly.

At three o'clock he called. She hurried around the room, fussing, and getting herself excited. He said not to hurry, they had lots of time to walk to the station. They walked along the street, talking agreeably, a stout little woman in a green felt hat, and a short blue coat a little tight around the waist, trying not to feel much older than the neatly dressed fellow. She let herself think they were going away together. She didn't think he would actually get on the train but it seemed as if he ought to. They talked about the Oddys. He said he would have a new job next week. When she saw the clock at the station tower she was uneasy because she couldn't bring the conversation to a point where she could explain her feeling for him.

"I'm glad I met you at the Oddy's, anyway," she said.

"Well, it was a relief to meet you," he said sincerely. He added that very few women knew how to mind their own business.

In the station she bought her ticket, fumbling in her purse for coins. She felt that something was slipping away from her. "He ought to speak to me," she said to herself fiercely, then felt foolish for thinking it.

"It's funny the Oddys had something against both of us," she said. He laughed boyishly and helped her on the train.

"What did they have against you?" he said.

"They thought I was seeing things in the mirror. How about you?"

"I was holding something back, something up my sleeve, I guess."

"Funny the way they linked us together," she said shyly.

"Yeah."

"Don't you think it was funny?"

"Yeah, you bet. The old dame was seeing things, not you."

She stood on the last step, looking down at him and smiling awkwardly. She got confused when the train moved. "You're a good sport," he said, "I have an aunt just like you."

He waved cheerfully. "Good luck, Mrs. Austin."

"Good luck," she repeated vaguely.

"Goodbye."

"Goodbye . . ."

A VERY
MERRY CHRISTMAS

After midnight on Christmas Eve hundreds of people prayed at the crib of the Infant Jesus, which was to the right of the altar under the evergreen-tree branches in St. Malachi's Church. That night there had been a heavy fall of wet snow, and there was a muddy path up to the crib. Both Sylvanus O'Meara, the old caretaker who had helped to prepare the crib, and Father Gorman, the stout, red-faced, excitable parish priest, had agreed it was the most lifelike tableau of the Child Jesus in a corner of the stable at Bethlehem they had ever had in the church.

But early on Christmas morning Father Gorman came running to see O'Meara, the blood drained out of his face and his hands pumping up and down at his sides, and he shouted, "A terrible thing has happened. Where is the Infant Jesus? The crib's empty."

O'Meara, who was a devout, innocent, wondering old man, who prayed a lot and always felt very close to God in the church, was bewildered and he whispered. "Who could have taken it? Taken it where?"

"Take a look in the crib yourself, man, if you don't believe me," the priest said, and he grabbed the caretaker by the arm, marched him into the church and over to the crib and showed him that the figure of the Infant Jesus was gone.

"Someone took it, of course. It didn't fly away. But who took it, that's the question?" the priest said. "When was the last time you saw it?"

"I know it was here last night," O'Meara said, "because after the midnight mass when everybody else had gone home I saw Mrs. Farrel and her little boy kneeling up here, and when they stood up I wished them a Merry Christmas. You don't think she'd touch it, do you?"

"What nonsense, O'Meara. There's not a finer woman in the parish. I'm going over to her house for dinner tonight."

"I noticed that she wanted to go home, but the little boy wanted to stay there and keep praying by the crib; but after they went home I said a few prayers myself and the Infant Jesus was still there."

Grabbing O'Meara by the arm the priest whispered excitedly, "It must be the work of communists or atheists." There was a sudden rush of blood to his face. "This isn't the first time they've struck at us," he said.

"What would communists want with the figure of the Infant Jesus?" O'Meara asked innocently. "They wouldn't want to have it to be reminded that God was with them. I didn't think they could bear to have Him with them."

"They'd take it to mock at us, of course, and to desecrate the church. O'Meara, you don't seem to know much about the times we live in. Why did they set fire to the church?"

O'Meara said nothing because he was very loyal and he didn't like to remind the priest that the little fire they had in the church a few months ago was caused by a cigarette butt the priest had left in his pocket when he was changing into his vestments, so he was puzzled and silent for a while and then whispered, "Maybe someone really wanted to take God away, do you think so?"

"Take Him out of the church?"

"Yes. Take Him away."

"How could you take God out of the church, man? Don't be stupid."

"But maybe someone thought you could, don't you see?"

"O'Meara, you talk like an old idiot. Don't you realize you play right into the hands of the atheists, saying such things? Do we believe an image is God? Do we worship idols? We do not. No more of that, then. If communists and atheists tried to burn this church once, they'll not stop till they desecrate it. God help us, why is my church marked out for this?" He got terribly excited and rushed away shouting, "I'm going to phone the police."

It looked like the beginning of a terrible Christmas Day for the parish. The police came, and were puzzled, and talked to everybody. Newspapermen came. They took pictures of the church and of Father Gorman, who had just preached a sermon that startled the congregation because he grew very eloquent on the subject of vandal outrages to the house of God. Men and women stood outside the church in their best clothes and talked very gravely. Everybody wanted to know what the thief would do with the image of the Infant Jesus. They all were wounded, stirred and wondering. There certainly was going to be something worth talking about at a great many Christmas dinners in the neighborhood.

But Sylvanus O'Meara went off by himself and was very sad. From time to time he went into the church and looked at the empty crib. He had all kinds of strange thoughts. He told himself that if someone really wanted to hurt God, then just wishing harm to Him really hurt Him, for what other way was there of hurting Him? Last night he had had the feeling that God was all around the crib, and now it felt as if God wasn't there at all. It wasn't just that the image of the Infant Jesus was gone, but someone had done violence to that spot and had driven God away from it. He told himself that things could be done that would make God want to leave a place. It was very hard to know where God was. Of course, He would always be in the church, but where had that part of Him that had seemed to be all around the crib gone?

It wasn't a question he could ask the little groups of astonished parishioners who stood on the sidewalk outside the church, because they felt like wagging their fingers and puffing their cheeks out and talking about what was happening to God in Mexico and Spain.

But when they had all gone home to eat their Christmas dinners, O'Meara himself began to feel a little hungry. He went out and stood in front of the church and was feeling thankful that there was so much snow for the children on Christmas Day when he saw that splendid and prominent woman, Mrs. Farrel, coming along the street with her little boy. On Mrs. Farrel's face there was a grim and desperate expression and she was taking such long fierce strides that the five-year-old boy, whose hand she held so tight, could hardly keep up with her and pull his big red sleigh. Sometimes the little boy tried to lean back and was a dead weight and then she pulled his feet off the ground while he whimpered, "Oh, gee, oh, gee, let me go." His red snowsuit was all covered with snow as if he had been rolling on the road.

"Merry Christmas, Mrs. Farrel," O'Meara said. He called to the boy, "Not happy on Christmas Day? What's up, son?"

"Merry Christmas, indeed, Mr. O'Meara," the woman snapped to him. She was not accustomed to paying much attention to the caretaker, a curt nod was all she ever gave him, and now she was far too angry and mortified to bother with him. "Where's Father Gorman?" she demanded.

"Still at the police station, I think."

"At the police station! God help us, did you hear that, Jimmie?" she said, and she gave such a sharp tug at the boy's arm that she spun him around in the snow behind her skirts where he cowered, watching O'Meara with a curiously steady pair of fine blue eyes. He wiped away a mat of hair from his forehead as he watched and waited. "Oh, Lord, this is terrible," Mrs. Farrel said. "What will I do?"

"What's the matter, Mrs. Farrel?"

"I didn't do anything," the child said. "I was coming back here. Honest I was, mister."

"Mr. O'Meara," the woman began, as if coming down from a great height to the level of an unimportant and simple-minded old man, "maybe you could do something for us. Look in the sleigh."

O'Meara saw that an old coat was wrapped around something on the sleigh, and stooping to lift it, he saw the figure of the Infant Jesus there. He was so delighted he only looked up at Mrs. Farrel and shook his head in wonder and said, "It's back and nobody harmed it at all."

"I'm ashamed, I'm terribly ashamed, Mr. O'Meara. You don't know how mortified I am," she said, "but the child really didn't know what he was doing. It's a disgrace to us, I know. It's my fault that I haven't trained him better, though

God knows I've tried to drum respect for the Church into him." She gave such a jerk at the child's hand he slid on his knee in the snow keeping his eyes on O'Meara.

Still unbelieving, O'Meara asked. "You mean he really took it from the church?"

"He did, he really did."

"Fancy that. Why, child, that was a terrible thing to do," O'Meara said. "Whatever got into you?" Completely mystified he turned to Mrs. Farrel, but he was so relieved to have the figure of the Infant Jesus back without there having been any great scandal that he couldn't help putting his hand gently on the child's back.

"It's all right, and you don't need to say anything," the child said, pulling away angrily from his mother, and yet he never took his eyes off O'Meara, as if he felt there was some bond between them. Then he looked down at his mitts, fumbled with them and looked up steadily and said, "It's all right, isn't it mister?"

"It was early this morning, right after he got up, almost the first thing he must have done on Christmas Day," Mrs. Farrel said. "He must have walked right in and picked it up and taken it out to the street."

"But what got into him?"

"He makes no sense about it. He says he had to do it."

"'Cause it was a promise," the child said, "I promised last night, I promised God that if He would make Mother bring me a big red sleigh for Christmas I would give Him the first ride on it."

"Don't think I've taught the child foolish things," Mrs. Farrel said. "I'm sure he meant no harm. He didn't understand at all what he was doing."

"Yes, I did," the boy said stubbornly.

"Shut up, child," she said, shaking him.

O'Meara knelt down till his eyes were on a level with the child's and they looked at each other till they felt close together and he said, "But why did you want to do that for God?"

"'Cause it's a swell sleigh, and I thought God would like it."

Mrs. Farrel, fussing and red-faced, said, "Don't you worry, I'll see he's punished by having the sleigh taken away from him."

But O'Meara, who had picked up the figure of the Infant Jesus, was staring down at the red sleigh; and suddenly he had a feeling of great joy, of the illumination of strange good tidings, a feeling that this might be the most marvelous Christmas Day in the whole history of the city, for God must surely have been with the child, with him on a joyous, carefree holiday sleigh ride, as he ran along those streets and pulled the sleigh. O'Meara turned to Mrs. Farrel, his face bright with joy, and said, commandingly, with a look in his eyes that awed her, "Don't you dare say a word to him, and don't you dare touch that sleigh do you hear? I think God did like it."

ALL RIGHT, FLATFOOT

A t midnight Karl came into the hotel lobby and approached the desk with a self-conscious air, asking for Mr. Bristow, the boxing promoter. He was only nineteen and in his first year of university and not accustomed to hotel lobbies at that hour. "Mr. Bristow?" said the neat, cool night clerk. "Why, there's Mr. Bristow right over there," and he pointed to a group of men standing by one of the marble pillars about ten feet away. "Mr. Bristow," he called softly.

A big shouldered, heavy man about forty-five, who was wearing a dark brown suit and a snap-brimmed brown hat on the back of his head, left the group and came toward the desk. He was good-looking with bold regular features and cold blue eyes and a face which in repose was like a piece of gray stone, but when he grinned as he came closer his expression changed and he seemed to have an engaging jolly self-assurance.

The clerk had merely nodded at Karl, and Mr. Bristow, without waiting for Karl to speak, put out his big hand. "You're Karl, aren't you?" he said. "How are you, Karl? So your uncle's laid up, eh?"

"He had a touch of pleurisy, Mr. Bristow."

"He sounded all right on the phone, Karl."

"He's all right, only he has to stay in bed."

"Well, it was nice of you wanting to come down and meet me, Karl."

"I've always wanted to meet you, Mr. Bristow," Karl said shyly. "I've heard so much about you from my uncle."

"It's nice having you want to sit around with us. You look just right to me," Mr. Bristow said warmly, as he took him by the arm and led him toward the two friends. Karl grinned. He liked Mr. Bristow immediately, felt at ease with him and decided quickly that he was even more impressive than he had expected him to be.

Ever since Karl had been a kid he had heard his Uncle John talk about his old friend, Willie Bristow, who had had such an exciting, successful life in the biggest cities on the continent. Willie had made money out of fighters and he had kept it. If Willie hadn't liked the easy careless sporting life he could have been a great politician or an industrialist, according to Uncle John, for he had a very remarkable quality: he had great instinctive knowledge of a man's weakness; he knew how to handle people.

They had only walked across the lobby, but Willie had already made Karl feel like an old friend and the two men to whom he was introduced seemed to accept him as someone who was important in Willie's life. Both these men were smoking fine cigars and they wore good clothes and they shared the same mellow nonchalance. The thin one with the tired eyes and the intellectual stoop was Pierre Ouiment, a fight manager from Montreal whose boy, a lightweight, had been knocked out two hours ago in the Garden.

The other was Solly Stone, who had been a fighter himself ten years ago, and now had an unmarked, bland, moon-like face and the soft chuckling assurance of a man with a rapidly growing bank account. They went on talking about the fight, teasing each other because they had all lost money. Then Willie said, "Just a moment," and he went back to the desk and Karl, who was more interested in watching Willie than in listening to his friends, saw what his uncle had meant.

Approaching the desk, Willie called, "Hey, you . . . " And the neat polite clerk, who had jerked his head around in indignation, quickly smiled. With his big hands flat on the desk, Willie gave the clerk some instructions about delivering a parcel the next day, and then he looked at his watch, returned to his friends, hardly listened to them and finally said impatiently, "Oh, come on up to the room and have a drink. That dame can come up to the room."

It was a big double room on the fifth floor and the window was open with the curtains bellying in the warm night wind and the sound of a tugboat whistling coming from the harbor. "Take off your coat, Karl," Willie said. The others, and Willie too, had quickly taken off their coats.

"I'm all right like this," Karl said.

"Come on, take it off, be one of us," Willie said and he took the coat from Karl. Then he opened a box of cigars and took a bottle from his bag. For his friends, he poured generous drinks, but for Karl he poured a very small one which hardly colored the water with which he filled the glass and he whispered sympathetically, "Nurse it along, Karl, as a favor to me. I don't want your uncle bending my ear about getting you into bad habits."

Advice of this kind might have offended Karl if Willie hadn't offered it so intimately, or if he hadn't had such a comradely touch which made Karl want to please him. Willie hadn't poured himself a drink: in fact he drank nothing until the girl he had been waiting for, a girl with thick shining hair in a black dress, who had a good-natured smile and a beautiful figure, came in with a bottle of special imported Scotch, which was Willie's favorite drink. The girl was the secretary of one of the directors of the Garden and she knew a lot about fight managers and promoters.

For ten minutes Willie was wonderfully considerate of her, and his friends smiled and winked at each other and watched him intently.

"You know," said Pierre, "I still figure Willie was right in betting on my boy. It was a sucker punch that got the kid."

"It was a sucker punch from where I was sitting," Karl said, and they argued about the fight.

"What business are you in, Mr. Stone?" Karl asked suddenly.

"Mr. Stone? What's this Mr. Stone stuff, Karl?"

"Well . . . Solly."

"That's better," Willie said. "And as for Solly, he's got a hundred and fifty thousand salted away."

"How did you make it, Solly?"

"That's easy," Solly said softly with a bland grin. "You see, Karl, when I was twenty I was a fighter. And in New York I won sixteen straight fights."

"For which he got three dollars and twenty cents apiece," Willie jeered.

"No, four dollars and eighty cents," Solly chuckled. They were all laughing heartily and didn't hear the knock on the door. At the second knock, Solly said, "The house dick for sure."

"Let me handle this," Willie said with real enjoyment.

When he opened the door, they could see two tall detective, one of them gray-haired and hollow-cheeked, peering into the room. Blocking the door with his huge body, Willie said quietly, "Why, you're my boys, come on in and have a quick one."

"No thanks, no thanks, Mr. Bristow," the detectives answered with false smiles and deprecating gestures. "You're making a little too much noise. Other people on the floor complain when they want to sleep and well, you know . . . "

"Sure," Willie said, and he walked out to the hall with him. When he returned he said with a shrug, "Flatfeet are all right, only you got to take a little interest in them. What were we saying, guys?"

Then they began a conversation about who was the most stylish fighter they had ever seen. It was the kind of conversation Karl wanted to hear, wise and salty, and his young face was full of eagerness. He felt happy. His one drink had warmed him: he began to dream of being in faraway cities with Willie Bristow and having a share of his exciting life.

He found himself thinking positively about fighters he had never seen and his opinion was respected because he was a friend of Willie's. First they talked about Benny Leonard, then about Kid Chocolate. "Chocolate, yeah, Chocolate, the nicest piece of fighting machinery I ever saw," Willie said. Solly and Pierre each longed to tell about the last time they had seen Chocolate in the ring, and their voices rose and they laughed happily, throwing their arms around each other's shoulders, each one trying to offer some splendid illumination about the perfection of the great black fighter's style.

"This is wonderful — wonderful," Karl thought, grinning gratefully at Willie, who was sitting on the edge of his chair, the collar of his expensive sport shirt pulled open, his bright expensive silk tie sliding across the shirt every time he threw his head back and laughed hilariously.

Karl forgot all about the time until someone knocked on the door, then he looked at his wristwatch. It was two-thirty. "The house dick again, I suppose," Willie said, and he chuckled to himself. On his way to the door he switched off the light, then he opened the door and there was the tall, hollow-cheeked, gray-haired detective standing in the lighted hall, blinking his eyes in surprise.

Willie stepped out, closed the door, leaving them in darkness. Before anyone could get up and turn on the light, he'd opened the door again, turned the light on himself and was leading the thin detective into the room. "Karl," he said, "pour this guy a real hooker. I can tell a man with an awful thirst."

"Okay, boys," the detective whispered, a guilty, apologetic smile on his face. "Only keep the noise down eh? Let's keep it quiet."

"Here you are, colonel," Willie said affably as he handed him the drink Karl had poured. "Get this into that parched gullet, then take your coat off."

"Well, just one," the house detective said, sitting down on the edge of the bed.

"A guy like you, an old-timer, looks as if he might have an opinion on a great fighter," Willie said.

"Now that's a funny thing, Mr. Bristow," the detective said. "I was a battalion champion in the war."

"Drink to the battalion champ, gentlemen," Willie commanded. As they all raised their glasses he went on, "These boys think Kid Chocolate was the nicest-looking fighter they ever saw. Did you ever see him?"

"That I did," the battalion champion said enthusiastically, "and right here in this town about fifteen years ago." With a quick smile he added in a pleading tone, "Keep the voices down, OK, boys?"

"We want to know what you thought of Kid Chocolate," Willie said in a whisper.

"For my money," the detective said, with a solemn glance at the glass which he had emptied in one gulp, "Chocolate was the real fancy Dan. A great artist."

"I knew it, he's one of us," Willie cried in admiration. "Fill up his glass, Karl."

Again they began to talk eagerly about Chocolate's great fights, about his ability to deliver a straight punch from any angle, and the detective's eyes began to glow. He felt happy and free. His opinions were being treated with respect and when he made a joke there was a burst of hearty laughter. Soon they were making more noise than they had made all evening.

"There's just one thing I can't understand," Willie said suddenly, as he sat down on the bed beside the detective and put his arm on his shoulder. "How did a fine guy like you ever become a snooper?"

"Well, you know how it is," the detective began awkwardly.

"Go on, tell me why."

"I don't know," he said, fumbling for words. In his deep, apologetic embarrassment he looked almost innocent. "It's a living, see. I've been at it ten years. I've got a wife and two kids. A married man has to have steady work, eh? It's something you get used to. Some guys look for trouble. I mean, well, it's not so bad."

The fumbling apology had moved Karl, who suddenly felt happy when he saw Willie, Pierre and Solly nod gravely to each other. The flushed face of the detective lit up. He relaxed again, took another drink, his eyes shone and he started to sing softly, "By Killarney's lakes and dells . . ."

"The man's got a voice too," Willie cried.

"A real baritone," Solly said enthusiastically.

"If only there was a tenor here," the detective sighed.

"I'll be the tenor," Karl said. So they sang "Killarney" with dignity and restraint, then swung easily into "Annie Laurie." In the happiness of the song and the noisy enthusiasm of the applause the detective forgot where he was; he forgot about his job and the lateness of the hour.

Karl, turning, looked at Willie Bristow with wondering admiration, for it was Willie who, with his magical assurance, had touched this man and drawn him in among them. Someone irritable who didn't know how to get along with people would have been intimidated by the detective's knock on the door and would have let him spoil the evening.

The detective, liking Karl's happy smile, had backed him into a corner and was telling how his father had taught him to use his fists and how he had dreamed in his youth of being the world's light heavyweight champion. The detective had a very fond memory of his youth and his eyes had softened.

Over by the window Willie and Solly Stone were having a serious conversation, keeping their voices low. A puff of wind from the open window blew the light curtain across Willie's face and he frowned and twisted his head and brushed it away and leaned closer to Solly. Pierre, who had been talking casually to the girl, turned away and stood behind the detective, listening and puffing methodically on his cigar. Suddenly, he blew a cloud of smoke at the back of the detective's neck and grinned in derision when the detective began to cough.

Some little memory of his youth had struck the detective as being so good, so amusing, that he wanted Willie to hear it, and he went over to him and tapped him on the shoulder. "Listen to this, Willie," he said with a strange innocent smile. Willie frowned and waved him away impatiently. "This is good, Willie," the detective pleaded. "You'll like this. I want you to hear it," and again he rested his hand on Willie's shoulder.

"I'm talking myself," Willie said abruptly.

"Sure. Go ahead," the detective said, drawing up a chair. The intrusion annoyed Willie, who looked at the smiling detective steadily for a moment.

"You finished that drink, soldier?" he said calmly.

"That I have," the detective agreed with a deprecating chuckle as he held out the glass, thinking Willie was going to fill it again. "And it's first-class stuff too."

"All right, flatfoot," Willie said crisply. "You've had a couple of drinks. That's your payoff. Now get out of here and don't bother us any more."

"What?" the detective whispered in a bewildered tone. He seemed to be trying to believe they were kidding him. Then he looked stricken, for Willie was waiting with an assured, hard smile and the detective's eyes shifted and he looked around as if he wanted to hide himself, but there was no place to hide, and he became obsequious and muttered, "Yes, sir," and walked quickly to the door. "Thanks, gentlemen, for the drinks," he said in a tone of comic dignity, but he did not look back.

"Nice work, Willie," Solly said, grinning in admiration. "I wondered how long you were going to put up with that crumb."

"Yes, Willie," Pierre agreed with a meditative air. "Easing him out might have been difficult."

"Him? Don't worry," Willie said contemptuously. "I know how to handle those flatfeet. He knows when his ears have been pinned back."

"But . . ." Karl began.

"But what, Karl?"

"I don't know," Karl said unhappily. He was struggling against a terrible disappointment in Willie. "He was letting himself go and feeling happy . . ." He could still see the detective's hurt eyes. "I guess I got to like the guy a little," he said awkwardly, as he looked from one face to another.

"You'll get wise to those guys later on, Karl," Willie said casually. "I've handled dozens of them. I know how to handcuff them."

"I guess you do."

"I'm going to take you out with us now, Karl, and buy you some first-class Chinese food. I know the place to get it. I want to have a real talk with you, Karl."

"It's getting late," Karl said, and he stood up slowly.

"Oh, nonsense, Karl. This is your night."

"No. I have to go," Karl said with surprising firmness, for as he dwelt on Willie's big, red, friendly, smiling face he felt himself pulling away in sudden fear, knowing that just as Willie had handled the detective and Solly and Pierre, he was now ready to handle him, too.

THE NEW KID

When Luke Baldwin was the new kid in town he was very lonely and didn't believe he would ever make any sincere friends. The trouble was that he was a city kid. When his father, a doctor, died he had come to live with his uncle at the sawmill two miles beyond the town. Uncle Henry, the manager of the mill, was a confident, important man, whom everybody respected, but he couldn't be expected to make friends for Luke. The only reliable friend Luke had in those days was the old collie dog, Dan, which was blind in one eye, and not much use to anybody around the mill.

The old dog helped Luke get better acquainted with the boys at school and particularly with Elmer Highbottom, the son of the rich merchant, who had Uncle Henry's approval. Luke himself was too reticent and too quiet; he spoke too politely; and so the other boys jeered at him and would not believe he was really one of them. But the dog was always with him when he showed up at the ball field behind Stevenson's orchard. The boys would talk to the dog and play with it and compare it with Elmer's dog, which also was supposed to be a clean-bred.

Elmer was a skinny red-haired kid, two years older than Luke, who had become the leader of the boys by the power of his abusive voice and his frantic bad temper. In the gang there were six others: Eddie Shore, the dark and muscular son of a grocer; Woody Alliston, the undertaker's son; Jimmie Stewart, the minister's boy; Dave Dalton, the left-handed first baseman, whose father owned the ice-cream parlor; Hank Hennessey, whose father worked in the shipyard; and Norm McLeod, whose father was the superintendent of the grain elevator. They all wanted to be big-league ballplayers. If Luke missed a fly ball, Elmer, the potential big leaguer, would scream at him in derision, and Luke secretly hated him. Lying in the grass by the third-base line with Dan, Luke would whisper, "He's a one-armed ballplayer himself. He just swings that glove at the ball, Dan. If the ball sticks in the pocket he's all right, but he might as well be out there swinging a broom."

He was not afraid of Elmer, but he never said these things to him, for he wanted to go on hanging around with the bunch of boys. Elmer had decided that he would become a great left-hand pitcher. One way of being friendly with Elmer was to stand behind him when he was pitching and say, "Gee, did you see that curve? How did you throw it, Elmer?" Luke, who was lonely and wanted to have friends, also would stand behind Elmer, and one day he said enthusiastically, "Gee, what a hook you had on that one, Elmer! I wish you'd show me how to throw it." It made him a little sick at his stomach to say it, for the ball didn't have a curve at all. "Maybe I will sometime," Elmer said, and that day he took Luke home with him to show him his valuable clean-bred dog.

As soon as Luke saw this dog, Thor, which was chained up at a kennel at the back of the big Highbottom house, he doubted that the dog was a clean-bred. Its legs were too long; it didn't have the long-haired coat of a collie; the hair was more like that of an Alsatian; but it was a big, power-ful, bad-tempered dog which was always kept on a leash.

"It's a thoroughbred," Elmer said, "and it can lick any dog in this town."

"If that dog's a thoroughbred, then our Dan isn't," Luke said.

"Then your Dan isn't. This is a fighting thoroughbred."

"Aw, go on," Luke said.

"Aw, go on yourself. Nuts to you."

"Nuts to you, Elmer. Why has it got that crazy look in its eyes?"

"Because he doesn't like strangers, see. And he doesn't like other dogs," Elmer said.

But then Mr. Highbottom, a plump, affable, sandy-haired man with rimless glasses and a round pink face, came out. He was a rich man and a good friend of Luke's Uncle Henry. When Elmer went into the house to get his new first-base-man's glove, Mr. Highbottom explained that Thor was kept as a watchdog; he had gotten the dog from some people in the city who had kept him locked up in an apartment; he had been badly treated. The first night he, Mr. Highbottom, had got the dog he had had to hit him on the head with a club to let him know who was the master. He was half collie and half Alsatian. Luke said nothing to Elmer about knowing the dog was not a clean-bred, for he wanted to keep Elmer's friendship.

In the evenings they would all go up to the fairgrounds, especially if a team from one of the grain boats in the har-bor was playing the town team. Luke was always ill at ease because he didn't know the members of the town team; he could not stand behind the bench when the home team was batting, and chat and kid with these great players. So he would listen, or wander among the crowd with Dan following him, or he would drift out to left field, where the gang would sprawl in the grass. They would stay there till it was dark, then Elmer would whisper with Eddie Shore, the swarthy and muscular son of the grocer, and they and the others would go off by themselves on some night adventure on the main street of the town. Luke and Dan were left alone. On the way home, with the stars coming out and the night breeze rustling through the leaves of the great elms along the road, Luke would try to imagine that he was following the boys furtively into mysterious places where he had never been.

But on Saturday mornings it was really worthwhile to be with Elmer's friends, for then they would go down to the old dock by the rusty grain elevator. There they would swim, with the collie swimming with them, and afterward they would lie in the sun, talking and dreaming. When they had gotten dressed they would go along the pier to the place where the *Missouri* was tied up, and sit there, peering into the darkness of the hold.

A seaman in a torn black sweater, whose face was leathery and whose hair was iron gray, was sitting on the pier smoking his pipe. He smiled as he watched Elmer Highbottom strutting around. "Hey, kid, how old are you?" he called.

"Thirteen. Why?" Elmer asked.

"Oh, nothing," drawled the seaman. "It's just that I remember when I was thirteen around here."

"Are you from around here, mister?"

"Believe it or not," the sailor said, "I was a kid here. It was a long time ago." Both Luke and Elmer, sitting cross-legged now at the seaman's feet, listened to him telling stories.

Maybe he was lying a little, but his voice was soft, his tone full of affection and his eyes were happy, and so Luke believed him. After a profound silence Luke said suddenly, "I could do that too. I could stow away some night. I could go down the St. Lawrence. I could sail to Siam."

"When are you going to make the break, son?" the sailor asked with a smile.

"One of these nights. I'll pick a night."

"You," Elmer jeered. "Listen to him, mister. He's never been on a ship. He doesn't know one end of a ship from another. He's just a punk around here."

"I was a punk once," the sailor said, in such a way that Luke felt grateful. He couldn't figure out why he endured Elmer's jeering insults. Gradually all the boys had adopted Elmer's tone with him.

One day they were in Johnson's lumberyard on the south side of the tracks, playing around the great pile of sawdust which was heaped at the back of a two-storey brick building. A ladder hooked to the wall of the building ran up to the flat roof. "Come on, everybody up on the roof," Elmer yelled, and they followed him up the ladder. Sitting on the edge of the roof they all looked down at the pile of sawdust, which was about twenty feet below.

"I'll stump you to jump down," Elmer said, and without waiting for them to yell, "Stumpers go first," he jumped.

One by one the boys began to jump, and as each one fell Dan barked excitedly. But the second boy to jump had taken a little longer to make up his mind, and the third one hesitated even longer, the jump becoming longer and more frightening as he kept looking down; and Luke, who was the last one, had had too much time to think about it.

"Come on, Luke," they yelled. "What's the matter with you, Luke? What are you scared of?"

"I'm taking my time. What's the matter with taking my time?"

He wanted to jump, he knew he was going to jump, only he couldn't bring himself to do it at the moment. It was really an easy jump, so he laughed and tried to keep on kidding with them, but he had tightened up and every time he got ready to jump a queasy feeling came at the base of his spine.

"I think he's yellow," Elmer shouted. "He's got glue" on his pants." Then they all began to jeer.

Luke wanted to close his eyes and jump, but he was ashamed to let them see that he was closing his eyes. That all this was happening bewildered him. And then the collie began to bark impatiently. "Okay, Dan," Luke yelled. Waving his arms carelessly as if he had been only kidding with them, he suddenly pushed himself blindly off the roof and fell heavily on the sawdust, where the dog leaped at him joyfully.

"Well, there you are, bigmouth," he said to Elmer as he got up, dusting his clothes.

"Who's a bigmouth?"

"You've got the biggest, loudest mouth in this town, Elmer," Luke said quietly. "You're a blowhard. A great big blowhard."

"Listen, punk, you want something?"

"You don't worry me, bigmouth."

"You want I should smack you stupid?"

"Go ahead, smack me, Elmer. I'll show you who's stupid."

"Come on!" Elmer yelled.

Then they were circling around each other and Luke now was happy. It was a crazy kind of happiness; it seemed as if Elmer had been pounding him for a long time and now at last he could openly smack him. As they feinted at each other Dan began to growl. Eddie Shore grabbed the dog by the collar. Impressed by the wild glare in Luke's eyes, Elmer feinted cautiously and then suddenly he ducked and charged, swinging his right, and Luke blindly stuck out his left hand like a rod. Elmer walked right into it. The fist got him on the nose, which spurted blood. Screaming like an old woman, he came clawing at Luke and got his arms around him and they rolled in the sawdust. He was heavier and stronger than Luke and had gotten on top of him.

"Let him up. Let him up and go on fighting," the others yelled. But Elmer, frantic now, his freckled face white, with the mouth gaping open and a trickle of blood from his nose running into the corner of his mouth, had grabbed Luke by the hair and kept banging his head on the ground.

The collie had growled; he lay back, growling, then suddenly jerked his head free and leaped at Elmer. He did not look like a wild dog, but looked like a dog being workmanlike. He slashed at Elmer's leg, only at the cloth, but the growl and the sound of the ripping cloth seemed to jerk Elmer out of his frenzy. He was scared. Jumping up, he shouted, "I'll kill that dog. I'll brain it. Where's a brick, gimme a brick!"

"Come here, Dan. Come here, quick," Luke cried. As the dog turned to him he grabbed him by the collar. "You're not hurt," he said to Elmer. "It's only your pants torn a little. Dan didn't bite you."

"I'll brain that dog," Elmer shouted. "I've got a right to kill it now."

"If you want to hit somebody, come on, hit me now I'm standing up. Here," he said to Eddie, "you hold Dan's collar — and hold him this time."

"I'll get you when your vicious dog isn't with you," Elmer yelled. "I'll get you after my father has that dog destroyed."

"You can get me anytime you want, Elmer. I'll fight you anytime you're willing to have a fair fight."

"Aw, go on, beat it. Do you hear? Beat it."

As Luke dusted himself off, taking a long time, he waited for one of the other boys to make a friendly remark, or invite him to stay with them. But they had all grown profoundly meditative. So finally Luke said, "Come on, Dan," and he went off by himself.

Luke got home just in time for dinner. At the table his Uncle Henry said, "Is that a scratch on your face, Luke?"

"I was playing up in the lumberyard with Elmer, jumping in the sawdust, Uncle Henry."

"Oh, you and Elmer are becoming great friends, aren't you?" he said approvingly.

Uncle Henry, in his shirt-sleeves, big-faced, thin-haired, his great shoulders hunched over the table, looked as if he had the strength of character to protect fearlessly everything that belonged to him. But Uncle Henry and Mr. Highbottom admired each other. Luke seemed to see Mr. Highbottom coming into the room and explaining that the collie had bitten Elmer. Luke could almost hear them talking as one practical man to another, and coming finally to a practical arrangement to destroy Dan. Suddenly Uncle Henry looked up, their eyes met, and Uncle Henry smiled. But no complaint came to Uncle Henry from Mr. Highbottom, and at school Elmer was as nonchalant with him as if nothing had happened.

On Friday afternoon Eddie Shore, Elmer's good friend, said to Luke, "Going to play ball tomorrow, Luke? Guess we'll see you there, eh?"

"Sure, I'll be up there," Luke said with a grateful grin.

That Saturday morning at about ten o'clock he walked up to the ball field with Dan. Only two other kids were there, Eddie and Woody Alliston, the undertaker's son. It was a cloudy day; it had rained a little early in the morning. While Dan lay under the hawthorn tree, Luke and Eddie and Woody played three-cornered catch.

"Here comes Elmer now," Eddie said laconically.

"Soon they'll all be here," Luke said. Feeling a little embarrassed about Elmer, he did not turn to watch him coming across the field. But Eddie, who had the ball, held on to it, a big excited grin on his face. With Elmer was the big dog, Thor, on a chain. The powerful dog was dragging Elmer along. "Why has he got that crazy dog?" Luke asked, turning. Then his heartbeat came up high in his throat and he felt weak, for now he knew why Eddie Shore had grinned. "Come here, Dan," he called quickly. As the old dog came to him slowly, he whispered, "You stay right here with me."

The big dog with the wicked, crazy eyes had already growled at Dan. Thor was three inches higher and years younger than Dan.

"I see you've got your dog with you, Luke," Elmer said with a smirk.

"Yeah, Dan's always with me, Elmer."

"That dog of yours is a mighty savage dog," Elmer said softly. "It goes around biting people, doesn't it?"

"Dan's not savage. Dan never bit anybody."

"Of course, I'm nobody. A dog that bites me isn't really a savage dog. That's not the way I heard it, eh, guys?"

With a grin he turned to Eddie and Woody, but they did not grin, for now that they were close to Thor and had heard him growl they were frightened.

"You better take that dog home, Elmer," Luke said placatingly. "I don't think your father would like it if it made trouble for anybody."

"I'm going to see if that dog of yours wants to growl and bite when there's another dog around," Elmer jeered. Slipping the chain off Thor's collar, he pointed to Dan. "Go get him, boy," he yelled. "Sic him."

Thor had growled, his lips trembling and drawing back from the long white teeth; he growled a little as Dan stiffened, then growled again, his mane rising. And Dan, too, growled, his head going down a little, waiting, and showing his teeth, which were blunted and old.

Suddenly Thor leaped at Dan's throat, trying to knock him over with the weight of the charge and sink his teeth in the throat and swing him over. But Dan pivoted, sliding away to the side, and Thor's snapping jaws missed the throat. Then Dan drew on the strength and wisdom of his breed. His strength was all instinct and heart, and it was against that instinct to snap or chew, or grip with his teeth and snarl and roll over, clawing and kicking and cutting until it was over. As Thor missed, Dan did not back away and wait again. Doing what he would have done five years ago, he wheeled, leaping past the big dog and slashing at the flank; then, wheeling again, returned for the slashing rip at the flank again.

These splendid, fearless movements were executed so perfectly that Luke sobbed, "Oh, Dan," but the slashes at Thor's flank had not gone deep.

The sun, which was now bright, was shining in Thor's wild empty eyes. Growling and scraping at the ground with his claws he charged again; it was like the pounce of a great cat. Again the snapping jaws missed Dan's throat, but the weight of the charge, catching him on the hip, spun him around off balance and bewildered him a little.

Luke was watching with both his hands up to his face. It was as if he was prepared to cover his eyes and scream but couldn't; he was frozen to the one spot. The two boys, Eddie and Woody, were close together, crouching a little and crazy with excitement. Elmer's jaw was moving loosely and he kept blinking his eyes.

The thin clouds overhead broke up, a blue patch of sky appeared. The damp grass glistened. Thor had learned that Dan was vulnerable on the left flank; the blind eye saw nothing, the good eye couldn't shift quickly enough. Whirling quickly, Thor charged in again on that left flank, knocking Dan over, but the weight of his own charge caused Thor to sprawl over Dan. The teeth could only snap at the flank, and though both dogs had rolled in the grass, snarling and clawing, Dan was soon on his feet again.

But Dan knew now that his instinctive style was no good. When this heavy dog came whirling to the left of him he couldn't see him in time, and he was bleeding just behind the shoulder. It was like watching a bewildered old dog suddenly becoming aware of its age, and yet with courage trying to break itself of a style of fighting which was the only one its breed had known. Circling and backing, Dan drew near the trunk of the hawthorn tree. There he stood with the tree on his left, protecting that flank, so that Thor would have to charge toward the good eye. His head dropped and he waited.

"No, oh, no, Elmer," Eddie said weakly.

"Elmer. Have some sense!" Woody Alliston pleaded.

"Elmer," Luke shrieked suddenly, and he grabbed Elmer. "I'll kill you. I'll kill you. Call him off or I'll kill you!"

But with a low exultant growl Thor had leaped in again to pin Dan against the tree, and as Dan swerved a little Thor got his teeth in the shoulder, snarling and shaking his head as he rolled Dan over, shaking and stretching his own neck away from Dan's teeth, and holding on tight till he could draw Dan underneath him on his back and then shift his jaws to Dan's throat and kill him.

The agonized growling and snarling was terrible and yet exultant, and Luke screamed, "Elmer, Elmer, call him off! He'll kill him, Elmer!"

And the other two boys, Eddie and Woody, awed and sick, yelled, "Do something, Elmer. Don't let him kill him, Elmer!"

Fascinated by the power and viciousness of his dog, which he believed he couldn't control, Elmer cried, "I can't stop it."

And Luke sobbed, for it was as if Dan was more than a dog. The collie seemed to have come out of that good part of his life which he had shared with his own father. "Dan! Dan!" he screamed. He looked around wildly for help. On the other side of the tree was a thick broken branch. It flashed into his mind that he should use this branch as a club; this was in his mind as he rushed at the snarling dogs. But instead he kicked at Thor's flank; he kicked three times with the good heavy serviceable shoes Uncle Henry had bought for him.

Thor snarled, his head swinging around, his bright eyes now on Luke, the lip curled back from the fangs. Luke backed away toward the club. As he picked up the branch and held it with both hands, he felt numb all over. There was nothing but the paralyzing beat of his own heart — nothing else in the world.

Seeing him there with the club, Thor tried to hold Dan down with his paws. Then he suddenly growled as he let go Dan's shoulder and whirled on Luke.

"Luke, come away from him!" Elmer screamed.

"Run, Luke," Eddie yelled. "Get someone at Stevenson's, Woody."

Woody started to run across the field to Stevenson's house as Luke, waiting, watched Thor's trembling lip. The big dog's growl was deep with satisfaction as he came two steps closer, the head going down.

In Luke's mind it was all like a dream. It was like a dream of Mr. Highbottom telling him he had once pounded Thor on the head with a club, and of a story he had once read about Indians pounding the heads of wild dogs with clubs. But it was important that he should not wait, that he should attack the dog and cow him.

Dan, free now, had tried to get up and then had fallen back and was watching him with his glowing eye.

With a deep warning growl Thor crouched, and Luke rushed at him and cracked him on the skull, swinging the club with both hands. The big dog, trying to leap at him, knocked him down, and when he staggered to his feet Thor was there, shaking his head stupidly, but still growling. Not waiting now, Luke rushed at him and whacked him on the head again and again. The crazy dog would not run; he was still trying to jump at him. Suddenly the dog lurched, his legs buckled, he rolled over on his side and was still.

While Elmer and Eddie were looking at him as if they were afraid of him, Luke did a thing he hated himself for doing. He went over and sat down beside Dan and put his hand on Dan's head, and then he started to cry. He couldn't help it; it was just relief; he felt weak and he ground his fists in his eyes.

"Holy cow," Elmer said in relief, "you might have got killed."

"Luke," Eddie said softly.

"Are you all right, Luke?"

"You better put the chain on that dog of yours, Elmer," Luke said when he could get his breath. "You'd better tie him up to the tree."

"Maybe he's dead. What if he's dead?"

"Not that dog. Not that crazy dog. It's Dan that's hurt."

When Elmer was linking the chain to his dog's collar, the animal's legs trembled convulsively. Opening his eyes he tried to get to his feet, but Elmer had no trouble dragging him over to the tree and looping the chain around it.

Across the field at the gate to the Stevenson house, Mr. Stevenson was talking with Woody Alliston. They could see him point and shrug — there seemed to be no trouble over there by the tree — then he turned back to the house and Woody came on alone.

"Let's see your shoulder, Dan," Luke said gently to the collie lying quietly beside him. The collie knew he had been hurt, knew the muscle above the shoulder was torn and bleeding, yet he lay quietly and patiently, regaining his strength while his flanks heaved.

"Okay, okay," Luke said softly. Taking out his handkerchief he dabbed at the blood already congealing on the fur. The other boys, kneeling down beside Luke, were silent. Sometimes they looked at Luke's white face. When he had mopped up the blood, he began to stroke Dan's head softly, and Dan, wiggling his tail a little, thumped the grass three times.

"Maybe he's not hurt so bad," Elmer said nervously, for Dan, swinging his head around, had begun to lick the wound patiently; the clean pink tongue and the saliva on the tongue were cleaning and soothing the slash, and Luke and the other boys seemed to be waiting for Dan to come to a conclusion about the seriousness of the wound.

"Can you get up, Dan?" Luke whispered. "Come on, try, boy."

Slowly the collie rose and hobbled on three legs in a little circle. Coming over to Luke, who was kneeling and waiting anxiously, the old collie rubbed his nose against Luke's neck, then flopped down again.

"I guess he'll be all right, will he?" Elmer asked anxiously.

"Maybe that leg won't be so good again," Luke said mournfully. "Maybe it'll never be good again."

"Sure it will, if nothing is broken, Luke," Elmer insisted, as he got up and thrust his hands into his pockets and walked around aimlessly, his freckled face full of concern. Once he stopped and looked at his own dog, which was crouched by the tree, his eyes following Elmer. Thor was a subdued dog now. Growing more meditative and more unhappy, Elmer finally blurted out, "I guess you'll tell your uncle what happened, eh, Luke?"

"You knew Dan was my uncle's dog," Luke said grimly.

"If you tell your uncle — well, your uncle will tell my father, and then there will be awful trouble, Luke."

"Well, you knew there'd be trouble, Elmer."

"I only wanted to scare you and chase Dan," Elmer insisted. "I thought Dan would run and howl. I didn't know Thor would turn on you. Gee, Luke, I was crazy. I didn't stop to think." With a sudden pathetic hopefulness he muttered, "I could have told my father that your dog slashed at me. Only I didn't, Luke. I didn't say anything, though he asked me how I tore my pants."

"Okay, you didn't say anything, Elmer. So what?"

"Maybe if you don't say anything, eh, Luke?"

"I can look after myself too," Luke said grandly.

"Well — in that case I'd sure think you were a great guy, Luke," Elmer said.

"Sure, he's a great guy," Eddie agreed firmly.

Eddie and Woody wanted to make friendly gestures to Luke, and they didn't quite know how to do it. They felt awkward and ashamed. They took turns petting Dan lovingly. They asked Luke if he wouldn't go swimming down at the dock after lunch. "I'll walk home with you, Luke," Eddie said. "I'd like to see if Dan gets home all right."

"I'm not letting him walk all that distance," Luke said, and he knelt down, gathered Dan in his arms and hoisted him up on his shoulder. On the way across the field Luke and Eddie took their time and worried about Dan.

"Let me carry him now," Eddie said.

"No, we'll see if he can walk a little," Luke said.

It was extraordinary how effectively the old dog could travel on three legs. He hopped along briskly. Sometimes he would stop and let the wounded leg come down firmly, as if testing it, then come hopping along until Luke picked him up again.

"We should take it easy," Luke said. "We should rest a little now and then." When they got to the road leading to the mill they sat down in the grass and took turns stroking Dan's head.

Going along that road, and resting every three hundred yards, Luke and Eddie were beginning a new relationship with each other. They both knew it, and so they were a little shy and very respectful to each other. While they were talking about Dan they were really trying to draw closer together. Eddie was offering a sincere admiring friendship, and Luke knew it and accepted it gravely.

"Well, I'll look for you this afternoon," Eddie said.

"At the dock. Sure, Eddie."

"Yeah. At the dock. Well, I'll be seeing you, Luke."

Halfway up the path Luke suddenly dropped on his knees and put his arms around Dan. It was as if the dog had really been struggling not only against the big wild Thor but against the barrier between Luke and the other boys. "You're some dog, Dan," he whispered, rubbing his face against the dog's nose, trying to show his gratitude.

But when he got back to the mill and saw Uncle Henry going toward the house, mounting the veranda steps, opening the screen door, his step decisive, his face so full of sensible determination, Luke longed to be able to tell him what had happened, not only because the dog was Uncle Henry's property — and property ought to be protected — but because he suddenly believed that Uncle Henry would have done just what he himself had done, and would be proud of him. "The sensible thing would have been to pick up a club and smack that crazy dog on the head," he could almost hear Uncle Henry say. "Why, that's just what I did, Uncle Henry," Luke imagined himself explaining as he followed Uncle Henry into the house. But of course he would never be able to see this glow of approval in his uncle's eyes.

THE DUEL

*I*n their light summer suits they kept coming up the steps
from the Christopher Street subway into the warm night,
their bright faces moving from the shadow into the streetlight.
Sometimes they came slowly in groups, but those who were
alone hurried when they reached the street. At first there were
so many girls that Luther Simpson, standing a little piece away
on Seventh Avenue, thought Inez would surely be among
them. "She'll be on the next train," he thought. "If she's not on
that, I'll only wait three trains more."

He grew more and more desolate, more uncertain and
fearful, and yet, looking along the lighted avenue and remembering how often he and Inez had been among these people
at this hour, he felt eager and almost hopeful. This was his
neighborhood, here among these people; they looked just the
same as they did on any other night when he and Inez were
together. At any moment she was apt to come hurrying along;
she would try hard to look severe, smile in spite of herself,
look very lovely, start to speak, and then maybe laugh a little
instead, and then they would link arms awkwardly and walk
in silence.

But because he could not help feeling fearful, Luther
started to walk along the side street toward her house, so he
would be sure of not missing her. When he was nearly there

a taxi stopped a few houses away with the engine running. The driver turned and hung open the door, and there was a little movement of his shoulders as he made himself more comfortable in his seat. Then the engine was turned off. After what seemed a very long time a big man in a gray flannel suit stepped out and then helped Inez to the pavement. He helped her out with a special tenderness, and when he made a little bow to her the light shone on his high forehead and black hair. "Good night, Inez. You're a darling," he was saying.

She was smiling; her face looked more lovely than Luther had thought it would look when he was thinking of her coming along and smiling at him. "It was such a super time," she said gaily.

"Dream about it," the man said, grinning.

"I'll try hard," she called as she turned, waving her hand. Her face in that light was full of a glowing excitement; there was a reckless, laughing joy in it that Luther had never seen before, as if she had just come from some kind of delightful amusement she had not known for a long time, something that had left her a little breathless. The sound of her laughter scared Luther. It seemed to be the very sound he had been waiting for so fearfully. Now, in her white linen suit and white shoes, she was going across the pavement. She was taking the key out of her purse. Pausing an instant, she pulled off her hat and shook her thick, dark hair free. And then, as she opened the door, he called out sharply, "Inez, Inez, wait a minute."

Startled, she turned, but she did not speak. She stood there watching him coming toward her, and when he was close to her she said in a cool, even tone, "What do you want, Luther?"

"What were you doing with that guy, Inez? Where have you been?" He took hold of her by the arm as if she had always belonged to him and now he was entitled to punish her, but when she pulled her arm away so very firmly he stopped speaking, as if he could not get his breath.

"It's none of your business where I was, Luther," she said. "I'm going in now, if you don't mind."

"Who was that guy?"

"I won't tell you."

"Was that the first time you were out with him?"

"I won't tell you," she said wearily. "I'm going in."

He was trying to think of something harsh to say that would hurt her, but as he realized how aloof she was, how untouched by his presence, he grew frightened, and he said, "Listen, I was only kidding the other night. I'm not sore now, I love you, Inez. Only you should have said you were going out with someone else when I phoned. You said you were going to see your cousin."

"Supposing I did."

"Well . . . you ought . . . Never mind that. I'm not sore. I can understand you might want to see a show sometimes like we used to. Were you at a show? See, I'm not sore. Look at me." Luther was trying to smile like an amiable young man who was happy to see people having a good time, but when Inez did look up at him she wasn't reassured at all.

She grew very agitated and said angrily, "You've got a nerve, Luther. You weren't content to leave things the way they were. Any girl would get tired of the way you go . . ." She didn't finish, she felt an ache growing in her for all the good times they had had during these last three years. Every trivial pleasure they had shared seemed to have an intense meaning now. And then she blurted out, "I'm sick and tired of the way you've been going on, Luther. That's all over, I've made up my mind."

"No, you haven't, Inez. I was irritable the other night. I was thinking I'd never get work. I was thinking we'd never be able to get married. I was thinking I'd go crazy."

"Did I ever complain?"

"No. You really didn't."

"You said yourself you were fed up."

"I wasn't fed up with you, Inez. I was fed up with borrowing money from you and letting you do things for me. It got so it was terrible having you buy coffee and things like that for us, don't you see?"

"I didn't say anything, but you kept yelling at me that I was discontented."

"I meant I'd like to be able to be doing little things for you. That's why I started to quarrel and shout at you."

"You kept saying it so often now I believe it," she said, taking a deep breath and then, sighing wearily, "Maybe I *was* discontented."

"Did I really make you feel it was all hopeless?"

"Yes, you did."

"Then I'm a nut. I love you."

With her face turned away, as if she dared not listen, she started to go into the apartment house. She did not want him to see how bewildered she was. As she opened the door she said so softly that he could hardly hear, "Goodnight, Luther."

"I won't go. You can't do a thing like that. Tell me where you were tonight," and he pressed his face against the glass of the door, catching a last glimpse of her ankles and then her shoes as she went up the stairs. At first he was so resentful that he wanted to pound on the door with his fist, but almost at once he felt weak and spent, and he walked away and crossed the road so he could look up at her apartment.

Standing there, he waited to see her shadow pass across the lowered window shade as she moved around the room, but there was no shadow, nothing to show she was in the room. At last he noticed the faintest movement of the window drape, low down, at the corner, and then a little thin streak of light. Someone was there, peering out at the street. She was watching him, he knew, trying to hide, probably kneeling on the floor with her eyes level with the windowsill. He felt a surge of joy. Inez could not leave him like that. She had to watch him. She had to kneel there, feeling herself pulled strongly toward him, unable to go while he was looking up at her window.

But it was very hard to have her up there and not be able to talk to her. He felt now a vast apology in himself for anything he might have done to destroy the tenderness she had felt for him. It was so splendid to be able to hold her there, making her watch him, that he longed to be able to do something that would coax her back to him; and he kept growing more hopeful, as if he had only to keep looking at the window faithfully for awhile and the drape would be pulled to one side, the shade raised, and she would beckon to him. The same summer night air, the same murmur of city sounds, were there around them now as they had been on other nights, when they had felt so close to one another. If only she could hear him, how he would plead with her. He whispered, "I'm not sore, only you should have said you were going out with someone when I phoned." He knew that she was kneeling there, feeling the struggle within her;

all her restlessness and the bitterness of the last few days were pulling her one way, and something much deeper, that weakened her and filled her with melancholy, was resisting strongly. He said aloud, "That guy didn't mean a thing, you just wanted a little amusement, right?"

As he kept looking up at the window, he grew full of persuasion, full of confidence because he still held her there. All the love between them that had been built up out of so many fine, hopeful, eager moments was offering too much resistance to the bitterness that was pulling her the other way.

Knowing her so close to him, he began to feel a new boldness; he felt that she must have been persuaded and had yielded to him. He began to move across the street, looking up at the lighted room.

But when he reached the middle of the street, it was as though the struggle had been decided: she had left the window he knew, for in the room the light was turned out.

Running ahead, he rang the apartment bell; he waited, and then rang again, and then kept on ringing. There was no answer, and he wanted to shout, "She thinks I'm crazy? All right. All right."

He ran to the corner, his thoughts raced with him: "She thinks she won't make a mistake. She thinks I'll never get anywhere, I can't show a girl the town, like that guy that rides in taxicabs. I'll get money, I'll get clothes, I'll get girls, pretty girls." These thoughts rushed through his mind as though he had become buoyant and confident. He reached the corner and stood looking up Seventh Avenue. There was no breeze, and the air was warm and muggy. He looked up the street as far as he could, and then he took a deep, tired breath.

THE THING
THAT HAPPENED TO
UNCLE ADOLPHE

When his mother died, Albert came from the country to his Uncle Adolphe's shoe-repair shop to learn his uncle's trade and go to school. His uncle was squat and broad-shouldered, and powerful, with a glistening bald head and a fringe of gray hair. It was fun working for him. Albert ran messages and delivered shoes and then came back and sat around watching his uncle trim the leather for a pair of soles with his short, sharp knife.

In the evenings, Uncle Adolphe often took Albert to the houses of friends in the neighborhood. On the way, Albert asked questions about anything that came into his head and got an answer that seemed natural and clear, and made the question seem important. His uncle, full of lively information about everything going on around him, also used to sing while he worked at the bench near the window. Standing in his old khaki-colored smock he pounded away with his hammer, singing at the top of his voice. If people passing on the street turned and gaped, Uncle Adolphe swung his hammer in the air and grinned cheerfully at them.

Then one day Albert noticed that his uncle was working very fast and watching the clock. "Albert, come here," he said earnestly. "Are you listening carefully, Albert? I want you to go down to the corner and cross the road and go along to Molsen's grocery store. Then go in and tell Mr. Molsen you are from your Uncle Adolphe and you have come for Mr. Zimmerman. He'll be sitting there in the back room. He's blind, understand, Albert? You take his arm, see? And bring him along here. And be careful. He's my good friend. You bring him here."

"I didn't know you had a blind friend, Uncle Adolphe," Albert said, getting his hat.

"I met him at Molsen's. He promised to come here and talk to me in the afternoon. He's a very important man. Be careful, whatever you do, Albert."

Albert was very shy going into the grocery store. "My uncle sent me for Mr. Zimmerman," he said. Pointing to a back room the grocer said, "He's been waiting. Go on in." And he called out, "Henry, here's the boy that Adolphe sent for you."

In the back room, a thin old man in a neat black suit sat alone in a rocking chair. His hair was long and white. It stuck out from under the wide-brimmed black hat he had just put on. But it was his calm, thin face which Albert noticed. While Albert was gaping at him Mr. Zimmerman said quietly, "Take my arm, boy." Mr. Zimmerman seemed to know Albert was standing beside him. It was startling. But then Albert told himself he didn't need to feel shy, for after all, Mr. Zimmerman couldn't really see him.

Albert walked him out to the street. Mr. Zimmerman touched Albert's arm very lightly. As they went down the street Albert grew fascinated by the ease and assurance with which Mr. Zimmerman strode along. Once he even said, "Faster, please." Albert wondered if he would notice if he withdrew his arm and let him walk on alone, and he did this, and Mr. Zimmerman kept on going, but then he suddenly stopped, waving his cane fiercely. "Where are you? Are you playing a trick on me?" he snapped. Outraged, he looked as if he were going to strike at Albert.

"I'm here," Albert said.

"Then you mind what you're doing, and no tricks," Mr. Zimmerman warned him.

They said nothing the rest of the way, and Albert was glad when they got to the shoemaker's shop and he saw his uncle through the window. He was so glad that he ducked away from Mr. Zimmerman as soon as he opened the door.

"Careful, careful, use your head, Albert," his uncle called sharply, for Mr. Zimmerman was groping around with his stick.

"No fuss, no fuss, please," Mr. Zimmerman protested, irritably. "I'm all right."

"It's just that Albert —"

"Albert's all right," Mr. Zimmerman said impatiently, as he sat down, "only tell him next time he's not to play games with me and let me go along by myself."

"Why, I'm ashamed. Is that so, Albert?" Uncle Adolphe said. He was so apologetic as he fussed around Mr. Zimmerman that Albert couldn't believe he was looking at his own uncle. He began to feel truly ashamed of himself, as if he had insulted a very great man. He got out of the way, working at little jobs around the shop, and listened furtively while his uncle and Mr. Zimmerman talked.

He couldn't make much out of the conversation. With both hands resting on the head of his stick, Mr. Zimmerman was talking like a man making a speech. He talked about China and Russia, and the march of history and the future of the people of America. The big-sounding, lofty phrases meant nothing to Albert, except that sometimes they sounded mocking, and sometimes eager or triumphant and seemed to fill Uncle Adolphe with restless excitement. He asked questions, and when he got the answer he scratched his head and looked puzzled. Albert noticed that Mr. Zimmerman never asked his uncle a question about anything, and it offended Albert. In a couple of hours, Uncle Adolphe took Mr. Zimmerman home and left Albert minding the shop.

Then one afternoon Uncle Adolphe said, "Now listen, Albert. I want you to go and get Mr. Zimmerman. This time put your mind on it, see? If you embarrass him again I won't like it and I'll certainly give you a smack, see?"

Hesitating, Albert asked, "Uncle Adolphe, why do you like the blind man?"

"Ah, he's a great scholar. You should have heard him last night."

"I'll bet he doesn't know half as much as you do."

"Me?" he said. "Why, I don't know anything. I'm just a poor, ignorant shoemaker. But if I listen to him then maybe I'll get to learn how to see things. Now go along, Albert."

Albert went down the street slowly, dreading the walk with Mr. Zimmerman. At Molsen's, he hung back. Four men from the neighborhood were there, listening reverently to the blind man. When Albert stuck his head into the room he expected Mr. Zimmerman to know he was there and stare at him suspiciously.

Letting Mr. Zimmerman take his arm, they started out. When they had gone only a little piece he found himself staring up at the blind man's impassive face and wondering, "How does he know so much? Why do they ask him questions? He can't see the streets, or people's faces, or anything in the world. You'd think he'd be the one who'd be asking Uncle Adolphe to come and tell him what's going on all over."

"Are you walking along staring at me, boy?" Mr. Zimmerman asked suddenly.

"I wasn't," Albert began, shocked. Then he grew scared. The other day Mr. Zimmerman had known when he was playing a little game. He seemed to have ways of knowing things that were frightening, and it was as if they were walking arm in arm, yet in different worlds.

"I was wondering how you knew so much?" he said.

"Does it surprise you?"

"I was only thinking —"

"You should be a polite boy and not keep on reminding me that I can't see," Mr. Zimmerman said. "So please don't stare at me." He made a sucking sound with his lower lip. He seemed to think Albert was trying to humiliate him. They went to the shop in silence, with Albert frightened by the hostility growing between them.

"It was a nice little trip this time, eh?" Uncle Adolphe asked, hopefully, as they came in.

"Oh, yes, indeed," Mr. Zimmerman said. But then he smiled reproachfully. "Just the same, I don't think the boy likes me. Do you, Albert?"

Albert shook his head helplessly at his uncle, who was scowling at him.

"What's he been doing now?" Uncle Adolphe asked, humiliated again.

"He keeps staring at me and not saying anything, eh, Albert?" Mr. Zimmerman said, his hand groping for Albert's arm, a knowing smile on his face.

"I just don't know what to say and I couldn't help it," Albert protested. His uncle's face was reddening, exasperated that Albert should always be doing some little thing to embarrass a man like Mr. Zimmerman. He knocked Albert spinning against the counter and scowled at him, daring him to make more fuss. "I guess he's a stupid boy," he apologized. "I haven't been paying much attention to him. I haven't noticed him much." Then he swung his arm at Albert. "Go 'way," he said. "Go on, go on, go on."

Albert stayed out of the store till his uncle took Mr. Zimmerman home.

For the next few days Uncle Adolphe paid no attention to him at all. Albert hung around the bench near the window, waiting for his uncle to be friendly. A couple of times he asked a few timid questions. "Don't bother me, Albert," his uncle said. Albert knew his uncle was seeing Mr. Zimmerman in the evenings. He could tell by the way his uncle stood with a shoe in his hand, his face all puckered up, worrying and muttering. He never sang any more.

Then a week later, in the afternoon, Uncle Adolphe said, "Go and get Mr. Zimmerman, Albert. He's waiting. Now mind, no woolgathering. It's disgusting that a boy your age can't walk a block with Mr. Zimmerman without making trouble. Do you hear me?"

"I hear, Uncle Adolphe."

"Then don't gape at me so stupidly. Go on," he said.

When Albert went down to the grocery store he took the blind man's arm tighter than ever before. Looking straight ahead, thinking only of his uncle's shop, he guided Mr. Zimmerman along the crowded sidewalk.

"You don't need to pull me like that," Mr. Zimmerman complained. "Just walk, just walk, if you please," he said. "I don't want everybody gaping at me."

Though he felt helpless and lost, Albert held on to Mr. Zimmerman's arm.

By the time they got to the shop Albert was trembling. He opened the door for Mr. Zimmerman, and was so eager to get away that he jerked his arm loose. Lurching to the side, the blind man groped for the door. He missed it and swung around, losing his balance and banged his head against the door jamb. A little blue bruise appeared on his pale high forehead.

"Oh, you stupid, careless, clumsy boy." Uncle Adolphe shouted. "Sit here, Mr. Zimmerman. Oh, what can I say? He's a stupid boy if ever there was one. Please wait. I'll get a little hot water in the back room."

He grabbed Albert by the scruff of the neck, dragging him along. Passing the counter, he snatched a long piece of thick, raw leather. He clamped his big hand over Albert's mouth when they got to the back room. He raised his arm, his face full of cold disgust and rage, and he pounded Albert. Then he pushed him on the floor and rushed to get a wet towel and hurried back to Mr. Zimmerman.

Albert lay there trying not to sob, hearing the drone of their voices, remembering how his uncle used to sing and how bright the world had looked to him until he had started listening to the blind man.

THE
SENTIMENTALISTS

It was at the scarf counter at noontime that Jack Malone, a young law student, saw the yellow scarf on the rack and thought he might give it to his girl for her birthday. His plump friend, Fred Webster, bored with wandering around from counter to counter in the department store, had just said, "Sure she'll like it. Take it," when a gray-haired woman in a blue sailor hat came gliding around the corner and bumped into Malone.

"Excuse me, lady," he said, but she was in his way, idly toying with the yellow scarf. "Excuse me, madam," he said firmly. Moving a step away, she said impatiently, "Excuse me," and went on fussing with the scarves without actually looking at them, and when the salesgirl approached she did not look up. Reddening, the salesgirl retreated quickly, leaving her there peering through the screen of scarves at the silk-stocking counter in the next aisle.

"Why get sore? She's the store detective. You got in her way," Webster said.

"Why shouldn't I? I don't work for her."

"She's checking out someone at the silk-stocking counter," Webster said, brightening. "Let's watch."

Because they were having a sale, silk stockings were out loose on the counter and sometimes there was a line of women and sometimes the line thinned out.

"If you were a betting man, who would you say it was?" Webster asked. He knew Malone was proud of his judgment of people and of the experience he got from talking to people of all kinds in the law office and in the police court. "I'll bet you five bucks," Webster said. "Go ahead, look over the field."

"It's too easy," Malone said. All he had to do was watch the detective behind the scarves and follow the direction of her eyes, watching three women at the end of the silk-stocking counter who had been standing there longer than the others. It was hard to get more than a glimpse of their faces, but one was a stout woman with a silver-fox fur and a dark, heavy, aggressive, and arrogant face. She looked very shrewd and competent. Her lips were heavy and greedy. If she were going to steal anything it would probably be something very valuable, and she wouldn't give it up easily. On the left of her was a lanky schoolgirl with no shape at all, a brainless-looking kid. And there was a young girl in a red felt hat and a fawn-colored loose spring coat.

All the women at the counter seemed to be sliding stockings over the backs of their hands and holding them up to the light. Getting a little closer, his excitement quickening, Malone tried to see into their faces and into their lives, and the first one he counted out was the girl in the fawn coat: she seemed like someone he had met on a train, or someone he had known all his life without ever knowing her name. In a hundred places they might have seen each other, at summer dances or on the streets where he had played when he was a kid. But while he was watching her and feeling sure of her, the schoolgirl sighed and dropped the stocking she was looking at and walked away.

"That leaves only the two," Webster whispered, coming alongside. His plump good-natured face was disturbed, as if he, too, had decided the stout woman was far too sensible-looking to be a store thief, and his estimate of the girl in the fawn coat with the dark hair and the brown eyes was the same as Malone's. "I was thinking it would be the school kid doing something crazy," he whispered.

"So was I."

While they stood together, suddenly disturbed, the stout woman made a purchase and walked away. They both turned, watching the bright-colored bank of scarves, and Malone suddenly longed to see the blue sailor hat go gliding behind the scarves, following the stout woman. But the detective was still there, waiting. You could see the motionless rim of her hat.

"Well, it's the girl in the fawn coat she's watching," Webster said.

"And what do you think?"

"I think the detective's crazy."

"Yet she's the one the woman's watching."

"Listen, I'll bet you that five bucks old eagle eye hiding over there is absolutely wrong about her."

"Not on your life. That's no bet. That kid's no thief," Malone said.

It wasn't just that the girl was pretty. But in the slow way she turned her head, swinging the dark hair over her raised collar, in the light of intelligence that shone in her dark eyes when she looked up quickly, and in the warmth that would surely come easily in her face, Malone was reminded that she might be someone like his own sister. Her clothes were not expensive: the fawn coat looked as if it had been worn at least three seasons. But his sister had looked like that the time they were all scrimping and saving to send her to collage. Suddenly, Malone and Webster were joined, betting against the judgment of the store detective. They wanted to root for the girl, root her away from the counter. With a passionate eagerness to see the woman detective frustrated, Malone muttered in her direction, "Lady, you're picking on the wrong party. Just stick around a while and watch her walk away."

But the store detective's blue sailor hat was moving slowly, coming around, closing in. Yet the girl stood motionless. A stocking was in her hand, or her hand was on the counter, and her absent-minded stillness, her lowered head — it became apparent — were a furtive awareness of the position of the salesgirl. Malone went to speak to Webster, and then he couldn't: they were both unbelieving and hurt. Yet there still was a chance. It became a desperate necessity that he should be right about the girl. "Go away, kid," he was begging her. "Why do you stand there looking like that? You're no thief. You're a kid. Get moving, why don't you?" But she bent her head, she hunched up her shoulders a little, and her hand on the counter was drawing a pair of silk stockings into the wide sleeve of her coat. As the store detective came slowly around the end of the scarf counter, Webster said, disgusted, "Just another little store thief."

Malone wanted to slap the girl and abuse her. It wasn't just that she had let him down, she seemed to have betrayed so many things that belonged to the most intimate and warmest part of his life. "Let her arrest her, what do we care?" he said as the store detective went slowly down the aisle. But in spite of himself he thought he would cry out if he stood there. He got excited. He walked along the aisle alone, taking out his watch as if he had been waiting a long time for someone. When he was opposite the girl he stopped, staring at her back, at the bunch of black curls under the rim of her hat, and he was sick and hesitant and bewildered. "Why, Helen," he said, reaching out and touching her, "have you been here all this time?" A wide, forced smile was on his face.

"Smile, please smile," he whispered, because he could see the store detective watching them. "Come away," he begged her. "They're watching you."

Before the scared smile came on her face, the silk stockings rolled in a ball in her palm and half up her sleeve were dropped almost naturally on the counter. She made it look like a careless gesture. "Hello," she said, "I was . . ." then her voice was lost. If he had not moved she would have stood gaping and incredulous, but he was scared for himself now, for he might be arrested as an accomplice, and he linked his arm under hers and started to walk down the aisle to the door.

They had to pass the store detective, and maybe it was because Malone instinctively tightened his hold on the girl's arm that he could feel it trembling. But the store detective, frustrated and puzzled, seemed to smile cynically just as they passed; he hated her for being right about the girl.

When they got outside, they stopped a moment under the big clock. It had been raining out, but there was bright sunlight on the wet pavement and the noonday crowd surged by. In that bright light, as he stood hesitating and the girl's head was lowered in humiliation, he noticed that there seemed to be a hundred little spots on her light coat, maybe rain marks or dust and rain. His heart was pounding, but now that he had got her safely out of the store, he wanted to get rid of her, and he didn't want her to offer any of that servile gratitude he got from petty thieves he helped in the police court.

"Thanks," she whispered.

"Forget it," he said, as if the whole thing had been nothing to him and he had understood from the beginning what she was. "I guess you'd better be getting on your way."

"All right."

"Well, there's no use standing here. Aren't you going along?"

"It doesn't matter," she said, standing there staring at him, her face still full of humiliation.

"You better be heading somewhere out of here. Where are you from?" he asked awkwardly.

"Out of town," she said. Then she touched him on the arm. "Listen, what was the idea?" she asked. While she waited for him to answer her face seemed to brighten. She was looking at him, looking right into his eyes. "Why did you do it? What's it to you?" They seemed to be alone on the street while she waited breathlessly because she had been offered some incredible promise, a turn that gave her a wild hope.

"We were standing there watching," he said uneasily, as he nodded to Webster, who had followed them out and was now standing by the window trying to hear what she said. "Me and my pal, we saw what was going on," Malone said.

Then, remembering their disappointment, he said bluntly, "We were betting on you."

"How do you mean?"

"When we saw the detective watching you —"

"Yes . . ."

"Our money went on you . . . that she was wrong . . . you let us down, that's all; we were wrong. We lose."

"Oh," she said, startled. As Webster came closer, she swung her head in wild resentment at him. Again they were both staring at her, watching her. She looked around the street at the faces of passing people as if everybody had suddenly stopped to watch her and make a little bet. "A buck she will, a buck she won't, eh!" she said as her eyes brightened with a crazy fury. "Get out of my way," she whispered. Swinging her foot she kicked him savagely on the shin.

As he felt the pain he could think only of how she had asked, "Why did you do it?" and waited breathlessly for some gesture from him. At that moment there did not seem to be a single good instinct, a single good thing in his life that he had not betrayed.

And she came walking right at him as if she would walk right through him if he did not step aside, and she had her head up and her fists clenched tight, going down the street, going deeper into the crowd with the sun touching her red hat and her good legs with the runs down her stockings.

EMILY

*F*or four years Dave had had a room in Mrs. MacDoug-
ald's house where Emily Sherwood also had a room,
and every night and sometimes in the mornings he used to
pass her in the hall. When he first knew her, he was twenty-
one and she was thirty-one, and so shapely and stylish with
her smart clothes, her lustrous black hair, and the faint dimple
marks in her smooth cheeks, that she seemed to him just the
kind of woman he had always longed to meet. For many
nights he had lain awake, thinking of her fine laughing mouth
while he made plans for coaxing her to go out with him the
next day. In the evenings he used to try to be in the hall when
she came home, so that he could follow her up the stairs and
call out, "Just a minute, Miss Sherwood," and then catch up
to her and make awkward gestures like a big, shy, serious boy
as he tried to persuade her to go to a show with him.

When he passed her door in the hall and it was not quite
closed, he listened, holding his breath and trying to get up
enough courage to call to her and urge her to let him come
into the room. But he was never able to suggest that to her.
Sometimes she was very kind to him, for his admiration delighted her, but she had explained that she had a lover named
George Hamilton, who had gone to Montreal, and to whom
she wrote long letters three times a week.

Dave became like a sullen, determined child. He was working in a broker's office and at noontime, once, he came home to see her and tell her hot-temperedly that she was a fool to be wasting her life for a man who might never return to her. She squeezed his arm so tightly and laughed so merrily, he was ashamed of himself.

But during the last two years he noticed Emily looking much older. She didn't seem so buoyantly cheerful either. Dave thought it was a shame that she didn't have to make herself look elegantly attractive for some man who might see her from day to day, instead of dressing like a woman with no place go. She spent too much time by herself reading the poems of Lord Alfred Tennyson and waiting for the man to return to the city and marry her. Once she showed Dave some pictures of herself that she was sending to Montreal. In the photographs the dimples in her plump cheeks were quite deep and, since she was laughing, there were heavy lines in her face. She looked too heavy. Dave thought at the time that she made herself worse by probably insisting upon wearing the same size shoes she had always worn when a girl, which made her walk sometimes, when she was tired, as though her feet hurt her.

But by this time Dave had accepted her devotion for her lover as something marvelous and mysterious that he ought never to disturb. And, besides, he no longer was anxious to be in love with a mature woman of thirty-five: he had a nice young girl of his own now. So he had made a kind of lasting joke out of his love for Emily, and when he passed her in the hall he always said, "Are you sure you wouldn't like to kiss me, Emily?" and they both laughed good-naturedly.

One night in the spring, after being to the theater with his girl, Dave returned to the rooming house and was passing along the hall by Emily's room. Her door was open and he could see her standing there with her coat on as if she had just come in. Outside the first spring freshness had been in the air. The first really mild, clear weather had come at last after a bad, long winter. Dave had been walking along the streets with his girl and they had felt so exhilarated they had started to laugh out loud and walk faster with long, swinging steps. They had suddenly started talking about getting married in the summer. So some of this exhilaration was still in Dave when he stood outside Emily Sherwood's room, wanting to be friendly with everybody in the world. He saw Emily, with her coat on, standing by the bureau, looking into the mirror with her hands up to her face. Her back was to the door, but he could see her image in the mirror. Her face looked drawn and tired, as though the image of an Emily Sherwood she had never really noticed before left her bewildered.

"Hello, Emily," he called. "Going out, or coming in?"

She turned, but before speaking she looked at him steadily, and she was holding her lower lip with her teeth. In a low voice she said: "Hello, Dave, won't you come in?"

As he went in he was embarrassed and he tried to figure out why she had at last invited him into her room. His heart began to beat unevenly because he couldn't help remembering how he used to want to have her call him into this room, and now he didn't know what she expected of him. Then she threw off her coat and he saw her in a new, flaming, red silk dress fitting far too tightly at the waist, so tightly that two of the fasteners had come undone. Dave didn't like the dress. It made Emily look older, heavier, and more flamboyant. She actually looked loud and gaudy in such a dress, and she was really such a modest woman.

With a solemn face and wide, dark, sad eyes, Emily stared at him till he began to grin uneasily. Just to be casual and frivolous, he said, as he had been saying for the last two years in the same mocking tone: "Why, what's the matter, Emily? Aren't you going to kiss me?"

"Do you really want to kiss me, Dave?" she asked, timid and hesitating. Then she began to crimson. "You can kiss me if you want to," she said, as though expecting him to be doubtful. She was acting like a woman who no longer believes that anybody could find her desirable. For the last two years Dave hadn't wanted to kiss Emily; he hadn't thought of her in that way for so long he couldn't help hesitating, and when she noticed it he was ashamed of himself. He went over and sat beside her on the bed, putting his arm with serious gentleness on her shoulder and he kissed her lightly on the cheek. Her head seemed to droop to his shoulder, her eyes remained closed, but her lips were moving with a strange girlish excitement. So there was nothing left for him to do but kiss her again. He began to feel uncomfortable. She didn't seem to be Emily. And, besides, he started thinking of his own girl whom he had been kissing only half an hour ago. Emily was holding on to his arm as though she would never let it go.

Then she said, "What do you think of me, Dave? How do I look to you?"

"You look like a peach to me, Emily."

"Oh, you're grand, Dave. Are you sure you're not teasing me?"

"You know how you always looked to me," he said, smiling.

"Do I seem just as nice to you as I used to?"

"You've always looked the same, Emily," he said at once.

She suddenly laughed out loud as she used to laugh when he followed her up the stairs four years ago. She seemed delighted to believe that she was so very desirable. She became quite sure of herself and smiled at him gaily as though expecting him to pursue her as he had always done. The rich warm blood surged back into her face and her eyes were bright and moist. As soon as he put out his hand and touched her again, she seemed delighted with what she thought was his eagerness and excitement. She no longer looked like a woman who is losing the last of her youth.

He didn't really know what was the matter with her; he only knew that she had been miserable and wanted comforting and sympathy. So he smiled at her and went to embrace her again. "Something's got into her. Maybe the fine spring nights outside have started her thinking about her lover," he thought. Some of his old feeling for her returned, and when with warm sincerity he began to plead, "Kiss me, please kiss me, Emily," he seemed to be saying exactly what she wanted him to say, for she smiled with delight, then looked more confused and more lovely.

Then he was astonished to find that she was resisting with a new, quiet confidence that exasperated him. "There, there now," she said, just as she might have said a few years ago. "Heavens, I don't know what you must be thinking of me. And what do you think George Hamilton would say if he walked in here and saw you kissing me?"

Laughing, he said, "I don't know. I don't know George."
He reached out to take hold of her hands, just to tease her.

"No, no, you mustn't touch me," she said gently. "It
wouldn't be fair to George. Now would it?"

"I suppose not."

"I mean it's like this. You have a girl yourself. You
wouldn't like somebody else to be hugging her, would you?
You'd want her to be square with you. That's the way it is
with me, too; I want to be square with George," she said
with simple dignity.

Now she looked much lovelier than when he had seen
her standing by the bureau looking into the mirror with her
hands up to her face. He was so pleased to see her feeling
cheerful again that he said, "Gee, Emily, I never could do
anything with you, could I?"

"You always worried me. You do to this day, Dave.
You're still so persistent. If it weren't for George . . ." she
added mildly, "You know, he might be upset if he knew
how much you like me."

A wistful expression was on her face, and Dave felt
uncomfortable, so he said, "That's a pretty dress you've got
on — where did you get it, Emily?"

"I bought it this afternoon."

"What for, some big celebration?"

"Do you like it? George always used to say I looked
good in red with my black hair. I bought these patent leather
shoes, too. I went down to the station tonight to meet
George."

"Lord, Emily, after all that time! Where is he?"

"I've just come back from the station," she said, looking worried. "I must have missed him."

As he looked at her in her red silk dress that was to make her look so attractive in her lover's eyes, and saw the fasteners that had burst open at the waist, and saw her wiggling her feet as though the new patent leather shoes hurt her, he had a sudden feeling that she never really expected to see George Hamilton again.

"Maybe something happened to him," Dave said. "Maybe he was broke and couldn't come. It's an expensive trip."

"Oh, no," she said. "I sent him the money when I wrote to him. I must have missed him. I've just come back from sitting there for hours. Don't you think that's likely what happened, Dave!" She seemed to be appealing to Dave.

"Sure," he said. "You must have been both looking so hard you couldn't see each other. So you missed him."

"That's it, all right," she said, taking a deep breath.

"And you were feeling so unhappy about missing him you called me in here for company, eh?"

"I was feeling blue, thinking I must have been careless in some way," she said.

Frowning and making an awkward gesture with his hand, he thought: "I ought to put her straight about that cheap guy; he'll never turn up." So he said, "look here, Emily, let me tell you . . ."

"Tell me what?" she said unwillingly.

"Just that you're lovely," he said, jerking his head, for he suddenly realized with wonder that he couldn't bear to disturb the happiness she had got from resisting him, as if the more he coaxed and urged her, the more she could believe she still had a lover, and that George Hamilton, wherever he was, must still want to marry her.

BIG JULES

*T*hey were having a lot of fun in the neighborhood with Big Jules Casson. Word had soon gone around that he had promised his old man he would never get into trouble again after he had been sent to reform school for stealing from Spagnola's fruit market. The boys whose leader he had once been, and who had been afraid of him for years, found that he wouldn't fight back; they mocked him on those winter nights when he came hurrying home from the job at the printing shop his father had got him. A big, raw-boned seventeen-year-old who seemed to have realized suddenly that he would soon be a man, he started running the minute he got off the bus. He trotted along with his head down and his hands deep in his overcoat pockets. When he passed the cigar store where the boys were playing the slot machines, and they saw him through the open door and yelled — "Hey, when did they let you out?" — he never turned his big serious face.

But one night in the middle of the winter, when it had been raining and half snowing for hours and he came trotting past the cigar store, someone called out, "Hey, Jules, what are you doing tonight?"

This time the voice seemed to be soft, friendly, and casual. So Jules stopped and turned. As he came into the light, his face showed how eager he was for companionship if only they wouldn't kid him. Near the cigar-store door were three fellows whom he had grown up with. There was Phil Harris in a new overcoat, tight at the waist, with a pearl-gray felt hat, lighting a cigarette for Alf Maguire in the same old dirty overcoat he had worn the last five years. But the one who had called to him was leaning against the window, in a leather jacket and peak cap — Stuffy Meuller, whom Big Jules hadn't seen for three months. It was hard to see the expressions on their faces through the light stream of snow. So Jules went toward them slowly.

"What's on your mind?" he asked.

"Well, if it isn't my old friend, Big Jules," Stuffy Meuller said enthusiastically. As he reached up and slapped him on the shoulder, Jules nodded warmly. "Maybe we could go to the fights, eh, guys," he said eagerly. "I haven't been to the fights for months."

But Stuffy Meuller, a little guy that Jules could have smacked down with one swing, kept up the elaborate enthusiasm. "Wait a minute, give me a chance to get used to you. I didn't know they had let you out."

When he saw that they were smirking at each other, Big Jules wanted to plead with Meuller to shut up. But Meuller, enjoying himself, went on, "If you weren't doing anything I thought we might take a little trip over to Spagnola's fruit market. What do you say, Jules?"

Jules was peering at their faces that looked so mocking in the light and the snow. Then he shook his head, as if puzzled. "Lay off," he muttered. He was leaning close to them, holding himself taut, as if he had just had an insight into what he would always be. His face suddenly frightened them. Scared, they backed away. But this only seemed to hurt him more. "What's the matter?" he pleaded, taking a step after them. Shooting out his hand, he grabbed Meuller by the shoulder. "I'm not going to hurt you." Now they were looking as frightened as if he had been going to pull a knife on them.

"Beat it, Stuffy," Phil Harris whispered, shoving Meuller away. "Get going. He's taking the plug out."

As they went up the street he stood there, helpless, for now it seemed that in some way, after digging at him for months, they had found out that he was still what he had always been. After a little while, he started to go home, thinking desperately that maybe they were right, that if his life belonged to the lanes around Spagnola's fruit market, if he had been pinned there forever the night the police caught him and the others rifling the till — even if he was just a kid when it happened — then the dream he had been carrying around in him for months of working hard and making something out of his life was all gone.

He suddenly began to walk faster, feeling a great longing to look into the faces of his own family and see if they, too, were really only waiting for him to get into trouble again; maybe they, too, were always thinking of the fruit market and the years when he was growing up near it. So when he went into the house, he hung back near the door of the living room, his hat still on his head, the melted snow dripping off the brim, and he looked around suspiciously. His father, who had been sitting in the armchair at the head of the table, his arms spread out over the evening paper on the table, did not look up. Nor did his mother. She was fixing the collar of his sister Alice's dress, and Alice kept saying, "Please hurry, or I'll be late." But as Jules stood there staring at them, they turned one by one. He looked so excited and suspicious that his mother's hand began to tremble. Her face showed that she was alarmed. Then his father, opening his mouth blankly, looked very grave and folded up the paper.

To Jules it seemed that they were just as frightened as the fellows at the corner, and he cried, "Why are you all gaping at me?"

"Why, son," his mother said, "what happened?"

"I ran into Meuller and some of the guys down at the corner," he blurted out, "and I didn't smack them. See, I didn't smack them."

Then Jules' father got up and began to walk up and down the room. Jules could see how worried he was. His head hung down a little and the patch of white hair at the back stuck up in the light; it was as if something he had been dreading for months were coming at last to a head: the anguish he felt, which he could not conceal now, gave Jules a painful but deep satisfaction. "I was right. This is how they've been feeling all along," he thought.

"What's Meuller to you, son?" his father said, stopping in front of Jules with his hands out appealingly. "You're a good boy, see," he said, taking a step closer, his worried face full of gentle concern. It was as if he wanted to put his arm around Jules but was too shy. "You're working and doing well, isn't that so? And we're proud of you." His voice broke a little, but he went on, "We're proud of the way you handle yourself, son."

"Cut it out," Jules said harshly. "That isn't what you're thinking."

"It's the way I've been feeling, Jules."

"Meuller's a bum, Jules," his mother said, taking him by the arm and trying to get him to sit down. "Sure you should smack him, but he's no good. Why should you put your hands on trash? Me and your father only want that you shouldn't let such things bother you, son, see?" When he didn't seem to be listening, she said desperately, "You don't need to worry, you don't need to worry about anything anybody says. We're sure of you, son."

But Jules was looking at his sister Alice, who sat down with her hat on and her hands clasped tight in her lap. She was two years older than Jules. She had never gotten into trouble, she was very pretty, and she had always seemed beyond the reach of any of the neighborhood boys. It was the way she carried herself. But now there was an angry flush on her face. In that flush, and in her silence, Jules thought he saw at last the true picture of the humiliation he would always bring to his family.

When Alice got up grimly and started to go along the hall, Jules followed her and grabbed her arm.

"Go on," he whispered, "say it."

"Say, what?"

"I never give you a chance to stop being ashamed of me!"

"Jules —"

"That boyfriend of yours — why don't you ever bring him around here?"

"You're going crazy, Jules. He was around here last night."

"Sure," he said. "When I wasn't here."

Then her eyes blazed, but she looked as if she were going to cry. "Why don't you get some sense?" she whispered.

"What's the use of hitting Meuller? Nobody's going around watching you, can't you see? Jules, can't you see?"

As she tried to take his arm comfortingly, he knocked it away. "Damn it all, stop sympathizing with me," he said. He didn't want to hear anything more. All he wanted to do was go out and find Meuller — or any other guy who would dare open his trap — and beat his brains out.

Going along the street, looking for Meuller, he kept gripping his hands tight, exulting in the release and freedom such violence would bring to him. But when he got to the corner and looked around, there was no one standing near the cigar store. There were no marks even in the snow, nothing to show that they, or he, had ever stood there. Then, as he looked up and down the street, wondering which way he should go, he felt an immense longing to have everything that had ever happened to him up to a few months ago wiped clean, just as the white falling snow had covered up and wiped out his footprints and Meuller's.

He turned to look into the store through the window, but he couldn't see in because of the way the snow, swept against the panes, melted and streamed down. Then it got so that he couldn't even see the window. Spagnola's fruit market kept coming into his head; he could see nothing but the old shed with the baskets of fruit, the little store, the lane behind. Turning away, he started to walk fast, trying hard to think of other things, like the little soft-eyed girl who had come into the shop where he worked. But it was no good. He couldn't get the fruit market out of his head. It began to grow feverishly bright.

It was there blocking him every time he tried to move away from it, and while it was there, he could have no big dreams, no great eagerness, no future to work for. Then the magnitude of this one spot in his life began to awe him. He felt he had to see it and look at it again.

He was four blocks away from home, going down the street where the fruit market was, and he knew within himself that he had been deliberately heading over that way. Keeping on the other side of the road, he walked slowly past the lighted fruit-store window. Through the glistening glass he could see the pyramids of oranges and lemons and purple plums and red apples; and then he saw old Spagnola himself waddle into the light. "There it is. Just like it'll always be," he thought.

To get closer, he crossed the road to the lane that ran past the side of the store, the lane where the kids used to meet at night. Out of the store came a shabby woman carrying a big paper bag, and Jules ducked furtively into the lane. As he went along by the fence, he looked back once at the trail of his footprints in the snow. Again he felt the longing to have this place and that couple of years in the reform school dumped magically out of his life.

Then he was at the old gate that led into the yard behind Spagnola's place. Hundreds of times he had hopped over it when it was locked, at first just to steal an apple or a peach with the other boys — and then go running madly along the lane with Spagnola shouting after them. The gate was open now. Slow, wondering, disbelieving, he went into the yard. There was the shed, the roof a white slope of snow. At the back of the store, on the stoop, was a big pile of empty baskets.

As he got closer to the place his wonder, his unbelief, kept growing. The place suddenly seemed shabby and unimportant. He wanted to cry out bitterly that it was a terrible thing that such a tumbling down blot of a place should always be in his head, should always be there in the eyes of his father and mother when they were worried about him, and in the eyes of everybody who knew him when they looked at him.

On the ground beside him was an empty basket. Swinging his foot savagely, he sent it crashing against the stoop.

At the sound of the crash, a shadow filled the lighted window; then the back door was thrown open — the beam of light fell on Big Jules, standing there, bewildered and motionless.

Rushing out old Spagnola yelled, "Hey, you, hey!" He came rushing at Jules, his arms wide, his white apron flapping like a sail.

Jules turned to run, but slipped in the mud and the snow, and when he looked up and saw Spagnola close to him, the man's short little arms opened wide to grab him, he felt crazy. It seemed that not only Spagnola but the years around the place when he was growing up, and Meuller and all the other guys, were trying to hold him tight, hold him there forever. He had to break the grip it had on him. He had to destroy it. So he took a leap at Spagnola, like a flying tackle, his head getting him in the chest, sending him sprawling on the snow. Instead of running, Big Jules looked around wildly. Then he started kicking at the pile of baskets. Yelling "Help! Help!" Spagnola got up and jumped on Jules' back, but he couldn't hold him. So he went on shouting while Jules crashed against the piled-up baskets and kicked at them and sent the splinters flying in the snow as if he had to keep it up till he smashed the whole place and Spagnola's fruit market was wiped forever from the earth.

But Spagnola's weight on his shoulders was pulling him down and exhausting him. At last he crashed on the stoop with Spagnola on top. "I got you, I got you," Spagnola grunted. But Jules wasn't even trying to move.

Then Mrs. Spagnola came waddling down the path of light. "Hold him, hold him!" she yelled. "I'll get the police."

"He's crazy. But I got him," Spagnola said.

Jules lay there dazed, hardly hearing anything, but when Mrs. Spagnola, bending down, cried, "Look, look would you! It's Jules Casson!" he began to tremble.

"So it is," Spagnola said.

"What was he trying to steal?" she asked.

"But there's nothing out here to steal in the winter," he said, astonished.

Hoisting himself up on one elbow, Jules sobbed, "Don't get the cops. Please don't get the cops. Can't you see? I only wanted to get a look at the place — because — because I couldn't get it out of my head."

He looked so stricken and bewildered that the Spagnolas shook their heads at each other and shrugged in wonder.

"Only yesterday his father was talking to me about his Jules, saying such good things," Spagnola said to his wife. Then he said to Jules, "What is this? You should tell us."

As Jules looked up at their wondering faces, he saw that there was nothing to fear from them. They were wanting to take him in and help him as if he were some trapped animal they had found when they opened the door. "I . . . I . . ." he stammered, and couldn't go on. But he kept nodding his head gratefully, as if in their friendly worried faces he had found a release from a bad violent dream about himself.

THE FIDDLER ON TWENTY-THIRD STREET

*T*he basement hand laundry on Twenty-third Street was closed for the night, so Joseph Loney got his fiddle and sat down at the end of the long table littered with shirts and aprons waiting to be ironed and began to play. He played his fiddle every night before he went down to the corner to have a drink with his friend, Jimmie Leonard.

His wife, Mary, stooped a little and thin, was at the window on a level with the street, and she felt sullen and resentful as she waited for her husband to put on his hat and coat and go off for the night. He would spend his money drinking, and sleep late in the morning, and then would have the same old sheepish grin as he scratched his head and tried to joke with customers who grew irritable when the laundry they had been promised wasn't ready.

Looking out the window Mary saw a little girl in a leather jacket leaning against the lamppost, listening to the fiddle music and, as Mrs. Loney watched, a boy came along and stood beside the girl and listened too.

Mrs. Loney, who had no children of her own, watched the boy and girl with a troubled longing that puzzled her. Turning, she glanced at her husband, whose hairless head shone more brightly under the light than any white stiffened garments hanging on the wall, and she felt she could hardly blame him for going out night after night seeking places where there was laughter and companionship.

Outside, another little girl, holding by the hand a small boy in a red sweater and a red woolen hat, had joined the other children, their faces turned toward the laundry window.

Mrs. Loney called out suddenly, "Play harder, Joseph; make it sound louder."

Joseph, smiling brightly, scraped away on his fiddle. Mary, pressing her face against the window, saw the little girl who had been holding the boy by the hand start to dance, raising her one hand over her head and putting the other on her hip, going around and around in a circle.

"The children on the sidewalk are listening, Joseph," Mrs. Loney called. "Maybe they'd love it if we asked them to come in and listen."

"Sure, ask them in," he said.

Mrs. Loney called to the children, "How would you like to come in and listen, children? Maybe you could have a concert in here."

They looked at her shyly; the girl who had been dancing took hold of her little brother's hand and the bigger boy began to shuffle away.

Yet Mrs. Loney was smiling and still coaxing them. "Do not be shy, children, maybe you'll be having a lot of fun."

At last the girl with the straight hair and the short skirt, the one who had first heard the sound of the fiddle, came forward boldly, and then the others, not so timid, followed her down the steps. They huddled together at the end of the long table, smelling the steam and the irons that were still hot, staring at the pile of freshly ironed shirts.

As soon as Joseph started to play again the children, fascinated at the way he puckered up his face and grinned and winked one eye and kept pounding his foot up and down in time with his music, began to smile. Suddenly he jumped up, still playing the fiddle, and danced around the table, grinning over his shoulder as he passed them, encouraging them to follow. He lifted his knees high. The children began to laugh. Mrs. Loney was delighted to see the bolder girl, whose name was Sally, get up and start to follow Joseph, and the boy, Phil, was grinning shyly, and the polite little girl, Margot, who never let go of her small brother's hand, was tense and wide-eyed with excitement. Mrs. Loney called to her husband, "Maybe you could play something, Joseph, they all could dance to, or maybe they'd all like to take turns doing something."

Wiping his red face with his handkerchief, Joseph said, "Which one of you is any good with his feet?"

"Margot can do a jig, Margot can do a jig," Phil shouted. The sedate little girl glared at him angrily, muttering, "You keep quiet, Phil Thompson."

"Yes, she can," Sally cried.

"I can't, I really can't," Margot said.

But they pushed her out on the floor, so she took a deep breath, nodded to Joseph Loney to play something for her, raised her hand, and with a gravely solemn face began to dance a jig.

Mrs. Loney coaxed the children to perform, and praised their talents lavishly. The bold girl, Sally, was a Catholic, and when it was her turn she told how her aunt had been dying for months and how she had got to like saying the prayers for the sick at the aunt's house, and she asked them if it would be all right if she knelt down and said the prayers that she liked best.

Soon, they were all laughing and praying and singing, and Mary Loney realized her husband had forgotten about going out for a drink. With the fiddle and bow clutched in his left hand, he sat on the edge of his chair leaning over the children who were on the floor at his feet, his voice rising and falling, and his face glowed. Mary Loney felt such a sudden contentment that she was afraid to speak for fear of distracting them. She was full of thankfulness that she had some little biscuits left from dinner.

That night she lay awake a long time, listening to her husband breathing steadily beside her, marveling at the look of pleasure on his face all evening.

Hardly a night passed after that when she did not say to her husband as soon as he had finished his dinner, "Aren't you going to play a tune on the fiddle tonight, Joseph?"

He lit his pipe, then got his fiddle, and she watched at the window for the children to come. Sometimes they all came together, sometimes one by one, all fond of Sally's prayers, and they loved to kneel down on the floor with her and repeat the prayers while Joseph plucked at the fiddle with his thumb in a kind of accompaniment.

The children grew to love Joseph Loney and often seemed to forget that his wife was there with them. Knowing this made the delight she got from their company seem like a precious secret. She hadn't felt so contented in years. She was ready to feed them when they grew tired and were thinking of going home.

But one night when the children came over Joseph Loney was not there with his fiddle. His old friend, Jimmie Leonard, had come looking for him, and they had gone out together.

The children came at the same time the next night. When Mary Loney let them in they saw she had been crying. "He didn't come home last night and he hasn't come home yet," she said to them.

"Oh, something terrible's happened," they said.

"I don't know what to do," she said.

Instead of going home, the children, fascinated by Mary Loney's despair, sat down on the floor and stared at her. It was silent while she worked her lips and swallowed hard, and then her eyes suddenly filled with tears, her lips trembled and she began to cry.

Growing frightened, the children felt that Joseph Loney was close to death wherever he was. Suddenly Margot asked, "Was he wearing a brown coat? I saw a man that looked like him wearing a brown coat and he was getting into a car near Madison Square."

The rest of the children looked at Margot in envy, and then Sally cried, "Oh, now I remember. I saw a crowd down at the corner last night and I was sure I saw Mr. Loney . . ."

Mrs. Loney, realizing the bright imaginations of the children were making them conjure up things that had never happened, cried angrily, "Please be quiet, and don't tell lies."

Sally said, "Oh, now is the time when we ought to pray for him. Let's all kneel and say a little prayer." She knelt on the floor, and the others knelt too, with their faces full of excitement.

"Look! Over there," Sally said, pointing at a little table against the wall that had a bowl of artificial flowers on a clean white cloth. "That will be the altar." She clasped her hands against her breast and bowed her head and had them repeat after her, "Oh, dear Lord, let nothing happen to him, and bring him home safe and sound."

This prayer that had such a simple beginning turned out to be long and rambling, with Sally pausing from time to time to hear her words repeated, and Mary Loney, listening to their childish whispers and watching their earnest faces, began to feel that somehow her life had reached a turning point.

Then they all heard the sound of a trumpet, a beautiful soothing sound, and then the sweet harmony of a cornet and a stringed instrument. The children got up off their knees, sure their prayers had been answered. For a moment they were too scared to move, and they looked at Mrs. Loney whose own heart began to beat unevenly and she, too, was frightened.

Crowding around and looking out of the window, they saw two men with horns and one with a mandolin, each with a little framed and printed sign hanging from a button on his coat, shuffling slowly along the sidewalk in the way blind men do, while they made their music, and a small boy walked a little ahead carrying a tin cup.

Still startled, Margot said, "Just the same, it was funny."

"Aw, I could have told you it was something like that," Phil scoffed, but his tone showed how serious and disappointed he was.

"Children, children," Mrs. Loney cried, but the simplicity of their belief had upset her. She began to wail, "Oh, you're so young. You don't know what I've had to endure. It's terrible to have had to put up with the things I've put up with in my life."

She knew by their silence and staring eyes that they would be unyielding in their resentment if she should try and make them feel her bitterness, yet she did not know why she wanted their sympathy, why she wanted them to feel close to her; and, with nothing to do but sit there and feel separated while they stared at her, she began to feel helpless.

Joseph Loney's sister, whom Mary had phoned, came in and sat down and sighed and tried to smile pleasantly. Joseph's sister, who looked like him and was as thin, was usually comforting but today her patient, understanding smile irritated Mary, who remembered suddenly that this woman had sobered Joseph up on the nights years ago when he came courting her.

"I know you're not worried at all," Mary blurted out. "But that's because from the beginning you never expected anything better of him. It's different with me. Year after year I've never stopped hoping."

"Did you hear from him?"

"Not a word since he went out with Jimmie Leonard."

"That Jimmie Leonard is a no-account man if ever there was one. I wouldn't worry if something put a blight on his life."

"But Joseph staying out all night when I was sure he was straightening up. Why, I let myself feel so hopeful for the first time in years. I was feeling contented. I was a fool."

Trying to smile soothingly, the sister said, "Joseph was picked up last night and taken to the station. He phoned me and asked me to break it to you. He's on his way home."

"Oh, my Lord!" Mary Loney wailed. "What will I do? Wait till I set eyes on him. A night in jail at this time in life! And me wasting my life trying to make him decent."

"Don't be too sure you've made his life any too easy for him," the sister-in-law shouted angrily. "If you weren't dogging him for one thing it was another till he had to turn to something to feel he was alive."

"Have you no shame, woman, to be talking before these children?"

"Why don't you send them home?"

The children were standing stiffly against the wall, and when Mrs. Loney looked at their white, frightened faces she saw they were staring at her resentfully. "Go home, children," she cried angrily. "You should have gone home long ago."

"I'll be the first to go," the sister-in-law said, and held her head high and walked out.

One by one with lowered heads, the children backed toward the door, keeping their eyes on Mrs. Loney as though sure she would jump at them. But they did not go far. Mrs. Loney, sitting at the window, saw them standing outside and she could hear their chatter. Their excitement made her frantic, but then she heard them shout. They came leaping down the steps, pushing open the door and shouting, "Here he comes, Mrs. Loney. Hurray, hurray, hurray! Here he comes," and then they rushed out again to welcome him.

Through the window she could see him coming down the street, his head lowered and body bent so he wouldn't have to look in the neighbors' windows, stooped and shuffling in his familiar, beaten way, and it was like watching years of her married life flow by, and the happiness and security of the last few months became like something held out to tease her.

The children were still shouting, "Hurray, hurray!" Then they came through the door. "Here he comes, Mrs. Loney."

She saw them grabbing his arms and hanging on to his coat, and then when they were at the door they pushed him into the room.

Her body rigid with anger, she tried to make him look directly into her eyes, but he succeeded in sitting down without appearing to see her. While the children gathered around him, he let his head droop, clenched his hands between his knees and waited.

His shame and silence were almost too terrible for the children to bear, and in bewilderment they looked at Mrs. Loney, unable to understand why she showed no gladness when she had worried and waited so long.

Then Joseph looked up and sighed, and spoke in a way he had not spoken for years. "I'm sorry, Mary," he said. "I didn't want it to happen again like this. I'm very sorry."

When Mary only shook her head bitterly, he shrugged and in shy apology smiled into the faces of the children. As Mary saw their faces light up with gladness and sympathy, the injustice of their childish disregard of her filled her with resentment.

Joseph got up slowly and went into the kitchen and came back with the fiddle, still moving in the same slow way, and sat down and twanged the strings with his thumb. Too bewildered and indignant to know what to say, she could only watch him.

He started to play one of the old songs. He broke off, took the fiddle from under his chin and seemed to look at it in disappointment. Then he started to play another song and tried two or three more old songs of his youth, and as each failed, he seemed puzzled. Mary, clenching her fists, shouted, "So that's all there is to it, eh? It's just going to be like that, eh, and you're going to sit there and have nothing to say? I'll show you." She rushed at her husband, grabbed the fiddle out of his hands and tossed it across the room. As the fiddle fell they heard one of the strings snap. The fiddle lay upside down near the little table with the flowerpot on it.

The children, with horror and fear of Mrs. Loney in their faces, began to edge to the door. Phil was the first to dart out to the street, and Margot, pulling her little brother after her, followed, and Sally bumped into Margot going up the steps. Frightened, Mrs. Loney whispered to her husband, "Joseph — the children."

But when he did nothing but smile at her in the puzzled, wondering way, she cried out helplessly, "Children, children," and rushed out after them, urgent and eager as she stood on the street crying out, "Come back, children, come back."

The children, who had retreated along the sidewalk, only backed away a little farther when they heard her calling. Realizing they would not return even if she ran along the street after them, she rushed through the door and pleaded desperately, "Joseph, oh, Joseph, do something! Don't let them go like that."

Joseph, picking up his fiddle, looked at his wife's frightened, pleading face and said, "What'll I do?"

"Call them, call them. They won't come back for me," she said.

Joseph hurried out and she heard him calling, "Hey, kids, hey, kids." She saw him take a few steps after them, holding his fiddle over his head, and she waited, looking out into the street, feeling old and frightened.

Then Joseph came in and sat down at the end of the long table and began to play a fiery tune on his fiddle with the broken string. He smiled and nodded to his wife, who still watched out the open door.

"They'll come," Joseph said confidently, as he went on scraping with his bow. She nodded humbly, and as the solemn faces of the children came closer a fearful eagerness kept growing in her.

MOTHER'S DAY
AT THE BALLPARK

W illie McCaffery, the burly International League umpire, had a splendid contempt for the crowd. No one
had ever heard him say a good word about fans in a ballpark.
Not only were they abusive and heartless, he had decided
long ago, but they had no sense of natural justice. They
were incapable of appreciating that beautiful coordination
of mind and eye that went into one of his decisions. They
were always resentful of his integrity. On and off the ball
field he avoided people, but he didn't feel lonely. He was
proud of his work.

Around the circuit regular fans who hated his imper-
turbable aloofness would try and ride him, and he would
show his contempt in the way he stood on the baseline, his
massive blue-clad body motionless, his big arms folded, his
shoulders hunched up, his cap pulled down over his eyes.
Some fans believed that he was deaf, for when they tried kidding him before a game, with a laughing sweet friendliness,
he wouldn't turn and smile. He despised their loud friendship
as much as he did their insults, and the crowd knew it, and
when he went swooping after a runner, crouched, shot out his
fist, and yelled, "Y'rrre out!" the fist remained held out like

a quivering spine, quivering with the crowd's angry roar, and they hated it. But they couldn't reach him with their insults. He had trained himself so thoroughly that words hurled at him had no meaning. They were just sounds.

One Saturday afternoon he was working the second game of a doubleheader between Buffalo and Toronto in the Toronto ballpark. Willie was having a difficult day. He was not himself. Last night he got a wire from his only brother, out on the coast, asking for money for an operation on his sick wife. Willie had wired some money, and then had felt conscience-stricken: he hadn't wired enough. On the train he had not slept. During the first game of the doubleheader he felt restless and impatient, then the sun got hotter; the second game dragged on, the fielding ragged and the home team un-able to do anything right, and Willie was disgusted.

In the sixth inning, the home team, three runs down, filled the bases with one out; then Watkins hit sharply to the left of second. It could have been a single, but the Buffalo short-stop made a fantastic stop, half spinning, and threw to second, where the second baseman, pivoting beautifully, got the ball over to first. Willie jerked up his fist and cried, "Y'rrre out!"

Henley, the Toronto manager, jumped out of the dugout, but Willie met his eyes and Henley backed away. Willie had the respect of every manager in the league and knew it.

Sauntering over to the grass behind the first base line, Willie took out his handkerchief and mopped his forehead. "Hey, McCaffery, you swine . . ." He not only heard the voice, he heard the words and found himself repeating them, and was so astonished that he tried to figure out why. It was a foghorn voice, coming from the rail behind first. Any other day he would have heard that voice but he wouldn't have dwelt on the words; it would have been just another insulting snarl having no meaning for him. But today he wasn't himself, his mind wandering from the game. Hunching up his big shoulders, he kicked at the grass and tried to conceal from himself that the voice had reached him.

Loafing near the foul line at the end of the seventh inning, he heard the voice again. "Hey McCaffery, you're blind as a bat. Where's your white cane?" He stooped and picked up a blade of grass, planted himself solidly on his feet and reflected, worried, for this one foghorn voice was breaking through his years of impenetrable aloofness; and when Smiley, the first batter up, hit into left and tried to stretch it into a double, Willie, calling him out, half turned to listen. "You bow-legged blind man!" the big voice jeered. As Willie moved into position behind first, it came again. "McCaffery! You got big bucks on this game. I know your bookie. He told me."

Willie was disgusted with himself, but the more he tried to concentrate on not listening, the more he became aware of the voice, and it shook him. He had a furtive curiosity about the owner of that voice. When he was stationed with folded arms near first and he heard, "You think your ass is a star," he turned in spite of himself, looked at the first row of seats behind the rail and picked out a balding, thin, middle-aged man with a bow tie. As soon as he had turned he realized how he was cheapening himself. He jerked his head away. The regular fans, who had never seen him take the slightest interest in them, howled with delight. The man with the bow tie roared out more insults.

Willie tried to tell himself he had looked up over the stands to see if a bank of clouds would soon hide the sun and throw a shadow over the hot infield, but he hated himself. It was all the fault of the ragged, endless game and the heat and his lack of sleep. He tried to show his contempt for the crowd with an even greater arrogance of style. He kept moving around. He stomped his foot and punched the air, calling, "You, out!" He felt sure he had become himself again. The insulting voice seemed to recede.

In the last of the ninth, the home team rallied and scored two runs; and with Spencer, the heavyset catcher on first with the tieing run, Ingoldsby came in to pinch-hit. He rapped one between first and second. The second baseman got his glove on it, tossed it to the shortstop, who had no trouble tagging the slow-moving Spencer, and Willie called him out, and the game was over. Removing his cap he sighed and came walking off the diamond.

At the rail the fat, pink-cheeked heckler stood up scowling. He felt big and important — he had provoked Willie. Passing only a few feet away from him Willie didn't look up. As if he felt slighted, the fat man, leaning over the rail, said so quietly and intimately that none of the other fans heard him, "McCaffery, me and your mother know you're a lousy son of a bitch . . ."

Willie felt himself go blind and his muscles quiver. Running at the rail he didn't know what he was doing. He swung himself over the rail. He lurched among the fans who blocked the aisle, gaping at him. He charged toward his tormentor who was wiping his pink forehead . . .

Dropping his handkerchief, the fat man put up his pudgy fists and with his short, heavy arms, he tried to flail at Willie, who punched him on the nose. Someone jumped at Willie and tried to drag him off. Soon two policemen had Willie by the arms. Fans who had come leaping over the seats tried to jostle Willie. A small boy gave him a poke at the back of his neck.

The fat man, also restrained by a cop, held his nose and cursed loudly and begged everybody to let him at Willie.

Willie suddenly became aware of the cops' uniforms and, his mind cleared, he realized that he had gone into the stands and had assaulted a fan. In a panic, he kept shaking his head in desperate protest. Not only had he lost his self-respect, he would lose his job, for coming toward them in a rush through the crowd was Collins, the home team's tall, weary-faced business manager, who yelled, "Out of the way! What is this?"

Faces came crowding closer to Willie and he felt very lonely. In his rage and remorse and fear he stared at these faces, and for the first time he felt he had to justify himself to a crowd, and he cried out blindly, "He's not going to insult my mother, he's not going to call my mother that . . ."

A big fellow, who looked like a truck driver, turned to the little man beside him. "What did the guy say about Mc-Caffery's mother?"

"I don't know."

The angry business manager was now standing beside Willie and the two cops. "What's the cause of this?" Collins shouted. "What are you trying to do, McCaffery?" He waited but Willie, breathing hard, only shook his head.

"The guy was riding McCaffery about his mother," one of the cops said.

"Yeah, the guy insulted his mother and McCaffery took a poke at him," said the other cop.

"I see," said Collins, baffled and embarrassed. Suddenly he swung around on the man with the bow tie on, then he turned impatiently to the cops. "I know this guy. He's in here on a pass anyway. Take him out and I'll see he doesn't get back in."

While the two cops were walking the fat man away Willie waited for the crowd to jeer at him, but nobody said anything; and, as he looked around, he felt bewildered, for he saw a kind of apologetic sympathy in their faces.

"Come on, McCaffery, I'll walk you to the dressing room," Collins said and, when they fell in step, he added, "You don't have to worry about this at all. Not with your record. As far as I'm concerned, nothing will be said about it."

"Thanks," Willie said. Still trembling and all mixed up, he tried to recall what he had cried out to the crowd that had made them feel he had so much in common with them. He kept going over it, but he couldn't remember.

JUST LIKE
HER MOTHER

*U*ncle Alec was a short solid man with a smooth unsmiling face. His clothes always looked too tight on him because, as his wife Marge said, he had a tendency to obesity. Yet in spite of his clumsy body and awkward gait he had an impressive quiet dignity. He and his wife lived in a flat over his small book and gift shop. He was not a good businessman. He was too independent and stubborn, and he had an annoying way of shrugging when a customer disregarded his advice on a book. He sold records but showed real interest only in the customers who liked the classical composers, especially Mozart and Bach.

When Georgie Miller's father died, it was Uncle Alec who offered to look after her. She was sixteen. Her beautiful young mother came up from Toronto, where she worked in television, and made the arrangements. She promised to send fifty dollars a month for Georgie's board, and then she returned to Toronto and Georgie moved in with Uncle Alec and Aunt Marge.

At first she found it hard to feel at home at her uncle's place. She knew she could never grow to love a sedate, methodical woman like Aunt Marge.

At the end of the month, when a letter came from her mother and no mention was made of the board money, Aunt Marge made a caustic comment, but Uncle Alec didn't complain. Georgie was his brother's child, he said, and he was going to look after her anyway. She wanted, then, to help him in the store. And she was of real help because the customers who bought pop records liked her to wait on them and she learned to talk their language. Soon the little cubicle where they kept the record player became her department.

Uncle Alec would sit at his big corner desk by the cash register and watch her and he would rub the side of his face slowly and meditate. Once, he said, "You're a bright intelligent girl, Georgie," and another time he said, "A girl like you with a little spark of something, well, she should have some distinction. There shouldn't be anything cheap and common about her. No, that's right." He seemed to be debating with himself, mulling over some plan and gradually finding pleasure in it.

He began to spend his spare time talking to her about books and when they weren't busy in the shop he played classical records and talked about the composers. If she offered an intelligent perception, his face would soften and his eyes shine. He took her to concerts with him. At home, even when they were having dinner, he would recite the poetry of Keats and Shelley and have her repeat it, and then explain that the wisdom of the race was in the language and when good poems were learned by heart a girl could possess that wisdom.

He had her read aloud to him while he leaned back in the big chair in the living room, his eyes closed, and if she slurred a word, or dropped a G, or sounded nasal he would throw out his arms and shout, "No, no, no," and tap his diaphragm.

"From here. From here, understand, Georgie?" It astonished her that he could get so excited and show such intensity and be so concerned. She was never to use slang, she was to speak slowly and with dignity. When he showed that he was growing proud of her she wanted to please him, and then it became good fun and she became proud of herself. Next year, he said, if they could get the money together he wanted her to go to the university.

His gentle patient concern began to touch every part of her life. In that neighborhood she knew few boys, but sometimes a young man who came into the store would notice her grave blue eyes. Her fair hair was drawn back into a bun on her neck and she dressed rather primly and wore no makeup, but he would take another look at her eyes and her beautiful figure and ask her out for an evening. But she would frighten him off with her tone and her conversation, and then wonder why he didn't come back again. Uncle Alec would be there to console her. "That's all right, my dear. Never hold yourself cheap. Never be easy. Always be out of their reach, a little beyond them, and later on, when the cheap ones have passed through their hands, they'll remember you with respect and come back."

He insisted that she write faithfully to her mother. She would take great pains with the letter and then read it to Uncle Alec, who would smile happily if she had expressed herself with distinction, and she began to believe they were both sharing a desire to impress her mother. Sometimes she would ask for money for a dress or a pair of shoes. Her mother would answer and send the money and say that they were not to worry about the board money; one of these days she would come for a quick visit and pay in full. The letter would be written in a breezy, careless style with little punctuation and a lot of exclamation marks and many commonplace phrases.

Once, Uncle Alec, himself, answered one of these letters to reassure Georgie's mother. He was not worrying about the money, he said. He came into Georgie's bedroom to read his letter while she curled up on the bed, and she was grateful that in the way he wrote he showed no hostility whatever to her mother. The whole tone of his letter was dignified and respectful and Georgie loved him for his generosity and for realizing how fond she was of her mother.

That night she asked, "What do you think Mother really does in television, Uncle Alec?"

"Does? Why don't you ask her?"

"I have asked her. I ask her all the time."

"And what does she say?"

"She says she works with directors and producers, but what does that mean?"

"She's having her life, Georgie, just as you'll have yours. All lives are different, and they should be completely different, shouldn't they?"

One day they got a letter from her mother in which she said she was coming for two days to see Georgie. "Well now, imagine," Aunt Marge said with a cynical smile. "I suppose she's worried about owing us money." But Uncle Alec took his time before saying anything. "Ten months since you've seen your mother, eh, Georgie?" he said finally. "Well, she won't know you. You've come a long way. You're quite a little lady," and he smiled to himself.

In the afternoon, two days later, Georgie's mother telephoned from the hotel where she had registered. She knew they had no room for her in the apartment. She was calling, she said, before she came up to the shop, to warn them she was counting on taking them back to the hotel for dinner.

Georgie put on her new dark-blue dress. It was a severely modest dress with a high neckline, but when she turned slowly under the close inspection of Aunt Marge and Uncle Alec, they told her that her mother wouldn't know her. For an hour, she waited at the window. It started to rain. It was time to close the store, though two men still browsed around, and Georgie got excited and fearful, and then with the rain falling hard a taxi stopped and her mother, in a mauve-colored straw hat and a squirrel cape, got out waving cheerfully to the driver and came running across the pavement to where she waited at the open door. "Why, Georgie, you dear soul, bless you," she cried, and they threw their arms around each other.

As her mother swept into the store the two men who were talking to Uncle Alec couldn't help turning to stare at her. It was her stride, her warm laugh sounding loud in the quiet store and her light careless elegant easy movements. She looked much younger than thirty-six and as she walked the length of the store, her arm around Georgie's waist, Georgie was very proud of her. They stopped to shake hands with Uncle Alec. On the way upstairs, Georgie felt a glow come over her whole being, and she enjoyed it when Aunt Marge, who had on her best brown dress, took on an apologetic manner in her mother's presence as if she felt inadequate.

Uncle Alec finally came upstairs and Georgie sat by herself and listened while they talked. It was a very polite and gracious conversation, and Georgie loved it when her mother, looking over at her, smiled. But she noticed things about her mother that she wouldn't have noticed before; she used a lot of slang and sometimes swore lightheartedly, just for emphasis, and she had a lazy indulgent smile that made profound conversation difficult.

Her hair was lighter than it used to be. She wore too much makeup. These impressions might have disturbed her if Uncle Alec himself hadn't made them seem unimportant. Her mother joked with him and laughed and listened, making what was said between them seem so sympathetically right and intimate that Uncle Alec, very reluctantly at first, yet surely, began to lose his superior aloofness. He began to make graceful speeches, he played up to her and once he laughed boisterously and warmly. When Aunt Marge became silent, Georgie smiled at her shyly.

When they had taken a taxi to the hotel and had had a fine meal in the big dining room, Uncle Alec wanted to pay for the dinner, but Georgie's mother reminded him gently that they were her guests. Everything seemed to be within her mother's reach, Georgie thought. They went up to her room and there she sat down at the desk and wrote a check for five hundred dollars, the amount she owed for ten months' board. "How do you like that, Aunt Marge?" Georgie wanted to say, but it wasn't necessary to say it. Aunt Marge, her eyes shining with vast satisfaction, made a silly embarrassing speech, and Uncle Alec had to say quickly that the money didn't mean anything to him, Georgie had become a valuable part of his life. He so plainly meant it that Georgie smiled at her mother and felt at peace with everybody.

It was arranged that Georgie would come down to the hotel next day and have lunch with her mother, and then they would go shopping. On the way home, Uncle Alec said to her, "I was proud of you, Georgie. Nice manners. A girl of some cultivation. It was showing, my dear, and your mother saw it." Lying in her bed that night, Georgie heard the murmur of voices in the other bedroom and she knew they were talking about her mother, and she wondered if they felt as good as she did about the evening. Her mother did everything wrong, she thought, and yet with her careless ease and her little laugh she could put a glow on the evening.

At noontime next day, Uncle Alec said to her, "We were in the way last night, Georgie. Have a good talk with your mother. Open up with her. Tell her all you've done and learned. Be yourself. Show her what you are interested in. A lot of water has gone under the bridge, Georgie."

"I've got so much to talk about," she said. "Last night I just didn't seem to get started, did I?" When she got to her mother's hotel room she intended to have this conversation but her mother was wearing a gray tailored suit and it looked very elegant and she began to admire it.

"It is nice, isn't it, Georgie? Oh, darling, we just don't look right together, do we? That little dress you have on makes you look like a novice in a convent. Do you want to look like that? Why, you don't look like my daughter at all. Are you sure Uncle Alec doesn't want you to wear horn-rimmed glasses?"

"My eyes are quite good, Mother."

"I'm kidding you, honey."

"Yes, I suppose you are."

"I mean, you don't have to dress like Aunt Marge, Georgie. Come here and sit down and let me fix your hair."

As she sat down, feeling awkward, she began to like the feel of her mother's hand running through her hair as she talked. "Why do they want to make such a sedate little lady out of you, Georgie? You're actually quite pretty, darling. You know what I'm going to do after lunch? I'm going to buy you the silliest gay dress, and you see that you wear it, too."

At lunch Georgie tried to find out what her mother was doing in television, but nothing was made very clear to her. She was doing executive work for a Mr. Henderson, a producer. She got away from Mr. Henderson, and talked gaily about Toronto and how Georgie would love it, but something was troubling her. "Georgie, you don't know how quickly time passes for a woman," she said finally, her eyes almost sad as she smiled. Her beautiful, generous, smiling mouth and the loneliness in her eyes seemed to Georgie to bring them very close together. "In a few years I'll be old, Georgie. That's the way it is. A woman wakes up and realizes she has suddenly fallen to pieces. In a year you'll be older and in a year I'll be so much older, and then we're going to live together, darling." She made Georgie feel a little sad and yet poetic, as she had felt when Uncle Alec had carried her away with his reading of one of Keats' poems.

She began to talk enthusiastically about Uncle Alec. "He's been everything to me, simply everything," she said, and she told how he worked with her and wanted her to have a good mind and about his consideration and patience. It all poured out of her. She used words Uncle Alec would have liked her to use, she showed off and laughed and wanted her mother to see she had a fine discriminating mind. Her mother nodded, listening thoughtfully, her elbow on the table, her chin cupped in her hand.

"Tell me something, Georgie," she said. "Is Alec, well, is he ever critical of me?"

"He wouldn't say anything about you. Why, that's beneath him. His mind is too fine and generous."

"Well, maybe you jumped right into his heart. Why not? You're an angel. And who knows, maybe angels talk like you do, darling. Your mother is light-headed and silly and anything very deep goes in one ear and right out the other, but I'll always be willing to listen to you. Come on and we'll do some shopping."

They loafed around the big stores and even the loafing made Georgie feel luxurious. The little things they encountered in idle moments became so diverting and so amusing. They bought a good brown-leather purse for Aunt Marge and an imported English pipe and a pound of tobacco for Uncle Alec. "Now for the dress," her mother said. "It must be something crazy, almost with a touch of high fashion." For an hour Georgie tried on dresses. They bought one of fluffy organdie in very pale mauve that billowed out like foam. It had two thin shoulder straps.

Her mother, who was leaving on the early train, came back to the shop with her to say goodbye to Uncle Alec and Aunt Marge. When they arrived with their parcels, Uncle Alec was just closing the store. He suggested they all have dinner, but Georgie's mother said she would eat on the train. Aunt Marge came down and they had a splendid time giving the presents. Uncle Alec and Aunt Marge were both surprised and touched.

"I've got half an hour, Georgie," her mother said, looking at her wristwatch. "Why don't you put on your dress and show it to them? Go on, dear. Hurry."

"Yes, I'll hurry," Georgie said, wanting to please her mother. She went upstairs and put on the dress, and when she came down she was trembling a little and didn't know why. Her mother was sitting on the edge of Uncle Alec's big desk, one leg crossed over the other, Uncle Alec was leaning against the poetry section of the bookcase, having lighted his new pipe, and Aunt Marge was holding her purse.

"Why bless you, Georgie, bless you, darling, a thousand times," her mother cried. "Now just look at her. Isn't she a picture?"

"It looks — it looks very expensive," Aunt Marge said.

"How do you like it, Uncle Alec?" Georgie asked eagerly.

There was a surprise in his eyes as he looked at her steadily, then he put down his pipe. "Yes, that's a very pretty dress," he said quietly. But the expression on his face was so unfamiliar it seemed to her that he had trouble recognizing her, and so she didn't know whether he liked the dress.

"Georgie dear," her mother said gravely, "you're going to be quite a looker. Yes, sir, quite a gal." She laughed happily and threw up her arms as if she had just come upon her own daughter. "Oh, I'd like to see you dancing around, Georgie. You're so young and beautiful I want to go away seeing you dancing and singing. Put on some records. Where are those records, Alec?"

"I'll do it," Georgie said, running to the little music cubicle. She felt that she and her mother were sharing some kind of new happiness. She rifled through the records. She came dancing out of the cubicle, dancing in slow circles, her eyes on her mother who suddenly laughed — it was such a warm rich pleased careless laugh — and got up and put her arm around her and began to dance with her. While her mother held her so lightly and led her so easily, Georgie felt all the stiffness and shyness leaving her limbs; she wanted to whirl as her mother hummed; she started to sing and her mother sang with her while they danced, and they kept it up till they were both out of breath. Then they started to laugh, not knowing why they laughed so gaily.

"You've got a nice little voice there, Georgie," her mother said when she could get her breath. "Do you sing much?"

"Not much popular stuff. Uncle Alec likes me to sing the concert pieces."

"Oh, nuts, Alec. Let her relax and be charming. Surely you can see she was born to be charming."

"It's quite true," he said.

"What time is it? If I don't get a taxi right at the door I won't have time to pick up my bag at the hotel and make the train."

"There's a taxi stand just twenty feet away. Come on," Uncle Alec said.

"Oh, you're all wonderful. Bless you, bless you," she cried. "Why didn't I plan to stay longer? Why are things always like this — I have to go just when I'm feeling so happy. It's always like this." She was half laughing, half tearful in the excitement of rushing away. At the door, she threw her arms around Georgie and kissed her. Alec was already out on the street beckoning to a taxi. Georgie, standing at the door, watched them shake hands and she liked seeing them with their hands out to each other, and she wanted to cry.

"Isn't she lovely?" she asked, when her uncle came in.

But he didn't answer. He was breathing hard as if he had been running, and he walked back to the desk and sat where her mother had sat. Now he was watching Georgie as she came toward him. His pale steady eyes and the heavy lines in his forehead worried her; he sighed and pondered and did not try to hide his disappointment.

"The dress must have cost a penny," Aunt Marge said. "Just what did it cost, Georgie?"

"I think it was almost a hundred dollars."

"Did she say where she got the money?"

"I didn't ask her," Georgie said, hardly listening to her aunt as she watched Uncle Alec, whose eyes now were hard and bitter when he stared at her.

"What's the matter, Uncle Alec?"

Ignoring her, he said to his wife, "She looked just like her, didn't she? So very much like her."

"She certainly did. Just suddenly — there they are — two peas in a pod."

"But what's the matter?" Georgie asked. "Isn't it all right if —"

"You won't be like her, do you hear?" Uncle Alec said harshly. "Singing with her, looking like her. She's no good." He tried to control himself but couldn't. He blurted out fiercely, "You won't be like her. That strumpet! Never anything else but a strumpet. She killed my brother. She broke his heart, running off with that cheap actor two years ago. Now it's a new one. And there's money there for a while. Georgie, Georgie . . ." As he came toward her, reaching out for her, his hand trembled. "Take off that dress." She screamed and ran up the stairs and pulled the dress off frantically and tossed it in the corner, and she knew Uncle Alec hated her mother.

She lay on the bed and wanted to cry, but couldn't; her loneliness frightened her. A little later she heard Uncle Alec and his wife come upstairs. She heard them sitting down for dinner, but a chair was pushed back, then Alec came along the hall. "Georgie," he called and he opened her door. "Georgie," he said, "I'm very sorry." He sounded so ashamed and apologetic that she looked up at him. "You see, Georgie," he said gently, "I shouldn't have said what I did, but maybe it's better that it was said, because nothing should be hidden between you and me. Later on you'll forgive me. Come on. We'll have dinner."

He sounded like himself now, calm and patient, and she had the habit of trying to please him, so she got up and went with him to the dinner table. They respected her silence and the fact that she couldn't touch her food. Once she raised her head intending to tell Uncle Alec that she understood why he had made himself her teacher and had worked with her so patiently; it wasn't just loving concern; he had wanted to make her into someone so different from her mother that she would feel completely separated from her whenever they were together.

But she couldn't tell it to him; the painful beating of her heart made it all too complicated. Instead she found herself saying gravely, "You're wrong about my father. He loved her till the day he died because he couldn't help loving her, no matter what happened, because she's like she is, and maybe that's what you have against her." Uncle Alec's hurt troubled eyes forced her to stop and she mumbled, "Excuse me," and hurried back to her room.

As she sat down in the chair by the window, knowing she had said the right thing to hurt Uncle Alec, the truth seemed to come tumbling at her, making her strangely happy. What had been true of her own father had been true of Uncle Alec and he knew it; he hadn't been a hypocrite with her mother, in her presence he had to be gracious and warm and available; he couldn't help it; he loved what was beautiful, it was the wisdom he had tried to cultivate in her, too, and when he was with her mother he felt compelled to respond to something beautiful in her nature, even if it left him feeling angry afterward.

She got up, slipped off the dressing gown she had been wearing and picked up the fluffy dress and put it on. With her cheeks burning she watched herself in the mirror as she walked the length of the room trying to look as her mother had looked yesterday when she swept into the shop.

A Boy
Grows Older

———◆———

*I*n the bedroom Mrs. Sloane sat down and folded her hands tight in her lap, swallowed hard, and said to her husband, "I've got something to tell you about Jim."

Holding the shoe he had just taken off in his hand, he said, "Were you talking to him today?"

"He's coming here for money. I've been giving a bit to him from time to time. I know I shouldn't, but he's got me completely distracted."

"He knows we've got no money to lend," he said, and as he got up and walked around excitedly with one shoe on she knew he was thinking of their little bit of money disappearing day by day. "He knows we've only got our pension," he said. He had worked hard all his life and they had both denied themselves many little comforts and now she could see a look of terror coming into his eyes that she had seen for the first time the day he had to quit work and they had thought they would hardly be able to live. "Why, what'll happen to us?" he said, turning on her suddenly. "Where does he think we get it?"

She only sighed and shook her head, for she had been asking Jim that question for months, yet every time he got behind in his insurance collections he came around, scared, and got a little more money from her.

"There's no use giving me a setting out," she said. "He'll never believe we won't give it to him till you tell him. If he understands we're through helping him maybe he'll get some sense."

As they sat there solemnly looking at each other and waiting for Jim, she had her old dressing gown wrapped around her and he was sitting on the bed with his white hair mussed from rubbing his hands through it. They took turns blurting things out, questions they never tried to answer, questions that worried them more and more and drew them closer together. When they heard Jim come in and call from the living room, she said, "Remember, I'm going to tell him I told you. I've done all I can. It's up to you now."

Jim was waiting for her, walking up and down with his hat on and his white scarf hanging out as if the wind had blown it free from his overcoat while he hurried along the street. He looked very unhappy but he tried to smile at his mother. His face was so good-natured it was almost weak.

"What is it this time?" she asked.

"Oh," he said, sitting down and starting to rub his shoe on the carpet like an embarrassed small boy, "the same thing, I guess."

"More money again, you mean," she said.

"I guess that's it."

"In God's name, what for this time?"

"The same thing — I'm behind in my collections."

She had intended to shrug and say coolly, "Speak to your father," but instead she found herself walking up and down in front of him, wheeling on him and whispering savagely,

"You'd take the last cent from us, and then what do you think is going to happen? Who are you going to run to then?" But he got up and took her arm and muttered, "I'll never ask you again — I promise — but I've got to have it. I'll give every cent back to you — I promise. I wouldn't ask you if there was a chance of getting it any place else." He felt sure of her. "I'll lose my job," he said.

"Maybe it would teach you to have some respect for yourself," she said, and then she added calmly, "I've told your father."

"You told him after all?" he said, terribly hurt. "You promised not to."

"I'm through," she said.

He started to work himself up into a temper which didn't fool her at all because he always did it when he was trying to abuse her.

"You're mean," he said. "Plain mean." His words had no real anger and she smiled grimly. When he saw her smile he stopped and said helplessly, "Please, Mom, please —" But she said firmly, "Speak to your father. It's his money."

"Mom, just this once more," he pleaded, and when she saw how he dreaded facing his father she was puzzled because he had never been afraid of him, they had never shouted at each other. "I've got to do it, I've got to do it," he kept saying to himself as he walked up and down, and then he turned to her, white-faced, and said, "Well, I've got to ask him, I can't help it," and he went into the bedroom with her following.

His father had gotten into bed and was reading and he could just see the crown of his white head rising over the edge of the newspaper. When Jim went into the room he stood under the light on the wall. That was where he always stood when he was in trouble. Years ago, when he had been caught in a petty theft at school he had stood there; when he had started to work he used to come in late at night and stand under the light and tell them what had happened during the day, and it was where he had stood the night when he was eighteen and had told them he was going to get married. He was tilting back and forth on his heels, waiting for his father to look over at him, but when the paper wasn't lowered, he said at last in a mild, friendly tone, "Dad, could you loan me some money?"

His father put down his paper, folded it, shoved it under his arm and took off his glasses and said, "What do you do with your money, son?"

As his father stared at him steadily, a silly half-ashamed grin was on Jim's face. "I don't know, honestly I don't," he said shaking his head.

"Well, tell me what you think you do with it. You must remember something."

"Salesmen and collectors are pretty much alike," Jim said. "They hang around together and it just slips through their fingers and then they're short at the end of the week."

"Then a man like you shouldn't have such a job."

"I guess you're right," Jim mumbled.

"Why don't you hunt for another job?"

"I will — I'll try hard," he said eagerly.

"How much do you need this time?"

"It's a lot, I've got to cover a whole week's collections," Jim said, his head down, his voice faint.

"All that?" his father said, and Mrs. Sloane knew by the way he swung his head toward her, startled that he was thinking of the money he had saved for himself for his personal expenses such as tobacco, newspapers, a trip to the movies and clothes for himself. As he swung the bedclothes off, his face was flushed a vivid red against his white hair and he kept on staring at Jim. Mrs. Sloane knew he had a bad temper and she grew afraid.

Jim, watching his father coming toward him in his bare feet, muttered hastily, "I guess you haven't got it. I guess I'll go."

"Wait," his father called, making it clear he was not going to challenge him. "I didn't say I didn't have it." He spoke as if Jim ought to understand they had always been close together. He was going over to his coat hanging on the closet door. When Mrs. Sloane saw how he fumbled in his pocket for his check book and how his hand trembled as he jerked his pen out of his vest pocket, she knew he was scared of something. She thought he was scared of Jim: she resented it so much she turned to abuse Jim herself.

But she said nothing to Jim because she had never seen him look so hurt as he did standing there waiting and watching his father as if at last he understood everything his father felt, and he said in a whisper, "What are you scared of?"

"Nothing," his father said.

"What's the matter?"

"Maybe I was thinking it might be worse."

"What do you mean?"

"Supposing I didn't give it to you?" his father said.

And while they kept looking at each other, Jim felt the fear in his father that came from knowing how weak he was, a fear that tomorrow or in a year something was apt to happen that would break him and jail him. He turned to his mother, begging her with his eyes to tell him what to do or say that would drive that scared look from his father's eyes. For the first time he seemed aware of their feeling for him. She nodded her head: she wanted to tell him she believed in him, but she was puzzled herself.

His father was writing the check on the top of the dresser. He wrote very carefully, and when he was finished he handed the check to Jim, saying only, "Here you are, son."

Looking at the check as if it were very hard for him to take it, Jim said in such a low voice he could hardly hear him, "I guess I've got to take it, but I'll pay you back. I wish you'd believe I'll pay you back. I don't want to take it if you won't believe it."

"All right, son."

"Well, thanks, thanks . . ." he said.

But at the door he stood for a while with his head down, waiting, as if he couldn't bear to leave them till he was sure they had some faith left in him. He was so grave it made him look years older.

When he had gone his father waited a while for her to abuse him scornfully for not being firm with him, and then when she didn't speak, but stood there looking at the door, he got into bed and pulled the covers over him. After a few moments she went over and got into bed too. But she couldn't lie down. She sat up stiffly, staring down at her husband's face. His head rolled away from her and his eyes were closed.

"I'm glad you gave it to him," she said.

He opened his eyes and said simply, "He's getting older. He was a little different. Didn't you notice it? It made me feel we hadn't been wrong helping him this far."

As she lay down beside him and reached to turn out the light, her hand trembled. She lay very still. Then she turned and put her arm around him, and they lay there together in the dark.

THE MAN
WITH THE COAT

*T*hat winter day in the corridor outside the courtroom where J. C. (Scotty) Bowman, the bank manager, was to be tried for fraud there was a gathering of people who would not have come together at any other time. It wasn't a big crowd but they had come from shops, brokerage offices and saloons, their own private homes, and even Chinese laundries. The corridor was wet and dirty with little pools of water from their wet overshoes. After the all-night heavy snowfall it had turned mild and the sun had come out and the melting snow had flooded the streets. Everybody had got wet from spray from passing taxis. They had all come there because Scotty Bowman was a well-known man, and his friend, Harry Lane, the public-relations director of the Sweetman Distillery, to whom he had loaned the fifteen thousand, was even better known in the city.

Harry Lane, of an old family that had lost its money, had been a flier in the Battle of Britain. When he had come home and had taken the distillery job at thirteen thousand a year, his picture had often appeared in the papers as the organizer of golf tournaments for Sweetman Cups and as the speaker at sport banquets and service-club luncheons. He knew everybody.

The branch of the bank where Scotty had been manager was near Stanley on St. Catherine, right in the metropolitan section of the city which was that neighborhood below Sherbrooke at the foot of the mountain, the district of the big hotels, department stores, railroad stations and restaurants, nightclubs, brothels and bookie joints. In this neighborhood Scotty had had a splendid reputation among the storekeepers and businessmen. Many shiftless and rootless neighborhood characters also used his bank because they liked and trusted him. Through Harry Lane he had also met at Dorfman's some celebrated sporting and theatrical people of rich taste and easy money.

In the corridor the troubled and wondering shopkeepers and small businessmen stood in little groups, all wearing their good suits out of respect for Scotty whose integrity they had always admired. Near the courtroom door the two tall neat clean-looking bond salesmen, friends of Harry Lane's, looked around at the others with some amusement. "Look at those two Chinamen. Notice anything funny about them?" the taller one said. "You mean they look alike?" "No, not that. Neither one is wearing a hat that seems to fit him properly. Look." The two Chinese had done business with Scotty's bank and had often invited him to Chinese banquets; two years ago Scotty had received a decoration from Chiang Kai-shek.

The two matrons from Westmount, walking up and down in their mink coats, gossiped in English accents that did not come from England. "Of course you know Harry's mother died without leaving him a cent." "Well, he certainly seems to have left this bank manager flat on his back without a cent." "I must say I was astonished when he took that job with Sweetman's." "That pushing Mrs. Sweetman. She'll do a little squirming over this kind of publicity."

The corridor began to smell of wet fur and rubber and there was a lot of coughing. The weather had been bad all week. A mild flu epidemic, an influenza that started with a head cold and coughing, was prevalent. Coming along the corridor was the newspaperman they called The Young Lion, because he was determined to outwrite, outdrink and out-smart all his older colleagues, and his grin widened as he recognized some older men he respected. A few paces behind him was Lonesome Harry, the saloonkeeper, and when he caught up he said, "I wasn't sure whether any of the boys would bother coming. Geez, there's Eddie." His camel-hair coat was expensive, but neither the coat nor his expensive suit nor his new hat seemed to belong to him. He made his way toward big Eddie Adams, the rich fight promoter who was talking to Haggerty, the sporting editor of the *Sun,* and Ted Ogilvie, a friend of Harry Lane's from college days.

In the hum of conversation there was a loud burst of laughter. "Less noise there, less noise," the gray-haired policeman at the door shouted belligerently. The laughter came only from the members of the sporting fraternity. The sedate little businessmen, still surprised that they were there, and still troubled and wondering, didn't feel like laughing. Those who did laugh, because it was their style, secretly felt the same kind of wonder that Scotty Bowman and Harry Lane should end their friendship in a courtroom. "Come here, Mike," Haggerty called to the tailor, Mike Kon, who had a shop on St. Catherine near Bleury. He was an old middle-weight fighter and Scotty had arranged for the loan that had started him in business. Standing off by himself dejectedly, Mike the Scholar had his hands buried in the pockets of his special black lightweight winter overcoat. He was thirty-five and he had a broken nose. "Don't be a brooder, Mike," Eddie Adams kidded him. "Why do guys who read books turn into brooders?" Joining them Mike said wanly, "For me this is no joke. Scotty was my friend."

"You say 'was.' Are they hanging the guy?"

"I mean is. Not was."

"We're all friends. These things only happen among friends. What's the point of having friends if you can't get them into trouble?"

"But Scotty loses his job anyway," Mike said earnestly. "He loses his pension and he has a wife and children. I know what that means."

"The case hasn't been tried yet," Ted Ogilvie said hope-fully. "Harry may be able to put Scotty in a very good light. It's a gift with Harry."

"I hope so," Mike said. "This thing is all wrong, you know. Something is very wrong. Never in his life did Scotty get out of line and Harry Lane is, well, everybody likes Harry. I keep asking myself why this should be."

The policeman suddenly opened the door and they all began to file into the big high-ceilinged paneled courtroom. Two spectators had been let in ahead of the others: Mrs. Bow-man and a gray-haired man, a family friend, had been allowed to enter with the lawyers from the side door. She was a plump motherly white-haired woman in a brown hat and a brown cloth coat with a little fur on the collar. As the benches began to fill around her, her neck and back grew rigid. The Chinese sat in one row and the shopkeepers who knew each other kept together in another row. They all seemed to know where they belonged. No one got out of place, and bright sunlight came through the high western window.

At the crowded press table Entwhistle, the dignified bald little court reporter for the *Sun,* couldn't find a suitable seat. "How can I work with someone sitting in my lap," he protested loudly. Then Mollie Morris, Judge Morris' daughter, who did a column for the *Sun* came in and everybody turned. She was Harry Lane's girl. No one had believed she would come and sit at the press table, but she came hurrying in with her fur coat open, her heavy goloshes making a flapping swishing sound, her high-cheekboned face with the bright brown eyes flushed from hurrying.

The noise subsided as Scotty Bowman was led to the dock. In the last two months Scotty had got older. He looked like the family man he was, with a plump wife and two children. He had lost weight. His hair had been quite gray anyway, for he was fifty-eight, but he had been plump and jolly, not stooping a little as he did now approaching the dock. In one quick furtive glance he took in all the spectators till he found his wife. In the bank, or at the ball game, or the fights, or sitting in Dorfman's, feeling so pleased to be there with more celebrated personalities who led expensive and glamorous lives, he had always met a man's eyes. All his integrity had seemed to shine in his candid blue eyes. He fumbled at his collar, then turned to the window and blinked at the shaft of sunlight that just reached the dock; then he lowered his head and his face became so pale his lawyer, Roger Ouimet, stood up and went over to speak to him. Scotty lifted his head as if the lawyer's consoling smile had given him some dignity, and then he smiled too.

When Judge Montpetit came in everybody stood up, although some of them couldn't see him at first, for he was only five-feet-four. His white plume rose above the heads of the lawyers and the clerks as he mounted the steps to his chair. He had a big head and heavy features. He glanced anxiously at the open window. He was afraid he was catching a cold and had taken a mixture of lemon juice and baking soda before leaving the house. His hearing was not good and the courtroom acoustics were bad and, as always, he looked up resentfully at the high ceiling. While the jury was being selected he fumbled with papers, read them, wrote on many notepads, leaning well over to the left, then folded his hands and waited.

The jury was selected quickly because there were no challenges from Roger Ouimet. They were salesmen, electricians, managers and an insurance man. One by one, they walked to their chairs, and when they were all together, their faces in two rows bunched against the sunlit window, they did look like men of common sense. Then Scotty stood up and the charge was read. "Not guilty," he said firmly.

They didn't need a special prosecutor to handle Scotty's case. It was too simple, and was being handled by George Henderson. His tired eyes, his gray mustache touched up a little, and the network of red veins in his cheeks, told everybody why he had missed having a distinguished career. "John Slocombe," he called, linking both hands behind him under his gown and swinging around to look for the bank superintendent.

The thin gray man in a gray suit, grimly doing a job he hated, clutched the rail and never let go, as Henderson, in his ponderous style, brought out that he had been with the bank for fifteen years and a superintendent for five. Then he told how he had discovered that Bowman had misrepresented the security he had got from Lane; he had represented to the bank that he had taken thirty thousand shares of Western Oil as security for fifteen thousand dollars he had loaned Harry Lane. The market value of these thirty thousand shares at the time he made the loan would have been equal to twice the amount of the loan. The fact was he had taken only fifteen thousand shares as security. Of course, by the time the deception was discovered the shares were worth about a thousand dollars.

"Did you ask Mr. Bowman why he misrepresented the amount of security he had got from Lane?"

"I did."

"What did he say?"

"He said he had wanted to have the loan cleared."

"And why the misrepresentation of what he had done?"

"I asked him why, of course, and he said that after he had committed himself to making the loan he felt he owed it to Harry Lane to go through with it; he believed in it. There seemed to be no risk at all. The head office couldn't have the confidence in Harry Lane that he had and he said it was all a matter of confidence."

"He admitted he misrepresented the conditions of the loan?"

"Well, there it was, and he admitted it."

"Will the witness please speak up," the judge said testily. "Speak out. You have nothing to be ashamed of. It's hard to hear anything in this court. Now what was it you said? Turn this way a little."

Clearing his throat the superintendent said, "It was the day the stock crashed — before noon, and I came in. He had been busy and hadn't heard about it, or I suppose he could have rushed out and bought shares to cover himself for next to nothing, but there I was confronting him — well, he said he was afraid he would be prosecuted," and Slocombe's voice faded as he looked at Scotty.

"I know this is an unpleasant task for you," the judge said gently. "But it is an honorable one."

"You said Mr. Bowman admitted that his misrepresentation of the security he had taken on this loan would leave him charged with fraud."

"Or possibly conspiracy."

"There's no charge of conspiracy with anyone. Just this admitted fraud."

"Oh, but I object," Ouimet said, rising slowly, "My friend goes too fast. Mr. Bowman has pleaded not guilty. All that the witness has brought out is Mr. Bowman's recognition of his awareness of certain facts that might lead to this charge."

"That might be very well put in the defense counsel's argument to the jury," the judge said, smiling.

"Well, those are the facts," Henderson said. He didn't want to make a big thing of it. It wasn't necessary. Linking his hands behind him under his gown he shrugged. "Your witness."

"Mr. Slocombe," Ouimet said, with a courteous little bow and a friendly smile as if he only wanted to be helpful, "how long have you known Mr. Bowman? I mean in your banking business."

"About fifteen years, sir."

"And what was your opinion of his character?"

"I had the highest opinion of him."

"Not a blemish on his reputation?"

"No, sir."

"In fact, would you not say that in your own bank he had always been considered a man of the highest integrity?"

"That's true," and for the first time he was at ease with himself.

"Mr. Slocombe," Ouimet said, walking slowly toward the jury, "supposing Mr. Bowman had made this loan to Harry Lane, just as he did — irregular and all as it was — and it had been repaid within a week with interest, as Mr. Bowman believed it would, what would have been the procedure?"

"Well, we might never have discovered that there had been a misrepresentation, I suppose."

"And he might not be here in the dock at all?"

"Well, I don't know. I can't tell about ifs and buts."

"Oh, I know bankers are cautious, but if Bowman's confidence in Harry Lane had been justified . . ."

"That wouldn't justify the misrepresentation."

"Now look here," Ouimet said amiably, and he smiled at the jury, "if Lane had repaid the loan, as he promised to do, in a few days, and picked up his security, where would we be?"

"But the thing was discovered."

"All right. Now has Mr. Bowman always shown good banking judgment?"

"The very best."

"Till he came to his friend Lane?"

"Well, yes, until this affair."

"By the way, when you questioned him about misrepresenting the security he had got from Lane, did you ask what in the world happened to his judgment?"

"I did."

"And what did he say?"

"He was upset. Seemed to feel he had committed himself, and had confidence in Lane."

"He seemed to feel under an obligation, a personal obligation?"

"As far as I could see," the superintendent said, with a helpless gesture, "it was just because he was Harry Lane."

"Just because he was Harry Lane," Ouimet repeated softly, and as he sauntered away and pondered, everybody, waiting and watching, heard him quietly repeating the words over and over. "Thank you, that's all," he said finally. When the superintendent left the dock Henderson said, "Call Harry Lane." They called "Harry Lane." The policeman at the door repeated "Harry Lane," and it echoed along the corridor.

They all turned as he came in, but the jurors had the best view of him as he approached the box, his head up, his shoulders back like a man with some military training. He was thirty-two, about five-foot-nine and slender, and he had curly black hair and good teeth. Pale as he was, he still had his distinguished air. He had on a navy-blue suit and a white shirt and a blue tie with a thin red stripe in it, and though Scotty too had on a good suit, it didn't look like Harry's; he couldn't wear clothes as Harry could, and the old fighter, Mike Kon, the tailor, whispered, "He probably got that suit from Saville Row. What a pleasure it would be to make a suit for him." Haggerty, grinning, needled him, "Better stick to those wrestlers and ball players who wear those suits of yours,

Mike. It'll be a while before you move up to the carriage trade."

They all expected Harry to have an easy confident manner, for he was always sure he belonged wherever he was. Coming from an old family he had always belonged to the places where people with money went. He belonged to the Royal Golf Club, the M.A.A., he had been a Zate, and his father, when he had been alive, had belonged to the Mount Royal Club. He had been incredibly lucky in the war, where he should have been shot down a dozen times, and his luck held when he came home and got his soft job with Sweetman. Everybody could see he didn't want to be anything else but what he was, alive and back home among his own people and feeling lucky with the beauty and joy of being alive. When he drove his Jaguar he waved to the cops at the intersections. He was a carelessly generous impulsive smiling man, who counted on everybody sharing his goodwill, and had had a lot of luck in this too, and seemed to appreciate it. But he was a man of many charming and slightly theatrical gestures. If he bought a pack of cigarettes he always bought one for the friend with him; he never passed by a panhandler. He overtipped everywhere. He wore bright checked English jackets and bright scarves and looked like a polo player in them. Two months ago he had bought an expensive English lightweight felt hat in New York, very light gray; he could roll it up in a ball in his hand without wrinkling it, and when Ted Ogilvie had admired the hat he had insisted on giving it to him. Standing out there in the corridor Ted had been wearing the hat. All these gestures seemed to be little tributes to something or other that nobody understood.

But he made a bad impression as soon as he got into the box. He went to yawn, then tried to suppress it quickly as his friends, watching him, smiled. But the yawn wasn't one of his gestures. He was really tired and troubled. He had been up nearly all night. He had gone home early enough, but before he could get undressed and into bed there had been a knock at the door. It was the young blond wife of the rich old painter, who was sixty, living in the apartment upstairs. For a month her husband's nerves had been going to pieces. Worrying about everything, he was really afraid of being left alone. Now he was upstairs, she said, repeating that he had no friends and threatening to kill himself. "I know it's silly," she had pleaded, "because he hasn't a worry in the world. He likes you, Harry, won't you come up? You're good for him." He had sighed and grumbled a little, then he had gone upstairs to drink with the old painter and cheer him up with amusing stories which he acted out for him. It had been comical really. All that was the matter with the painter was that every time he looked at his young wife he felt old and insecure. "Things look different when you're around, Harry," he kept saying and wouldn't let him go till four in the morning.

Back in his own place he couldn't sleep. He kept going over and over the story he had to tell about Scotty Bowman, starting with that day on the street when they had met accidentally. He himself had been feeling lighthearted and he had told Scotty about his luck. A few months ago, his friend McCanse, of McCanse and Ashworth, the brokers and investment financiers, had given him five hundred shares of Western Oil. McCanse, an old air force comrade, insisted he owed his life to him. The stock then had gone to a dollar a share. He was feeling good that day because McCanse had just got a wire from the drilling superintendent telling him of reaching oil in the sands; in three days the well would be brought in. If the stock merely repeated the pattern of the other oil stocks, McCanse insisted, it would be worth five dollars a share in three days.

"Things come your way, Harry," Scotty had said enviously. "Lucky in war, lucky in love." He knew McCanse, of course, and had the highest respect for his word and judgment. It had been snowing a little and as he slowly raised the collar of his coat his eyes turned inward. "Don't you understand, Harry," he said, "if you had fifteen thousand shares you would make at least seventy-five thousand; maybe a lot more," and his eyes were like a shrewd businessman's; he seemed to be concerned as a banker might be concerned for a client. "I haven't got fifteen thousand, Scotty," he said, laughing. But that was what banks were for, Scotty said, smiling. "Scotty, there's the question of security." And as a banker Scotty seemed to ponder over this. It was too bad, really too bad, and then he had said, what about McCanse; would he let him have fifteen thousand dollars' worth of the stock, trusting him for a few days? If he would, the bank might take it as security at the present market price for a very short-term loan. "But, Scotty, wouldn't you have to get the approval of God Almighty for such a loan?" Smiling, Scotty said, "That's right, and it's a good thing," and he thought it over. "Of course, bank loans are made as much on reputation as on security, Harry. I don't know. I'd have to think it over. You have a good reputation. Anyway, it would be up to the head office. Don't let me build you up. But why don't you see if you can get the stock?" And he had said, "I can get the stock all right, Scotty. But for heaven's sake, why don't you go to a broker and buy some for yourself?" Holding up both hands and smiling broadly, Scotty had said, "Don't talk about me now. Very much against the rules, you know, Harry. Anyway, I'm broke. Harry, I'll think it over — yes — no harm in that. I'll see if it's worthwhile sounding out the head office. If it is, I'll call you." He hadn't expected to hear from Scotty.

The next day Scotty had telephoned and asked him to see if he could get the stock. McCanse had been willing to wait a few days for payment. A day later Scotty had phoned and asked him to come in again, and he had, and Scotty told him the loan had been approved. So he had paid McCanse at once for the shares, and then he had come back and gone out for lunch with Scotty at Drury's. Afterwards, when they were crossing the square in the bright crisp sunlight, some pigeons had come waddling toward them on the walk and he had thrown an empty cigarette pack at them, and then Scotty had said quietly, "As for me, Harry, I may have been of some service to you, how would you like to let me have five thousand of those shares now the thing's gone through?" "How would I like to?" He laughed, hiding his embarrassment, as he wondered uneasily if this had been in Scotty's mind from the beginning. Not that he minded him getting the shares. He felt taken in, and he didn't like it. "Of course, they're yours," he said. "You can pay me for them when you're able to."

After the collapse of the stock, bank officials and then detectives started asking questions. They said Scotty had fraudulently misrepresented the security on the loan to the head office. One night Scotty came to see him and told him he was going to be arrested. "I've heard it said there's a bit of larceny in everybody, Scotty," he said harshly, and he started to abuse him for getting him involved in the fraud. But Scotty, standing at the door, looked like a beaten old man. When he came in he wouldn't take off his overcoat, and when he sat down in the chair by the window there were two little pads of snow on the toes of his rubbers. "All right, Scotty, this is all yours," he said, but he couldn't take his eyes off the toes of those old-fashioned rubbers.

"Harry, listen to me," Scotty pleaded. "I've told them you're not involved at all. I've told them I was trying to be big and do you a favor, and you're blameless. The blame is all mine and I've taken it. All you need to do is tell the truth," he said.

"Why did you do it, Scotty? I'd have bet my life on you."

Looking bewildered Scotty said slowly, "I don't know, Harry. I got thinking it over and for just a few days I lost my head. Money in chunks never seemed to come my way and I was handling it all the time, Harry." Their eyes met and he knew Scotty had been corrupt about the thing from the beginning. Then he looked away. It was a painfully embarrassing moment for they had been friends, and he was sure he knew what had happened to Scotty: in the last two years he had spent too much time in the company of promoters and entertainers who sat in Dorfman's and talked about throwing their money around, and they had made him feel poor. "It seemed to be such a sure thing, Harry," Scotty said. "The kind of thing that always happens to a guy like you and not to me. I believed in your luck and you, Harry, and wanted to get in on it, don't you see?"

"No I don't," he said, but he did, and it upset him. It was sudden remorse that his own life could charm and seduce a good man like Scotty. He wondered if somewhere along the

way he should have lit a candle; there and then he touched
wood on the arm of the chair as Scotty watched him with a
bitter smile. Then Scotty talked about his wife and children
and how he would lose his job and his pension. "There's just
one thing, Harry," he said desperately. "About those shares I
asked for after the loan. It was after the loan, you know. All
they want to know is about getting the loan. If you mention
those shares it'll look like a cooked-up deal," and then he
patted the top of his gray head nervously. "Anyway, it
might look to people — I know that wouldn't stop you —
but if you mention it they'll go hard on me. You know my
wife, Harry. For the sake of my wife and children."

"Scotty, I've got to tell the truth."

"I know you'll tell the truth, and everybody else knows
it. Harry, you don't have to add everything up for them."

"Oh, hell, Scotty," he said, and he was ashamed that a
man who had once had so much integrity should be there
abjectly pleading with him for the sake of his wife and children. "I'll tell the truth, Scotty, I mean all about getting the
loan and where I stood and no more. After all, it's not for
me to say what was in your mind."

Facing them in the witness box Harry wanted to tell the
truth and nothing but the truth as he affirmed he would do
taking the oath; then he turned and looked at Scotty, who
was watching him with a friendly trusting expression in his
eyes, and then he looked to the right of Scotty, under the
clock, where his wife was sitting, and he watched her fumbling in her purse for her glasses which she put on, and as
she eyed him steadily the fear in her face disturbed him.

Then Henderson asked him who he was. "I want to start
right at the beginning with you," and he had to tell about

the meeting that afternoon on Crescent. He told the whole story as it had happened up until the time he got the loan.

"Now Mr. Lane, I put this to you," Henderson said, hitching at the shoulder of his gown, "when the subject of the loan came up you were sure you were going to make a lot of money, weren't you?"

"Yes, I thought it was a sure thing."

"I put it to you that you and Bowman got together to work out a way of getting this money."

"I don't follow you," he said uneasily.

"Tell us how you got together on it."

"After listening to me it seemed to him that I would be silly if I didn't go after a loan and make some real money."

"Did you hold out any inducement to him to make the loan?"

"I did not."

"And he was only trying to be helpful with business advice in his field."

"Like any other businessman, I suppose, he saw that I ought to be able to make a lot of money."

"You mean like a banker looking for business?"

"No, it was just a businessman's observation, I thought."

"Then he suggested a loan?"

"Well, he smiled and said banks made loans."

"Did you offer him any inducement at all to make such a loan?"

"None at all. He offered to look into it."

"When did he tell you his head office wanted twice the security that you could get?"

"Well, the truth is," Harry said reluctantly, "he never told me."

"You mean you thought you were meeting all the requirements?"

"Well, he had said that reputation was as important as security to a bank. They both added up to the loan."

"Hm," Henderson said, with his dry old smile. "So he didn't tell you about his little difficulty with the head office. A most helpful friend," and then he turned to Ouimet. "Your witness."

Smiling politely Ouimet came close to Harry and he had cold sharp eyes. In one hand he was twisting a little gold knife on a gold chain, and the hand was thin and pale. His hair was clipped tight at the temples to conceal the grayness. They had known each other casually for two years, but Harry had never felt any real friendliness in him, and they had shied away from each other. Ouimet was a strict Catholic, and in his private life he had a spinsterish aloofness from any kind of self-indulgence and Harry had always felt he disapproved of him.

"What is your occupation, Mr. Lane?" he asked gently.

"I'm the public-relations director for the Sweetman Distillery."

"And your job, I take it, is to promote goodwill," and he smiled, making a joke. "Should I say to soften people up?"

"No, you shouldn't say it."

"Then I apologize. But a man to be successful at your job would have to be affable, know everybody, have a winning personality, be persuasive."

"A man with those qualities would do well even in the legal profession," Harry said, smiling.

"But they are the necessary qualities for your job, I take it. Now how long have you known Mr. Bowman?"

"About three years, I think."

"How did you come to meet him?"

"One day I was in the bank with a friend and I was introduced to him and then on and off I would see him at the ball games or at the hockey games and sometimes at the fights."

"He was very fond of sport and you were too. Was that the basis of your friendship?"

"No, I liked him the first time I met him. He had a kind of dignity, a simple integrity, a wonderfully kind open simple friendliness," he said slowly.

"Qualities rarely found in your world, I take it?" Ouimet said dryly.

"Very rare in any world," Harry said simply.

"And you knew that this honest bank manager, making six thousand a year, admired you?"

"I knew he liked me, as I liked him."

"And being fond of sport you knew that he had a naive admiration for champions, sporting figures and great entertainers, the kind of people you ran into every day, and did you ask him why he didn't drop into Dorfman's?"

"I knew he would like sitting around listening to the gossip."

"In this world of easy money, I suppose this bank manager was impressed by these celebrated figures, and Dorfman's is a famous old expensive restaurant catering to the elite, isn't it?" Among the spectators, Eddie Adams, Haggerty and Ted Ogilvie in their row looked at each other with a new and grave respect.

"He only came there about once a week, and sometimes he brought his wife."

"Of course," Ouimet agreed sympathetically. "It was a little out of his reach, but he felt at home with you and your friends. It was a big thing for him, wasn't it? In truth, between us, wasn't he a little stage-struck?"

"Well, maybe he had a naive admiration for some famous visiting firemen who weren't good enough to lace his shoes."

"The methodical banker, twenty years older than you, with a wife and two children, living in the suburbs, was secretly stage-struck, wouldn't you say?"

"Any time I was ever around," Harry said, wondering at how Ouimet had got so close to the truth, "I could see that he was liked and respected for what he was in himself."

"I see," Ouimet said, leaning amiably on the rail of the jury box so he could join with the jurors in watching Harry. "To come back to this rainy day . . ."

"It wasn't raining, it was snowing a little."

"Oh, that's it. You want to be accurate. Good. You had just come from a funeral parlor. No?"

"That's true. Old Professor McLean had died."

"And when you ran into Mr. Bowman what did you say you had been doing in the funeral parlor?"

"You want me to remember the jokes?" Harry asked impatiently, and Henderson rose and said he didn't see the relevancy of the question, and Ouimet protested sharply that it had to do with the character of the witness. "I'm not sure myself where this is leading," the judge said, and he started to cough. His left nostril began to run and he wondered why he had wasted his time trying a preventive like lemon juice and baking soda. "Continue, continue," he said irritably. "And speak up, please."

"I joked with Mr. Bowman. I said I was a public-relations man for half the city. About thirty-six old classmates had phoned me, knowing I'd be going to the funeral parlor, and they asked me to sign their names on the book." Everybody snickered.

"I hope I wasn't one of those who phoned you," the judge said brightly.

"Not that I recall," he said gravely; then he laughed.

"Your friends are all a bit cynical," Ouimet said.

"No, they knew I'd be at the funeral parlor."

"And they knew you'd go through the cynical performance of making it look to the dead man's family as if they had come to pay their respects."

"Well, I was there, so I wasn't cynical," he said uneasily. Ouimet's little smile and the glitter in his pale-blue eyes made him stiffen. "Well, now you and Mr. Bowman, standing on the street, have joked and you've told your cynical little story. Now how did the subject of the loan come up?"

"Well, I was feeling good. I knew I was going to make some money on the stock. I trusted Mr. Bowman. I told him about it."

"By the way, have you anyone else to support but yourself on your thirteen thousand a year?"

"No, sir."

"A free spender, easy come, easy go, I suppose," Ouimet said indulgently. "You go to New York to see the big fights, and to the World Series, and see all the new plays, eh?"

"Now — now — now . . ." the judge warned Ouimet.

"Surely it's important to establish the nature of Mr. Bowman's relationship with the witness — the fact that he saw the places and did the things Mr. Bowman only dreamed about," Ouimet protested.

"Well, only as to his credibility," the judge said. "Never mind these beautiful pictures of the witness."

"Only as to his credibility," Ouimet said, turning to Harry. "You've told your good admiring and stage-struck friend, who happens to be a banker, that you need money, eh?"

"Quite the opposite. I told him I was going to make some money, and he saw how I could make a lot more."

"And finally he mentioned the loan, eh? That is to say, you let him mention it first. That's good salesmanship, isn't it?"

"What was I supposed to be selling?"

"Isn't that the art of letting the customer come to you?" Ouimet asked blandly.

"I wouldn't know. It isn't my style. Naturally, the question of security came up."

"With you raising the obstacles, of course?"

"I saw the objections. Yes."

"You put up the obstacles, and he came leaping over them — should I say eagerly?"

"No, you should be accurate. Let's say there seemed to be no objections to him."

"Let's get the picture straight," Ouimet said with an amused smile. "This banker influenced you to take a loan from him?"

"He didn't influence me. I said it was his suggestion."

"And I suppose it was also his suggestion you go to Mc-Canse, and McCanse would let you have the stock, trusting you?"

"Well, yes, he did," Harry said reluctantly.

"And you would have been shocked if he had told you he hadn't got the loan approved?"

"There wouldn't have been any loan."

"He was afraid to tell you the money was tainted — afraid you'd let him down by not taking it?"

"If that's the way you want to put it."

"Really," Ouimet said softly, and then he turned to the jury and some of them tried not to smile. Harry looked around and saw that they all believed that in trying to protect himself he had gone too far and was willing to blame Scotty for everything. In the last row of spectators his own friend Ted Ogilvie, astonished and disappointed, had leaned close to Eddie Adams to whisper, and Scotty's wife, her mouth trembling, had turned to the elderly man who held her arm. Nobody believed him. Bewildered, he turned half pleading as he looked at Mollie Morris at the press table. Leaning back in her chair she tapped her teeth with her pencil, and as their eyes met she slumped in her chair and let her chin fall on her chest, dejected.

"Mr. Bowman will stand here and tell exactly the same thing," he said angrily.

"Are all your friends anxious to do you favors?"

"I don't go around with my hat in my hand," he said straightening up with his distinguished air. But someone had snickered. There was a little titter and the titter spread and there was a scraping of feet and everybody was smiling. Banging his gavel the judge threatened to have the courtroom cleared. Turning suddenly Harry stared at Scotty, the whole swing of his body angry and challenging. But Ouimet took advantage of this deftly, "Oh, let me reassure you," he said sarcastically, "Mr. Bowman may still believe that all the suggestions came from him, even if he's somewhat bewildered at how it could happen that he found himself doing — shall we call it — this favor?"

"At no time did I ask him to do me a favor."

"Oh, come now, surely by this time you'll have to admit that Mr. Bowman was trying to help you out — just a little — be generous."

"As I understood it," Harry said doggedly, "it was a loan to be acceptable to the bank in every way. Who gets loans from the bank by way of a favor? Is that the only way you, yourself, can get a loan?"

"Ah, now, let me ask the questions."

"Well, stop distorting everything I say."

"The witness shouldn't lose his temper," the judge said mildly.

"Let's go on," Ouimet said softly. "You admit you didn't use money as a bait?"

"I certainly didn't. It wasn't at all necessary." Taking out his handkerchief he wiped his mouth. It felt dry, and he moistened his lips, and said truthfully, "I asked if it was to be a regular loan, an approved loan, and it was as far as I was concerned."

"You didn't use money as a bait — but you did use friendship, knowing this stage-struck manager believed completely in his distinguished friend."

"If I'm supposed to be the distinguished friend, that's absurd." Then he added slowly, "Mr. Bowman is a shrewd man — a banker — a much shrewder businessman than I am."

He couldn't take his eyes off Ouimet's feet. The black and shiny shoes were very narrow and sharply pointed and Harry despised such shoes.

"A shrewd man," Ouimet said, his tone changing. Dropping the soft insinuations he came closer, coldly aggressive, and Harry hated him. "If you were a clever man, a little cynical and reckless with money . . ." Ouimet began.

"Now, now," the judge complained. "Counsel should make his speeches to the jury and not to the witness."

"I'm sorry," Ouimet said, bowing deferentially, and then he whirled on Harry. "I put it to you that you were looking for money, that you knew that no bank in town would give you a loan on such security."

"It's not true."

"I suggest to you that you went to work on Bowman and he told you he doubted the head office would approve the loan."

"It's not true."

"And knowing he trusted you completely, didn't you insist that only three or four days were involved and you weren't asking him to take much risk and you wouldn't let him down?"

"It's absolutely untrue," Harry said.

"And didn't you appeal to his friendship and faith in you when he spoke of getting the loan approved by the head office?"

"I did not."

"Don't you see, even now, that you simply took advantage of his strong sense of friendship — that he was a dupe?"

"That he was a dupe — really! Nothing of the kind. There's not a word of truth in it. I tell you I was completely in the dark."

"But now isn't there enough light for you to see that if it could be shown that you collaborated on getting this loan that you'd be here charged with conspiracy?"

"You know why I'm not charged with conspiracy. He'll stand here in his turn and tell you."

"Have you still got that much confidence in your influence over Mr. Bowman?" Ouimet asked, smiling as if Harry had said what he wanted him to say. "Well, that's all. Thank you."

But Harry stood there, troubled and yet grim, then half turning to the judge, he hesitated.

"Is there something the witness wishes to say?" the judge asked.

"There is," Harry said, with dignity. "There's one fact that may have been lost sight of and rather deliberately, I'm afraid. The root of the whole matter. And it is this: I was not told that this loan did not meet the requirements of the head office and that it had been misrepresented." As Ouimet got to his feet, protesting, he raised his voice. "And Mr. Bowman will stand here and tell you I was kept absolutely in the dark —"

"A speech, this is a speech," Ouimet cried, and in the hubbub the judge pounded his gavel. When Harry stepped down Ouimet, recovering himself, smiled. "I can sympathize with the witness wanting to make a speech to the jury. He seems to think that he and not Mr. Bowman is on trial. Oh, I won't ask that he be recalled," he said, and Harry, after turning belligerently, went to the seat near the door where he had left his overcoat. There, he stared at Scotty and waited confidently for him to take the stand.

But Ouimet, having made exactly the impression he wanted to make on the jury, turned blandly to the judge and said almost idly that he wasn't putting Mr. Bowman on the stand; he didn't think it was necessary.

Harry half rose, his mouth opened in astonishment; his face turned a dull brick red and he slumped back on the bench while Henderson began his address to the jury.

Reviewing the facts without any harshness, Henderson pointed out that there was no question but that there had been an admission of wrongdoing. The jurors should not be confused in judging the nature of the bank manager's guilt. He had fraudulently misrepresented the loan to the head office. That he might on one particular occasion have been influenced by another man had nothing to do with his guilt or innocence . . . And Harry kept staring at Scotty, despising him. Scotty took out his handkerchief, wiped his face, then his eyes wandered around the room and finally were drawn to Harry. Their eyes met and then it seemed to Harry that Scotty was pleading with him, saying with his eyes, "Please don't be sore. You're established and so well liked and popular. In a little while this won't matter to you." It upset Harry and he waited for Henderson to finish and Ouimet to begin.

Ouimet had a conversational, intimate style. He hardly raised his voice; he took the jurors into his confidence. He talked movingly about Scotty's family life and how he was respected by everyone who knew him. "Now we come to Harry Lane." Every time he used the name all the spectators turned and looked at Harry thoughtfully. His hands clenched on the seat ahead of him, he kept bending down pressing his chin against his knuckles, his face flushed.

"You saw Harry Lane," Ouimet said. "Of course, he's not the kind of businessman Mr. Bowman dealt with every day, a man of charm and grace. Mr. Bowman was very fond of this man. If Mr. Bowman committed a crime, why did he do it? Out of avarice? Oh no. What was there in it for him? He was very vulnerable to his dashing friend. Now you are men of common sense. At some time in your lives you may have been running around wanting to borrow money. Well, can you really imagine that the idea of a loan came from Mr. Bowman, that all the suggestions came from him, that he actually pressed Lane to take the loan when he knew, on the face of it, he was risking his job and his freedom? Does this offend your intelligence? Can't you see him yielding reluctantly to the corrupting pressure of friendship, saying to himself, 'It is only for a few days. He won't let me down.' And why isn't the man who took the advantage here in the dock with Mr. Bowman, charged with conspiracy? Because Mr. Bowman still retains his pathetic loyalty to him . . . He takes all the blame."

"No," Harry shouted, and he jumped to his feet, his head caught suddenly in the last rays of the sunlight sweating and shining, and crazy anger in his eyes as he glared at Scotty, and he thought Scotty was also going to stand up and protest for he looked ashamed and miserable, but he didn't; he shook his head helplessly. Then Harry turned, his hand up, facing the judge, who had been momentarily startled. Ouimet, too, had turned indignantly, caught off balance. The words Harry wanted to use were on the tip of his tongue. "I want to be sworn in again. This is a disgrace. I have something more to say. Mr. Bowman came to me pleading. He knew he could get shares from me. He asked for them. Let me be sworn in again." But in the moment, the little moment while they were all startled and facing him, his instinct made him aware with a swift frightening clarity of the consequence of such a statement now: it would look as if he had held back through fear of being charged with conspiracy. Ouimet would cry out that Harry Lane should be in the dock too; he had bribed Mr. Bowman with the promise of shares; and Mr. Bowman still could remain silent, for from the beginning he had known if he could get as far as the trial in this way, without being denounced by his friend, free of any resentment or hostility from his friend, his silence could protect him from the sentence he deserved.

While the light suddenly changed in the courtroom as if it were clouding up outside, and the judge cleared his throat angrily and raised his gavel, his face stern, Harry lowered his arm, looking stricken. Swiftly and intelligently he saw his real mistake. His mistake was in the beginning when the police were questioning Scotty, and him too; why didn't I protect myself by denouncing Scotty? I should have been Scotty's accuser. I, as well as the bank, was the victim of his deceit; the police should have had my story. Long before the trial they would have had him face Scotty; as an accuser. Even Ouimet, who was an honorable man, mightn't have tried to pillory him, and Henderson would have been speaking for him as well as for the bank and for justice.

"Order, order," the judge shouted. "I won't have this in my court. You'll be ejected." But Harry, his mouth trembling, hurried toward the door, and the policeman opening it for him watched him go along the corridor where the wet blotches and muddy footprints had all dried, and he saw him stop and wipe his forehead, his hand trembling.

❖ II ❖

W hen the courtroom door opened two hours later, three
St. Catherine Street businessmen, coming out slowly
and putting on their coats, blocked the door. Then Mollie
came around them hurrying to get ahead of the others. Her
beaver coat swung back like a sail and her open goloshes flop-
flopped with each long angry stride. She was a very proud
woman and she was pale and sick with humiliation because
everybody knew she was Harry Lane's girl. She had known
him since she was seventeen, although only in the last year
had they felt sure they belonged to each other. In the old
days he hadn't liked her. Those were the days when her
father had spent ten thousand on her coming out at the St.
Andrew's Ball. Harry had teased her about her father being
the greatest authority on indecent literature in the city, because
the judge used to make speeches on the need of strong cen-
sorship, and he also used to tease her about her mother being
a born convener of committees, jockeying for social position.
In those days they had been very rude to each other.

But when he came back from the war he found her working at the *Sun,* where she had started on the women's page
doing society notes, until they found she had a gift for gay
malice and gave her a column, and she had left home for her
own apartment on Bishop, and she seemed like another girl.
She could sit with him in the Ritz Bar or in a little joint like
Jimmie Aldo's and have her lovely easy laughing tolerance
of stockbrokers or old fighters while newspapermen said, "I
get a kick out of her. She gives the job a little class, always
dressed for high tea."

The flopping of her open goloshes irritated her and she had to stop and bend down to zip them up, but the sound of footsteps behind her coming closer flustered her and she got up and hurried on. She couldn't bear to hear them talking about Harry, running from her own secret conviction that Harry had the kind of nature that could easily have influenced Scotty, and she tried to hide from this conviction by scolding away at him bitterly in her mind for his jokes about her own sense of prudence. She had a sneaking respect for the way he saw through her, but not now. The secret solid steady side of her nature was scandalized and angry; yet, with all her heart she wanted to hurry to him.

When she looked around at the end of the corridor and he wasn't there, she was glad. But then, it wasn't like him to have waited. Outside, the street lights were coming on, the sidewalks were still wet and the air was damp and heavy. It looked like rain. She got a taxi and told the driver to go to the Ritz and she lay back and closed her eyes, thinking, "This could ruin everything for me."

At the Ritz she hurried downstairs to the bar and there he was sitting alone with his Manhattan. It was too early for the cocktail crowd. Both his elbows were on the bar and his chin was cupped in his hands, and she had never seen him look so dejected. Then he turned. "Mollie, what did they do?"

"Gave him four months," she said grimly.

"I've been framed, Mollie," he whispered fiercely and he kept clenching and unclenching his fist. His lips were white and the crazy anger in his eyes frightened her. "I've been ruthlessly framed."

"Why did you let them do it?" she blurted out.

"I was on the hook. You saw I was on the hook."

"You could have got right off the hook by telling about those shares Scotty wanted for himself."

"Could I? I stood up there when Ouimet was talking. Even then — well, it was too late. It would look as if I had made a deal with Scotty. All he had to do was keep quiet and who'd believe it wasn't a cooked-up deal, a conspiracy, worse than ever for me. Come on," he said, as two strangers came in and sat at the bar. "I'll take you home. People are watching us."

"A fine time to care about anybody watching us," she said, as he took her arm and led her out up to the street. From the hotel to the first corner they were silent and he seemed to think she was sharing his anger; then at the curb he stepped out into six inches of water and slush and as it came up over his ankle he cursed. "I left my goloshes back there in the courtroom."

"Harry, you left more than your goloshes back there."

"Cut it out," he said savagely, but when he had gone on only twenty paces he muttered to himself, "I still can't believe it. For the guy to sit there looking so ashamed. He was hoping for a suspended sentence or what he got, instead of five or seven years he knew he deserved, and he let me be crucified." Then he blurted out, "The cowardly bastard."

"Harry, from the beginning you were careless."

"How was I careless?"

"I wondered at the time why you didn't do a little more investigating."

"Whoever heard of a man investigating a bank manager who wanted to make him a loan?" he asked angrily. "Am I stupid?"

"Nobody thinks you're stupid."

"Everything I said was absolutely true."

"The truth. Don't you know you can't tell only part of the truth? The thing ends up as a lie. Right at the beginning why didn't you add it up for the judge?"

"At the beginning I was sorry for Scotty. Don't you understand? I was sure he'd go on the stand. An old beat-up friend. Didn't I practically give him a character certificate? I was sure of him. I don't know, his wife was sitting there."

"I was there, too, Harry. Am I not supposed to have any shame?" she asked fiercely. "Why didn't you say to hell with Scotty when he was first arrested?"

"But if Scotty had gone on the stand . . . Look, please stop trying to explain it to me." They kept quiet while they turned down Bishop to her place, an old stone house a half block below Sherbrooke. "It's your optimistic nature, Harry," she said. "It's good and generous, but sometimes I think it blinds you and everybody else, and then it does bad things for everybody."

Following two steps behind her up the stairs he watched the little sway of her hips as he had always done, in spite of his anger, waiting for her to turn and put out her hand as she used to do, and then when her face came into the light on the landing by her door and she fumbled with her key in the lock he saw how thoughtful she was and he felt a sense of dread. Tossing her coat on a chair she went into the kitchen to get him a drink, and as he folded his coat slowly over the same chair a trace of her perfume seemed to be all around him; he could still smell her hair.

The room, done in white with yellow curtains and a black mantel, was spotlessly clean. Everything in the room seemed to join with her to ask him why he hadn't been shrewd and prudent enough to foresee that his compassion for Scotty could only lead to a humiliation. His wet shoes squeaked; his right foot felt icy cold.

"For heaven's sake, Harry," she said, coming from the kitchen with the bottle and glasses. "Why don't you take off those shoes? I suppose it'll help a lot if you get pneumonia."

"I'll keep moving around," he said, and then he turned, stricken. "A man shouldn't go against his own nature, Mollie. That's when he gets hit on the head. It's my nature to be absolutely candid. I've never had to conceal stuff. The trouble was, it wasn't my nature to kick Scotty any deeper in the gutter than he was. I couldn't. Do you see?" But her back was to him as she poured a rye on ice. "Well, to faithful old Scotty," he said, taking the glass from her.

"No, to Scotty's faithful friend."

"Oh, cut it out."

"That's right," she said wearily. "Just have a drink." As she sat down on the chesterfield and lay back with her eyes closed, sighing, her dress tightened across her breasts. He watched her face and it was beautiful. She had very clear soft skin with a little mole high on her left cheek. He had always liked that little mole. It was a clean well-cut face with a good jaw and chin, but with her eyes closed, and without the laughter that came in them, there was a grimness to her face, and he wondered why he had never noticed it before. Then her full red mouth quivered.

"These easy associations," she said wearily. "This fast money. This sticking together. Harry, why should you ever have got involved with Scotty Bowman?"

"Well, he was around. We're people around. We bump against each other. We get to like each other. People."

"People, people. Too many people. It's your business, Harry. All this comes from the rootless kind of life we lead. I do my bright little column and sit around being gay with the boys, and I feel grand, feel I'm not a nobody if some alderman waves at me. I'm twenty-seven, Harry, do you think I want to go on being one of those women no one ever really expects a man to live with, and if she has a husband he irons his own shirts so she can do her work?"

"Well?"

"This can ruin you. How long do you think it's going to take you to live this down?"

"You don't have to live down the truth. What's all this about?"

"It's about you and me," she said fiercely.

"It's Scotty who's going to jail. Not me. They tried to throw some mud on me. Well, I can stand it. Why talk like this to me now?"

"I feel like it now." But she was going to cry and she hated her tears. "A crooked deal, and it looks as if you'd taken advantage of a bank manager and left him in jail. I know what people are like about money. I know what this looks like to respectable people."

"How things look, the appearance of things," he said impatiently. "That's you. Never look under the covers. It's indecent. For heaven's sake, I thought you had left home." He walked over to the window. It had started to rain. The bare branches of the tree in front of the house were shining in the reflected light from the street lamp. A girl went running down the street holding a newspaper over her head and somewhere a monastery bell was chiming. But he wasn't watching or listening. His head had jerked back, his lips curled a little, then he suddenly rubbed vigorously at the clouded pane.

"What's out there?" she asked impatiently.

"Nothing. It's raining. That's all."

"Then what's on your mind?"

"I don't know. Two weeks ago they were praying for snow in the Laurentians for the skiing. It looked as if the lodges and everybody connected with them were going to be ruined. Then it snowed heavily, didn't it? And they rang the church bells and gave thanks. Now it may rain for a week."

"Harry, what were you thinking?"

"Well," he said, turning to her. "Maybe I was thinking of your people and what they will say."

"I know you never liked them," she said, standing up, "but since you brought them into it I know exactly what my father will say. You won't get sore?"

"No, go on."

"Were you afraid, in the beginning — with the police — of mentioning these shares Scotty asked for, afraid it would look like a deal?" and the pain in her eyes told him she had been trying to hide the doubt in her own mind.

"And you think I was only trying to protect myself? Look, Mollie," and he was hesitant, almost shy. "About the whole thing beginning with Scotty . . ."

"Oh, Harry," she said bitterly. "What does it matter how it began. Who's going to listen now?"

"I see," and he half smiled, wanting to say, "but you, yourself, you don't quite believe me." He didn't say it. Putting his hands in his pockets he walked around the room feeling like a stranger; then he turned, white-faced. "You forgot something. Scotty once had a lot of integrity, and right now he's so ashamed he knows he could never come out and face me. Don't worry. I'll hear from him."

"Harry," she said, but the real pity in her eyes hurt his pride painfully and then she came over to him and, half ashamed of her need and the sympathy it made her feel, she tried to put her arms around him and it seemed to belittle him more than anything said in the courtroom. "No," he said fiercely. Jerking away, he slapped her on the face.

Her hand went up slowly to her cheek, rage in her eyes, for never in her life had she been hit, and then her quivering face shamed him.

"Mollie, I'm sorry. I don't know why . . ."

"Well, I know why," she said breathing hard.

"No, you don't, you don't at all."

"Well, you figure it out, Harry."

"I do."

But he couldn't hold on to his anger. Her wrong understanding of him, in their love, filled him with terrible sadness; he felt stricken; he had to hide his desolation, and he quickly picked up his coat and hat and hurried out.

The Man with the Coat

◇ **III** ◇

*H*e lived in a neatly remodeled old house just two
blocks west of the Ritz on Sherbrooke and across the
road were the big apartment houses screening the mountain. He had always liked coming up the streets on the lower
slope and seeing the shadows of the trees against the night sky
and below, the pattern of street lights. In the old days his family home had been on Clarke Street on the west of the mountain, but one winter in his second year at college when his
mother had been in Florida he had roomed with a fellow just
a few doors west of where he now lived. On summer nights
when all the trees were in bloom and the old stone mansions
gleamed with light, he used to think that this one fine street in
the city was as fine as any street in Paris or London.

His apartment was on the ground floor, a big high-ceilinged room that had once been a drawing room, and a bedroom and a small kitchen. The big room was done in gray
with coral drapes and yellow chairs, and on the mantel was
a picture of Mollie and one of his mother who had died of
cancer a year ago. In this picture, taken only five years ago,
she still had some of her beauty, and it showed in her fine
eyes. She was a Quebec Catholic whose marriage to a Protes-
tant hadn't affected her happiness at all, although at the end
she had worried about Harry never going to church as she
had worried too about him being killed in battle or dying in
a hospital without the last rites of the church, and for her
sake he had worn a religious medal around his neck so that
he could be identified and prayed for, if he lay dying among
strangers.

When he came in, and before he turned on the light, he saw the chair by the window, just touched faintly by the street light, and he seemed to see Scotty sitting there as he sat that night with the snow on the toes of his old-fashioned rubbers. That I should be such an open book to any man, he thought bitterly. Sitting there in the chair, Scotty had counted on being able to touch his heart, just as he had also counted on getting the shares from him. His face burning with humiliation he suddenly wondered why his heart hadn't been as open to Mollie as it had been to Scotty, for she had his love.

Then he felt all mixed up about himself and a little wild and betrayed by both of them. He hurled his hat and coat at the chair. "You ruthless disloyal bastard," he said. "Well, I know something about you too. Your Calvinistic soul will be tormented. Soon you'll know you can't come out and face me."

Switching on the light he sat down, breathing heavily, and listened. From the street came the sound of car wheels licking loudly through pools of water, then a young woman's voice talking baby talk to a little dog on its night walk with her. The front door opened. The old painter and his wife came in and went upstairs. These familiar sounds made him feel lonely, then his head began to sweat and burn and he jumped up and paced around the room.

But the fact is, he thought, jerking open his collar, the fact is nobody now can know the truth but me and Scotty, and the walls of the room seemed to come against him. Then he thought he would call Ouimet, then he thought he would call the newspapers, then enraged and helpless he said, "To hell with it, that little Judas can't cheapen me."

His mahogany desk in the far corner of the room caught his eye and something he saw there began to bother him.

Frowning, he walked slowly over to the desk. Opened letters and unpaid bills were scattered on the desk top, all mixed up and pushed aside. Some of them had been there for weeks. He always paid his bills and sooner or later he answered all the letters. But the careless disorder of it worried him and almost furtively he began to straighten out the papers, separating the letters from the bills and putting them in neat piles, which he put in different drawers, getting it done before anybody could come in and get the impression that he was careless in these simple business matters. Then he looked down at his wet shoes and slowly wiggled his cold foot. It felt numb and he went into the bedroom and pulled off the shoes and socks and lay on the bed, feeling exhausted, and was soon asleep.

The sound of the phone ringing on the table beside him woke him up, and he grabbed it. "Hello, Harry," the voice said. Suddenly he was wide awake and worried. It was Sweetman. "Have you seen the morning paper, Harry?"

"No. What time is it?"

"Around midnight. You won't like the story, Harry. What in hell happened?"

"What happened?" and then he started to curse Scotty.

"I'm just over here at the Colony with my wife and some friends. If you'd like they can go on home and you run over here. I'd certainly like to hear your story."

"I'd certainly like to tell it," he said, vehemently. "I'll be there in twenty-five minutes." When he put down the phone he stood in his bare feet for a few moments, smiling grimly. The enormous importance of those few words from a man who knew him. "I'd like to hear your story," was wonderfully comforting to his pride.

Outside it had stopped raining. On the short walk along Sherbrooke, he began to tell his story to Sweetman and grew wildly impatient. A taxi passed and he waved and jumped in and was at the Colony in two minutes. Most of the regular patrons knew him, and when he strode in brusquely, he didn't even wonder if any of them had read the morning paper. "Hello, Harry, hello, Harry," he heard the different voices calling to him, but he was looking for Sweetman. He saw him sitting at a little corner table by the window, wearing a jacket of the same cut and color as the one he, himself, had bought a month ago. "Sweetman must have liked that jacket of mine," he thought, and he felt better.

Sweetman was a slim and elegant cultivated Jew of forty who had gone to Oxford and who tried to preserve some of the English mannerisms; he wore his handkerchief in his sleeve, had a soft accent and got his clothes from a London tailor. Yet, somehow, he managed to sound like a remittance man. He had smooth, slightly sallow skin, a rather heavy British military mustache and a little black curling hair on the top of his head, and he played good tennis and golf. He had a handsome, hard, ambitious wife who wanted him to be a member of the Board of Governors at the university, and he kept giving them large donations without having any luck.

"Sit down, Harry," Sweetman said. "You wanted your rye, didn't you, Harry?" and then he handed him the folded newspaper, and watched him while he read it, for as a businessman he felt involved himself and was worried.

On page two was a simple factual report of the trial, with a quotation from Ouimet's speech to the jury, and a quotation from the judge, expressing great sympathy for Scotty as he sentenced him so leniently. The name Harry Lane was mentioned only six times but it seemed to Harry to be all over the page, and his face began to burn and he scowled. "You see, Harry, it makes it sound as if you led that little bank manager right down the garden path," Sweetman said. "It doesn't sound like you at all. What in the world happened?"

"I was framed," Harry said, grimly, and he told about Scotty coming to his apartment and asking him for the sake of his wife and children not to mention the shares, and how Scotty had taken advantage of his friendship.

Chatter and laughter coming from the other tables made him raise his voice a little, his blue eyes blazing, and yet he was apologetic that he had been taken in. "You've got to understand that Scotty had been a good man. Probably all his life. Then the itch suddenly got him. I was sorry for him. It's terrible. All that integrity suddenly in ruins."

"It's quite a story," Sweetman said, reflecting. Then he took out his briar pipe, his pouch, and filled the bowl. "Put a little pressure on some of these nice fellows, and, well, there is such a thing as a gentleman, you know," and he smiled. "Harry, it all sounds like you. You go around with your chin stuck out. Take it easy." And he reached over and squeezed his shoulder reassuringly. "People soon forget a little unfavorable publicity."

"Oh, I can stand it."

"Water off a duck's back, old boy."

"Just the same, Max old boy, I appreciate this."

"You're a well-liked man, old boy."

"At least I hope I've got a few friends of my own."

"A well-liked man doesn't have to do too much apologizing, Harry." He lit his pipe; he took a few deep meditative puffs. "You're indignant, of course. Just the same, if I were you, I wouldn't start explaining the thing. Keep away from people for a few days. Let the important ones come to you, Harry. And they will. You've got a good story there. Glad I had the sense to call you," and he got up.

They went out together and stood on the sidewalk talking amiably until a taxi came along. "Can I give you a lift anywhere, Harry?" Sweetman asked. "Thanks, Max. I think I'd just as soon take a little walk." "As you say, old boy," Sweetman said, and he got into the taxi and Harry watched it pull away.

He's all right, he's really all right, Harry thought, feeling ashamed of the amusement he used to get out of Sweetman's affectations. He stood there pondering over the unexpected ease with which Sweetman had offered his faith in him; a man who had been a friend, an employer with whom he had never felt truly intimate; then he contrasted this faith and understanding of his nature with Mollie's doubt and fear and it hurt him painfully. It was hard for him to believe that in their intimacy and desire there was no real knowledge of each other or that the deeper one went into knowledge of the other the less certainty there was. Why should Sweetman be more generous than she is? he thought.

As he looked up the hill the life he had lived in the neighborhood seemed to be all around him, reassuring him. The trickling at the curb of the water from the melting snow flowing down the hill had a peaceful friendly sound. He looked at the rolled-up copy of the morning paper in his hand, then dropped it at the curb and watched it make a little dam in the slush. A pool formed around it, then the dammed-up water suddenly flowed over the paper.

◇ **IV** ◇

*I*n his heart he knew Mollie was waiting for him to
phone; he knew the slap would torment her unless she
believed it came from some wild struggle against his need
of her and his need to be absolutely honest with her, and his
shame that he hadn't been. She would want him to need her
more than any friend he had. That was like her. The next
day, in his mind she had all her silken round firmness, but
overnight she had lost her mystery for him and he didn't
need her at all.

On the second day, at a quarter to five in the afternoon,
his secretary came into his office and told him Mr. Sweetman
wanted to see him. Sweetman was sitting at his desk, his head
in both hands, reading the afternoon newspaper. It was an immense office. It had once been gloomily impressive but Mrs.
Sweetman, who often came there, had redecorated it herself.
The dark-oak paneling had been bleached, the ceiling done in
pale green and the drapes were wine-colored with a thin gold
pattern. On the wall behind the big mahogany desk was a
painting of Mrs. Sweetman, looking very smooth, golden, intelligent and determined.

"Have you seen this, Harry?" Sweetman said and he
pushed the paper across the desk. "What is it, what's up?"
Harry said, sitting down. On the front page was the picture
of Scotty Bowman. Scotty had killed himself in his jail cell.
It said in the story that he was to have been taken away in
the morning to begin his sentence. But last night he had cut
his wrist with a razor blade and had lain down and covered

himself with a blanket and bled to death. He had been convicted of fraud after letting Harry Lane have an unauthorized loan. There had been general sympathy for him but he had lost his job and his pension. He had a wife and two children.

"God Almighty," Harry whispered. His hand holding the paper began to tremble and he was ashen, and then was almost apologetic. "I knew — well, I knew the guy was tormented."

"My wife was downtown, saw the paper and phoned me," Sweetman said uneasily. "This is a terrible thing, you know. The other day it didn't worry me so much, but look how it's snowballing."

"I know," and he leaned back in the chair staring blankly at the shiny surface of the desk, and then he looked up, but all he could think of was that he ought to have been nicer to Mrs. Sweetman who had counted on him getting her into the homes of those old families who remained grimly anti-Semitic.

"Harry, old boy, I know this is an awful shock for you. Very poor show. Very poor show for a chap to flake out like that. Probably knew he couldn't face his friends when he came out, couldn't face you. I said I knew you didn't take advantage of that man, didn't I?"

"It was decent of you to say so."

"Well, we know each other and all that kind of rot," and he cleared his throat, fumbling for his pipe but he seemed to have forgotten where he had put it, so he leaned back in the chair and let his chin sink glumly on his chest. Neither one said anything for a long time. They seemed to be staring at the same point on the shiny desk and it held them raptly. Harry heard his own heart beating, then the loud ticking of the clock on the desk, then he became aware that Sweetman was rubbing the side of his nose and shifting around in the chair uncomfortably as he waited and yet dreaded to break the silence himself. "You're in a poor frame of mind now, Harry," he said uneasily. "Why don't you go home and tomorrow —"

"What do you think this is going to do, Max?"

"I don't know, Harry. You know the public. It's your job to know the public. "

"I do your public relations, Max. Are you thinking I might be an embarrassment?"

"I don't know, I really don't," he said awkwardly. "I know these things pass off. I said so." But he drooped heavily in the chair. All his indecision and unhappiness was in his eyes and in the slump of his body.

"What do you think I'd better do, Max?"

"About what, Harry?"

"Well . . ."

"I know you're a sensitive man, Harry. Right now, of course, I know you don't want to appear in public places representing us or anybody," and then half believing the Harry Lane he had known might be able to stand even this scandal he said hesitantly, "Or do you?"

"That's up to you, Max. "

"Harry," he said uneasily. "You know what I'd do? I'd take a two-month vacation. Yes, that's it," he added more confidently. "Take two months' pay now. Go to Florida and let this stupid little bank manager be forgotten." Again he waited, but the shock of Scotty's death was still with Harry.

Gradually a flush came on Harry's face. "You know, Max," he said angrily. "Nobody's going to pin the disgrace of Scotty's death on me. I'm not running away. I can stand this.

You don't think so. All right, have you thought of this? People are rather unpredictable and when they hear you thought it was good business to get rid of me till you saw whether you could afford to take me back — well, you know, loyalties among gentlemen are deeply respected."

"I wish you hadn't said that, Harry. That's damned unfair and you know it. I made the sensible suggestion. I'm not an insensitive man," he muttered, but he was begging him with his eyes to go so he could sit with his head in his hands and wonder if everybody would say he had been no gentleman.

"Well, I also am not an insensitive man," Harry said, and he walked out and went to his own office, cleaned out his desk and looked around the office with his heart taking a sudden painful uneven beat; then he put on his overcoat and hat and got out before his secretary could come in and speak to him.

Why all these blows to me? he wondered uneasily. In a few hours he had been asked to leave his job, and his faith in Mollie had gone. He had always had faith in his own life, yet now he wondered uneasily if somewhere he had pushed his luck too far and taken a little extra risk that was resented; yet all he had done was to try and interfere a little, out of compassion, with the course of justice and the punishment that should have come to Scotty.

Then he remembered how ashamed Sweetman had looked and it suddenly cheered him up. "If I know the Sweet-mans, they'll be running after me in a week," he thought. The shame of the thing had been too much for Scotty, the truth had got to him even in jail. All he had to defend himself with was the truth, he thought, but it could be a grimly satisfactory weapon.

With his head high and his distinguished air he began to go up the hill and along Sherbrooke, and by the time he got to the Ritz he was acting beautifully. He called out cheerfully to the doorman, he stood talking with the hat-check girl, teasing her, and then he hurried down the stairs to the bar for his Manhattan.

◆ **V** ◆

*T*rying stubbornly to get another job he talked to advertising executives and financial men on St. James Street. These men had always seemed to like him and he talked to them in his opulent manner without any sense of disgrace at all. Finally their uneasy embarrassment began to worry him. They didn't mention Scotty, nor did he. All week he tried to cope with their apologetic reticence without mentioning Scotty. Then it seemed that these men were telling him they couldn't feel free with him unless he discussed his case openly, so he began to say confidentially and quietly, "You know Scotty wanted some of those shares for himself. He knew me. Knew he'd get them. You see how he was working it? Do you see how it clears it all up? The irony of it is that he let people think I was taking advantage of him. My only mistake was in feeling sorry for the guy. But how could you help it?" It made them all the more uncomfortable. He couldn't see he was offending their sense of justice by denouncing Scotty after he had had his day in court, with Scotty ruined and dead. But he felt the resentment of these businessmen. It troubled him and he felt compelled to explain the whole case to anyone who would listen. In the M.A.A. Club, where he had always come for his after-dinner drink, and where he had always felt at home among the college men in the paneled room with the tables and the little bar, he became aware that his friends were overly polite and uncomfortable when he sat down with them. To some he had talked about a job. When he sat down he tried to brush away their embarrassment with his old candid charm,

saying, "You know the notion that I took advantage of Bowman is fantastic. The guy had me on a hook." Only the barman listened to him with the sympathetic tolerance of all
bartenders.

One day at five he came downstairs to the Ritz bar, smiling and refusing, with a stubborn splendid courage, to be embarrassed, his cheeks tingling from the icy wind as he rubbed
his hands together. "That's the coldest corner in town out
there," he called cheerfully to the bartender. "I mean the
windiest corner," and he grinned at those who were at the
bar, and he sat down beside his old friend Ted Ogilvie.

"Didn't see you at the fights last night, Ted," he said.

"Didn't see you either, Harry."

"Johnny Bruno looked very good but he'll never have
a punch."

"Why does he need a punch when he's one of Rosso's
boys? How do we know when they go into the tank for
him?"

"I don't think the kid would believe anyone ever went
into the tank for him. He's a very honest boy," and he hesitated. "Look Ted, what goes on? I talk to people. I tell them
the facts about Scotty. I have to if I'm to get a job. What else
can I do when the general impression is that I took advantage of the guy and broke his heart? I'm entitled to a little
justice, you know. Yet people seem to be . . .well, half resentful. What is it?"

"I don't know, Harry," Ted said slowly. He was a pro-
fessionally unruffled man and his smile behind his tortoise-
shell glasses meant nothing. He was feeling very cross. He
didn't get along with his wife, and that afternoon he had heard
that she was asking his friends, "Don't you notice a great

change in Ted?" It was very effective. He had wondered why his friends were looking at him as if he were an alcoholic. It was all so obtuse. Now Harry sounded obtuse too. "Maybe it's the fact that you're here and Scotty's six feet underground. That's an advantage, isn't it, in any league, Harry?"

"But when the guy killed himself he really ran out on me, don't you see?" and then he started to explain that Scotty was tormented; he wasn't cut out to be a fraud. "But he was a coward about his trial. And he was a bigger coward to die without clearing me."

"I don't know, Harry," Ted said, as he got up to go. "But with Scotty not here, as he was in court — well, who am I to say what people think? Take it easy, Harry. So long," and Harry watched him resentfully as he stood at the door. Ted had put on his hat. It wasn't the very light-gray hat he had given him. It was a brown felt hat. "Why isn't he wearing that hat I gave him?" he thought uneasily.

Then he turned to the man on the stool to the left, a gray-haired, gray-mustached man by the name of Wilf Tremblay, the personnel manager for one of the railroad companies, who called himself an economic adviser. Tremblay had been listening, and so had James, the bartender; they had been smiling at each other thoughtfully. "Well, these are the facts anyway, Tremblay," Harry said.

"Sure," Tremblay said dryly. "But I'd like to hear what Bowman would say."

⬥ VI ⬥

*F*or two days it snowed and in the railroad stations there were gaily dressed skiing parties entraining for the mountains, and automobiles with ski racks were always passing him on the street. Only a few weeks ago he had been wondering who would invite him to the Laurentians for skiing this year; only two months ago he had been putting off invitations from ambitious hostesses in big houses. Now he wasn't being invited anywhere. Nor was he hearing from any of those people who had said they would keep him in mind for a decent job. But there was always Dorfman's with its gleaming white tablecloths, polite waiters, and its warmth after the icy wind blowing down the hill.

In Dorfman's Harry had one very small advantage. Alfred Dorfman's son, John, had been in his air squadron. When he lay dying in the hospital in England John had written some letters to his father about Harry's kindness. So now, Alfred was Harry's friend, and on his side no matter what he did.

He came into Dorfman's at the cocktail hour. He came in proudly as though he still had his good job and was bringing a little distinction to the place. The old crowd was there; Ogilvie, Haggerty, Eddie Adams the fight promoter, and even Mike Kon, the tailor; they were always there too in the evening after the dinner parties had gone home. But they had found out how to protect themselves if he tried to talk about Scotty Bowman.

Laughing and joking they would brush him off and get away from him and he would show no resentment.

That day Mollie was sitting with a lawyer friend named Jay Scott, who had been devoted to her for a long time. He had a calm intelligent face and a little gray in his thick black hair. When Harry passed their table she said quietly, "Hello, Harry."

"Oh, hello," he said with a quick smile, as if a stranger had surprised him by speaking, and he sat down by himself in the chair by the window. A little flush, starting low on her neck, rose to her cheeks, then her whole face burned. Her friend was watching her as she tried to conceal her embarrassment, and couldn't; she couldn't get used to being slighted. She had known Harry, coming in, would rebuff her. The others, the old crowd, watching, knew he had deliberately humiliated her. It didn't help his case at all with them, and she was aware of this too. Today at least she had had an excuse for not coming there. It was the day in the month when her father and mother came to her place for dinner, yet she had had to come, waiting, wearing the dress, the hat, the little touch of perfume Harry liked, yet knowing she would suffer when he passed her by.

"Why doesn't old Harry go to Europe or South America?" Jay Scott asked idly.

"Because he hasn't got the sense. Because he's too pig-headed," she said, contemptuously, and she looked over at Harry sitting in lonely dignity. "He'll sit there," she said scornfully, "till someone sits down with him, then he'll work his way round to explaining what a coward Scotty Bowman was from the beginning."

Still watching Harry, she tried to control her resentment. Alone and indifferent to her presence he waited for someone to sit down and talk to him; somehow it made her remember the slap on the face he had given her and her mouth tight-

---

ened and her eyes hardened. It's just as important to him to come here and try and humiliate me, she thought, as it is for him to go on talking about Scotty's cowardice, and she wondered if his twisted pride had made him hate her because everything had turned out as she had predicted, only more cruelly for him.

"I have to run, Jay," she said, her hand going out to his arm. "Dinner with my people, you know. No, you stay here. I'm late." She stood up in full view of Harry as Jay helped her with her coat, then hurrying out with a pleasant bright smile for everyone who nodded to her, she believed Harry was following her with his eyes.

Outside, the cold wind hit her flushed face as she ran toward a taxi, worrying now about her father and mother getting to the apartment before she did and waiting to ask what had delayed her. It put her into a very bad temper. At her place she ran up the stairs, hung up her coat and went into the kitchen. For these monthly dinners she had a caterer provide a maid who cooked the dinner and waited on table. Fussing around in the kitchen she scolded the maid for having put the rolls in the oven too soon. She tasted the soup. She scolded the maid again for having forgotten to warm the plates. But when she heard her father and mother coming up the stairs she rushed to the door, looking untroubled and happy. "Hello, hello," she called cheerfully. Her mother in a mink coat, three years out of style, was leading the way, her thin nervous face with the lonely eyes flushed from the climbing, pride and affection in her smile, and behind her was the judge in his black Homburg hat and dark-blue double-breasted coat, and clipped gray mustache, his big nose looking bigger because it was red from the cold. He had never been a brilliant lawyer, but he had a remarkable sense of responsibility and it had got into his manner. She fluttered around them taking their coats and chattering. She brought them a drink. "You've got everything so nice, everything so nice," her mother said, sipping her Scotch and soda. The judge was in a jovial mood. Last night he had made a speech to an educational association on the failure of the schools to teach history properly. "I really think I said some good things," he said. "Remember how I used to drum your history into you, Mollie?" "That's a fact, Mollie," her mother said, her long thin hand with the big diamond ring going out to her husband's arm. That's my own gesture, Mollie thought, remembering how she had often turned to Harry, her hand going out to his arm. Then the conversation, intimate, easy, lazy and dull, with dinner finished, began to get on her nerves. She said idly, "I saw Harry Lane today."

"You did?" her father asked. "Well, there's a man who must be bent on his own destruction. I hear he's going around town telling the wildest cock-and-bull stories about that dead bank manager framing him."

"If you saw Harry Lane," her mother said, "I hope you didn't let him work on your sympathy."

"I said I saw him. I wasn't talking to him."

"You're well rid of that young man, my dear."

"We shouldn't be surprised that he turned out to be a bit of a bounder," her father said gravely. "I used to be uneasy about his father. Those grandiose schemes of his. Those companies he floated and the money he threw around. He was an unstabilizing influence. It's the promoter's temperament and I distrust it."

"And his mother was a bit showy too, don't you think, James?"

"A good-looking woman, but yes," the judge said, meditating. "Showy. That's a good homely word for it."

"How was she showy?" Mollie asked, a little edge in her voice.

"Well, take the matter of the decoration of a house, or clothes one wears. People of real taste like quiet soft colors, neutral shades, don't they? Nothing about her was ever subdued, was it?"

"What has that to do with Harry now?"

"Your mother is merely saying, Mollie, that these little things in a family shape a boy's attitude to life."

"I don't believe it. Oh, it's absurd," Mollie said vehemently. "Let's drop the matter." Smiling indulgently her father said, "I'd be glad to." But now, in her own mind, she couldn't, feeling that she and her own family had been put in a light that mocked her own unhappiness. They were at home with her, she had always been at ease in the family silences, at ease, too, with the sudden comfortable opinions, but now she seemed to have drawn away. All her life her father had been kind and gentle with her, but afraid to show any warm affection, and the orderliness of his thinking even now, sitting there gossiping, began to irritate her. She'd always admired her mother's nervous energy, and her active social life, but now, watching the changing expressions on her sensible face, she was troubled by the loneliness in her eyes, some untouched secret in her heart. She felt disloyal, then full of affection for them. Finally her mother yawned, then laughed; the judge said he had to sit on the bench in the morning and he always liked to feel fresh, and she got them their coats and kissed them and they left.

Feeling upset she stood by the door, frowning; then sighing, she went into her own bedroom and kicked off her shoes.

She looked around for her slippers, then jerked at the clothes-closet door. It swung back sharply against her big toe. The pain made her limp around on one stockinged foot, tears in her eyes. "Oh, damn you, Harry Lane," she said, and suddenly and savagely she kicked at the door, then moaned with the pain. Crying softly she limped over to the bed and held her foot in both hands.

When she got into bed she lay listening for sounds on the street, listening really for the sound of the front door opening, then Harry's step on the stairs; she would let him in, then get back into bed and he would sit on the bed and tell her that he had felt lonely in Dorfman's watching her leave without him and as the hours had passed he had realized that it was her love for him that had prompted her to try to accept the reality of his disgrace while still needing him. He seemed to be there in the dark, sitting on the bed beside her while they talked intelligently. She told him that she knew his careless impulsive wildly optimistic nature had got the better of him in dealing with Scotty. Agreeing, he told her he hadn't realized how he had been leading Scotty on; he had felt so sure of the huge profit that he had thought nothing of letting Scotty feel he was entitled to some of the shares. Oh, Harry, you have that extravagant nature, all your pleasures, your kisses are extravagant. Well, they are. She heard herself say these things, she heard him answer, then she began to toss and turn in the bed with the ache in her heart, her body warm and open to him as never before, if he could only be there.

The most extravagant thing of all is his foolish courage in trying to confront people without shame, she thought, and then she sat up suddenly as though hearing him crying out,

"I'm a fool, stop me from going on like this." It was so real she turned on the light and got out of bed very worried, and walked into the other room in her nightdress, still limping a little, the nightdress falling off one shoulder, and she looked ardent and shameless. That side of her nature that Harry had called flighty, which had spoiled her evening with her parents and made her feel like a stranger to them, was out of hand now and with all her heart she wanted to get dressed in a hurry and go out and find Harry and tell him she believed in the goodness of his nature; all the facts were unimportant and should never have counted with her. Going over to the window she looked out. It had started to snow again. The wind drove hard sleet against the windowpane. Suddenly she shivered and there were little goose pimples on her bare shoulders, and she began to rub them. The draught from the window, chilling her, seemed to get into her thoughts and calm her and touch her common sense, that secret steady side of her, which gave her all her pride, and she felt herself draw-ing back in anguish from the shame of going after someone who had rejected her. Whether she was there in her night-dress, or in her fur coat on the street, he didn't want her, she thought. Her face, her hair, the shape of her, her voice, her laugh meant nothing to him; he had rejected everything she was; her honesty, her breeding, her intelligence, her people, and he tried to make this humiliatingly clear every time she spoke to him. Then her fierce pride suddenly revolted. "Oh, you fool, Harry," she whispered fiercely. "Whatever there's left of you to ruin you'll do it, and I won't mind. I won't mind at all. It's you who'll get really slapped." The sleet drove hard at the window but she kept looking out, her firm jaw set and her eyes angry, wondering where he was at that hour.

❖ VII ❖

*H*e was in the Press Club in the hotel, sitting by himself at a corner table instead of standing at the bar with old newspaper friends as he used to do. Engrossed in his news magazine he paid no attention to the others, yet secretly he waited for a newspaperman to come over out of curiosity and get interested in his story; a newspaperman, he had told himself, would be the best of advocates. But they left him alone, and he hardly touched his drink. He was afraid if he started drinking he would go to the bar and start bothering someone with the truth and touch that vague resentment that so exasperated him. He wanted someone else to mention Scotty, the interest to come from someone else, and he looked over at the bar and put down his magazine, wondering at the powerful and baffling advantage Scotty had over him. Then he concentrated on Scotty, not as he had been in the courtroom, taking advantage of him ruthlessly, but as he had been a few months ago, smiling warmly with his air of fine integrity. That was it; he was up against Scotty's monumental reputation for integrity. Again and again the word integrity had come up in the courtroom, but always about Scotty who had built it up as fundamental public asset with great prudence. Until now he had never wondered if anyone had even thought of him as having integrity, and again he would look over at the bar where the newspapermen talked noisily and forgot that his own integrity had been a private thing of feeling and imagination. The truth seemed to be that he had nothing to put against Scotty's overpowering business reputation; it didn't matter that he, himself, had never cheated anybody and didn't lie.

The fact was that no one had ever called him prudent; he was careless with money and lived from day to day like a lily of the field. Everything that was good in his nature suddenly seemed to be bad and he wondered if he had all the qualities that could corrupt a solid prudent man. Suddenly he felt self-conscious sitting alone and got up and went out, and walked east against the wind, his head down, and his collar up. It was snowing, the wind was damp and raw, the snow was wet and turning to heavy sleet.

A priest was coming toward him, the wind flopping his black coat and black soutane around his legs, his nose a little pinched and blue from the cold. He smiled faintly at the priest. It was a city of churches and monasteries and ringing bells, and there were hundreds of priests on the streets. He had called them the Black Hawks and had never bothered smiling at them. Yet a priest on the street reminded him that there was always someone who would regard it as a sacred obligation to listen to him and see the justice of his case. In a confessional a priest would believe every word he said and give him absolution. But he didn't want to be forgiven; he wanted to be told he deserved a little justice.

He turned the corner to go into the Tahiti Inn, a smoke-filled small place with a gleaming bar. He sat beside a girl called Annie Laurie. He had often seen her around and sometimes he had talked to her. She was a dark soft-eyed girl with golden skin, a gentle manner, and she had slim legs, good shoulders and large breasts, and looked as if she took a size twelve from the hips down and a sixteen from the waist up. She never wore a hat. Sometimes she worked and sometimes she didn't. She fell in love and men fell briefly in love with her. She followed her heart, though she was shrewd and expensive. She had no reputation and it didn't worry her at all, for everyone conceded she was a very unlucky girl. A boy she had been engaged to had been killed in a motorcycle accident; the man she finally married, a naval officer, had gone down with his ship in the war. She was always there in the well-known places and often someone from out of town was introduced to her and fell in love with her, but was afraid to stay with her too long because of the jinx on her.

Leaning close to him, her hand on his arm, she said suddenly, "Harry, I used to go into Scotty's bank. When I had any money I kept it there. I've spent a lot of time talking to Scotty, and you know, Harry, I never could see you letting him down."

"You couldn't?" he said, startled, then smiling suspiciously. "You don't know me any better than you knew Scotty."

"Yes, I do," she said calmly. "I know something about men. Everybody liked Scotty. He had that smiling straightforward businessman's air. But who do you know who ever could say what went on behind those steady blue eyes of his? Not me. Never. Oh, we used to laugh and kid each other. But, as a matter of fact, I don't think Scotty believed in getting himself into a position where he'd be the one left standing on the barricades. On the other hand," she said smiling, "I knew a lot about you the first time I talked to you. Tell me what really happened, will you?"

"You're sure you want to know?"

"Go ahead."

He told her the whole story, and when he had finished, the belief in her eyes and the way she leaned over and kissed him gently, upset him. He was surprised. In his gratitude he could not speak for a while. He had come upon her too quickly and easily. He wanted to go on sitting there beside her, then he grew afraid someone would come in and take her away from him, so he asked her where she lived and if he could go home with her. "Sure. Come on," she said.

Outside they couldn't get a taxi. There was a hard driving sleet, the taxis were all moving slowly. It was bitter cold, and they shuffled on the corner, their heads buried in their coat collars. "We might as well walk," she said. "It's only ten minutes away as the crow flies. The only trouble is a crow couldn't fly in this weather. Why don't we all live in Cuba?" "And play the tuba," he said laughing, as they started along Dorchester past the old limestone houses and along by the board fences where there was only a narrow path through the snow. She led the way, her head down against the wind, and he followed five feet behind, and neither could hear half the other said, their words coming from their mouths buried in their collars, carried away on the wind.

She had a small ground-floor apartment, a very clean place in the new building opposite the monastery. At first he felt a little shy with her and very respectful, waiting for her to mention Scotty Bowman again, and then he saw it wasn't necessary. For her the whole matter had been settled, and he smiled, the look in his eyes making her wonder; then she said she was going to make some spaghetti. Following her around the little kitchen he got in her way till they sat down together. She ate with a wonderful appetite. She was bright and intelligent and she didn't try to be at all seductive. "I'm really very refined, you know, Harry," she said grandly. "My father was a school superintendent, and I spent two years in a convent." While they were talking and laughing the phone rang three times and she answered it impatiently and returned to him grumbling. Suddenly he became aware that he was very happy sitting with her in her kitchen.

"I like being here with you," he said, smiling.

"I always admired you, Harry, so I'm really the lucky one."

"Lucky? I thought you were supposed to be unlucky."

"I am, but I make the best of it now. It's easy too, when you get the hang of it. You just don't care."

"But you look happy, Annie Laurie."

"Why not? I've been happy enough since I stopped using my head. I play strictly by ear now. All the trouble comes for people who are bent on using their heads. They look for angels in people, they always expect people to be better than they are and they have their little schemes. Not me, I don't care. But when there's any good in anybody, don't worry, I can feel it."

"You're wonderful."

"No, I'm just me, now. Let's go in and listen to a little music."

She sat in the big soft chair by the steaming rad and it got late and he kept trying to entertain her so he wouldn't have to go home. Finally she yawned and laughed and curled herself up in the chair. With her dress slipping up over her knee, she fell asleep, her mouth open a little and her chest rising and falling. She had a pretty mouth. Then her shoe, which she had undone, fell off her foot, but she didn't waken. Picking up the shoe he went over and stood beside her, looking at her hand hanging near the floor. For the first time in a month he had been with someone who made him feel he was himself and nothing in him was spoiled, so he looked at her for a long time. He didn't want to go home. But he kissed her gently and went out without waking her.

✦ VIII ✦

*A*fter that night he had her come to his place as often as
she could, although he knew it didn't help his case at
all to have a girl like Annie Laurie as his friend and advocate; she had no reputation herself and had too often made
it plain that she was indifferent to those who had. She could
only make other people believe they could see the way he
was going, having her as his only friend.

One night when he had come home alone after eating
with her, there was soon after a knocking on the door. It
had a friendly sound. When he opened the door and saw the
plump little woman in the brown coat with a little fur at the
neck staring at him, his heart beat heavily. "Oh, Mrs. Bowman, come in," he said, hopefully, for he was sure she had
come to tell him that she knew the truth about him and
Scotty.

"Thank you, Mr. Lane," she said. It had been snowing
out and the snow on her arm had melted and as she brushed
against him her wet sleeve touched his hand.

"Sit down, sit down," he said, moved by her resolute
manner, and when she sat down in the chair by the window
where Scotty had sat, he circled around her, waiting nervously. "What can I do for you, Mrs. Bowman?"

"Mr. Lane," she said, taking off her gloves and fold-
ing them and clutching them with both hands. "It was very
painful for me to come here. You're really the last man I
want to see, but my bitterness is strong enough to drive me
here."

"I thought — I hoped you might know the truth."

"Mr. Lane," she said, and her voice broke with anger. "I know what you're saying all around town. How could I not help hear about it?"

"Mrs. Bowman, you don't understand, I'm telling the truth. I've lost my job. I can't get a job. This thing follows me around. I'm entitled to a little justice. I don't lie about people. I don't have to lie about Scotty." But her head had jerked up and the glint in her round brown eyes made it hard for him to go on pounding away at her husband's lack of integrity when her good memory of him was all she had left. "What's the use," he said, wretchedly. "I say I was not to blame."

"I didn't come here to portion out the blame, Mr. Lane."

"Then why do you come here?"

"I come here," she said bitterly, "hoping, as there's a God in heaven, I can show you something. So I can throw at your heart all that's happened to us because my husband was unfortunate enough to like you, and ask if it's fair. No, not to ask! To throw it at you."

"Tell my why you come here."

"Why? Why for the sake of my children, my home. Would anything else drive me here to you?" Then even the strength of her bitterness failed her, and her voice broke and her eyes filled with tears, but her desperate determination, no matter how it humiliated her, was in her wet and shining eyes. "Oh, my God, don't you understand? I have two boys. One is fifteen and one seventeen. Scotty lost his job and his pension. There's a mortgage on our house. In the last two years he's saved nothing. Do you know why? He was attracted to the life of men like you. I can look after myself. I've got a job in a chain-store. My seventeen-year-old boy is to go on with his education. Do you hear? I say he's to go

on," she said fiercely. "He's not going to quit school, do
you hear that? Not for our home or me or his brother.
Neither is his brother if I work my fingers to the bone. Do
you hear me? I'll lose the house. I don't care." She began to
weep while he walked up and down helpless and ashamed. "I
was driven here by my own sense of justice. Now, my God,
I'm pleading with you. My children have to go on with their
education. I don't care about me. Scotty is dead. He suffered, he was sentenced, but you escaped scot-free. Is that
fair? You're well off. You're somebody. Is it fair you escaped
scot-free?"

"I escaped scot-free?" he said. "Everybody's sore because I escaped scot-free. Well, thanks, thanks very much."
But she kept up her sobbing, her voice broke and rose as
she repeated herself drearily over and over again, and it
made him desolate.

"Please, Mrs. Bowman, please stop," he said, taking
her arm and trying to draw her out of the chair. "You won't
like yourself for going on like this to me. This is awful for
both of us." All he wanted to do was get her out of the room
and out of his life. But the feel of her plump arm as he tried
to lift her, the weight of her, the anguish and shame in her
round motherly face bewildered him; he was stricken by his
own crazy painful regret. "Please, please, please," he said,
and then he couldn't bear her or her friends to believe he
had turned her away. "Oh, Lord," he said, dropping her arm,
angrily. "I don't have any money. They made a great point of
that at Scotty's trial, didn't they. I'm careless. I'm a spend-
thrift. What does the injustice of the thing matter to me?" and
driven to make one of his reckless gestures he rushed over
to his desk and got out his check book. "I got two months'

salary from Sweetman, sixteen hundred dollars. Here," he said, writing the check rapidly. "Take it for your children." He got up, holding out the check to her. "Now go Mrs. Bowman, please go and leave me alone."

Dabbing her eyes with her handkerchief she stood up and took the check, then she looked around his fine apartment and hesitated half resentful. "You're young, Mr. Lane," she said, putting the cheque in her purse. "This will mean very little to you. Well," and taking a deep breath to recover her grim dignity, she went out.

Trembling, he rushed to the window and watched the plump little woman go along the street in the snow. "No dignity left for anybody," he muttered. For a long time he stood there watching the falling snow, and pondered over what he had done, and what it could mean. When people heard that he had given money to Mrs. Bowman they would smile and say he had a bad conscience. But he didn't care. Nobody believed him anyway. No one among the people who knew him was offering him a job, and suddenly he didn't want to talk about his case any more.

In the morning he went to the garage and made arrangements to sell his car. He spent the rest of the week getting a tenant for the apartment, selling all but two of his suits to a secondhand dealer, and he sold his furniture too. At the end of the week, it was the last week in February and very cold, he went down to the Windsor Station late in the afternoon and bought a ticket for Cornwall, seventy-five miles west. He left no forwarding address and told no one where he was going.

W hen he got off the train and went to the hotel he registered under the name of Harry Lansing. The next
day he got a job at a gasoline service station and he took a
room near a church with two elderly spinsters.

His employer, James C. Wilson, a stocky man of forty-
five, with a heavy nose and heavy lips and a nice little business, tried to find out something about him. He laughed and
told him he had been in many cities. Wilson protested that
he wasn't being nosy, he was only wondering where he had
learned so much about cars. But Harry couldn't keep to himself. He liked Wilson, who was the manager of a midget
hockey team, and he liked Mrs. Wilson, a young, plump, jolly
woman, who was always inviting him to dinner. In the evenings he began to go with Wilson to the rink to help coach the
kids' hockey team. Everybody in town got to know him.

Wilson used to kid him about wearing gloves working
on the cars so his hands wouldn't get too badly soiled and
roughened, and he would smile to himself and take off his
gloves and look at his hands and know he didn't intend to
stay here. He hadn't made any plans, and yet every night before he fell asleep he felt a little better about himself. All his
natural good feeling for people had come back to him. At
night, listening to the snow sliding from the roof and the
cry of a freight train so very lonely in the country hills, and
going over what had happened since the trial, he saw that
he had made a bad mistake in trying to attack Scotty. These
attacks had provoked people to defend him in their own
minds and hearts because he wasn't there. Scotty's silence

in death had become more effective than his silence in the courtroom. To explain and explain is no good, he thought. It's like a picture, a poem. There the thing is. There we are. Now it seemed all wrong to try and get people to look back on it and consider his explanations. People wanted to live from day to day in the charm of new things that would destroy all the bad memories. If a man wanted to live he had to be able to forget. Yesterday's resentments and indignations had to go like the snow on the roof melting in the sun. By the lightness of his thoughts he became aware that in his heart he felt sure the whole case had been dropped.

When summer came he began to dream of his own neighborhood, of women going into hotels and the trees heavy with leaves on the mountain and the floodlit ballpark and the sessions afterwards in Dorfman's. He missed the strange, piping whistle of the canal boats and the sound of the church bells. He would lie awake with not a sound outside on the quiet street and the moonlight, broken in patches by the leaves of the tree stretching across his window and touching his bed, and remember that he used to think that no city had as much willingness to live and let live as his own city had, and it was because of the necessary toleration between the French-speaking Catholics and the English-speaking Protestants, the way they got used to each other and learned to live together, and it touched the life of the whole city in all the little ways, and even where it wasn't wanted; the brothels opened and closed and opened again, and the gambling places put up patiently with police raids, and life went on. In such a city people could always tell, he thought, when a man had goodwill and was willing to live and let live and forget.

◊ **X** ◊

*H*e came home at the beginning of the heat wave when the city all day had been drenched in sunlight and the thermometer was at ninety-seven degrees. The heat seemed to cling to the pavement and lick at the ankles of people on the street, and French priests in the sunlight in their long black soutanes looked depressingly hot. At night the city seemed to have held in its oven all the heat of the day and there was no evening breeze. People going out to the ballpark for the night game passed the long rows of houses with the outside stair-cases and balconies jammed with half-naked children, men naked to the waist and women sitting with their legs spread wide, all perched up there as if watching a parade.

Harry took a room on Mountain Street in a decent house next door to one with a liquor license and girls. A little way up the street in another house a barbotte game had been running all year. It was a mixed-up street, yet it was in his own neigh-borhood, and he only intended to stay in the front room on the ground floor till he looked around and saw where he stood with his friends. He had saved four hundred dollars. He felt hopeful and prudent and full of goodwill. His landlady, Mrs. Benoit, a lean stern angular woman, who was determined to keep her place respectable, never read the papers and had never heard of him, and he liked this too. Unpacking his bag, he sweated, wiped his head and felt his pants sticking to his legs. He had two suits, the dark one, which he was hanging up, and which had a tear in the leg from a nail on a chair in his room in Cornwall, and the gray suit he had on, both of a win-ter weight. He made up his mind to get a lightweight tropical suit in the morning; then he washed, shaved and changed his shirt and went out, thinking of Annie Laurie.

He didn't want to start off with her, but she was the only one he felt sure of, the only one who had really believed him and he felt a fierce loyalty to her. He went down to the Tahiti looking for her. The smoke-filled beer-smelling place depressed him. In his mind now she didn't belong there any more than he did. When he saw her sitting at the bar in a pretty oyster-shade dress, her shoulders bare, her dark curly hair just covering the nape of her neck, laughing loudly with a tired sad-eyed girl, he felt angry; then, in the mirror over the bar she saw him standing behind her and swung around on the stool, opening her arms to him. "Harry, is it you, is it really you?" she cried. Even in that room reeking of cheap perfume and beer, she seemed to have all her warm prettiness, and his feeling as he laughed and hugged her bewildered him, for he couldn't believe he longed for Annie Laurie. "Let's get out of this dive. Come on," he said. Outside he said, "Let's take a walk, just loaf along. I seem to have been away for ten years."

If he wanted a long walk, she said, he could walk her home; she had a fine new place on University near the campus, a place she had got very reasonably because she was decorating it herself. Walking along Dorchester he listened eagerly for the sound of the canal boats and the shunting of engines in the station yards, and at Peel, by the hotel, he looked down the hill where the old barouches with their battered horses were lined up by the curb. "Everything in the same place," he said. "Everything looks good." He told her where he had been, and she understood why he had gone away and she said she rarely heard anyone mention Scotty

Bowman now. About two weeks ago, passing Scotty's bank, she had heard a man standing at the door say to another man, "Well, about this time Scotty would have been coming out of jail." Both men had laughed. "I hadn't thought of that. I mean I didn't realize he would have been coming out about now," he said uneasily. "You're absurd," she said, giving him a little push. Then she told him that her own luck had been mixed up. When the ball season opened the business manager of the ball team, a wonderful guy, amazingly generous, had met her, and he was like an eager boy. He had said she was the kind of girl he used to dream of on fishing and hunting trips, and he had sent her wires from every city on the circuit. He had told her he wanted to marry her, and then he had suddenly dropped out of her life.

"You'll hear from him, Annie," he said consolingly.

"Oh, I'll hear from him, sure."

"Maybe he got amnesia or something," he said, slipping his arm around her waist, for he understood that someone had got to the business manager and told him there was a jinx on her and that like all ball players he was superstitious; she wouldn't hear from him again.

The crowd on St. Catherine Street ambled along in the sultry night under the neon signs. Young fellows, carrying their coats, ogled girls with light print dresses clinging to their legs, who glanced over their shoulders and either slowed down or hurried when a fellow turned. Everybody was lazy, hot and restless. For Harry there was a quiet happiness in loafing along with the crowd. Then they turned up to Sherbrooke and there was the campus with a hot heavy moon throwing a pallid light over the roofs sloping up the mountain with the trees stark and still in that light.

She had the ground-floor apartment, and on the bare living room floor were two cans of paint on a spread-out newspaper. A stepladder stood near the end wall which she had already painted a shade of pastel green. "I'm doing it all myself," she said proudly, standing with her hands on her hips, a cigarette hanging from her lips. "Who could do it any better? I think I'm a great natural painter, don't you think so?" she asked, turning. "Hey, watch out for that paint." His foot had bumped against one of the cans, and as he looked down, he saw he was standing on an open page of the *Sun*, and there was Mollie Morris' column with her picture at the top, the chin raised, the smile bright. "I wonder what she'd say if she saw me here tonight?" he thought; yet he didn't care what she would say; whatever happened to him he would never need her, and if he did, he could never have any faith in himself again, and he looked up, smiling, for Annie Laurie was gliding around the room, pointing at cracks in the wall she had mended neatly with plaster of Paris, and he compared her with Mollie. She had a simple truthful nature, and it led her to the truth in other people, but she had had no luck, and now she didn't care what other people thought, and so she was no good; she didn't have the self-respect to get a job and lead a decent life. But Mollie, in spite of her beauty and fierce self-respect, did not have a simple truthful nature and could not respond to one; she was only wonderfully aware of what other people thought. Part of her identity lay in other people, which seemed to him to be a kind of whoring of the mind in the sepulcher of her sense of respectability.

"Annie Laurie," he said gently. "You're a fine woman."

"When you say something like that I feel as cold as charity."

"It's the simple truth."

"No, the truth is that when I'm with you I'm always wishing I wasn't such a bum. I've got no guts. You've got courage. I know I'm a bum."

"I say I know you're an honest woman," Harry said, and he knew his words were true; for her shrewd slow smile and the wisdom in her eyes had revealed suddenly the enormous self-possession which sustained her and kept her indifferent to bad fortune, and tough and loyal to her own heart. There's nothing common about her at all, he thought, and stirred by this mystery in her he put his arms around her and drew her close.

At four o'clock in the morning, monastery bells tolling woke him up, and he thought, "Harry, you haven't got a case any more, you've dropped your case, everybody's satisfied." He wished Mollie could see him there with the bells ringing all around him.

◇ XI ◇

*I*t was another very hot day and he wanted to get the lightweight summer suit, and he went out intending to go to his
own tailor, but on the way along St. Catherine in the strong
sunlight making the street look so shabby, he passed Mike
Kon's shop, which was on the other side of the street. Stopping, he looked over at the small store with the oaken door
and window frames and the bolts of cloth in the window.
Mike Kon made clothes for the members of the sporting fraternity. He rarely made a suit for a man like him. But Mike
had been Scotty Bowman's good friend, and he had been at
Scotty's trial.

Then he crossed the road slowly, wondering why he
should not have Mike Kon make him a suit. It would be a legitimate excuse to make a little gesture to a man who had been
a friend of Scotty's and see if he was willing to be friendly
with him. The more he thought of it the more he liked it.

In the days before the war, when some of the newspapermen had claimed Mike had a chance of winning the title,
he used to watch him fight at the Forum and liked his style
— a rough, mean, crowding type of fighter, with a broken
nose and some scar tissue over his eyes. In those days Mike
had been an illiterate young hoodlum very much respected
by other young hoodlums in the east end. He had gone on
and done a lot of fighting in the smaller New York clubs;
then he had settled down to fight out of Philadelphia for a bad
and powerful character named Sleepy Ferraro. After five
years, washed up and with his eyes damaged, he came home.
But something must have happened to his mind and heart,

for around Dorfman's they used to joke about Mike, wondering why he had changed his life and educated himself. He was always reading books. He used big words and talked slowly and deliberately. All his friends called him Mike the Scholar. They joked about him reading books aloud to his father who had had a paralytic stroke and who lived with him in the apartment over the store.

But I really don't know him well, Harry thought, inspecting the cloth in the window. In Dorfman's, Mike had never been quite sure of himself, never quite certain he belonged, so they had always greeted each other good-naturedly and that was all. But suddenly he wanted to have Mike Kon, Scotty's friend, put out his hand to him and greet him with pleasure and respect as he would have done in the old days.

It was a smart shop done in limed oak with materials draped over pillars and he was agreeably impressed; then Mike, himself, came from his office, wearing a good worsted jacket.

"Hello, Mike," he said, and he put out his hand, smiling with his old distinguished air.

"Why, hello, Harry," Mike said, squinting with surprise; he refused to wear glasses.

"Thought I'd drop in and try one of your suits, Mike. What about it?" Harry said casually, and turned to some of the bolts of cloth.

"Why, sure," Mike said, a little flustered. There was an awkward moment and neither one of them knew whether it was from embarrassment or because Mike was impressed that he was being asked to make a suit for a man whose clothes he used to admire. As Mike pulled out bolts of cloth and draped the ends over the table, they talked casually. Harry said he had been out of town. Nothing was said about Scotty Bowman. Mike seemed to be concerned only about the suit. When Harry picked out a lightweight tropical very light gray with a fine blue check Mike remonstrated; he said those tropicals didn't keep a press no matter how you watched them. Harry couldn't agree with him. Any suit needed a lot of pressing in the summer, he said, and he asked for a fashion book. While Mike listened respectfully he pointed at a conservative model with natural shoulders and made some suggestions. There were to be real buttonholes on the sleeves and hand-stitching on the lapels. "Fine, fine. I like all this. I do," Mike said. "Now to measure you," and he got a tape measure. Hesitating, he said, "Willie is the real expert, Harry," and he called for his middle-aged English fitter who came from the office, a tape measure around his neck, and wearing the vest he always wore even in the hottest weather. Everything went well. The suit was to be finished in a week. They shook hands. Outside, Harry stood in the sun lighting a cigarette and smiling to himself for he hadn't noticed in Mike that embarrassed vague resentment he used to feel in people who had known both him and Scotty; he hadn't noticed it at all.

He knew Mike Kon would tell everybody he was back but he took his time that week about appearing in the old places. He wanted the word to get around; for a while he wouldn't go to the Ritz bar or the M.A.A. Club, he decided; it would be better to wait until old friends, who heard he was back, came looking for him. When that happened it would be time to start talking about a decent job.

In the middle of the week when he went into Mike's place for a fitting, only Willie was there. That night he went into Dorfman's for the first time. Alfred Dorfman, of course, was glad to see him and bought him drinks and insisted he come out to the house some night and have dinner. When Ted Ogilvie and old Haggerty came in, Alfred called them over and bought drinks for them, too, and got them all drunk.

At the end of the week, at noontime, he got the suit and took it home and tried it on. It looked like one of his own suits, a good-looking piece of cloth, well cut and worth the money Mike had charged him for it.

That night he went to Alfred Dorfman's home and had dinner with the family. They welcomed him warmly but Alfred would have seen to this, he knew. Alfred would have welcomed him affectionately if he had just come out of the penitentiary. He was also very encouraging. "I'm telling some important people you're back, Harry, and I see them all," he said. Never at any time since the trial in the winter had Alfred mentioned Scotty Bowman, and he didn't now.

◇ XII ◇

Next day in the afternoon sunlight Harry walked over to Annie Laurie's place, wondering if she had finished with the painting.

The door was open and she called, "Come in," and he found her in her living room, kneeling in the corner painting the last of the woodwork white. "I'll be right with you in just a minute," she said. "Just this little corner to do."

"You could paint a three-story house," he said, admiringly. "How are you on the high ladders?"

"Harry, look out," she called, for he had come around her, close to the window trim shining white; he had brushed against the paint. "Oh, Lord," she cried. "I should have told you it was wet. I just painted it this morning. Your new suit."

On his shoulder and sleeve there was a smear of paint a foot long, and as he cursed she rushed into the kitchen and came back with a rag soaked in some cleaning fluid and she rubbed at the smear fiercely. The paint came off but there was a faint stain discoloring the cloth right down the arm. His wondering expression as he stared at it made her feel stricken. "Oh, don't take it so seriously," he said, smiling. "All I have to do is take it to the cleaners before it really dries. There's one right down on St. Catherine there. They can clean that coat in an hour."

"Yes, maybe if you take it at once before it dries," she said, and he gave her a kiss and went out, carrying his coat.

In the cleaning establishment the young fellow, a Greek with long sideburns, looked at the coat and shrugged and said it would clean up without a blemish and to come back in an hour. He went out, bought *Time* and *The New Yorker* from a newsstand, then entered a restaurant and had some coffee and read. In an hour and a half he went back to the cleaners.

When the young Greek saw him coming in he glanced at him nervously, hesitated, then went back to the office, and returned to the counter with an older man, bald, in a white shirt with a black bow tie, who was carrying the coat. "My friend," said the older man, shaking his head solemnly. "This you won't like," and he opened the coat and spread it out on the counter. The lining seemed to have light crisscrossing veins running through it, but these veins were really thin fine tears. "See, I do this," the young one with the sideburns said, and he nicked one of the cuts with his finger and it fell open. "You see?" he asked.

"Good God," Harry said, staring at the lining blankly. "What are you going to do? I bring the coat in to you and you tear it to pieces. It's that rotten stuff you use."

"Wait. Now wait. Look at the cloth, the rest of the coat. Is it all right?" the older man said, spreading it out on the counter. Getting excited, both cleaners grabbed at the coats on hangers that had been cleaned that morning. They showed him the linings. "That's a faulty piece of material you got there, mister," they said. "Look, every part of the lining. Now look at the cloth. If it was the cleaning fluid it would have hurt the cloth. No? Take it back. Where did you get it? — Mike Kon. It's a gyp. Make him put a new lining in it. Tell him to come to us," and they both pounded the counter belligerently as they gesticulated to each other, and grabbed at other coats, showing him how these linings couldn't be torn. They convinced him and he put on the coat and went out slowly, looking troubled.

⋄ **XIII** ⋄

*A*fter he had had his lunch next day, Mike Kon came loafing along the street in the sunlight, saying hello to any shopkeeper standing at a door and waving to clerks at the windows. He liked greeting these businessmen at noontime. He liked to think that in a few years' time he might be asked to be president of the neighborhood business association, and then be asked to run for alderman. These hopes helped him to feel secure and established and confident that in a year's time his business would be a success and the loan he had got from Scotty Bowman's bank would be paid off. He liked selling suits to young fellows of the sporting fraternity, but he also dreamed of being accepted as a tailor by people who wanted fine suits and wouldn't care whether or not he was an old fighter. He still wasn't quite sure whether he was accepted as a solid businessman.

Just to the right of the entrance to his shop was the door and the stairs that led to the upstairs apartment, and after lunch, before going into the store, he always climbed these stairs to see his father and spend a few minutes with him and the nurse, Mrs. McManus. The remodeling of the old apartment, which he had paid for himself, had been costly; he had wall-to-wall broadloom on the floors; there was a smart modern living room and three bedrooms, one for himself, and one for his father, and one for the nurse. He could not be sure that his father, now that he had had a stroke, appreciated how different this place was from the old one, and it always saddened him. His father was in the living room in his wheelchair, the light glistening on his bald head, his big nose shining too. On the right arm of the chair they had rigged up a board about a foot wide, and on this board there was a pad and a pencil on a string. Old Mr. Kon had been paralyzed on the left side; he couldn't speak, but sometimes two fingers on his right hand seemed to have a little life in them. Every morning Mrs. Mc-Manus, would stick the pencil between these two fingers and urge him to scratch on the pad. Often there were lines scratched on the pad but whether they were made by a nerve twitching in the finger or by the old man trying to write they didn't know. "Hello, papa," Mike said, cheerfully, as if he believed his father heard and understood every word he said. Every day he tried to have a little more faith in this, and he talked to him sometimes for an hour about everything going on the city. "How are you doing today, papa?" he asked. The one good eye, the right one, glittered at him fiercely till he pressed the hand gently. It was always hard for him to do this. He could not bear the touch of the inert, watery and swollen hand.

"Mrs. McManus," he called. "Is that you, Mr. Kon?" she said, coming from the kitchen in her white smock. She was a gray-haired jolly Scotswoman who seemed to have some affection for the helpless old man. "He seems to be pretty much himself today," she said, looking at the old man reflectively. "Don't you think so?"

"Look at those scratches on the pad," Mike said. "I think they're getting firmer all the time." He sat down, smiling at his father, as he always did, and began to talk to him about what was happening in the world, then about a book he had read last night as if he believed his father understood and had unspoken opinions of his own and showed it with that one lively blinking gray eye.

Years ago he couldn't have sat beside his father as he did now, feeling at ease and with speech unnecessary between them. In those early days he had had no understanding at all of his father. As a boy he had been ashamed that the old man had sold newspapers and had a bad accent and wore ill-fitting clothes, and that in the winter, at his corner newsstand, his red nose had been always running. His father used to wear a cap and earmuffs and had called out hoarsely the names of his papers while he danced around to keep his feet warm; this middle-aged newsboy used to come home and waste his time trying to read high-school poems aloud in a heavy accent. In those days just being near his father had offended him.

"Michael," his father had said, looking up, his finger on a sentence on the page. "This I don't get. Make it clear, please."

"Why don't you call me Mike like everybody else does?"

"Because with you and me it is not like it is with everybody else," he said mildly.

"Aw, hell, why don't you lay off those kids' books. Just be what you are. Everybody knows what we are anyway."

"What is it you say we are, Michael?" he asked gravely, as he closed the book, his finger between the pages, and looking down over his glasses.

"We don't rate. Why does a newsboy want to use big words? Who the hell cares?"

Closing the book, his father let it rest on his knee, and stared at the cover, and then he stood up and turned on the gas to heat the kettle and make himself a cup of tea. It was his only dissipation, the only one he could afford, the drinking of too many cups of tea. Mike had waited, hating the silence, his own uneasiness, and his father's familiar movements as he bent over the stove. "To insult your father, Michael, is not good," he said finally. "I'm a poor man, okay . . . The way it is with me there are no big jobs for me. But you are very wrong. Nobody knows what we are in this place but you and me. Maybe nobody but you knows what I would want to be . . . what we should be. The books — yes. Money — no. A poor man can have some dignity. If I'm rich, can I buy it? No, it has to be here," and he tapped his head, "and here," and he tapped his heart. "Someday, see this . . . then you are my son."

"And then I go peddle the papers too," he said, contemptuously. But his father sat down again and picked up the book. The kettle began to boil. Waiting stiffly, Mike hoped his father would get up and pour the water in the teapot. The expression in the steady gray eyes began to bother him; he tried to outstare him, feeling big and belligerent. Then the very calm, innocent, steady eyes began to insult him, and he trembled. "Have a cup of tea with me, Michael," his father said mildly.

"I don't drink tea. To hell with it," he said, and he swaggered into the bedroom and got undressed quickly. Yet the sounds of his father making the tea, the cup going down on the table, then the silence, then the knowledge that he was sitting out there, patient and untroubled, reading the grammar, the high-school poems, became an even deeper insult. At the end of the week he had left home, left that little room and his father and the few books and the silly, lofty, biblical talk.

After the years in the ring when he had hurt the optic nerve in his right eye and wondered what would become of him he found that he often thought of his father. On train trips and in cheap hotel rooms he began to read as if his father were beside him encouraging him to become an educated man. The more he read the more he was impressed by all the things his father had wanted. He had saved a little money and he came home and met his father, that is, he seemed to know him for the first time. Even now, when he thought of that day and how he had impressed his father, he would smile to himself. He had told Scotty Bowman all about it. At the time he had applied for the loan he had had to tell Scotty a great many things about himself.

On his lunch hour now he said the things he might have said if the stroke hadn't cheated them of the satisfaction of interesting conversation. It was a monologue, of course, but by this time he had learned to handle it naturally. Smoking his cigar, he would talk a little, look out the window reflectively, then turn feeling pleased when the one shining eye was on him, and sometimes sit for a long time saying nothing as he would have done with a man who could share the silence of his thoughts.

A buzzer in the room was connected with the store and whenever anyone came in at this hour wanting to see him personally, Willie, his fitter, rang this buzzer. Today he had been only ten minutes with father when the buzzer rang. "Well, so long for now, papa," he said amiably and he went down the stairs to the store.

Harry Lane, his arms folded, leaning against the long oaken table, was wearing the new lightweight gray tropical with the fine blue check.

"Hello, Harry," he said

"Hello, Mike," Harry said, straightening up.

"Anything I can do for you?"

"Yes, there is," Harry said coolly. "Something I thought I'd show you," and taking off the coat he spread it out on the table and showed him the torn lining. "What do you make of that, Mike?" he asked crisply.

"My God, what did you do to that coat already, Harry?" Mike said, and he looked indignant.

"I took it to the cleaners. That's all."

"But you just got it a few days ago."

"I got some paint on it."

"Paint."

"Yes, paint. What does it matter what I got on it?" he said impatiently. "I took it into the cleaners and they cleaned it at once. The Acme cleaners, about five blocks along the street. It came out like this."

"And what did they say?"

"They said it was a rotten lining."

"Of all the nerve," Mike said fiercely, but his face began to burn, for he could see that the cleaners had convinced Harry. He grew afraid that Harry, who had always patronized only the best tailors, was only too willing to look down on a piece of material from him; all his prestige seemed to be involved. "You know what did this lousy job?" he said quickly. "That stinking cleaning fluid they're using. Why, it's happening all the time with these cleaners. They're always getting sued. Who are they trying to kid?"

"Look here, Mike," Harry began; then he wouldn't go on; he was sure Mike was bluffing him; all he could think of then was that in the old days, before his disgrace, Mike wouldn't have been arguing with him; he would have had too much respect, but now he felt he didn't have to care. "If it had been the cleaning fluid," he said, trying to hold his temper, "it would have damaged the cloth as well as the lining, and you know it."

"Harry, I know what a hot iron can do to a lining."

"I don't know anything about hot irons. Are you going to put another lining in that coat?" Harry asked, losing his temper.

"Well, all right, I'll put a lining in the coat."

"You're damn right you will."

"Wait a minute," Mike said, also losing his temper. "If I put a lining in this coat I do it as a favor," and he straightened up and they faced each other. They were both the same height, though Harry was slimmer. But something in Harry's peremptory tone had reminded Mike of Scotty Bowman and of his own conviction that Harry had taken advantage of Bowman and escaped scot-free. When Harry had come into his store to order the suit he hadn't held this against him at all, but now some hidden resentment flared up. "Don't try and push me around," he said. "You can't get away with it with me."

"With you? What do you mean?" Harry asked, waiting white-faced. But Mike didn't answer. His eyes shifted; he wasn't sure what he meant; it just came out. "I'm not asking any favors," Harry said angrily. "Just cut out all this cheap bluffing."

"Cheap bluffing. You insult me. Don't insult me. You can't make me do anything by walking in on me. I'm not dirt. To hell with the coat."

"Okay," Harry said, and his hand trembled as he grabbed the coat and hurried out.

Mike took a few steps after him, bewildered by his own

unreasonable resentment. Although he was sure he was right about the cleaning fluid having damaged the lining, he wished he hadn't thought of Scotty Bowman. Angry and ashamed, he turned and walked slowly back toward the office where Willie, the fitter, had been standing at the door, listening. "That was the high-handed Harry Lane, Willie. Thinks he was slumming when he got a suit from me," he said bitterly.

Taking off his glasses and rubbing them with his handkerchief as he held them up to the light, Willie said sympathetically, "A little thing like that and you and a customer lose your tempers. Why, Mike? It isn't like you."

"He was snotty with me, Willie. Trying to look down on me. You heard him."

"Think about it a little, Mike. It could have been the pressing, yes, but if it had been the fluid it would have damaged the cloth too. You know that, Mike. Once in blue moon we get a piece of defective lining, don't we? It's not our fault. Why should you feel it's such a disgrace this time, with him?"

"I don't know. It's the guy. That guy," Mike said uneasily. "I guess I was wrong, Willie," and then he cursed and the more he cursed the more humiliated he looked. "I'll have to get the coat back," he muttered bitterly. "I'll have to go after him and apologize. Why does it gripe me so? I don't even know where he's living now. Well, he'll come into Dorfman's. I'll see him in Dorfman's," and then he sighed. "Why did he have to come to my store?"

◊ XIV ◊

*H*urrying away with the coat on his arm Harry looked like a man with a fine new suit finding the weather too hot for comfort. When he stopped at the corner to put the coat on it still looked like a handsome garment, although now he didn't care how he looked. He was blind with anger. His rage was deepened by a secret lonely desolation coming from his knowledge that he had sought from Mike Kon some reconciliation. He felt rejected.

Back in his room he sat down by the window and pondered, wondering if he might have been a little on edge and over-suspicious with Mike. With all his heart he longed to believe that he might have misinterpreted some of Mike's remarks. Granted that Mike had been bluffing about the lining it was possible that he hadn't been thinking of Scotty at all. In fact Mike might be astonished to hear that he was suspected of being capable of such a gesture, and laugh and say, "Oh, I see, I see. Now look here, Harry . . ." This seemed to him to be the natural and human explanation. The little things that make the world go round, he thought, and he lay down on the bed feeling tired, and soon fell sound asleep.

A knock on his door woke him up. It was dark in the room, and outside the street lights were lit. "Just a minute," he called, groping his way to the door. Annie Laurie was there in the hall light. "What time is it?" he asked.

"About ten," she said, coming in. "Why don't you turn on the light?"

"I forgot," he said, turning it on. "Have a drink."

"You were going to let me know what Mike did about the coat."

"Well, it was embarrassing," he said awkwardly. "We got off on the wrong foot. Maybe it was my fault. I don't know. He blamed the cleaners, and of course I knew it was not the cleaners, then he said I wasn't going to take advantage of him, and of course I thought he had Scotty Bowman in mind."

"Oh, Harry."

"I'm sure I was mistaken. But, well, you know, he was Scotty's good friend and all. That was in my mind. That was the trouble, see?"

"I know, but over a little thing like a coat lining, Harry."

"You don't think Scotty was in his mind at all, do you?"

"I'd certainly be surprised. If I thought . . . Why I'd go over and and break his store windows. Oh, Harry, you're wrong about the guy. He knows he has to fix that coat. Are you coming to Dorfman's?"

"I don't know. I've got to put on a shirt, and shave," he said, rubbing his hand over his face. "I guess no one will see the lining of that coat?"

"Who's going to look at a coat lining?"

"That's right," he said, grinning. "I'll see you later in Dorfman's."

"Okay," she said, then hesitating, she bent down and kissed him gently on the forehead.

"Why did you do that?" he asked.

"I don't know," she said awkwardly, and then she laughed, and he laughed, and she left him sitting on the bed.

◊ **XV** ◊

*M*ike was going up the street toward the big cool shadow across the sky which was the mountain slope with its pattern of lights, and leading up to it was the big glow of light at the hotel entrance, the lighted window of the exclusive little women's shop, then the single hanging wrought-iron light over the steps to Dorfman's, whose roof was touched with the pallid light from a hot red moon.

Mike had never felt that he was really established in the old expensive restaurant. Patrons who sat around at night in the paneled barroom had substance, they had families, even the sporting editors who came there were the ones who had wives who had gone to college. It seemed to Mike that these people, welcoming him freely, encouraged him to talk out of a half-amused curiosity, although he was never sure of this. He liked to talk about what was going on in Indo-China, or Germany, or about the bomb, and he always got a hearing, but if a visitor from out of town sat down with them he would hear someone say, "He's Mike the Scholar, an old fighter, but you should listen to the guy. Go on, talk to him. He's got an angle — fresh," and Mike would feel embarrassed.

Standing by the bar he looked around to see who was there. At the table by the window Mollie Morris was sitting with Ted Ogilvie, and Eddie Adams, the fight promoter, and old Haggerty, the sporting editor. Mike always felt at ease with Haggerty, though the sporting editor had a son at college and a very dignified wife; and, of course, he was sure of himself, too, with Eddie Adams, who was a very rich man, owning two apartment houses even if he didn't have much education. With Mollie Morris, though, Mike was never quite sure of himself; it was her kind of prettiness, her kind of style, and her cultivated voice; her friendly smile, too, always seemed to him to be good-naturedly indulgent. Yet he was glad Mollie was there for he was sure she would understand his difficulty with Harry. He was sure she was disgusted with Harry herself, not only because he had taken advantage of Scotty Bowman and got away with it, but because of his lofty manner of avoiding her, as if she ought to have approved of him for being a heel.

A little man with oily black hair, beady eyes and a small heavily tanned face, who didn't belong in Dorfman's at all and knew it, was standing behind Eddie Adams. He was Ray Conlin, who called himself the manager of Johnny Bruno, the fighter, and thought he was big enough for Dorfman's because his picture had appeared in a photo magazine as one of Rosso's handmen, riding around in Cadillacs and controlling the boxing industry. Everybody who knew the facts had laughed when they read this story. Conlin was merely Bruno's trainer.

Even with the air conditioning, it was hot in the bar and Adams and Haggerty and Ogilvie were in their shirtsleeves with their coats draped over the backs of their chairs.

"Good evening, Miss Morris," Mike said.

"Hi, Mike."

"Sit down, Mike."

"How are you, Mike?" Haggerty said, pushing out a chair to him with his foot. Tilting back in his chair, Mike saw Annie Laurie coming in, coming over to their table and he glanced at Mollie; maybe because Harry Lane was in his mind. Mollie's mouth twisted a little as though the sight of

Annie Laurie cheapened her intolerably, yet she didn't get up and go, for Annie didn't sit down at her table. She took a chair from the nearest table and pulled it over so she was on the fringe of the group, and Adams and Haggerty, who liked her, pushed back their chairs so their backs wouldn't be to her and Adams called the waiter. As far as Adams was concerned, if he wanted to buy Annie Laurie a drink he would buy her a drink and if Mollie didn't like it she could go home.

"Hey Mike," Annie Laurie said bluntly. "What did you do to Harry's coat?"

"What do you mean, what did I do?" and he was startled.

"I saw the lining."

"You mean already you've seen that lining?" he asked angrily. "You mean to say he's showing that coat all around? What's he trying to do?"

"I said I saw it, Mike."

"What lining?" Ogilvie asked. "What's this, anyway?"

"The lining of the coat, a suit Harry got from Mike."

"When did you become Harry Lane's tailor, Mike?" Haggerty asked.

"I made the guy a suit last week."

"I heard he was broke," Adams said, teasing Mike. "But was he afraid no one else would make him a suit?"

"What does Harry say?" Mike asked uneasily.

"He said you blame the cleaners."

"Why not?" he asked. "All over town people have got claims against cleaners. Would I gyp the guy?"

"Oh, come on Mike," Annie Laurie said. "Never mind the explanations. Why don't you simply put another lining in the coat?"

"Who said I wouldn't put a lining in his coat?"

"Why don't you tell him you will?"

"All right. I'll tell him. Give me a chance."

Little Ray Conlin, who had been hovering around the table, waiting for a chance to get into the conversation, suddenly saw his opportunity. "Maybe he won't want you to put in another lining," he said suddenly; his small, dark, narrow-eyed and shifty face all screwed up in happy surprise. "Maybe Harry Lane will be too smart to let you touch that coat again, Mike." His eyes were mocking. "Maybe he'll be afraid this time you'll try your own special lining — yellow. You always had a yellow lining, eh, Mike?" He slapped his knee and danced around, his hard little face full of happiness. It was the only time in his life he had ever been quicker than anyone else with a clever remark. "Ah, ha, aw, aw, aw ha," he snickered and they all laughed and waited.

"Yellow was never my color, Conlin," Mike said quietly.

"You mean to say those trunks you used to wear in the ring didn't have a yellow lining?"

"That's right," Mike said, smiling disdainfully.

"What about that night in Philadelphia ten years ago. Remember?" he jeered, trying doggedly to hold his audience. "The night you went into the tank for Walters. Wasn't the yellow lining showing then? Ho, ho, ho, ho," and again he looked around for approval, as Mike eyed him steadily. It was true Mike had gone into the tank for young Walters who was on the way up; he had been told to do it; it was part of the life he had lived then; but he hated Ray for reminding them now of the days when he had been an illiterate unprincipled washed-up young hoodlum, when they were accusing him of gypping Harry Lane. His smile slow and patient, he said, "When it comes to tanks, Ray, you'd know all about them. You and the Rosso mob."

"Come on outside," Ray blustered fiercely. "Come on and I'll show you the color of the lining in your own coat." Then he jerked away as though expecting Mike to smack him. Keeping his voice and his anger buried under a vast superior calmness and a slow lazy smile, Mike said, "Oh, go and peddle your papers, Ray." He found it easy to be quiet and patient with the others smiling approvingly. Feeling unwanted, Ray moved over to the bar.

"Nice guy, Mike," Ogilvie said. "Conlin can't help being a poor little rat."

"Ray's just another rubber mouth," Mike said, shrugging.

Then they all saw Harry Lane come in carrying the coat over his arm. When he saw them all together, he stopped; he looked at Mike, then at Mollie, and then at Mike again; the two of them being there together seemed to disturb him. Turning away abruptly, he sat down at another table.

"Harry, old boy," Haggerty called, chuckling to himself, and he rose and went over to Harry with a fine judicial air. His gray-haired solemnity and plump white face fooled Harry, who looked up blankly. "What's it this time, Haggerty?" he asked. "How can we have any opinion on the deal unless we see what you got for your money," Haggerty said, and he picked up the coat and held it open so they could all see the lining. "Why the moths certainly got into it, that's a fact," he said innocently. "Moths in the cleaning fluid. Never heard of it."

"Come on, come on," Harry said, very embarrassed.

"Haggerty, cut it out," Mike called, "What are you trying to do? Sit down."

"What is this?" Harry asked, rising with a blank, incredulous expression. He had always been a neat fastidious man, and wherever he was, drunk or sober, he always dressed with immaculate correctness and now his coat was being waved around as if it belonged to a buffoon. He looked over at Mike, knowing he must have been talking about the coat, for all the laughter came from that table; then their eyes met and Mike knew he was despising him for talking about the coat and making him the butt of a joke. Harry's mouth twisted, his angry eyes still on Mike, as if he were getting from him only the kind of cheap treatment he should have expected. Never had Mike felt so looked down upon, or judged to be so unworthy, and it seemed to Mike to be so unfair, so untrue, that he glared at everybody indignantly.

"Put the coat down, Haggerty," Harry said.

"What do you say if we take up a collection to have it mended," Haggerty said, as he hung the coat on the back of the chair.

"A great idea. And pass the word along old Harry'll match every contribution dollar for dollar," he said, trying to behave with some grace and dignity, and when Haggerty left he took the coat and folded it so the lining would not show and leaned back against it, and Mike watched him intently.

When Haggerty came back to his own table Mike said bitterly, "That you should do such a very stupid thing, Haggerty. Why can't people mind their own business? Look how hard you make it for me to speak to the guy, now. Already I've had words with him. I can see he wants to have more words." He stared fascinated at the coat. "Maybe he came in here to make trouble." Still bothered by that contempt and hostility in Harry's expression he wondered if it would be better if he went home and tried to speak to him in the morning. Then he saw Harry turn to someone at the next table, laughing, making some bright, sharp joke about being taken to the cleaners.

"That's fighting dirty, real dirty," Mike said, standing up. "This must go no further. This cheapens my shop. This is a public slander. He's not going to use that coat to belittle me." He stepped over to Harry and said angrily, "Look here, Harry Lane, I told you once I'd fix that coat."

"Who's ordering me around?" Harry asked.

"Do you want the coat fixed?"

"Don't push me around. I'm going to think about it," Harry said slowly. "Yes, I'll think about it. Mind you, I appreciate that you're very anxious to get it and fix it now — now it's in the public domain." He smiled, enjoying his success in defending himself. Mike shrugged and turned away.

On the way back to his table he brushed against Ray, which was what Ray wanted. "Take it easy, Mike," he said, hoping for a little friendly grin in return. But Mike was too worried and angry to notice him.

"What did you say, Mike?' Ted asked.

"I told him to bring the coat in."

"Good, and what did he say?"

"I don't like his attitude." He was very stiff and still, his hands clenched on the table, and the others, feeling his frustration and anger, were sorry for him.

"Have you heard anything about the Bruno fight, Mike?" Ted asked, helpfully.

"Those New York fights of his never looked right to me, Mike," Haggerty said.

Little Ray Conlin, edging closer, heard them talking about his boy, Johnny Bruno, and it hurt that they were listening to Mike and not to him. He could see now that Mike had solid support, a following which he had underestimated. All his life Ray had had a profound respect for any man who had a following. On his own he would have judged that Harry Lane would be a top man in Dorfman's and Mike a nobody, but Harry Lane had lost his prestige. Ray had no convictions at all about the Scotty Bowman case. He didn't care. But he wanted to be always on the side of public opinion. He was a born meddler. He could see that Mike now was getting all the sympathetic attention.

Then he heard Mike say bitterly, "All this talk about Bruno and the Dutchman. All I know is I'd give fifty dollars to get that coat for a few hours."

They've got no sense of humor, Ray thought profoundly. I make a joke about a yellow lining. Why has nobody got any sense of humor tonight?

As he stared at the coat himself he tried to think of doing something very comical that would make even Harry and Mike laugh. He thought of grabbing the coat and tossing it up in the air, but he wasn't sure this would get a laugh. As he passed he stared at the tattered lining and grinned at Harry. It was not only that he needed fifty dollars, he always needed money, but he could see himself slipping the coat to Mike outside or at the entrance. "I know how you feel, Mike. We'll see that Lane gets it back." Mike could put a new lining in the coat and it would be a big joke around Dorfman's and Mike would be his grateful friend again.

As it hung there on the chair, it became more than a coat to Ray, it was now something that would give him back his place in Dorfman's and he watched and tried to make a cunning plan.

Then Harry, his drink only half finished, got up and began to go in the direction of the washroom, leaving the coat on the chair. Tightening up, Ray grinned but Harry came back and picked up the coat and went on to the washroom. Ray, watching him, had no particular plan, and as he loafed toward the washroom himself, he thought he might speak to Harry and make a joke about the coat, yet he knew the joke wouldn't come easily.

In the washroom, he saw the coat hanging on a wall peg. He stared at it, making no sound, wondering if Harry Lane could see his feet. His little dark face puckered up in a frown. Bright happy thoughts came to him. The coat was just there within his reach, his hand only had to go out and lift it neatly off the peg and then he could go hurrying out and home, and late that night he could go around to Mike's place, killing himself laughing, and let Mike have the coat and keep it all that next day so he could put a lining in it, and then early the next night Mike could come sneaking back with the coat and hang it on the peg. There it would be found, and it would be a joke on Harry Lane; the boys would talk about it for weeks. Mike, then, would certainly slip him fifty dollars, and he would see too that he was the friend who had actually done something for him.

All his life Ray had been running and ducking. When he had been a kid in Brooklyn he had heard himself called a rat of a boy. He had tried to be a fighter, and he had carried water pails around Stillman's gym, and there he had attached himself to Waxi Rosso. He had learned how to train a fighter and do everything that was expected of him. All

his life he had been able to get along by doing little things
for people, jobs no one else would do, and he had shown
Rosso that he could count on him.

Grinning, he took a slow step toward the coat and reached
out and unhooked it, and as soon as it fell across his arm he
knew it was the thing that would reestablish him in Dorfman's. Then there was a move behind the cubicle door. As he
went to run the coat slipped off his arm and when he grabbed
it, some papers fell out of the pocket. The cubicle door opened
suddenly. He ran. But Lane came charging after him, shouting, "You thief, you dirty little thief."

When he got back to the bar he started to laugh, so
everybody would see it was a joke. But Lane was right behind him, he had him by the shirt collar and jerked him and
spun him around and tore his shirt.

"Cut it out," he said angrily.

"Stealing my wallet, eh," Harry shouted. Ray was surprised at the strength in the hand of so light a man and now as
he looked at the white angry face with the hard blue eyes he
felt scared; as scared as he had felt when he was a kid and an
enormously powerful, coldly superior detective had cor-
nered him hiding behind a counter in a bakery shop.

"Lay off, Harry, it's a joke," he said, laughing. He tried to
brush Lane's hand away, while he kept on snickering. But
the others had got up from the tables and Alfred Dorfman had
come hurrying over.

"What's the matter, Harry?" Alfred asked.

"The little bastard was trying to lift my wallet."

"To hell with his wallet," Ray said. "It was just the coat.
The guy's crazy. Don't you see, Harry, the coat. It's a joke,"
and he appealed to the others to share the joke with him.

"Why don't you call a cop, Alfred," Harry said crisply. "He's a little gangster anyway. Why do you have him around here?"

"Jesus, you guys," Ray said turning helplessly to the others, for it frightened him to think of the local police looking into his life. If that happened everything would go, Rosso would turn against him. Rosso knew how important it was that his trainer in Montreal should be legitimate. "Tell him, you guys," he pleaded desperately with Ted Ogilvie and Haggerty. "It was only the coat. It's a joke. Mike Kon said he'd give fifty dollars to have the coat for a little while. You heard him. What the hell do I want with Harry's wallet? I've got friends. I've got connections. I've got a piece of Bruno. I get a cut of his purse. I'm no . . ."

Angry and frightened he cursed, he pleaded with them, till Ogilvie started to laugh. "He's right, Harry. It's a joke," he said.

"I say the guy was after my wallet," Harry said coldly. "You didn't see him. I did."

"Harry, don't be such a fool," Mollie said, blurting it out as if the whole thing outraged her. "I heard Mike say he'd give fifty dollars to put a lining in the coat. And Ray heard him."

"Yeah, I did say it," Mike confessed.

"So you put the little bastard up to stealing the coat."

"You're off your rocker, Harry. Sit down. It's a joke. What are you beefing about?" Ogilvie said. "Take it easy, man." Ray, taking his cue from them, laughed and then they all laughed heartily.

The laughter, the unbelief turning to laughter, seemed to be frighteningly new to Harry. With courage and dignity, some months ago, he had accepted that vague uneasy resentment in his friends, when he'd tried to explain his case. Now it seemed to him that they found relief in laughing at him.

"Is this all part of the big practical joke? Am I supposed to be a clown now?"

Facing them at bay, his eyes still blazing, he turned first to Mike, wanting to strike at him, then baffled, because he could prove nothing against him, he whirled around on Ray. "Okay," he whispered. "Laugh yourself out of this, Conlin," and he swung his right; it caught Ray high on the temple and he spun and fell.

Jumping up, Ray danced around, his narrow little eyes glittering with hate. Thrusting his finger out, he whispered, "Just wait, I'll fix you. You'll get it, but good!"

"Why wait?"

"I've got friends, you haven't. Nobody slaps me around. You'll see."

"Get out of here, Conlin. What kind of a place do you think this is?" Alfred suddenly shouted. "Look what you're doing. Is this a cheap little dive where I phone for the cops every hour?"

"You ask for it, Alfred," Harry said angrily, "if you have these little hatchet men for gangsters and cheap suit-and-cloak men here trying to palm off rotten goods — look at the coat, Alfred."

"Stop insulting me," Mike said, going closer. "You came in here with that coat looking for trouble. You came in here to disgrace me. Your mind's all twisted. You don't want me fix that coat. You want to flaunt it around and try and ruin me."

"You came in here making the whole thing public property, holding me up to ridicule," Harry said, disgusted. "You're as phony as a three-dollar bill."

"I'm no phony," Mike said, fiercely. "It was your little tramp who came at me about it." Then, with all the scornful resentment of Harry he was sure the others shared with him, he blurted out, "I know a guy who has disgraced himself is apt to take it out on anybody. But I'm not Scotty Bowman. You're not going to ruin me."

"To throw that up at me . . ." Harry whispered. For the first time he heard himself accused publicly, with the others, silent, uncomfortable and embarrassed, standing behind the morally outraged tailor. Looking beaten he turned to the door; he wanted to go, and then, as if this seemed cowardly, he turned again, very pale, and faced them with his old courage, struggling to find words to express his contempt. "You accuse me of these things with fine moral courage, thinking you have the good conscience of everybody behind you. Well, never mind, I know that over this little thing like a coat lining, you're hiding behind your friend Scotty. I think you thought you had a right to take advantage of me, and could get away with it in the eyes of everybody. That's what you're doing now. Could anything be more shameful for everybody?" Suddenly he laughed. "Well, if that's the way you want it, anybody who comes around here is going to see a lot of this coat."

⬦ XVI ⬦

*H*arry knew now that all his hopes of the Bowman business being forgotten had blown up on him, and that he had been mocked by his own goodwill, by the innocence of heart that had led him to go to Mike Kon. It seemed to him that Scotty's ghost was using Mike Kon to pursue him and drive him out of town again, or force him to go on defending himself against his accuser, to nag away, protesting till the boring insistence of his innocence finally destroyed him. All he had to defend himself with was the coat, he thought, but it could tell his story. Others now could do the explaining and interpreting.

He began to wear the coat everywhere, and when he had it on his back it looked like a well-cut handsome garment, but the story of what had happened in Dorfman's got around town much faster that he did, and people who used to be embarrassed by his presence and prefer to hold aloof would smile, seeing him wearing this coat they had heard about, and out of curiosity, ask to see the lining. When they tried to question him he kept his untroubled dignity and refused to give an explanation. As the story spread more people laughed at him and wanted to see the coat, and in Dorfman's especially he became a figure of fun. People, clowning with him, tried to get him to talk about the coat and defend himself. He would not. Unprovoked by their amusement, he hung onto his unruffled good humor. When really pressed for an explanation by someone who didn't know the story, all he would say was, "Why don't you ask Mike Kon?" and let it go at that, smiling when a questioner who had been laughing grew reflective.

He used to come into Dorfman's with his easy opulent manner. He didn't care who laughed at him. The only one who bothered him was Annie Laurie and he had found that he could never locate her at the hours when he went to Dorfman's.

On his way there late one afternoon he went into the hotel barbershop for a haircut and coming out he saw Annie Laurie in a yellow dress talking to a well-dressed gray-haired man who was buying some magazines at the newsstand. Feeling lonely, he turned away. But she had seen him, and caught up to him at the hotel entrance.

"What's the matter with you, Harry? You saw me," she said.

"Who's the guy?"

"Oh, him. I used to work for him ten years ago when I was a model. An utterly harmless man. He always sends me a Christmas card."

"Oh," he said, relieved.

"I know a girl has to live, Harry, but I don't want any guy near me while you're around, don't you believe me?"

"I do," and smiling, he took her arm and said, "Come on into Dorfman's with me."

"No, Harry," she said. "I'm not going into Dorfman's with you, I don't like it in there when you're wearing that damned coat. I can't bear the clowning that goes on in there, people looking at the lining and you refusing to say anything. I feel lonely, Harry, all the loneliness in the world seems to hit me right on the head." He looked worried for he could not bear hurting people who had all his affection, and he couldn't clown with Annie Laurie about the coat. "I respect you, Annie Laurie," he said, turning her toward him. "But can't you see I'm trapped around here. Scotty Bowman is on my back again. Old Mike Kon put him there. I didn't want it. I'm trapped around here because I won't go away again. I won't. This is my town. They think I can't get up off the floor. Annie Laurie," he said, quietly, "there's the principle of the thing. This coat," and he touched his shoulder, "this is the Scotty Bowman coat. Mike Kon put it on me when he accused me."

"Oh, Harry, now nobody has a chance to forget."

"So much the better," and he shrugged. "They'll laugh the pair of them, the ghost and his friend, right out of this town." But the way she was looking at him made him falter a little and he waited, ready to resist her stubbornly. Her dark head and the yellow dress suddenly looked lovely to him. "You're a stubborn man, Harry. But God knows, about the right things. I wish I could have been as stubborn myself," she said with a hurt and strange respect. "You've a right to fight in your own way, Harry. I don't care as long as you know I'm with you," and he laughed a little, satisfied.

"Coming with me?" he said.

"Not this time. Some other time," and she watched him go up the street alone and turn into Dorfman's.

⬧ XVII ⬧

*H*e always sat at the bar joking and paying no attention to Mike at all. At first Mike didn't mind being questioned about the coat even with Harry at the bar only twenty feet away. He was sure he had public support; he was sure public opinion had long ago condemned Harry Lane, so he explained patiently that he had offered to fix the coat lining and that Harry had insulted him. "But why did you have Conlin try to steal the coat?" someone would ask, and with patience and dignity he would explain that he hadn't offered to pay Conlin fifty dollars to get the coat. It had been only a joking remark. They always laughed knowingly when he repeated Conlin hadn't been acting for him. They enjoyed hearing him defending himself. In a few days he began to see that they didn't believe him, or at least they pretended not to believe him; he wasn't sure, and he could not understand it.

Late one afternoon Ray Conlin, who had met Eddie Adams on the street, and had attached himself to him so he could get back into Dorfman's, came in, hoping Alfred would not notice. Even the cigars smell better in Dorfman's, Ray thought as he looked around. Mike was sitting by himself near the window, the shaft of late sunlight touching his ear and heavy jaw as he watched people passing on the street with a very affected untroubled air. Anyone could see that he was determinedly there at that hour.

At the end of the bar, Harry Lane was wearing the coat and smiling peacefully, with his back to the table where Mollie Morris was sitting with Ted Ogilvie. People who came in glanced at the coat, smiled, made little jokes with him while he laughed good-naturedly, and then these same people would look over at Mike and smile.

Everybody was smiling at Mike and Harry, and Harry didn't mind, but Mike couldn't stand it.

Ray was afraid to follow Eddie to the bar and invite attention from Harry, who hadn't noticed him come in, so he hurried over to Mike's table. When Mike paid no attention to him he said sympathetically, "You see the item in Mallon's column, 'The Man with the Coat?' You see it?"

"I saw it," he said bitterly. "And tomorrow my lawyer'll see it too."

"So what do you do, Mike?"

"I have rights, and I know what that item means. People read that item and then they ask Lane about it and he laughs and refuses to say anything. I get slandered." His face white, he looked over at Harry who didn't seem to be aware that he was in the room; reaching out with his eyes to the coat, he longed to get his hands on it for only a few minutes. "No. How can I sue?" he said, half to himself, with an embarrassing despair. "I think he'd like to get it in the papers." Then as Ray eased himself into the chair beside him, he said quickly, "No, Ray. Not here with me. There's been trouble with you here. Alfred told you to keep away. Please."

Just then Alfred Dorfman passed by Ray and looked right through him. I'm not here, Ray thought resentfully. I'm a ghost. He and his waiters walk right through me. Staring at Harry shrewdly, Ray thought he saw something, a real weakness in him; the man had too much imagination. Any fighter he had ever known who had too much imagination was no good, and what he liked about his own boy Bruno was that he had no imagination at all.

It seemed to him to be such a shrewd and interesting observation that he leaned closer to the next table where Ogilvie and Miss Morris were sitting, but he had to wait to get a word in.

"For Harry to sit there and take it," she was saying, her voice breaking. "No shame at all left. Not a scrap."

"If he's able to keep on laughing long enough," Ted said, "he's apt to laugh the ghost of Scotty Bowman right out of town. Why should you feel ashamed now, Mollie?"

"Because . . . because . . ." and her voice was low and resentful. "I'm sure he thinks that somehow he's humiliating me. I'm not crazy, Ted. I know it's so. Why do you think he's always bringing that pushover, Annie Laurie, around?"

"Ah, now there, that's interesting," Ted said philosophically. "I've thought about that. Any guy who stays with Annie Laurie knows his number's up." When they both became reflective, Ray, leaning closer and putting his hand on the back of Ted's chair with professional firmness, said, "Look, I get paid to watch for a fighter's weakness. I spot it in Harry. It's his big imagination."

"Shut up, Conlin," Ogilvie said sourly.

"Run along, little man, you're annoying me," Miss Morris said, looking around impatiently for Alfred.

"Excuse me," Ray said, getting up quickly and hurrying out. Little man. I annoy them, he thought fiercely, as he went on gloomily down the hill to his hotel opposite the railroad station.

With all his heart he wanted to get back to Dorfman's, and he sighed and wiped his forehead and cursed his luck. Maybe he wasn't very high-toned, he thought, but he was a human being and he had a right to some justice. His only crime was in trying to show he had a sense of humor. He had had no ill will toward Harry. Yet he was the one who was now the outcast. The injustice of it made tears come to his eyes. No one cared about Harry knocking him down; the only thing that registered on them was that he had taken it. That was it, he thought, pondering. He had done nothing and so people despised him. Mike Kon was making the same mistake, sitting by the window and trying to tell his silly tiresome story with dignity. I won't go on making that stupid mistake, he thought grimly.

◆ XVIII ◆

*E*ven when Ray was doing road work with Bruno next day, pedaling slowly on the bicycle while Bruno, in beautiful condition, his breathing rhythmical and effortless, his eyes clear and happy, trotted along beside him, he went on making his plan. He was sure he could afford to show a little audacity in dealing with Harry; public opinion was so much against Harry that everybody would see the justice of having him slapped down and view it with an amused and vast satisfaction. The thing to do, he thought, would be to have him punished so everybody in Dorfman's, where he still hung on the ropes, could see it and make their enjoyment of the rightness of it so plain that Lane might never want to put his nose in the place again.

That night he went down to St. Lawrence in the east end to a neighborhood where Johnny Bruno was really a great hero and where he himself was an important figure. When he climbed the long stairs to the Coq d'Or he took care to carry himself with dignity. It was a big crowded garish hall with a dance floor and a quartet. The tables were crowded with young punks in sharp suits, most of them speaking French and they laughed noisily and clowned for each other and paid no attention to Josette, the singer, but when he, Ray Conlin, made his way through the tables, leaning well back, his hands in his pockets, his head high, taking his time, he heard some young fellow say, "Hey, look, Bruno's manager," and he smiled slightly but didn't turn. All around the dance floor he went toward a table where a huge smiling gray-haired man sat alone. "A little business, a little monkey business," Ray said casually, and he sat down. They tried to hold the conversation in whispers. Ray gave the details about Harry Lane, handed over a small roll of dollars, and left his phone number for further details.

When he was outside he began to feel great pride in his resourcefulness. On the hot summer night St. Catherine was crowded. The girls drifted by with linked arms, trailed by pimply-faced boys. The middle-aged couples looked in store windows. It was Bruno's neighborhood. So Ray swaggered and brushed through these little people who were trying to brighten their lives looking in shop windows on a hot night.

He didn't need Mike at all, he thought. The nice part of it was that by this time everybody would be figuring that Mike ought to have had Harry beaten up long ago, and he smiled.

Now he could see that all the trouble for him at Dorfman's had begun because he has associated himself with Mike Kon, a mistake he wouldn't make again. Last night Mike had looked worried and old. He remembered hearing Oscar Strauss, the promoter at the Garden, saying, "There's a rule for getting along. Never associate with people on the downgrade." Mike Kon was definitely on the downgrade.

⬦ XIX ⬦

*T*hat day in Mike's store business had been slow and at five o'clock he went into his office and took out his books so he could compare this week with the week of a year ago. The comparison told him nothing. A year ago the business had only been building. Yet aside from the comparison it had been a dull week. I'm a fool, he thought. I sit here waiting for lightning to hit me. From the back room came the sound of Willie moving around and Mike went to the door and looked in, wanting to talk to him about "The Man with the Coat" piece in the paper, yet balding Willie's impassive face as he stood there, the tape measure around his neck, now seemed alien; in the beginning Willie had said bluntly, "What's the matter with you, Mike? It couldn't have been the cleaning fluid." Even now, as their eyes met, it seemed to him Willie was pretending, in his wooden British manner, to be unaware that there had been any further trouble.

At noontime next day I.L. Singerman, himself, a short broad man with a paunch and glasses, came into the store and said he had just dropped in, being in the neighborhood, and he talked about the hot weather, the textile strike and the damned union agitators.

Looking out the window Mr. Singerman asked what was this story he had heard at the Variety Club where he had been lunching with some movie exhibitor, about a coat for Harry Lane that had fallen to pieces.

"Mr. Singerman, I told your man about that piece of lining," Mike said.

"Mike, I've got money in this business."

"So have I, Mr. Singerman. All I have in the world."

"So why didn't you fix the man's coat — like that?" he said, snapping his fingers.

"I asked him to let me fix the coat."

"So?"

"He wouldn't. It's just spite."

"You asked him and he wouldn't. Spite. Is it possible? Does it make sense? A man everybody talked about for months."

"What could I do, Mr. Singerman? I offered to fix the coat," Mike said, and he leaned wearily against the long oaken table.

He knew he couldn't explain his resentment of Harry to Mr. Singerman. The man had never read a good book. His knowledge of Mr. Singerman's basic illiteracy suddenly helped him, it made him feel sane and patient. "It's a complicated story," he said. "A story that has to be figured out."

Singerman said irritably, "So why should we hear any more about the damned coat? Go to his place, speak to him in a nice way as one substantial man to another. Make him a new suit, if he wants it, with an extra pair of pants. Handstitching on the lapels. Make it three pair of pants. But get that coat back from him. Well, go to it," he said grimly on the way out, and Mike moved over to the window and watched him get into his car. How quick he is to push me around, he thought, trembling. How quickly he'd drop me if he thought I had a bad name. As he watched the people hurrying by his window he longed with all his heart to get the coat back so he could fix it.

When he tried to concentrate on making a plan he thought his head would burst, then suddenly he seemed to know what he could do; he could go to Harry and say, "I was wrong in throwing up Scotty's death at you. I've thought about it and I've come to the conclusion I've no real knowledge of the facts. You could be blameless."

Then he actually felt himself blushing. To say these things against all his conviction would be intolerably unworthy of his self-respect, he thought, and what was worse, anyone who heard of him doing it would despise him. All I need to do is to hold out in Dorfman's till he cracks, he thought.

◇ **XX** ◇

*A*t that hour Harry was in his room waiting in the chair by the window, the morning paper on his knee, and the radio his landlady, Mrs. Benoit, had loaned him, playing softly. It was hot and he kept dabbing restlessly with his handkerchief at the little beads of moisture on his forehead.

He stayed in his room because he didn't want to go to the Ritz bar, or the M.A.A. Club or to any of the old places until the issue had been settled in Dorfman's. Every day at noontime he waited in his lonely room for two hours, and he was there for the same time after dinner, but not really according to any plan; he didn't admit to himself that he was waiting. Yet all his faith in himself prompted him to keep on believing that someone would come soon and tell him the stand he had taken had made people realize he must have been wronged. The power of his own imagination, the truth he was sure was in everybody's imagination seemed to him to compel someone to take this step. Someone soon would have to come. Back in his mind he hoped Mike Kon would be the one. So far nobody had come.

A knock on the door made him turn hopefully. Any step in the hall, someone outside his door, always quickened him. It was only Mrs. Benoit. "Why, come in, Mrs. Benoit," he said, graciously. His unaffected simple goodwill always made her feel she was a dignified and interesting person. Her gray hair was curled and she was dressed to go out, and she smiled apologetically. It had been so hot last night she said, and she wondered if he had been able to sleep. While she talked she poked around the room, straightening the magazines on his table and picking up his slippers, which she put in the clothes closet. The grim, humorless woman, who knew nothing about him, had taken a liking to him. She found excuses for coming into the room when he was there, knowing he was lonely. She believed he was looking for a job. Straightening the pillows on his bed while he smiled at her, she told him she had a cousin who was an insurance company executive; he needed someone to translate the French correspondence into English, and had told this cousin about the young man staying with her who spoke perfect French. "You could do it at home," she said, "and it would carry you over. Why don't you go over there now and see him?"

"Why, I will," he said. "I'll go down there right now," and he thanked her.

On the way out he stopped and thought, to carry me over, and he smiled, and the radio was still playing. Mrs. Benoit hadn't turned it off. He went down the street and across the square, and there were pigeons waddling on the walk, and he remembered the day he had crossed the square with Scotty Bowman. In the insurance company office he talked with Mrs. Benoit's cousin, a plump jolly man with a little black mustache and round bright eyes. "Harry Lane. Oh, Harry Lane," he said, as if trying to remember, and then suddenly, half turning away he smiled. Waiting uneasily, Harry flushed. But the man told him he could have the work; he told him what he wanted done. But his smile, the way he had placed him with the smile, remembering something he had heard, bothered Harry till he got outside. Then he thought suddenly; no one used to smile remembering something they had heard or read about me and Scotty Bowman. It was only a little thing for the man was a stranger, yet it seemed to be remarkably significant. In that man's smile, he told himself, there certainly hadn't been any of that old uneasy resentment. The more he thought of it the more hopeful he felt, and for a change he went to a movie and when he got home, after eating, he telephoned Annie Laurie and told her about the job. From now on he would have a little income, he said, something to tide him over. They should celebrate, she said gaily, there was a circus in town, how would he like to take her to the circus, and he said he would be right over. Then he went to the window and looked out; it had clouded up. The window curtains hung straight and still. It might rain. Rain might end the unseasonable heat but he didn't want anything to spoil the few free careless hours he could have at the circus before it was time to go to Dorfman's.

The circus was on the outskirts of town and it was much cooler even under the lanes of lights than it was in the city, and he liked the way she walked through the crowd in her yellow dress. It was not a big circus, the side shows were nothing, although in the main tent there were three old clowns that made Annie Laurie laugh like a young girl. The Ferris wheel was small. Then they found the little red cars with the rubber bumpers and the unpredictable steering wheels and they took to them; for ride after ride he tried to master the tricky steering wheel. In the small area the cars bumped crazily into each other while the drivers tried to avoid a jam in the middle of the floor. Again and again Harry crashed into three other cars, though he jiggled the steering wheel frantically, yet he was always happy-eyed and laughing; he couldn't successfully disengage the car and back out. "Look at me, Harry, look at me!" Annie Laurie screamed suddenly. Waving grandly she cruised freely around the other uncontrolled little cars, and twice again she circled them serenely before the ride was over. "Well, anyway, one of us did it," he said, taking her arm and walking her toward the hamburger booth. "I guess it's one of those things a woman is good at." "Sour grapes," she said. "I do the right things and crash into everybody," he protested. "You do all the wrong things and sail merrily on your way."

Sitting down at the counter stool he suddenly looked at his wristwatch and was uneasy, then their eyes met, and she knew he was thinking of getting to Dorfman's on time, but she was afraid to say she wished he didn't have to go there tonight. Now they never spoke of Mike Kon. While she was eating her hamburger he watched her, smiling to himself. He liked the enjoyment in her eyes and the way her small tongue touched her lips, and the way she kept moving the shoulder straps of her dress on her warm bare shoulders.

"You know, I have such a good appetite," she said, swinging round on the stool. "I know I, too, am going to live to be an old woman."

"You too?"

"Well, I had three uncles and they all lived to be over ninety. So in the family there's this longevity or lonjevity, which is it, Harry?"

"It's like lonjevity."

"But why? It doesn't make sense. Long is long."

"Of course it doesn't make sense," he said. "But long is from an old Anglo-Saxon word, and longevity had a Latin source."

"Well, fancy anyone knowing that. How about your people?"

"Both my mother and father died young."

"Which one are you like?"

"Well, I don't know," he said thoughtfully, his elbows on the counter as he reflected. "They were very different in every way." Gradually, as he remembered, he began to look troubled, and she waited. Finally his head went back proudly, "In their different ways they both had great self-esteem." Then he seemed to be bothered by some implication in his own words, and he looked at her, expecting some comment, the stubborn light in his eyes. But she didn't know what he wanted her to say.

He had looked at his watch for the third time like a man who knew he was going to be late for an appointment he did not really want to keep, and she turned away quickly, moved and understanding he was happy there and didn't want to go to Dorfman's; all his natural generosity was against it. He had picked up a paper napkin and was wiping his mouth. Out of the corner of her eye she watched him, then again she had to turn away from his silence and his ravaged face to hide the tears that came to her eyes, and hide too her knowledge that he was struggling with his pride which was driving him to Dorfman's. In the uneasy silence between them the strident brassy music from the merry-go-round seemed to be far away. And while he struggled with himself she felt the anguish of half understanding, just by way of feeling and the look in his eyes, that his innocence which, in spite of his war years and his background, had made him Scotty's dupe, the innocence which he had asserted and which everybody had rejected, had turned into a monstrous pride, and it was driving him on.

"The smell of that food cooking there isn't right for such a hot night, come on," he said, awkward and apologetic, and they started home.

On the way he said to her, "I've noticed something, Annie Laurie. When I suggest we eat someplace you always name a little place in the east end. Or we go to some place like this circus. Out-of-the-way places. Why?"

"Well, you don't want to be seen everywhere with me, Harry?"

"Why don't I?"

"In a little while you'll want me to drop out of your life."

"Annie Laurie, till the day I die I want you to be somewhere in my life."

"Oh, you'll drift back to your own place, the place you should have in this town. I can see that coming. It started today with that little job," she said.

"Why not? Why not?" he said, then they both kept their thoughts to themselves. All evening she had been aware of his hopeful cheerfulness; now she was thinking that underneath his anger and disgust with so many people was his naturally optimistic nature prompting him to grasp at some happy little sign, like the talk with the insurance man, to strengthen his faith in himself and his imagination. He, on the other hand, was wondering if she believed his cheerfulness hid some despair and was trying to cheer him up, and suddenly he smiled at her.

When they got to her place it was only eleven, but she said she was going to bed. Standing at her door, half in the shadow, she laughed. "I'll dream that everybody in town drives a little red car with a broken steering wheel. Everybody but me, Harry." "Good night," he said, and he kissed her. "I should get some sleep myself." Still, she didn't ask him where he was going.

He looked ahead at the light over Dorfman's. Each night it got a little harder for him to go in, and now, the same as last night, he thought of his father and mother and how they used to go to Dorfman's. There it was just ahead with its door under the wrought-iron light, a place full of familiar memories, always touching him so freshly now, and troubling him: it was that time when he was nineteen, a month after he had started college, and he had gone in there and had seen his father standing at the bar in his gray suit, his hair prematurely white, and wearing a red tie, and he had been embarrassed. Beckoning to him, his father had said to Alfred, "If my son is going to come to this bar, Alfred, then he should have his first drink here with you and me."

Night after night in those days he had been there and had seen his father coming downstairs from the Peacock dining room. What would they say if they could see me in there tonight, he thought, looking at the slits of light coming from the curtained windows. No, they'd be with me, he thought. His father, a little flamboyant and explosive, would curse the shame of the whole thing and shout, "By God, you're my son, Harry, don't let them do this to you," and his mother, her fine blue eyes fierce with indignation, would say, "I'd never be ashamed of anything you do, Harry, if you believe it's right."

Maybe Mike Kon won't be there tonight, he thought. Each night he said this hopefully to himself before turning in at the steps, and each night he felt a little more optimistic. Now he wanted this to be the one night when he could go in and sit there with the time passing till finally everyone realized that Mike had not shown up. If this could only happen two or three times in a row, he told himself, it would mean that Mike had grown ashamed of sitting there in his presence. It had to happen. All the signs were there. The focus of attention had shifted from him to Mike and therein lay the significance of the whole thing. The others, with their laughter, their derision and kidding, were putting it up to Mike. Soon there would be nothing for Mike to do but return from the place, laughed out of court, as the spokesman for Scotty Bowman, or come to him, shamefaced and good-natured, and try and negotiate a truce. In a sudden flight of fancy he seemed to see Mike coming over to him saying, "I can see how a man can get himself in a bad light with people. Maybe they don't want to believe me, I don't know. This could ruin me, just as people talking have tried to ruin you. Only a badly wronged man would go on like you do, Harry. Maybe I had no right to jump to conclusions." If Mike could only have the simple human charity to make this gesture, it would be enough, he thought, and he could stop wearing the coat, for people would ask Mike what had happened, and Mike would have to explain; with these explanations of the dropping of his accusations, Mike, whether he liked it or not, would really become his advocate.

Two men who had been looking in the dress-shop window on the other side of Dorfman's had come down the street. "Got a match, pal?" asked the one in the powder-blue suit, stopping at the Dorfman steps. "Sure," he said, shoving his hand in his pocket. As his fingers touched the match folder, the other fellow, the one without a coat, who had taken a few steps past him, turned, came closer and swung. Out of the corner of his eye Harry saw the arm looping in the light, but his own hand was in his pocket; the blow caught him on the left temple and he half spun, trying to keep his balance, then the taller one who had spoken to him came in punching hard with both hands while he staggered, trying not to go down. He felt the pain on his eye and jaw and he yelled wildly, "Help, help, help." As they both came at him he punched savagely with both hands at the nearest face, a cruel young vicious face in the Dorfman light, the mouth sagging open, and he felt his own fist crack against bone, and heard the moan, then the whimper, but the other one had dived at his legs, pinioning them, and he went down. One of them got an arm lock on him; his arm seemed to be breaking. His face was against the sidewalk. "Give it to him." The blows came on his face and he tried to roll away.

There was a flash of light; it was in his own mind; then the darkness closing down and new voices; a mob seemed to be beating him and he cursed with rage. Suddenly he was free, lying on the ground. The other voice had come from a car that had driven up and stopped, the motor running. His two assailants were getting into the car, one still whimpering.

Raising himself to his knees, he shook his head to clear it, and blood from his nose and mouth fell on his hand. He stood up slowly and lurched toward the steps. His left arm hung heavy and numb at his side and he blinked but could hardly see it. He wanted to get his handkerchief but it was in the left trouser pocket. Climbing the steps he trembled all over but his head had cleared and when he took a deep shaky breath and then another deeper one, sucking in the air, his strength came back to him and he opened the door and went in.

The patrons had crowded around the window, having heard the cries from the street, and Ted Ogilvie was the first one to turn and see him standing at the door. "Harry, it's Harry," he shouted and he came hurrying to him with Haggerty.

"Sooner or later, this had to happen," Haggerty said.

"Give me a drink," Harry said, breathing heavily as he leaned against the bar.

"Take this, Harry. It's brandy."

"To hell with brandy. Give me my Canadian Club."

"What's happened? Who was it, Harry?"

"They're gone in a car."

"Who were they?"

"Two hoods I've never seen in my life," and he sat down by the bar and took the cloth the barman tossed to him and wiped his eye slowly, staring at the blood on the cloth, then he concentrated patiently on wiping his face.

"Did they get your wallet, Harry?" the barman asked.

"My wallet! Hell, they weren't after my wallet," he said, looking up blankly. "It was me, you understand. It was a job, a job," and he closed his eyes and swallowed hard. His left arm was bothering him and he raised it slowly very delicately, and then he winced. "I thought the damn thing was broken," he said, with a grotesque smile for his puffed-up left eye was closing.

"Take it easy, Harry. I'll get a doctor," Alfred said.

"Where did they come from?"

"A thing like that on this street."

"They were waiting for me," he said, impatiently. "Which means they knew I'd be coming here at this hour. Two hoods planted there to jump me. Who planted them there? Who do I know who's crazy enough to have me beaten up?" and he looked around. Just back of the circle of patrons was Mike.

Only a few feet away, at the bar, was Ray Conlin smoking his cigar, his black eyes bright and amused.

"Everybody knows the one guy who'd like to have me beaten to a pulp," Harry said bitterly. "So you still know where to go to get a job done, eh, Mr. Kon?"

"Now I know you're out of your mind," Mike said.

"So you finally called in your hoods," Harry said, his swollen face twisting into a laugh. "Still hiding behind others."

"Wait a minute," Mike said fiercely. "I won't take this. I don't need the help of any hoods. That twisted mind of yours!" Then he took on an air of scornful dignity. "Nobody believes you anyway. I don't stoop to take you seriously. Nobody any longer takes anything you do seriously."

"Has Kon been coming around here this early, Alfred?" Harry asked.

"Well, not this early, Harry."

"Then why does he show up tonight? Just to have a ringside seat, of course."

"I show up here because I like it here," Mike said. "I sit here minding my business. Ask anybody."

"Yes, he's in here," Haggerty said, looking at Mike so thoughtfully that Mike felt insulted. "But you don't expect him to admit anything, do you?"

"Do you think he'd have the courage to act on his own? Him and Conlin, I say."

"Not me and Conlin," Mike said furiously.

"You see, Alfred," Harry said. "Him and Conlin," and he laughed again. "A pair. Kon and Conlin. Konlin. Little Kon," and then he turned on Ray. "You threatened to get me, didn't you, little Kon. You and Mike fixed it, didn't you?" and he came closer and Ray made a move to defend himself, scowling ferociously.

"Maybe you're right, Harry, only you can't prove anything," Haggerty said, and he grabbed at his arm, for Mike had hunched up his shoulders trying to control himself.

"I'm not going to hit him," Harry said. "That's been done before. He's just Kon's hatchet man anyway."

"I'm nobody's hatchet man. I'm Bruno's trainer. Don't you forget it," Ray shouted. "Bruno's a national name."

"Trainer! You're just that gangster Rosso's water boy."

"Tell it to Rosso when he comes up here for the fight."

"You tell him this, Conlin. Tell him you worked on the side for Mr. Kon and he ran out on you. You know what I'm going to do? I'm going to have you deported for having a hand in planting those hoods out there."

"A big man. He runs the government now," Ray jeered.

"Come on, Harry, and wash yourself up," Haggerty said soothingly, with his good-natured patronizing half-contemptuous tolerance of him.

Motionless and rooted there, Mike glared at Ray, but couldn't catch his eye; Ray seemed to be off by himself, scaring himself, feeling the touch of a mysterious new fear in Harry's threat.

Alfred took an angry step toward Ray. "Listen Conlin," he said. "Beat it. If you come around here again I'll have you thrown on your face in the middle of the road." Turning his back on Conlin he looked around and Mike met his eyes; he held his angry eyes, feeling himself being pushed out of the place and down the street and back to the cheap neighborhood where he had grown up; then Alfred beckoned to him and went over to the door, out of earshot of the others.

"What's on your mind, Alfred?" Mike said.

"I've never had any trouble in here, Mike," Alfred said, his face reddening. "It's not that kind of a place. I won't have this happen to Harry in my place. I don't care what you and the rest of the world have against him. I'm asking a favor of you. You're all right too, I guess, but as far as I'm concerned you've taken a mean advantage of him in my place. I'd be awfully obliged to you if you'd keep away."

"That's a real insult, Alfred," Mike said, the blood draining from his face, and then he added proudly, "It's not a thing I'd choose to argue about." As he walked out stiffly he said to Ray, "You rat. But they'll deport you right back to 14th Street." The light caught the gray at Mike's temples and the heavy lines on his forehead and he looked tired and old, and a little wild.

⋄ XXI ⋄

*T*he night after Harry had told Ray he was going to have him deported, Ray was in his small room in the second-class hotel near the Windsor Station with a view overlooking an alley shaft. The carpet was worn threadbare. All night long he heard the shunting of engines and if he turned out the light a neon sign on a nearby roof kept flashing its pinkish light across the foot of the bed. But in the three months he had been there the room had become truly his home.

He had never had a home until now where he could feel that he was by himself with some life that belonged to him alone. When he had been a boy in New York on Tenth Avenue he had been scared of the police, and his mother in her turn had always been scared she couldn't keep her family together. When Ray had made his connection with Rosso he had been sure he had found someone who could give him protection, although he had never been able to figure out why he needed this protection. Policemen had only a few small cases against him, honest men ignored him, and yet he had a secret hidden knowledge that someday he might be grabbed by nameless people and accused of some crime he wouldn't understand if he didn't have a big fellow there to fix it for him.

Yet in this room, far away from Rosso where he could pretend he was Bruno's manager, for the first time in his life he had that appearance of some authority of his own. Boys who worshiped young Bruno were proud to be invited to this room, and so were two-bit gamblers. Waitresses he brought there were awed when he showed them with a little flourish the picture-magazine story on Rosso with his own picture on the next page. On these occasions, when he rang for room service he felt compelled to toss a dollar tip to the waiter. He used to lie on the bed with his shoes off, smoking cigars and wondering why he felt so warm, lazy, loving and opulent.

Sighing, he sat down to take off his shoes. He had weak arches, and if his heels got worn a little his feet ached. Holding up one of the shoes he squinted at the heel, then suddenly he hurled it across the room, jumped up, and began to pad up and down, telling himself that Harry Lane couldn't have him deported; nothing had been proved against him. But he knew that people in authority would like to do something for a famous broken-down war hero, if it cost them nothing. Lane had been a big man, and he knew all the big men. So right now the police were probably hunting for the two who had beaten up on Lane. When they were found they would squeal, and he would be convicted. If they deport me I'll be finished with Rosso, he thought, and he began to sweat. His little black eyes were bright and staring. Someone else would have to come from Rosso to handle Bruno.

Undressing, he got into bed and lay there while the pink light flickered across the bed and tried to understand how he had got involved in the beginning. The trains shunted, the canal boats whistled and later the monastery bells chimed; the day came, and there was the hum of the station opening its doors to the city business. Still he couldn't sleep. He dozed a little. At ten o'clock the maid opened the door with her master key; she wanted to clean the room. He scowled at her, then quickly apologized; now he needed all his friends. He got dressed, walked up to St. Catherine, got some coffee, then came back and slept on the made bed, and at three he went to the gym for Bruno's workout, his mind made up that he would forget all about Harry Lane.

While he was rubbing the boy down, his fingers working surely and patiently, he started worrying again. "Everything's clowning and horsing around in this town," he complained, his fingers slackening their pressure as he stared, unseeing, at Bruno's gleaming limbs.

"What's the matter, Ray?"

"You know this Mollie Morris?" Ray asked.

"The column in the *Sun*? Sure, Ray."

"Right. She has a big following, wouldn't you say?"

"They give her a big play in this town."

"High-class stuff? High-class readership?"

"My old man reads her," Bruno said with dignity, raising his head and smiling, "Is she doing a story on me? I would like that very much."

"I'm going to see what I can do, Johnny." He got the telephone book and looked up Miss Morris' address. She lived on Bishop, three blocks away from the Ritz.

He tried to kid with Bruno so he wouldn't notice that he was worried. When they were both getting dressed, Bruno asked him if he could drop him off anywhere. He had a nice Ford convertible, and Ray, with a light air to impress Bruno, told him he could drop him off at the Ritz.

When he got out of the car to wait until it pulled away, the big-nosed Ritz doorman looked at him very stuffily and Ray tried to make it plain he had a low opinion of him too, then walked west, with the sun in his eyes, turned halfway down Bishop to an old stone house, climbed the stairs and stood listening at the door before he pressed the bell.

When she opened the door the words he had prepared wouldn't come easily because she was wearing a black sweater and white slacks, her black hair was hanging on her shoulders, and her eyes were unfriendly. "Oh, Mr. Conlin," she said. "What do you want?"

"Could I speak to you a minute, Miss Morris?"

"No, I'm busy, Conlin," she said, and he knew she did not want him in her house.

"This is so damned important to me, Miss Morris," he pleaded. "It's about Harry Lane."

"Well, come in," she said reluctantly.

The spotless whiteness of the walls and the black mantel and the gold rug upset him, and she left him standing there uneasily while she fumbled in the white pants for her cigarettes.

"Look, Miss Morris," he blurted out. "Harry thinks I'm responsible for that beating he got."

"Well?"

"He's going to have me deported. I've already been thrown out of Dorfman's. Harry's still got some big government friends who'll do things for him for the sake of the old days. I've had a lot of publicity. I mean that magazine story, and it'll be used against me to hound me out of here."

"So you'll be deported. What do I care?" she said, walking away from him to drop the ashes from her cigarette on the tray at the end of the ivory-colored sofa. "You disgust me," she said.

"You don't know how I feel," he blurted out desperately. "I'm entitled to a little justice. Do I get no justice because I get mixed up with people like Harry and you? You're a judge's daughter," he said angrily. "Why do you want to work on a newspaper and go everywhere alone with that smile? You sit around with the guys in Dorfman's and you go to the fights, and it's all just slumming. I've read your column. All those little guys you write about don't touch you. All for laughs. It don't put any spots on those nice white pants. You don't know what goes on inside people. What counts with a woman like you? There don't have to be no justice for a woman like you."

Then she turned on him wrathfully. "The nerve of you coming here like this and insulting me about Harry Lane."

"I don't want to insult you," he insisted desperately. "I don't want to insult nobody. That's my point. I make a practical joke about the coat. I goofed. I'm not quick. I'm good-humored, not quick, see, and I get a punch on the jaw for my joke. Is that justice? Miss Morris, who do you respect who takes a punch, and does nothing? I was happy around here, my nose clean, too. So I'm to be deported. Nobody speaks to me. Justice, justice." He was following her around the room and then over to the window, growing more desperately baffled by her grim silent anger, the stiffness of her body, her folded arms and her eyes that didn't see him — anger all turned in on herself, tormenting her, since he had told her the kind of woman she was. He couldn't cope with this silent inward-going anger and the slow reddening of her neck. "You, that slut Annie Laurie, Harry. The kind of woman I am," she whispered, yet she seemed to have forgotten that he was there. He was frightened now by her silence and its sadness, and some kind of strange passionate regret in her tormented eyes and she had this very clean smell with a little touch of perfume on her and her mouth began to tremble as if she were suffering. She was looking down at the back gardens, and he looked out too. In the garden next door were many flowers and a pear tree. Two visiting nuns were there in the garden. As they moved under the pear tree in the shade, Miss Morris, half angrily, muttered to herself, "Why is it that nuns look so well under a pear tree in the sunlight?"

"I don't know," he said blankly.

"What?"

"What do you mean?"

"You little fool," she said, turning on him fiercely. "Harry Lane have you deported! He doesn't expect anybody to take him that seriously. All he wants to do is make a fool of himself. Hasn't he turned away from everything decent, from common sense, remorse, from love, the pity and pride of love, to make himself nothing with sluts and morons like you? Go on, you fool. He won't have you deported. People won't stand any more from him. No more, not even the ruin of a jerk like you. People won't stand for it, I tell you. Now get out of here. Get out!"

"Okay, okay, Miss Morris," he said quickly. "I see you have great readership, great respect," and backing away from her to the door he was glad to get out.

On the street he stood looking up and down mopping his head. "The people I'm in with now," he thought. "Nuns looking well in the sunlight under a pear tree. Christ!" and then as his success with her began to dazzle him he grinned happily, and walked along whistling.

When he got to Peel he stopped, looking down at Dorfman's, where people were going in. He wanted to show a little defiance to someone so he loafed down the street and when he saw Ted Ogilvie getting out of a taxi he was delighted.

"Hi, Ted," he called waiting with a big friendly grin.

"Why, you little rat. I heard we had seen the last of you around here," Ted said sourly.

"Hell, all you're doing is believing that crazy guy Lane's story," and he started to chuckle. "I don't have to help him break his neck. He's doing it himself."

"You won't be here to see it. You'll be deported," Ogilvie said, taunting him.

"Deport me. Who? That crazy guy?"

"It's a good idea, and he'd have lots of support."

"Who can Lane count on?"

"Who can you count on?"

"I can count on Mollie Morris."

"Mollie Morris," Ted said incredulously.

"Yeah, Miss Morris. She's in my corner. With her behind me, to hell with Harry Lane," and he laughed defiantly. The surprise in Ogilvie's eyes delighted him. I'll be back in Dorfman's after the fight, he thought.

❖ XXII ❖

*A*ll night Mike lay awake twitching like a middle-aged man dreading the future, and in the dark he heard voices repeating, "Kicked out of Dorfman's just like a bum. Kicked out of Dorfman's . . ." But the night was long, and in moments of dreadful clarity, free of the tossing and twitching, he saw his Dorfman disgrace as a big step toward his ruin, for Singerman, hearing of it, would believe, of course, like everybody else, that he had actually had a hand in the beating, and say his advice had been answered with violence. As a businessman, Singerman might say he couldn't afford to be associated with an old fighter who was an outcast from a place where the best people went. "I won't be an outcast," Mike said so loudly that his own voice in the darkness startled him and he sat up in bed. Then he heard a cat in the lane behind the building. The window was open a few inches. The weeds that bothered his hay fever grew in the lane. Again he heard the cat dragging at the lid of the garbage pail. The lid clattered and rolled and he jumped up, slammed the window shut, then he clenched his big fists with the broken knuckles and stood in a trance for a long time.

At four o'clock, the bells began to chime in the monastery down the street and he went to bed and lay in the dark counting the bells, hoping sleep would come to him when the monks had done all their praying. But at five there were more bells, and Harry Lane seemed to be ringing them wildly and happily.

In the morning he was so tired he felt sick, and he went down to the shop and told Willie he had a headache, and needed some sleep. All afternoon he stayed in the office. He stayed there till nine in the evening, then he went upstairs and into the room where his father sat by the window, the pencil stuck between the thumb and forefinger, the swollen hand resting on the big pad. "Hi there, papa," he said, patting him on the shoulder affectionately as he looked at the little lines and scratches on the pad. His father's one good eye was blinking at him fiercely. Tonight he longed to believe there was more than intelligence and understanding in that gray eye and that his father could see how worried he was. Day after day he had been talking to his father about the coat and Harry Lane just as candidly as he might have talked to himself.

"It's still that Harry Lane," he said, walking around the room, his hands linked behind his back. "I'm to keep out of Dorfman's. I'm thrown out of Dorfman's. Imagine — the disgrace. I don't know what I've done," he said sighing. "I honestly don't. In this little thing wouldn't you think people would stand behind me? All this snickering at me. Why do they want to believe I got Conlin to lift the coat? Why believe that I had Lane beaten up? What are they trying to do to me? Nobody believes me. Why are the facts all against me? What is there about me now . . . now . . . that makes them snicker? What do I have to do to get someone to believe me?"

Stopping by the window he pondered, looking down at the street lights and hearing all the familiar street sounds coming through the open window; the voices of passing people in the warm sultry night, the voices sounding loud, then the rattle of the trolley, then the cars, always the cars.

"Singerman's car'll be stopping out there tomorrow or the next day," he said, turning again to his father. "He'll hear about me being told to keep out of Dorfman's. It'll mean a lot to him. He's apt to drop me. What'll I do?" Suddenly he banged his fists together. "Where's the justice in people? Everybody could see the terrible injustice of Scotty going to jail and killing himself, and Lane going free, and now the same Harry Lane, waving that coat around, ruins my character and business, my life — he tortures me — why don't they see the injustice of it for me? Do I have to kill myself to get some respect? A few months ago they froze Lane out. Their sense of justice! Is it there for me now when he turns on me? Do they freeze him out? They laugh and they needle me. I'm everybody's pin cushion. I'm just about off my rocker. Maybe compared with Lane I'm an ignorant man, but I know what's going on his crazy mind. He's in disgrace. I was Scotty's friend. This little quarrel about the lining — I give him this big guilt feeling. He's taking it all out on me. Everybody can see it, and everybody should be with me. Why don't they believe me? What do I have to do?"

Facing his father, his hands out, while the one eye blinked fiercely, he waited, telling himself there was understanding, above all belief in the one eye, and then as the eye went on blinking at him it seemed to mock all the candor and hope in his heart. Good God, he thought, the only one who would believe me doesn't hear anything I say, and he tried to laugh, but his face only twisted into a cracked despairing smile, and he went over to the window and sat down, leaning back with his eyes closed.

Suddenly he sat up, leaning forward, sure he saw his mistake; he hadn't been acting like an innocent, indignant good man who was being outraged. Like a fool he had been acquiescing in Harry Lane's antics. Like an apologetic fool he had been sitting around hoping he would be believed, a weak man without the courage in his heart to be silent, or the honest rage to demand respect.

But that night at Dorfman's, Mike thought, when he had thrown it at Harry that he had ruined Scotty, he had put himself above Harry openly and with the straightforward courage that other people lacked who shared his resentment. Now, when he himself was being ruined by Harry, they waited to see what he, who had had the courage to speak out, would do. They had waited a little while, then they had begun to laugh at him, sure he was bluffing about everything, bluffing about his indignation over Scotty's death, and his denunciation of Harry, bluffing to hide his big bluff, the mistake he had made over the coat. "Everybody's waiting. Well, they don't need to wait any longer. I'll get that coat. I'll tear it off his back," he said, jumping up. "I'll show them what I am," and he banged his fists together as though he had boxing gloves on.

His father's eye, still blinking wildly, followed him to the door. "I'm going down to the store, Mrs. McManus," he called, and he hurried downstairs, opened his shop, went back to his office and picked up the phone, called Dorfman's and asked the girl on the switchboard if Harry Lane had come in. He hadn't, she said, so in a nice friendly tone he asked her if she could give him Harry's address. In a minute she gave him the rooming house address on Mountain Street.

For a while he sat quiet and still at the desk, a hard smile on his face, his fingers drumming on the desk, then a tightness and tension gripped his whole body in the joy of knowing he had the strength to do what he had to do. Suddenly he got up, went to the window and looked at the street lights; a light in Harry's room would tell him whether Harry was in. He

didn't want to go to the house and miss him and have someone say that he was looking for him.

Then he heard the office buzzer that was connected with
the apartment; a long buzz, then a series of short ones. Afraid
for his father, he ran out and went leaping up the stairs, filled
with dread. At the head of the stairs was Mrs. McManus, pale,
and beckoning nervously.

"What's the matter, Mrs. McManus?"

"He wrote something," she said, trying to smile. "It upset
me, Mr. Kon," and he knew then by her stark astonishment
that in spite of what she had said day after day she had never
expected the old man to communicate with anybody again.

"What did he write?"

"It's right there on the pad," she said, following him
into the room. "I came in to fix him up and there it was. Just
two words . . ."

Grabbing the pad, he knocked the pencil from his father's
fingers, but he could hardly read the two words, the letters
were so crooked and faintly marked.

"It's different this time, it is something, it is two words,"
he said exultantly. "That first word is — what is it?" His hand
was trembling so badly now he could hardly make out the letters. "The other word — Not. It must be Not. Not, is that
what you thought it was, Mrs. McManus?" He felt wildly
hopeful that the life he had wanted to have with his father
would soon begin.

"I don't know," she whispered, and then they both stared
at the old man sitting there lifelessly, his bright eye fixed
straight ahead. "What does it mean?" she asked, still shaken.

"I — I don't know. He used to say religious things,"
Mike said uneasily.

"Oh, I see," Mrs. McManus said, sighing with relief. "Well, I was so excited myself. From now on I'll feel different about him. Why, we'll have to watch what we say, won't we, Mr. Kon? Oh, dear," and she went back to the kitchen.

"I knew you were with us, papa," Mike said, his hand on his father's shoulder and tears in his eyes.

Still shaken he sat down, the page from the pad in his hand, and again he tried to make out the words. The first letter of the first word could be a J and then a U, and he pondered. All week he had been talking to the old man about the injustice of the whole thing, and the two words could be a try at a sentence — justice not — then he remembered that years ago when he had been sore at the old man for being content to be a newsboy, the old man used to say, "The justice of a man's lot is hidden from him." The old man could still be having these thoughts. I'm the best judge of that right now, Mike thought, and he looked again at the writing. The word could be Judge — Judge not. The same idea, about the injustice of the whole thing. Bewildered he turned to his father. Do you want me to close down my shop and knuckle under to Harry? I know you don't, papa. I don't quite know what you mean.

Then he told himself the written words were intended to be some kindly comforting remark of a general nature that his father used to make about everybody, to hold his own life together and give him peace of mind. He told this to himself, knowing that if he sat there brooding he would feel handcuffed, just when he had freed himself by seeing his mistake, and he got up quickly to go out looking for Harry Lane.

When he looked back he saw the pencil lying on the floor and he picked it up and put it carefully between his father's fingers, then he ran down the stairs.

He went over to the rooming house on Mountain Street and Harry wasn't in. He phoned Dorfman's, he tried the Tahiti, he tried to recall where Annie Laurie was living now and couldn't and just before midnight he climbed the long stairs to the Dark Venus on St. Catherine where Harry used to go a lot.

To the left of the door were the tables, the dance floor and the band and to the right, across the wide expanse of broadloom, was the bar of studded pigskin, the stool seats of pigskin too, and at the far corner of the bar, Mollie Morris. She was in a dinner dress and with the handsome lawyer, Jay Scott. As Mike sat on the vacant stool she glanced at him, and he went to speak; then she pretended she didn't see him.

When he got the drink he gripped the glass in both hands, and he stared at Miss Morris puzzled, because he had known she had shared his disgust with Harry Lane. Finally she fumbled in her purse, then she whispered something to her lawyer friend, snapped the catch on her bag grimly, and came over to him.

"Good evening, Miss Morris," he said.

"I'm glad you came in here, Mike," she said, and he did not like the grim tilt of her jaw or her tone. "There's something I want to say to you."

"Go ahead, Miss Morris."

"Your elegant playmate, Mr. Conlin, came to see me. He's scared he's going to be deported because he and you had Harry beaten up."

"I didn't have that maniac beaten up," he said angrily.

"Oh, of course you did," she said impatiently.

"Well, I'm going to show you and everybody else, Miss Morris, I don't have to get somebody else to do the dirty work. I'm above it, do you hear? Above it."

"Well," she said, angrily, "I hear from Ted Ogilvie that your friend Conlin is going around saying I'm standing behind him against Harry and I'll use my influence to prevent him being deported . . . To try and mix me up in this . . ." She had to pause to take a deep breath, and watching her he grew flustered; she was trembling; she could have been in love with Harry, or she could be hating the sound of his name. "To drag my name in this thing and have it bandied around in this contemptible disgraceful business . . ." Mike felt himself drawing away in his uneasy glimpse of her wound and her humiliation. "If you were more of a man, you'd have settled this thing. You're not enough of a man," she said, goading him bitterly. "I think he goes on and on wondering why you don't end it." Her neck and her throat were scarlet. "You don't know how to behave, but you could do me a favor. Tell Conlin that if he goes around using my name in any way, connecting me in any way with this thing, I'll do all in my power to see that he really is deported. Just tell him that, will you?"

"Why don't you tell him yourself, Miss Morris?"

"You'll see him and I won't."

"I don't care what you and Conlin do, Miss Morris, or what arrangements you care to enter into," he said with heavy disdain. "If I see him I'll be courteous enough to give him your message."

"You'll see him, you know," she said with her elegant and insulting assurance, and as she walked away calmly, his heart started pounding. He turned and walked out, stumbling on the steep flight of stairs; then he was out on the street on his way over to Mountain and the rooming house. It was sticky and hot, there wasn't a puff of air. A few drops of rain fell. Going up Mountain he watched heavy clouds gathering and rolling together in a monstrous threatening black weight settling on the mountain's summit; then it started to rain heavily. The rain came lashing at the trees and thunder rattled off the mountain and came banging down at Mike and he rushed to get under a tree. A young mother and her little boy had also taken shelter under the tree, and the thunder rolled down the mountain, down the sloping street at Mike and the mother and her boy. Mike had never been able to get used to thunder low on the mountain; it wasn't like a thunderstorm in any other city he had been in, and he was glad when it stopped just as suddenly as it began. Now his shoulders and pants were soaking wet but he went on up the street.

There was a light in the ground-floor front window which was Harry's room, and he turned in eagerly, and then he saw a young fellow and a girl standing on the step making love and blocking the way. They didn't even turn. Backing away, Mike went up the street a little way, then hated himself for retiring as if he didn't want anyone to see him. Turning back, he brushed by the boy and girl. "Excuse me," he said, and he opened the door, walked in, and closed it.

"Who's there?" Mrs. Benoit called from the head of the stairs. "Why don't you ring? What do you want?"

"Mr. Lane."

"The door right there," she said, coming down the stairs a few steps, her hand on the banister, her head thrust down under the light to get a look at him. "And ring next time will you? This isn't the Windsor Station," and mumbling to herself she went back up the stairs.

Mike looked at the doorknob, hesitated, then he knocked. "Who is it?" Harry called.

"Mike Kon," he said, ready to heave with his shoulder against the door.

"Oh," Harry said, and Mike waited, his hand on the doorknob, then Harry called, "The door is always open. Why don't you come in?" and he went in.

Harry was on the bed, in his shorts, lying on his belly, his head twisted so he could see the door, and kneeling on the bed beside him so she could massage his legs, was Annie Laurie. Seeing her there with her hands on Harry's bruised legs hurt Mike for he had always liked her, and he scowled at her disgust.

"Take it easy, Mike," Annie said gently. "He was in bad shape after that beating. What do you want?"

"Just to put an end to his joke," Mike said grimly, looking around for the coat.

"You know, Mike, there's a way to put an end to my joke," Harry said, and he seemed to be moved by Mike's grim, harassed wildness, the ruin in his mind and heart, and all that had been magnanimous in his own nature was touched. "I've been wanting you to come and see me, Mike. When I heard you there at the door . . . well, in the whole thing maybe I've needed you, Mike," then he faltered, his head on one side, half puzzled by his mixed-up recognition of his need of Mike. Then, almost pleading, "Now that you've come here, Mike, why don't you say you could have been all wrong about me. You're not the kind of man who wants to make himself an accuser."

"You think I've come here to get down on my knees to you now — now?" Mike said, laughing harshly. "There's an apology to be made here, all right, and I owe it to myself." He went over the chair where Harry had flung his clothes, but the coat there belonged to another suit. "How you disgust me," he said. Then he saw the clothes closet to the left and near the room door. His back had been to it.

"Listen to me, Mike," Annie Laurie said indignantly, and she came close and grabbed his arm. "All right, so you feel insulted. What about Harry? People like you think he should run or hide his face. Well, he can't because he doesn't know how to run or hide. Don't you think it breaks my heart to see him wearing that stupid coat? If you're going crazy thinking no one believes your story, don't you think he has a right to go crazy knowing no one has believed him since last winter?"

"Whoa there, Annie Laurie," Harry said gently as he sat up on the bed, his legs folded under him. "You're only a poor little character witness, you know. Mike doesn't want to be a human being, making mistakes. He wants to go on in his big role of public prosecutor," and his smile and tone, regretful, almost affectionate in his compassionate aware-ness of what they had to be to each other, taunted Mike and made him feel looked down on more than ever. Breathing hard, Mike clenched his fists, moistened his lips, and bal-ancing on the balls of his feet he wanted to jump at Harry and choke off his words, yet he tried to remember it was the coat he wanted to destroy; beating him was no good if he was left with the coat. "Come on, where is it?" Striding toward the clothes closet he jerked the door open. Only one suit was there, a blue one, and then bewildered he looked at the gray one lying on the floor, for he hadn't been able to imagine Harry wouldn't have the coat.

"Old boy, you want to know where the coat is?" Harry asked mildly.

"Wherever it is you won't wear it again, you mocking maniac."

"Oh, yes, I will. The coat got dirtied up. Your boys, you know. The pavement outside Dorfman's hasn't been laundered recently. The coat's at the cleaners. I'll have it tomorrow. Made them promise not to touch my beautiful lining. Or is it your lining, or old Scotty's lining? Have to wear the coat tomorrow to the fights, you know."

"I'll tell you something, Harry Lane," Mike said going over to the bed and hating the white tired desperate face with the laughter in the eyes, "if you wear that coat again . . ."

"Got to wear it tomorrow night to the fights. Just told you," he said, putting the tips of his fingers together with great repose.

"And I'm telling you this," Mike said trembling. "If I see that coat on you, no matter where you are, I'll tear it off your back," and he felt all his physical strength and hard hatred and the toughness of his youth in the words as he leaned closer.

"I'm not at all drunk," Harry said, and he got up, smiling, and stood in front of Mike. "The nerves in my legs went last night, that's all. That coat is the mantle of Scotty Bowman. You pinned it on me. I'm trying to wear it with the distinction it deserves. I'm not crazy. I'm not degenerating fast. I'm not in collapse at all. So everybody's laughing at me? All right, that's fine. I don't mind. But how about you and old Scotty, your friend? Ghosts can't stand up under laughter. You and good old Scotty. When are you both leaving town?"

"You're mad," Mike said, but there was something in Harry's eyes that held him back; it was an unyielding fierceness beneath the smile, a blind wild rejection of the threats no matter how grave they were; it touched something far beyond Mike and held him, just for the moment, helpless and wondering, for he saw that Harry would never give up the coat, couldn't and wouldn't, for if he handed the coat over now there was nothing left for him in the world, nothing left of himself. It made Mike feel frightened and frantic, and then he wanted to meet him head on fiercely. "Well, I told you," he said. "You heard me, Annie Laurie. Now it's up to me. I'm satisfied," and he walked out.

In the hall he stopped to take a deep breath, then he opened the front door, and the boy and girl were still on the steps, only now the girl had her head down on the boy's shoulder; her fair hair had fallen away from the back of her neck and the hall light just touched her neck. Again he had to brush past them. The heavy clouds were drifting and breaking up, some of them all silvered, then the moon came out. But still there was no breeze.

❖ **XXIII** ❖

*A*t the Forum, after the semi-final when the lights came on, the officials for the Bruno fight got into the ring and the big crowd relaxed. Some who were sitting at the ringside left their chairs and stood around the press row. The Dutchman in a purple robe and his handlers were coming down the aisle, and getting a good hand. Then Ray Conlin led Bruno down the aisle and the roar rolled and then murmured on long after Bruno had sat down in his corner.

When those who had been loafing around the ring began to go back to their seats, Ray saw Harry Lane in the fifth row with Annie Laurie, who was leaning close, talking to him. Lane was in his shirt sleeves, the coat folded across his knees. Then someone called, "Hey, Conlin!" It was Mike Kon, on his way back to his seat and now at the Bruno corner. He had a crazy light in his eyes as if he had seen Harry with the coat and wanted to get at him.

"Later," Ray called casually, for he was no longer impressed by Mr. Kon.

"Come here, you little lug. I've got a message for you," Mike said angrily, so Ray ambled over to him and bent down.

"What gives, Mike? A message from who?"

"Mollie Morris. She tells me, you understand? Me, you little rat! Mention her name again as being behind you and she herself will have you deported. She insults me, phoning me. But I give you her message with pleasure."

"You're a nobody, Mike. And to hell with her," Ray snarled. "Tell that to her. A message from me. An old newspaper broad," and he spat.

Standing there in the ring with sixteen thousand of Bruno's own people behind him, he felt entitled to have contempt for anyone who was against him and he looked over the ringside seats. Suddenly he grinned happily, for there in the second row behind the Dutchman's corner, was Rosso, himself, sitting with little Augie Silone.

Then the house lights were dimmed, the big cone of light fell on the ring and the announcer shouted, "The next bout for the middleweight championship . . ." and Johnny Bruno did a little jig, his hands over his head while the crowd rose and screamed and even the sporting writers yelled encouragement. The Dutchman got a generous tribute too.

At the bell, Johnny moved out fast popping him with a light left on the nose.

He was faster and much prettier to watch than the Dutchman, he had the legs, and the Dutchman with his bull shoulders fighting from a crouch, his head bobbing, kept his long arms half hooked and held high ready to move in with the terrible short hooks. "Keep away from him, Johnny," Ray yelled, "Away, away, away, away. That's it, you're my boy, away — away," and he grinned as the Dutchman missed, and plodded on. Johnny, who kept popping him with the left, doing no damage, but piling up points, nailed him with a right high on the side of the head and the Dutchman looked startled. The crowd laughed exultantly. Standing flatfooted the Dutchman let go with a half-hearted right swing, just to keep Johnny dancing away. It glanced off Johnny's nose. Blood gushed from the nose. Dancing back, Johnny shook his head and drops of blood sprayed over the canvas and on his own shoulders. When he grabbed and held on the blood streamed down over the Dutchman's shoulder blades. "Hang on, Johnny, hang on," Ray screamed. "Ten seconds, baby, ten seconds," and they wrestled and the referee tried to break them, and Johnny backed away, the Dutchman very slowly followed him, and the bell sounded.

"It wasn't much of a punch," Ray said. "A very little bruise, Johnny. I'll get it." But Johnny kept spitting the blood bubbling from his nose into the pail and Ray cursed. He did not know where the blood came from that covered the towel, and Johnny's eyes now were frightened; yet when the bell sounded there was no blood on the clean spot on the towel. "Ah, baby, baby, keep away."

Standing up slowly, Johnny danced across the ring, but before he reached the Dutchman the blood drops fell on his gloves and his chest. Shaking his head he backed away, leaving a little trail of blood on the canvas. Grabbing him the referee backed him into the corner and yelled for the commission doctor, who came climbing into the corner, pushing his bag ahead of him and chewing cloves. He felt the nose, applied a medication but couldn't stop the bleeding. "Get him to the dressing room. It may be a minor hemorrhage. He's lost too much blood anyway." Then the referee, shouting, raised the Dutchman's hand and the crowd was silent, as Ray, pressing a towel to Johnny's nose, led him to the dressing room, where Johnny lay on the table while the doctor worked on his nose. Blinking his eyes nervously and feeling a tightness around his heart like an old fear from his boyhood days, Ray sat by himself in the corner. There was a lot of pounding on the door. Eddie Adams came in with his hard cynical smile; then the sporting writers, all but Haggerty.

Then Ray saw little Augie Silone at the door, beckoning, and he followed him out to the corridor. Augie had on a pearl-gray hat and a pearl-gray lightweight suit and a plain yellow tie and his thin dark face with the big lips was twitching nervously.

"Rosso wants to know what happened to the kid's nose," he said quietly. "The kid's no bleeder. Why didn't you fix his nose?"

"The doc says a blood vessel popped. I did all I could, Augie. The doc couldn't stop it himself till now."

"Rosso says the kid's no bleeder."

"No, he's no bleeder. It's got me beat. I don't know, Augie." Augie smiled mournfully, his eyes hard and suspicious. "See, it don't figure, Ray. The Dutchman says, why did the kid walk into the swing? Johnny was to have the title tonight, Ray. So Rosso wonders."

"Let him talk to the doc."

"He told me to talk to you." But three men were coming along the corridor, one of them Bruno's brother, older, heavier, the same little patch of hair on the balding forehead, and wearing a red shirt and sharp navy-blue pants, and Augie said, "Be seeing you," and he ambled on his way, and Ray went back to the dressing room and kept circling round the table where Johnny sat.

When they told him to hurry and get dressed, Johnny would drop him off in the convertible, he said they should go ahead without him, he would take his time; he had an appointment at the hotel. But the arena was dark and empty when he finally left.

Outside on the corner a newsboy was yelling, "Morning *Sun*," and Mike Kon was standing by himself, his hands in his pockets. He kept looking all around, waiting and looking as if he couldn't believe he had lost the one he was waiting for in the crowd. He was agitated, uncertain and very grim and full of trouble for someone. Ray was afraid to speak to him. He bought a paper and, under Haggerty's name, was the bare news that Bruno had lost in the second round to the Dutchman by a technical knockout. In the last three lines, it said, "Bruno had suffered a nosebleed two days ago and although it had been slight, the question was why hadn't his handlers asked for a postponement?"

"No," Ray whispered. "No," and he felt weak. Rosso will find out I was worrying about being deported, and Harry Lane, he thought. Suddenly he yelled "Taxi" at a passing cab, and jumped in. "The Mount Royal," he said, scared and lonely.

At the hotel he hurried through the rotunda, into the elevator, and on the sixth floor, the paper still like a club in his hands, he half ran along the corridor and rapped on the door; he could hear voices in the room; Eddie Adams was in there. Augie Silone opened the door.

"I want to see Rosso," Ray said. He liked the sound of his own voice, all the defiance he had ever possessed was now in the set of his shoulders and in his little black eyes, his thrust-forward head.

"You do, eh? I wouldn't if I was you," Augie said sourly, and he closed the door and Ray tried to stop his heart from pounding. The door opened again. Augie said, "Rosso is busy. Don't get in his way."

"Augie, I've got to see Rosso," he pleaded. "It says in the paper —"

"Rosso can read too."

"But that creep Haggerty . . ."

"You weren't on the ball, Ray."

"I was on the ball. All the time I'm on the ball. I'm the guy who knows the facts."

"Rosso has got the facts. Maybe now he is good to you, you should like it that he don't want to see you to ask why you so sudden go dumb and careless. Be a bunny, start hopping."

"Augie, I'm broke."

"We're all broke. Be a bunny, I said," and he closed the door.

Ray wanted to get away from that closed door; he hurried, but going down in the elevator he realized that the farther he got away from Rosso, the more alone he was, and he hadn't paid for his room. He couldn't go to Eddie Adams and ask for a share of the Bruno purse, and now everybody would cheer if he was deported. Back in New York, if Rosso was against him, he might be found some night in the gutter.

Hurrying, he took a cab down to St. Antoine and the *Sun* and climbed the stairs to the sporting department and asked for Haggerty. Haggerty came from an inner office, in his rolled-up shirt sleeves, and with his white hair tousled. "What's on your mind, Ray?" he asked, sitting down. "I want someone to get this right," Ray blurted out. "You got to get behind me, Haggerty." Squatting on the corner of the desk, his little dark face full of his terrible anxiety, he said, "Haggerty, if I ever had anything to say I always said it to you because you got a big following. I looked at Johnny's nose. I'm not careless and never was and worked with him in all his bouts. The whole thing now they pin on me. So I'm out with Rosso. I go to New York and hang around and nobody'll touch me. I'll have no job here, no money. It'll be easy for Harry Lane to get me deported, and with Rosso against me everywhere. Everybody listens to you, and maybe at Dorfman's tonight, Rosso goes there, and you say it was a little thing, you exaggerated, and I'm the best. I should be back with Bruno. Put in a word for me. Tell it in your column because somebody's got to put in a word for me."

"Damn it, Ray, it's none of my business," Haggerty said uncomfortably, avoiding Ray's eyes, bothered by his own compassion. "Well, look here, if I see anybody in Dorfman's I'll say I think you always were a good handler for the boy. I'll say it because it's true. I've got to get back to my column. Take it easy, Ray."

"Thanks, Haggerty," he said, and he had to go.

The street was dark and quiet, and as he looked up at the lights on the mountain, he thought, "Rosso and Eddie'll go to Dorfman's. I can see Rosso in Dorfman's — and if Haggerty's there — I've got to go to Dorfman's."

Near the hotel he heard fire reels; then he saw one fire truck parked across the road; a crowd had gathered. The police had blocked off the road. Firemen were dragging a hose across the road. A cop tried to turn him back but he ducked around him and without even looking back at the fire he hurried up the Dorfman steps, his heart beating heavily, for he was afraid he might encounter Alfred in the hall before he even got into the lounge. No one was in the hall. When he looked in the lounge he saw Harry Lane and Annie Laurie sitting at the bar. No one else was there. Lane was always in the way. It's those damned firemen blocking off the street, he thought. Everybody would be down the street at the fire, and in a panic he hurried out.

A thin stream of smoke was coming from an upstairs window. It was the Wishing Well, the night club, that was burning, and now there was a very big crowd. He cursed softly. Nobody'll get here, he thought. But the boys might be down there, and he started to run, all his natural hopefulness returned.

Searchlights were playing on the face of the night club and big-booted firemen dragged hoses across the road, shouting. A policeman pushed Ray back toward the sidewalk and, blocked off, he could see no one he knew. When he got out of the crowd he saw a taxi that had come around by way of Sherbrooke Street in front of Dorfman's, and he started to run that way again, then up the steps and into the hall to the lounge and there was Haggerty talking to Harry Lane and Annie Laurie.

Haggerty still had that tolerant, half-contemptuous ease with Harry. Annie Laurie had just turned. "It's not next door to the Wishing Well. It is the Wishing Well," she insisted.

"Get out. It's that restaurant next door," Harry said.

"No, it's the old Wishing Well."

"But they just had the place redecorated."

"So what?"

"Maybe they didn't pay the decorator, and he's burning the joint down."

"Imagine the Wishing Well burning," Annie Laurie said, sighing. "I remember the first night I ever went there. I was nineteen. My beautiful youth. It's all going up in smoke," and she was so much at ease with Harry that Ray hated her. Then his eye fell on the coat which Harry had tossed on a bar stool when he went to the window. The coat was there within ten feet of Ray, lying on the stool while the others laughed and watched the fire.

Very nervous, yet motionless as if in a trance, he stared at the coat. All his troubles had begun with that coat and the sight of it frightened him. In the beginning he had tried to be bright and witty with Mike Kon about a yellow lining; if it hadn't been for the coat he wouldn't have felt that he had to reestablish himself with Mike and he wouldn't have gone to the washroom and he wouldn't have got the punch on the jaw from Harry and he wouldn't have felt compelled to get even with him. Because of that coat, here he was now with Rosso against him and terrified that Harry could get the police to deport him. "Why was I such a meddler?" he thought. "That coat meant nothing to me. Why am I here at all having this guy on my back?" and he went toward Harry.

"Mr. Lane," he said huskily. "I've got something to say. Please listen to me."

"You. What's this?" Harry asked, turning to Haggerty and then to Annie Laurie, both of whom looked as astonished as he did.

"Mr. Lane," Ray went on desperately, "if you'd look at it this way. What should there be between you and me? Nothing, nothing at all. So why did I ever bother you? A guy gets drawn in. I made trouble. I get way out of my depth. About that beating — I apologize. For you I've been a big trouble-maker."

"Well, well, well," Haggerty said, and he started to laugh and the laughter frightened Ray.

"What's the matter with an apology?" he said fiercely. "A sincere apology is a good thing. A big man can take an apology, Mr. Lane. I want to make things right with you." Then he grew frightened again by Harry's silence and the mournful wondering expression on his face, as though some belief or hope he held was being mocked. He seemed to be off by himself like a man hearing ironic laughter, then he smiled, more at himself and his thoughts than at Ray, and he turned to Annie Laurie.

"You know," he said, keeping his face straight. "This is a very great moment."

"What do you mean, Harry?"

"A great historic moment," he said solemnly. "For a long time I've waited for some troubled soul to come wanting to make things right with me, someone to say I've been wronged. Well," and he bowed, "at last he's come. Here he is," and he burst out laughing.

"I'm on the level," Ray cried, bewildered.

"And who is it who comes along?" said Harry, his face straight again. "Who's the emissary? A scared little outcast with no one else to turn to. Driven out. No hole left to hide in. So he comes to me with a contrite heart. Conlin," he said, mockingly solemn again. "Don't you realize you may be making a grave mistake?"

"I don't get it," Ray said, brushing his oily hair out of his eyes, and feeling lost again. "I'm not so educated. I told you I know my mistake. I didn't mind my own business. That's all. This is no way to treat an apology."

"You're wrong, Conlin," Harry said. "I really appreciate the event. I thank you," and he grinned and linked his arm under Annie Laurie's and led her back to the window.

"Haggerty, just a minute," Ray said, grabbing his arm. "Is the guy really off my back or is he laughing at me?"

"The absolution seems to be in the laughter," Haggerty said, grinning, and he joined them at the window, leaving Ray there by himself, hesitant, yet full of hope, as he wondered what he would say when he, too, joined them at the window; then he heard a noise at the door and he turned and saw Mike Kon, and he said the right thing; going closer he touched Harry on the arm and said, "Harry, it's Mike Kon."

⋄ **XXIV** ⋄

*I*n the crowd at the fight Mike had lost sight of Harry, though he had waited at the exit, and later, on the street. Then he had gone into a bar, and had sat there drinking and brooding. In a little while he could think only of Harry saying, "I'll wear the coat at the fight," and of his own threat, which had been frustrated. Again he would appear to be bluffing. The fact was that he was left sitting alone in a little bar where he was a stranger. All year, after a fight, he had gone to Dorfman's. Now he couldn't go there. Yet Harry was probably there right now wearing the coat. This is an outrage, and I'm letting him get away with it, he thought. Suddenly he left the bar, took a taxi over to Peel, and was blocked off from Dorfman's by the crowd watching the fire. The smoke and the flames and the cops who drove him back every time he tried to go up the street inflamed his imagination. He felt hemmed in and wild because he could see the light over Dorfman's. For a while he tried to stay quietly in the crowd and wait, but he had to jerk open his collar so he could breathe more evenly, and finally he went back to the corner, and east a block, then all the way up to Sherbrooke and back, and now Dorfman's was down the hill, with the crowd on the street there smaller, and not so many policemen, and he edged his way slowly from door to door till he was through, then suddenly he trotted toward Dorfman's.

Flushed, with his collar opened and his tie pulled away, he stood near the bar, bewildered for a moment, seeing Ray Conlin there with Harry, then all his anger showed in his hard eyes. When he sat down on a stool at the end of the bar, Charlie hurried over to him.

"What'll it be, Mike?" he asked nervously.

Taking his time Mike dropped his cigarette in the ashtray.

"Don't you remember, Charlie? I'm not welcome here," he said.

"Alfred was at the fight, Mike. He phoned and said he wouldn't be in."

"I'm very lucky, eh, Charlie?"

"Alfred has a touch of gastritis. What'll you drink, Mike?"

"Since Alfred won't be in, eh? This insults me, Charlie."

"Nobody's in tonight. Everybody must be down the street. They'll want to come in just when I'm closing up."

But Mike had swung around on the stool, staring at Harry, who looked absolutely unimpressed as he put his hands in his pockets with a nonchalant and happy air.

"I told you, Harry Lane," Mike called over. "If I saw you wearing that coat again I'd tear it off your back. I saw you at the fights. I couldn't get near you." He stood up suddenly. "But I knew you'd be here."

"Mike," Ray called, hurrying over to him. "You're doing this thing all wrong, Mike. I know how you should behave. Listen to me."

"You little rat," Mike said, and he swung the back of his hand and caught him on the mouth and knocked him to one side against a stool and the stool squeaked as it spun round.

As Mike went toward the window there were cries from firemen high on ladders down the street; a bell was clanging, and then came a murmur from the crowd as flames shot from a window. Haggerty sat down, his elbow on the table, and watched him reflectively, and Annie Laurie picked up a glass, her eyes fierce. But for Mike, there was only Harry, who, smiling a little, took Annie's arm. "We were watching the fire, Annie," he said. "Come on," and he turned to the window.

Harry's easy indifference enraged Mike, who took three quick steps to get close to him. He shot out his hand and grabbed the coat by the collar, and with the other hand he reached around and jerked it open. A button, snapping off, bounced on the floor. He wanted to get the coat off in one powerful motion and walk out with it.

"Go away, you fool," Annie Laurie cried, and Haggerty stood up anxiously for Mike looked so much heavier and more powerful than Harry and he had the craziness in his eyes. Harry had said nothing. The coat, being jerked down his back, was pinioning his arms. He hardly struggled, and Mike thought it was going to be easy. Then Harry pivoted suddenly; he jerked himself free of the coat which Mike held onto; the light caught Harry's pale face and his wonderfully bright blue eyes, and balancing, flat on his feet and set, he punched Mike hard on the jaw. It was an astonishing punch, beautifully timed, for he was set right, and when he landed it, Haggerty stood up, his mouth open in surprise and admiration as Mike went down heavily on his haunches.

"Come on, Annie," Harry said, picking up the coat and taking her arm. "Let's get out of here," and he didn't even hurry.

"Remember — remember," she said hysterically, as she put down the glass. "That street out there is full of cops right now."

Sitting on the floor, Mike shook his head, jerking it from side to side spasmodically, his eyes glazed, and then he looked up at Haggerty, who was wiping a flake of tobacco from his lower lip. The astonishment in Haggerty's eyes seemed to degrade him, as if all along Haggerty, like everyone else, had been sure that he had been trying to behave with superior restraint because he was a great old fighter who could beat up Harry any time he wanted to. Yet now he saw him sitting on his pants in Dorfman's in the worst moment of his life.

Suddenly he bounded up, lurched a little, then rushed at the door, with Ray and Haggerty and Charlie crowding after him.

Harry and Annie Laurie were at the door which he had just opened. Annie Laurie had stepped out, then Harry turned, standing under the wrought-iron light over the door which made Annie Laurie's bare shoulders look golden. Then Mike shouted, "You — you —" and Harry half turned.

Then Mike went down into his crouch, his eyes, just slits now under the scarred brows, gleaming with a hatred and contempt for himself for all the indignities he had suffered. His head bobbed a little to the left, and his right foot slid forward, then he suddenly shifted, and in the doorway Harry had no room to move away. He could have retreated quickly down the steps, but, defiant, not scared at all, his eager shining eyes tried to follow Mike's shift; in that space he had no room to shift with him, and Mike's right, as straight a punch as he had ever thrown, caught him on the point of the chin. Everything that Mike used to be was in the punch, and they heard a crack, and a kind of a little snap; and Harry lurched backwards, not tumbling, but falling stiff like a post, toppled down the steps to the sidewalk.

He rolled past Annie Laurie who had both hands up, her purse hiding one side of her face, and she screamed and the wild lonely wail echoed down the street, then she screamed again, "Harry," and stumbled down the steps and dropped on her knees beside him.

The circle of light from the doorway reached only as far as her ankles and green pumps.

"My God," Haggerty said, and he started to wheeze as he ran out, but Ray, the first one down the steps, knelt beside Harry. Even in the shadow Harry's face had a strange pallor, his neck was twisted awkwardly to one side, and there was a little blood on the sidewalk at the back of his head. Mike watched Ray give Harry's face a little slap, then feel for his pulse, and then coming from what seemed to be a great distance away, he heard Annie Laurie sobbing, "Harry, oh, Harry, Jesus, Mary and Joseph," and he turned, still dazed and trembling, and watched her touch Harry's forehead and smooth back his hair. It made Mike feel lonely, and he thought, "What have I done? Why am I here with this man?" Then his own thoughts, wondering and desolate, frightened him, and he blurted out, "He asked for it."

"Get an ambulance," Haggerty shouted. Charlie ran down the street toward the crowd and they watched him stop halfway down the street and talk to a policeman who had heard the shriek and come running toward Charlie. The policeman pointed across the road at another policeman and then at the street beside the hotel, and Charlie started to run again, and the policeman came on toward them.

"That crack, that snap," Ray said to Haggerty, as he stood up.

"Never heard anything like it," Haggerty whispered.

"I think it broke his neck."

"He hit his head when he fell," Mike said quickly.

"I think he's dead," Annie Laurie cried. "My God, he's dead."

Two puffs of smoke came from the night club windows, followed by a little flicker of flame; then Mike came over to Harry and looked down at him. The coat had flopped open, the torn lining showing, and Mike stared at it stupidly, and then he stooped and furtively folded it in on Harry, and he didn't look up until he heard the policeman's steps coming closer.

Grabbing Haggerty's arm, he said, "You saw what happened."

"I saw it, Mike."

"You saw him hit me. You're my witness."

"That's right. He certainly smashed you, Mike, when you touched that coat."

"Anyone who hears the story will say I had a right to do it and that I should have done it long ago. When he hits me — have I a right to hit back?"

"Certainly you have. Take it easy. The three of us saw what happened."

Then Mike turned to Annie Laurie, for she was the one he was afraid of now. She was sitting on the Dorfman steps with the light on the back of her neck and on one leg. Her skirt had got pulled up and her round knee showed, and a hole had been rubbed in the knee of the stocking when she had knelt beside Harry. Mike couldn't take his eyes off this hole in the stocking. She kept putting her fingers up to her lips to keep them from trembling but her hand trembled too. Over and over again she did this, as if she were cold and shivering, and she seemed to be watching raptly something across the road, but there was nothing there. "Annie Laurie," Mike said, huskily. "You see, he knocked me down — you saw me on the floor."

"You poor driven fool, Mike," she said, bitterly, and he didn't know what she meant.

Now the cop was there, kneeling beside Harry and listening while Haggerty explained what had happened. He was French and young and had a black mustache. "Who's Mike Kon? You?" he said, looking up. "Me," Mike said. "I don't understand this about the coat. You'll have to come to the station." "I don't mind at all," Mike said. Then they heard the ambulance, which had been parked up the side street, called there because of the fire, coming up the street, its red light flashing off and on. They put Harry in the ambulance. Annie Laurie insisted on going with him. Haggerty helped her in. Then they were gone, and there was only the little blotch of blood on the sidewalk.

"Get this down right here," Mike said to the cop. "He hit me, then I went after him and hit him back. That's all. These guys saw it. He hit me once and I hit him once."

"That's right," Haggerty said. "You have to tell about the coat, Mike."

But the cop, snapping his book closed, said, "We'll go to the station," and they all walked down the street to the hotel where the cop called a police car.

In the station they stood before the sergeant's desk while the policeman made his report. The gray-headed, gray-faced, gray-eyed sergeant pondered, then shook his head. "Where's the coat? We better get hold of this coat, for your sake, Kon."

"Harry's got it on," Haggerty said impatiently.

"You saw all this, Mr. Haggerty?" the sergeant said respectfully.

"I certainly did," Haggerty said. "And this guy Conlin saw everything too."

"We'll have to wait until I hear from the hospital, but a man seems to have been killed," the sergeant said. "We'll have to book Kon on suspicion of manslaughter charge."

"It was a fight, a couple of blows struck," Haggerty said. "Where's there any suspicion of manslaughter?"

"What do you want me to do, give Kon a medal?" the sergeant asked.

"Charge him if you want to but you won't make it stick," Haggerty said sharply, and he turned to Mike, almost apologetically. "Don't worry about it, Mike," and Mike was astonished.

Until tonight, Haggerty, like the others, had laughed at him and needled him. Yet now he was showing this indignant concern for him. Even now he was turning to Ray Conlin. "Is that right, Ray?" "You're telling it just right, Mr. Haggerty," Ray said enthusiastically. "I'm with you all the way, Mike. My story is Mr. Haggerty's story." His oily little face was friendly and almost happy. He was a witness; he was needed and Haggerty seemed to count on him.

Mike put his shoulders back though he still had the inner trembling from his growing fear that he was disgraced and ruined. "At least I can get hold of my lawyer, can't I?" he asked. "Sure, who's your lawyer?" the sergeant said. "Louis Applebaum," Mike said. "I want to get him right down here. I shouldn't have to stay here. I want him down here."

They let him phone his lawyer and it took a little time; Applebaum was on his way to bed. When he heard what had happened and that Mike had three witnesses, he said he would be down to the station in an hour.

"I'm going to stay here with you, Mike," said Haggerty, now worried and unhappy. With the excitement gone, he spoke out of a long reflective troubled silence. "I'm staying too," Ray said earnestly. "I'm not walking out on you, Mike. I'm a witness," and the sergeant told them they could wait in a little room, a detective's room, to the right of his desk, where they sat around the long table sprawled out in the chairs.

The waiting seemed to drive them in on themselves. They said nothing. Finally, Mike took a cigar out of his pocket, but when he went to light it his hand trembled; he stared at the shaking hand and let the light go out, and as he put the burnt match carefully on the table he thought of his father and his shop, and he closed his eyes to hide his despair. A big detective came to the door, looked at them and went away. Then Haggerty, frowning and grappling with some aspect of the matter that bothered him, said angrily, "I liked Harry. Where could you have met a nicer guy? But you can't go against people like he did. You can't get away with it. People like people. That's the thing. People have to go on liking people and respecting the general sentiment." But these words didn't comfort Mike at all; he had lost all confidence in people; the phrases about people made him think of the coat, and how the story would be told in the newspapers, and how he had known the coat would ruin him. Now he was in the police station where he had once been when he was a boy. The years since then had counted for nothing. The mysterious sureness of the fate awaiting him filled him with dread. He had no anger left. Slumping heavily in the chair he chewed hard on his cigar, then thought suddenly of Annie Laurie, kneeling on the pavement, brushing back the hair from

Harry's forehead as he lay on the sidewalk; it seemed all wrong, terribly wrong, and he took the cigar from his mouth, to say angrily, "To see him there in that coat, the lining all torn, with only a little stray kneeling beside him . . ." He didn't say it — he was ashamed, and afraid of insulting Annie Laurie.

"Until he had the trouble with Scotty, I liked Harry Lane," he said suddenly. "He never knew it, and nobody else did either, but I used to look up to him. We should have been good friends. I used to admire the guy. I mean," he said, groping desperately for the right words, "I used to admire the way he seemed to feel he didn't have to impress people, he didn't have to try. I used to watch him come down the street, or sit at a table, and I used to think he made people want to act their best. Lots of times I wanted to talk to him about things. I was embarrassed, you understand — afraid I'd say or do something and spoil it and he'd look down on me. I wanted to be proud like he was — without trying or caring. But a guy can be so proud he thinks he doesn't have to care about anybody else, and I figured he was that way with Scotty. I thought he felt he just didn't have to care what happened to Scotty, my friend, and it made me feel that if anything went wrong he'd look down on me too, and it hurt me, and it led to this — to this."

Another detective came to the door, chewing gum, and regarding them impassively. He took out a nail clipper and worked on his fingers, until they satisfied him; then went away.

Haggerty had pulled the morning paper out of his pocket. "Look at my column, Ray," he said idly.

Turning to the sporting page Ray began to read the column. When Mike saw tears come to Ray's eyes he got up and stood behind him. He had to do something to get the picture of Annie Laurie kneeling beside Harry out of his head. Leaning over Ray's shoulder he read the long paragraph in the column about the fight. In this paragraph Haggerty had written that the one tragic figure in the comedy of errors in the ring was little Ray Conlin. The little guy, the most loyal handler a fighter ever had, had slipped maybe in not screaming for a postponement when Johnny got a nosebleed in training two days ago; but a doctor could have made the same mistake. For Eddie Adams to boot Ray out and leave him unpaid and wandering around, bewildered, was worthy of that exalted code of ethics that was now dominating the fight game since Rosso took over. "For shame, for shame, Eddie," he had written.

"Somehow I think that'll bring Eddie around to you," Haggerty said, grinning. "He likes things to be done in a nice way."

"Oh, geez, Mr. Haggerty," Ray said, then he couldn't go on, and Mike, feeling envious and lonely, walked around the table and back to his chair, and stared morosely at Ray who sat clutching the paper in both hands. "I must have done the right thing," Ray said. "I couldn't think of the right things, but I did them. How is it a guy like me, when things get tight, knows what to do?"

"You'll always survive," Mike said, irritated by Ray's relief.

"That's a great trick — to know how to survive."

"Paying no attention to Ray," Haggerty said. "Mike, listen Mike, are you listening to me?"

"Sure, I'm listening," Mike said glumly.

"Well, look Mike. This thing will come up in a magistrate's court to see if you'll be committed for trial and, of course, you can elect whether you'll be tried by a judge or jury. If it comes to that take a jury. But listen. Tell this Louis Applebaum, as soon as he comes down here — right now, and for this, the preliminary hearing — get Roger Ouimet. Tell him to get Ouimet at once. Understand?"

"Yeah, yeah," Mike said slowly as he pondered. Then he jerked his head back more confidently. "That's a real idea. I don't care what it costs. It must be Ouimet."

◇ **XXV** ◇

*I*t had turned cooler. The weather was much more seasonal the morning at ten when Mike was brought into the police court to answer to the charge of manslaughter in the death of Harry Lane. The police court was in that courthouse where Scotty Bowman had been tried. But the magistrate's court had none of the distinction or solemnity of that courtroom where Judge Montpetit's court had presided. Before Mike had been called three drunks and a burglar had been sentenced by the beery little magistrate with the rimless glasses, the red nose and dandruff on his shoulders. The courtroom was crowded because the story about the coat had appeared in all the newspapers. While Mike was out on bail his telephone had rung all day long; people he hardly knew had called to express their sympathy. Again and again they had said, "Mike, rest assured, you only did what you had to do."

Carrying his head high, and with a stern expression, Mike was led into the courtroom, wearing a dark-gray suit. Again and again he had been assured he had nothing to be ashamed of. He had the manner of a man who believed he had the confidence and support of decent people who had a respect for justice. Stepping into the prisoner's box he looked around calmly. The Dorfman crowd was there and Mollie Morris sat in the back row, not at the press table, dressed in black, with a veil.

When Roger Ouimet came in the little magistrate bowed to him and Henderson, who was already at the lawyers' table, also bowed. Ouimet was bringing some legal distinction and elegance to the common police court.

Then Mike was told to stand up while the charge against him was read. He was asked how he pleaded. "Not guilty," he said quietly.

Haggerty, the first witness, a very gray-headed, gray-faced, embarrassed witness, did a lot of wheezing as he told what he had seen in Dorfman's the night Harry was killed. When Henderson, questioning him, asked him gently to speak up, Haggerty got impatient and determined, and he told a good clear story.

"Now for the coat," Henderson said, and he turned to the magistrate. "This is exhibit A," and he held up the coat so the whole court and the magistrate could see the ragged lining. Nobody laughed. "You say animosity developed between these two men, although Kon offered to fix the coat. Tell us what you heard," and Haggerty told what he had seen and heard in Dorfman's.

"Let's see that coat," the little magistrate said, and it was passed up to him. "You say Harry Lane deliberately wore this coat when Kon was around."

"I do."

"A garment like this," the magistrate said, squinting at the coat again. "Was he drunk all the time?"

"He was drinking a little more toward the end."

"And finally Kon tried to get the coat."

"That's right."

"And he got this punch on the jaw."

"That's right."

Ouimet, smiling appreciatively, said he had no desire to question the witness, and then Ray Conlin was called. Mike didn't know what Conlin might say and he leaned forward nervously. Ray had his hair slicked back and he wore a tie, for the first time all summer he wore a tie, his little black eyes gleaming eagerly. "I was in this thing from the beginning," he said importantly. "Just answer the questions as they're asked," Henderson said and Mike smiled faintly. Conlin said he had seen that Harry was trying to torment Mike by refusing to let him fix the coat and it seemed unfair. After he had put himself in this authoritative light he told about seeing the blows struck in Dorfman's, his hands moving as he talked and his body weaving with the punches. His story was Haggerty's and Ouimet, almost bored, said he didn't wish to question him.

"Annie Laurie McNiece," Henderson said.

"Annie Laurie McNiece," the policeman at the door called along the corridor. People who had known her for years turned, startled; they had forgotten she had a surname. She came in wearing a black dress with a little white collar and a small white hat, her eyes in her pale face looking enormous. As she approached the witness box Mike didn't know why she upset him. Unless it was that he hadn't realized that she could look so elegantly sedate. When Henderson questioned her about the fight in Dorfman's she answered as Haggerty had done, and truthfully, and Mike relaxed — she didn't sound at all hostile.

"You recognize this coat?" Henderson asked, holding it up.

"Yes, sir."

"You've seen a good deal of it. "

"Yes, sir."

"And Lane was wearing it just to spite Kon?"

"Oh, no."

"No?"

"No, you see at the time Mike and Harry quarreled about the coat and Mike accused Harry of trying to ruin him as he had ruined Scotty Bowman, Mike was being brave enough to say what everybody thought."

"But you say Lane wasn't wearing the coat to spite Kon."

"Not just to spite him. It was the injustice of the whole thing," and she turned to the magistrate. "You know, sir, just like you might light a candle on Good Friday."

"Really," the magistrate said, leaning closer to her.

"I think so."

"And Lane felt wronged?" the magistrate asked.

"Oh, he was wronged all right," she said shrugging. "I knew both Harry and Bowman. All Harry did was try and save Bowman from the full force of the law. Maybe if you do a thing like that the full force falls on you. But Harry was a gentleman."

"Your Honor, your Honor," Ouimet protested angrily. "This is outrageous. This is not evidence at all."

"It may be outrageous," the magistrate said testily, thrusting out his red nose at Ouimet. "I'm trying to understand something about the background of this case. I'm also trying to decide whether the accused should be committed for trial. If you want to object you can do all the objecting you want to in a higher court. How am I hurting your client?"

Mike was afraid that Ouimet, with his cold superiority, might irritate the unpredictable stubborn little magistrate, waiting with his evil little smile, yet he wanted Ouimet to stop Annie Laurie, who was making him feel ashamed and afraid of his own thoughts, and Ouimet pondered, weighing whether Annie Laurie might not be actually making Mike a more sympathetic figure; then he sat down slowly, his eyes on her.

"You say Lane believed he was wronged, not just by Kon, but by everybody," Henderson asked her.

"That's right, sir," she said. "Mike was being wronged, too."

"You saw that he was being wronged," Henderson asked and Mike, relaxing, saw Ouimet smile with relief.

"Yes, sir. Everybody knows now he must have been wronged because he punched Harry on the jaw," and then she added quickly with a shrug, "The trouble was Harry didn't have a chance to punch Bowman on the jaw so nobody believes he was wronged."

Again Ouimet half rose, disgusted, but the magistrate, smiling, said, "That may be simple enough to be profound, but I don't think we should have any further reference to the Bowman case from the witness."

"Listening to the witness is like listening to a judgment from the appeal court," Ouimet said jovially without bothering to stand up.

"One thing more," Henderson said to her smiling. "You're doing a lot of thinking, but you can't vouch for any of these things, can you now?"

"Yes, I can," she said.

"How so?"

"Harry Lane told me the whole story."

"Oh, and you believed him?"

"I believed him."

"I see," Henderson said, still smiling. "Now when Kon tried to take the coat . . ."

"I think Mr. Kon was goaded into it," she said quietly.

"Goaded into it — by Harry Lane."

"Oh, no. Goaded into it by everybody."

"Everybody?" Henderson said, astonished, and there was an indignant murmur from the spectators.

"Yes, everybody," she said firmly, "because of the way they felt about Scotty Bowman and Harry going free, and Mike being Scotty's friend, although I know you don't want me to mention that again," and she turned apologetically to the magistrate.

Mike's scarred brow had come down over his eyes and he flushed. He felt enormously belittled and in the moment's pain he seemed to lose all his dignity as an outraged man taking his fate into his own hands and striking at the man who was ruining him.

Taking a little time, Ouimet walked up and down in front of the lawyers' table, for he was still wondering whether Annie Laurie had helped or hurt Mike's case with the magistrate. Then he turned to her almost genially. "By the way," he said, "how do you earn your living?"

"Well, one way and another," she said stiffly.

"How do you live? Tell us, please."

"I live well enough."

"On money you get from men?" When she didn't answer he said, coolly, "And I suppose in return you have to give them a certain amount of sympathetic understanding and belief, if they pay for it?"

"I know I'm not respectable," she said defiantly, "but that's just the point you're missing. A man doesn't have to lie to me to impress me. Do you think Harry's being with me helped him with more respectable people? Figure that out, and also this one, too — whatever Harry Lane was, it ought to be clear now he wasn't a coward. Somebody was, don't you think, and I don't mean Mike Kon."

"All right. All right," Ouimet said impatiently, wanting to get rid of her. "I defended Mr. Bowman once. I don't think the case is going to be reopened."

"Is that all the evidence?" the magistrate asked Henderson.

"That's all, your worship."

"Your worship," Ouimet said deferentially. "I'm prepared of course to discuss this evidence, if you think it would be helpful. But right now I'm moving for a dismissal of the charge."

"That all depends," the magistrate said, turning to Henderson. "Are you pressing for a committal?"

"I'm not pressing if you have already formed an opinion."

"Well, I have. It seems to be that the accused under extreme provocation was trying to defend himself. Once the accused had been struck by Lane, it was not unreasonable that he should strike back. It was unfortunate that the steps were there. I see no justification for making the accused stand trial. Case dismissed."

There was a burst of applause which the magistrate did not try to restrain. The policeman, standing beside the dock, said to Mike, "All right. On your way," and Mike, taking a deep breath, and then letting it out slowly in vast relief, stepped down. Ouimet, smiling, shook hands with him.

In the corridor many friends, and many who Mike did not know, crowded around to shake hands and pat him on the back. It all added to his relief, especially the surprising real indignation in their faces. Only Mollie Morris did not come near him. He saw her hurrying along the corridor alone, her head down, hurrying as though someone pursued her, no matter how fast she walked, although no one was following her at all.

The hands kept coming out to Mike, each handclasp buoying him up a little more, until he saw Annie Laurie come out of the courtroom. She was watching him, an odd smile on her face. Gradually he grew ashamed of the hands coming out to him, and when she moved away he broke loose from his well-wishers and caught up to her.

"Annie Laurie," he said awkwardly. "I'm sorry it happened."

"Oh, I was sure you'd get off, Mike," and she started to go.

"Wait a minute," he said uncomfortably. "That stuff about me being goaded on by everybody. Well, thanks, I think it helped me. But what am I supposed to be — the public executioner?"

"Oh, Lord, no," she said, shrugging. "Those guys are never popular. So long, Mike," and he watched her saunter away. She had a very lazy, indolent, very beautiful walk, and it bothered him.

When he got away from his friends he went home and climbed the stairs to his apartment and sat down beside his father. Since the night the old man tried to write the words on the pad he hadn't talked to him about Harry, nor had he told him that Harry was dead. Aside from worrying the old man, he had felt he might arouse in himself some remorse. Even now the one sharp eye seemed to be questioning him. I have killed a man. I'm a human being. I don't feel good, he thought. It began to bother him, remembering how he had felt goaded. Again he wondered why he had stopped talking to the old man, and why even now he hesitated to tell him the end of the story. Then he thought, supposing, as Annie Laurie had said, Harry had rushed across the courtroom and had punched Scotty on the jaw. A hard thing to do in a courtroom. A hard thing to do when the man is in jail, or when he is dead. Only a girl like her would have said such a thing. Then he wondered why he had been so sure that his father, trying to write the words Justice or Judge and Not, had only him and his case in mind, and not Harry and Scotty Bowman. This too began to worry him. Then he turned to his father as though pleading with him. "Everybody was sure of Scotty because he was so prudent. Harry, an imprudent guy, an open book. Such guys ruin themselves and others, don't they?" But thinking of prudence gave him no comfort. Scotty could have kept silent out of a fine sense of prudence, it could have kept him off the stand. Who knows what goes on in a prudent man's mind? They're too prudent to ever let you know. I never thought of that before, and standing up suddenly he cursed Annie Laurie.

The phone began to ring; it was some well-wisher he hardly knew; then the office buzzer sounded and he went down to the shop. A customer shook hands with him and offered him sympathy. Old customers kept coming in and new ones too. It kept up all day, and they all expected to see him and they all expected to shake hands with him warmly and talk about Harry Lane.

The story of what had happened at the preliminary investigation, very colorfully done by the reporters, appeared in the newspapers next day and more people came into the store. Some of them bought suits. Haggerty, who came in to see him, was astonished when Mike said, "This thing, of course, has made me think a lot about Harry and Scotty Bowman and

I can't help wondering now why Scotty didn't open his mouth at the trial. I know he didn't have to. But I mean, did he want to? Why didn't he want to?"

When he went to Ouimet's office next day to pay him, he asked him how well he knew Scotty Bowman. Until Bowman came into his office, Ouimet said, he knew nothing about him. All he knew about the fraudulent loan was what Bowman had told him. If it had been necessary to put Bowman in the stand he would have done so, he said, but Bowman had told him he preferred not to open his mouth at all. Bowman might have had a very shrewd head, Ouimet said dryly, but if that were the case it turned out that he also had a shamefully weak heart.

All week business picked up, and all month; Mike realized that he was becoming more solidly established, being greeted with great and friendly sympathy wherever he went, and he willingly talked about Harry Lane. He could go everywhere; that is, everywhere but Dorfman's, for while Alfred was alive, of course, he could never go there. He found a new place down the street on the other side with murals depicting scenes from Paris life and the place caught on with the high-class customers. His celebrity and quiet reserve soon gave him a following. He accepted the public sympathy with a lonely dignity.

More and more often he would begin a discussion about Harry Lane. He would liked to have talked to Mollie Morris but she had done what she thought Harry should have done; she had fled to Paris and nobody knew when she planned to return. Mike had a persuasive manner of beginning a discussion about Harry's case. "You know I was Scotty's friend," he used to say, "but if you have a friend you don't stop to ask what's going on in his mind. If a man says nothing, you naturally supply the answers. More and more from this distance I wonder why Scotty let people draw their own conclusions. That's what he did in court, you know." He was listened to with respect because he had proved he had no prejudice in favor of Harry.

Business continued, he was getting a better class of trade, but now he had no desire at all to be president of the local businessmen's association, to be an alderman, or ever to be appointed to any public office. Everybody still called him Mike the Scholar, and wherever he was he never missed a chance to put a doubt in the minds of people about the rightness of their judgment of Harry Lane.

It had taken a little time but Harry had finally found a tireless advocate who had won the right to be listened to with respect.

Dates of Original Publication

The Red Hat, *The New Yorker*, October 1931

Timothy Harshaw's Flute, *The New Yorker*, February 1934

A Regret for Youth, *Scribner's Magazine*, July 1928

A Very Merry Christmas, *Harper's Bazaar*, December 1937

All Right, Flatfoot, *Maclean's*, August 1948

The New Kid, *Saturday Evening Post*, September 1948

The Duel, *The New Yorker,* September 1934

The Thing That Happened to Uncle Adolphe, *John O'London's Weekly*, November 1939

The Sentimentalists, *Harper's Bazaar*, November 1938

Emily, *Household Magazine*, January 1933

Big Jules, *Yale Review*, September 1940

The Fiddler on Twenty-Third Street, *John O'London's Weekly*, October 1936

Mother's Day at the Ballpark, *Morley Callaghan: The Complete Stories, Volume Four*, 2003.

Just Like Her Mother, *Chatelaine*, 1957

A Boy Grows Older, *Esquire*, December 1937

The Man with the Coat, *Maclean's*, April 1955

Questions for Discussion and Essays

1. What are the essential ingredients in a Morley Callaghan short story? What does he choose to include and what does he choose to leave out that makes his stories successful? In her introduction, Margaret Atwood discusses Callaghan's style. What are its attributes?

2. How does Callaghan create a sense of realism in his stories? Does this style leave the reader intrigued, or puzzled, or unnerved?

3. What are the key differences between some of the shorter stories in the volume and some of the longer stories? How does Callaghan create a short short story, and when necessary what ingredients go into creating and sustaining a longer short story

4. Margaret Atwood calls Callaghan "a profoundly ironic writer." What makes Callaghan's stories ironic or, at least, what makes his voice, sensibilities, and style ironic? From reading the stories, how does Callaghan present and define what is "ironic?"

5. Critics such as Wayne C. Booth have pointed out that there are two modes or approaches to presenting a story: showing (the dramatization of events in real time through dialogue and direct action) and telling (the voice of an omniscient authorial presence in the narrative who is able to collapse time and editorialize on events and ideas). Is Callaghan a showing author or a telling author? What makes his stories one or the other?

Selected Related Reading

Allen, Walter Ernest. *The Short Story in English*. Oxford University Press, 1981. (Contains a chapter on Morley Callaghan.)

Anderson, Sherwood. *Winesburg, Ohio*. Introduced by Malcolm Cowley. New Edition. Milestone Editions, 1960.

Callaghan, Barry. *Barrelhouse Kings*. McArthur & Company, 1998.

Callaghan, Morley. *A Literary Life. Reflection and Reminiscences 1928–1990*. Exile Editions, 2008.

Conron, Brandon. *Morley Callaghan*. Twayne, 1966.

Dennis, Richard. *British Journal of Canadian Studies*, 1999. (Contains an essay by Richard Dennis: "Morley Callaghan and the Moral Geography of Toronto.")

Farrell, James T. *Studs Lonigan* (A Trilogy). Pete Hamill (editor). Library of America, 1998.

Flaubert, Gustave. *Madame Bovary*. Margaret Cohen (editor). Norton Critical Editions, 1998.

Hemingway, Ernest. *The Complete Short Stories*. Charles Scribner's Sons, 1998.

Joyce, James. *The Dubliners*. Penguin, 1999.

de Maupassant, Guy. *The Complete Short Stories of Guy de Maupassant*, 1955. Artine Artinian (editor). Penguin, 1995.

May, Charles Edward. *The Short Story: The Reality Of Artifice*. Twayne, 1995.

O'Connor, Frank. *The Lonely Voice: A Study of the Short Story*, with an introduction by Russell Banks. Melville House, 2011.

Snider, Norman. "Why Morley Callaghan Still Matters," *Globe and Mail*, 25 October, 2008.

Walsh, William. *A Manifold Voice: Studies in Commonwealth Literature*. Chatto & Windus, 1971.

White, Randall. *Too Good to Be True: Toronto in the 1920s*. Dundurn, 1993.

Wilson, Edmund. *O Canada: An American's Notes on Canadian Culture*. Farrar, Straus & Giroux, 1964.

Woodcock, George. "Callaghan's Toronto: The Persona of a City." *Journal of Canadian Studies* 7-2 (1972) 21-24.

Of Interest on the Web

www.MorleyCallaghan.ca
– The official site of the Morley Callaghan Estate

www.cbc.ca/rewind/sirius/2012/03/01/morley-callaghan/
Rewind With Michael Enright: An Hour With Morley Callaghan.
Thursday, March 1, 2012, CBC Radio One. This hour-long
broadcast features conversations with Morley Callaghan and a
splendid commentary.

www2.athabascau.ca/cll/writers/english/writers/mcallaghan.php
– Athabasca University site

www.editoreric.com/greatlit/authors/Callaghan.html
– The Greatest Authors of All Time site

www.cbc.ca/lifeandtimes/callaghan.htm
– Canadian Broadcasting Corporation (CBC) site

Exile Online Resource

www.ExileEditions.com has a section for the Exile Classics Series,
with further resources for all the books in the series.

Editor's Endnotes

In April of 1955, Ralph Allen, the now legendary editor of *Maclean's* magazine, published — complete in that month's issue — a *Maclean's* $5000 novel award — *The Man with the Coat*, by Morley Callaghan. There were nine pages of full-colour illustrations painted by Oscar Cahén, as well as the essential bones of the regular magazine. *Maclean's* sold for 15 cents. The prize, in present day terms, was in the area of $50,000. Astonishing.

Particularly so, because there had never been a *Maclean's* prize for fiction, short story or novel, and after *The Man with the Coat*, there never was such a prize again. Ralph Allen had read the story in manuscript, had loved it, and had created the prize so that he could print it. And print it he did in the weighty issue of April 16: pages and pages of wide-column type, and then some narrower columns snaking between ads for Nugget Shoe Polish, Beaver Power Tools, Christie's Cremo Biscuits, the '55 Dodge V-8 or V-6, and articles about General Isaac Brock and "How He Founded the Canadian Myth" and the honey-blonde school teacher, "Jacqueline Mac-Donald, Who Wants to Be the World's Strongest Woman."

The Man with the Coat is a novella, but it began as a short story, and it ended up as a full-length novel, *The Many Coloured Coat*. The intended short story — it lasted as such for about two days — was the last short fiction he attempted. "I just grew bored with the form," he said.

After he died, a little story was found among his papers as they were being prepared for the National Archives. It cannot be dated exactly, but it must be from 1923-4. If *The Man with the Coat* is the last of his shorter fiction, then "On the Way Home" is his first story in a "modern" style, written when he was twenty or twenty-one.

On the Way Home

The wire fence was low at the dip in the hill. Lou put one foot on the top wire and stepped over and down the embankment to the railway track. He walked along the track lifting his bearded face to the sky. It looked like rain. It was getting dark and he wanted to be down to the grocery story before it rained.

He heard voices on the bank above the track. A young fellow and a girl had come up from the wooded ravine to the right and were climbing the wire fence. Lou wondered what they had been doing down in the ravine so late. The young fellow tossed a coat and a leather bag and a book over the fence before helping her over. The girl had riding breeches under a long coat and she had a black band around her head. They did not see Lou. They walked along the top of the bank hardly speaking to each other. Lou could see that the fellow was very angry about something. He was swinging the bag at the tall weeds. The girl kept looking over her shoulder at him. They walked straight ahead. She tried to put her arm around his waist but he pushed it away. She laughed and started to tease him.

Lou didn't want them to see him so he walked slowly along the path by the tracks. It started to rain a little. The girl snatched the fellow's cap and put it on her head, the peak to one side. The fellow still pouted. Lou could have laughed out loud. He didn't mind the rain. The fellow and his girl came down the bank to the track. The street lights were a little way ahead.

Lou could hear her say, "Give me your handkerchief, and . . ."

"Go chase yourself," the fellow said.

The girl strutted along the ties. Lou saw her take a handkerchief from her pocket and knot it in the four corners. It was almost dark and raining steadily. The girl waited until the fellow came up even with her and slyly put her arms around his neck and kissed him until he let her put the knotted handkerchief on his head and turn up his coat collar. He put his arm around her waist, lifting her on to a track rail, balancing her while they walked. Lou followed vaguely excited.

The bank on the right flattened out. They stood on the track looking down the dark ravine. The girl must have been poking or pinching the fellow because he yelled, "Ouch, damn you," and she ran along the track, laughing out loud. Lou wanted to laugh out loud. The fellow chased her and caught up with her. She struggled while he tried to twist her over his knee, but finally submitted and he slapped her behind. She ran ahead again, to run and yell mocking, "Oh my big bad man, you're so strong." She came back giggling and put her head on his shoulder. He wouldn't say a word.

Lou wanted to lift up his head and whistle happily but he had never been a very good whistler. They didn't mind the rain and he didn't mind the Kingston Road radial car southeast of the track that hooted mournfully. The fellow and the girl were past the ravine and the track became a ridge on the level ground. Then they saw Lou and straightened up, walking respectably and rapidly along the track. By a guard rail on the track a path went down the bank to the end of a street. Lou started down the path and stopped, watching the fellow and the girl going along the track in the rain, the girl with the fellow's hat pulled over her ear, the fellow with the handkerchief knotted on his head. Lou turned up his coat collar and went down the path to the street and along to the grocery store. He could have kicked himself for thinking of the fellow and the girl trudging along the track to the stars. It was raining hard.

THE EXILE CLASSICS SERIES

THAT SUMMER IN PARIS (No. 1) ~ MORLEY CALLAGHAN
Memoir 6x9 247 pages 978-1-55096-688-6 (tpb) $19.95
It was the fabulous summer of 1929 when the literary capital of North America had moved to the Left Bank of Paris. Ernest Hemingway, F. Scott Fitzgerald, James Joyce, Ford Madox Ford, Robert McAlmon and Morley Callaghan... amid these tangled relationships, friendships were forged, and lost... A tragic and sad and unforgettable story told in Callaghan's lucid, compassionate prose.

NIGHTS IN THE UNDERGROUND (No. 2) ~ MARIE-CLAIRE BLAIS
Fiction/Novel 6x9 190 pages 978-1-55096-015-0 (tpb) $19.95
With this novel, Marie-Claire Blais came to the forefront of feminism in Canada. This is a classic of lesbian literature that weaves a profound matrix of human isolation, with transcendence found in the healing power of love.

DEAF TO THE CITY (No. 3) ~ MARIE-CLAIRE BLAIS
Fiction/Novel 6x9 218 pages 978-1-55096-013-6 (tpb) $19.95
City life, where innocence, death, sexuality, and despair fight for survival. It is a book of passion and anguish, characteristic of our times, written in a prose of controlled self-assurance. A true urban classic.

THE GERMAN PRISONER (No. 4) ~ JAMES HANLEY
Fiction/Novella 6x9 55 pages 978-1-55096-075-4 (tpb) $13.95
In the weariness and exhaustion of WWI trench warfare, men are driven to extremes of behaviour.

THERE ARE NO ELDERS (No. 5) ~ AUSTIN CLARKE
Fiction/Stories 6x9 159 pages 978-1-55096-092-1 (tpb) $17.95
Austin Clarke is one of the significant writers of our times. These are compelling stories of life as it is lived among the displaced in big cities, marked by a singular richness of language true to the streets.

100 LOVE SONNETS (No. 6) ~ PABLO NERUDA
Poetry 6x9 225 pages 978-1-55096-108-9 (tpb) $24.95
As Gabriel García Márquez stated: "Pablo Neruda is the greatest poet of the twentieth century – in any language." And, this is the finest translation available, anywhere!

THE SELECTED GWENDOLYN MACEWEN (No. 7)
GWENDOLYN MACEWEN
Poetry/Fiction/Drama/Art/Archival 6x9 352 pages
978-1-55096-111-9 (tpb) $32.95
"This book represents a signal event in Canadian culture." —*Globe and Mail*
The only edition to chronologically follow the astonishing trajectory of Mac-
Ewen's career as a poet, storyteller, translator and dramatist, in a substantial selec-
tion from each genre.

THE WOLF (No. 8) ~ MARIE-CLAIRE BLAIS
Fiction/Novel 6x9 158 pages 978-1-55096-105-8 (tpb) $19.95
A human wolf moves outside the bounds of love and conventional morality as he
stalks willing prey in this spellbinding masterpiece and classic of gay literature.

A SEASON IN THE LIFE OF EMMANUEL (No. 9) ~ MARIE-CLAIRE BLAIS
Fiction/Novel 6x9 175 pages 978-1-55096-118-8 (tpb) $19.95
Widely considered by critics and readers alike to be her masterpiece, this is truly a
work of genius comparable to Faulkner, Kafka, or Dostoyevsky. Includes 16 Ink
Drawings by Mary Meigs.

IN THIS CITY (No. 10) ~ AUSTIN CLARKE
Fiction/Stories 6x9 221 pages 978-1-55096-106-5 (tpb) $21.95
Clarke has caught the sorrowful and sometimes sweet longing for a home in the
heart that torments the dislocated in any city. Eight masterful stories showcase the
elegance of Clarke's prose and the innate sympathy of his eye.

THE NEW YORKER STORIES (No. 11) ~ MORLEY CALLAGHAN
Fiction/Stories 6x9 158 pages 978-1-55096-110-2 (tpb) $19.95
Callaghan's great achievement as a young writer is marked by his breaking out with
stories such as these in this collection... "If there is a better storyteller in the world,
we don't know where he is." —*New York Times*

REFUS GLOBAL (No. 12) ~ THE MONTRÉAL AUTOMATISTS
Manifesto 6x9 142 pages 978-1-55096-107-2 (tpb) $21.95
The single most important social document in Quebec history, and the most important aesthetic statement a group of Canadian artists has ever made. This is basic
reading for anyone interested in Canadian history or the arts in Canada.

TROJAN WOMEN (No. 13) ~ GWENDOLYN MACEWEN
Drama 6x9 142 pages 978-1-55096-123-2 (tpb) $19.95

A trio of timeless works featuring the great ancient theatre piece by Euripedes in a new version by MacEwen, and the translations of two long poems by the contemporary Greek poet Yannis Ritsos.

ANNA'S WORLD (No. 14) ~ MARIE-CLAIRE BLAIS
Fiction 5.5x8.5 166 pages ISBN: 978-1-55096-130-0 $19.95

An exploration of contemporary life, and the penetrating energy of youth, as Blais looks at teenagers by creating Anna, an introspective, alienated teenager without hope. Anna has experienced what life today has to offer and rejected its premise. There is really no point in going on. We are all going to die, if we are not already dead, is Anna's philosophy.

THE MANUSCRIPTS OF PAULINE ARCHANGE (No. 15)
MARIE-CLAIRE BLAIS
Fiction 5.5x8.5 324 pages ISBN: 978-1-55096-131-7 $23.95

For the first time, the three novelettes that constitute the complete text are brought together: the story of Pauline and her world, a world in which people turn to violence or sink into quiet despair, a world as damned as that of Baudelaire or Jean Genet.

A DREAM LIKE MINE (No. 16) ~ M.T. KELLY
Fiction 5.5x8.5 174 pages ISBN: 978-1-55096-132-4 $19.95

A Dream Like Mine is a journey into the contemporary issue of radical and violent solutions to stop the destruction of the environment. It is also a journey into the unconscious, and into the nightmare of history, beauty and terror that are the awesome landscape of the Native American spirit world.

THE LOVED AND THE LOST (No. 17) ~ MORLEY CALLAGHAN
Fiction 5.5x8.5 302 pages ISBN: 978-1-55096-151-5 (tpb) $21.95

With the story set in Montreal, young Peggy Sanderson has become socially unacceptable because of her association with black musicians in nightclubs. The black men think she must be involved sexually, the black women fear or loathe her, yet her direct, almost spiritual manner is at variance with her reputation.

NOT FOR EVERY EYE (No. 18) ~ GÉRARD BESSETTE
Fiction 5.5x8.5 126 pages ISBN: 978-1-55096-149-2 (tpb) $17.95

A novel of great tact and sly humour that deals with ennui in Quebec and the intellectual alienation of a disenchanted hero, and one of the absolute classics of modern revolutionary and comic Quebec literature. Chosen by the Grand Jury des Lettres of Montreal as one of the ten best novels of post-war contemporary Quebec.

STRANGE FUGITIVE (No. 19) ~ MORLEY CALLAGHAN
Fiction 5.5x8.5 242 pages ISBN: 978-1-55096-155-3 (tpb) $19.95

Callaghan's first novel – originally published in New York in 1928 – announced the coming of the urban novel in Canada, and we can now see it as a prototype for the "gangster" novel in America. The story is set in Toronto in the era of the speakeasy and underworld vendettas.

IT'S NEVER OVER (No. 20) ~ MORLEY CALLAGHAN
Fiction 5.5x8.5 190 pages ISBN: 978-1-55096-157-7 (tpb) $19.95

1930 was an electrifying time for writing. Callaghan's second novel, completed while he was living in Paris – imbibing and boxing with Joyce and Hemingway (see his memoir, Classics No. 1, *That Summer in Paris*) – has violence at its core; but first and foremost it is a story of love, a love haunted by a hanging. Dostoyevskian in its depiction of the morbid progress of possession moving like a virus, the novel is sustained insight of a very high order.

AFTER EXILE (No. 21) ~ RAYMOND KNISTER
Poetry/Prose 5.5x8.5 240 pages ISBN: 978-1-55096-159-1 (tpb) $19.95

This book collects for the first time Knister's poetry. The title *After Exile* is plucked from Knister's long poem written after he returned from Chicago and decided to become the unthinkable: a modernist Canadian writer. Knister, writing in the 20s and 30s, could barely get his poems published in Canada, but magazines like *This Quarter* (Paris), *Poetry* (Chicago), *Voices* (Boston), and *The Dial* (New York City), eagerly printed what he sent, and always asked for more – and all of it is in this book.

THE COMPLETE STORIES OF MORLEY CALLAGHAN (NO. 21–25)
Fiction 5.5x8.5 (tpb) $19.95
ISBN 978-1-55096-304-5 (v. 1) 328 pages
ISBN 978-1-55096-305-2 (v. 2) 320 pages
ISBN 978-1-55096-306-9 (v. 3) 344 pages
ISBN 978-1-55096-307-6 (v. 4) 334 pages

Attractively produced in four volumes, the complete short fiction of Morley Callaghan appears as he comes into full recognition as one of the singular storytellers of our time. Introductions by Alistair MacLeod, André Alexis, Anne Michaels and Margaret Atwood.

CONTRASTS: IN THE WARD. A BOOK OF POETRY AND PAINTINGS
Poetry 7x7 168 pages ISBN: 978-1-55096-308-3 (tpb) $24.95

In 1922, while the Group of Seven was emerging as a national phenomenon, Lawren Harris published his only book of poems – *Contrasts* – the first modernist exploration of Canadian urban space in verse. Harris also wandered the streets of Toronto, sketching and creating a powerful set of city paintings. *Lawren Harris ~ Contrasts: In the Ward* brings together for the first time Harris' original book of poems, and sixteen colour images of the artist's early urban paintings in this compact, beautiful-to-hold-and-read, genre-crossing collection. Edited and introduced by Gregory Betts.